Praise for Robert Dunn's musical novels:

Meet the Annas:

"In *Meet the Annas*, Robert Dunn has brought the world of
'60s pop to life with the precision and veracity of Nabokov.
Every detail is a thing to savor. This is a fully musical work
of literature, a book with a beat so good you could almost
dance to it. —David Hajdu, author of *Positively Fourth Street*

"From New York's Brill Building to a certain L.A. studio
with a golden touch, *Meet the Annas* has it all: suspense,
spot-on detail, and a big helping of true romance.
Anyone who felt a pang of loss as Merseybeat invaders
drove girl groups off U.S. airwaves will get a major charge
from Dunn's latest." —Lewis Shiner, author of *Glimpses*

Pink Cadillac:

The characters are larger than life and yet believable
in the way that it takes giants sometimes to effect cul-
tural change. The author knows blues and early rock
in the intimate way of a guitarist caressing people's
lives out of his guitar strings. This is one super book.
—Book Sense citation

The pervasive passion for music provides the novel
with a steady heat. —*Kirkus Reviews*

Cutting Time:

A heady mix of blues myth and blues nitty-gritty by
a writer who knows the passions and pleasures of
music from the inside.
—Michael Lydon, author of *Ray Charles: Man and Music*

Soul Cavalcade:

• *Soul Cavalcade* ma⋯⋯⋯ a time
lost now in histor⋯⋯⋯ to life
in a hugely entert⋯⋯⋯ *ookviews*

Meet The Annas

Annas

A musical novel by
Robert Dunn

A Coral Press original
First Published June 2, 2007

ISBN-10: 0-9708293-5-3
ISBN-13: 978-0-9708293-5-1
Library of Congress Control Number: 2007900784
Manufactured in Canada
1 3 5 7 9 10 8 6 4 2
First Edition

Cover Design: Linda Root
Cover Photograph: Chris Carroll
Author Photo: Nancy Ramsey

Come see more Annas' pictures and listen to Annas related recordings at:
www.coralpress.com.

To BD—we're walkin', yes indeed, we're talkin'....

Chapter One
The Ring in the Rubble

THE NOTE WAS PASSED to me by Punky Solomon himself—a surprise because here I was in this New York courtroom suing him—and its thought-you-should-know message was simple: Our old recording studio in L.A., SilverTone, was being torn down to make way for a minimall.

The note was an unexpected kindness, and I gave him a nod of thanks while we sat there in the courtroom. I spent the rest of the day fidgeting as my lawyer, Sandy Kovall, worked through preliminary motions, but by the time Judge MacIntire finally slapped down her gavel, telling us to be back in court promptly at nine Monday morning, I knew what I had to do. I dashed out into the rainy March afternoon and did my damnedest to get a cab. Sheets of water crested up my legs as I waved my new black umbrella. Finally, one pulled up, and I told the driver: Two stops, Midtown, the Edison Hotel; then Kennedy.

That morning, without any real reason, I'd made sure I had a few things in a small suitcase; my instincts were working again—they'd mysteriously fired up, like a long-damped coal burner, once I'd committed to my lawsuit—and I guess I wanted to be ready for whatever the weekend might bring. I never expected I'd be heading to L.A., though. Fortunately, I was able to get an 8:10 p.m. flight, which would get in about eleven their time. I'd worry about a room when I got there.

All this was a rush, and my head, as it had been for weeks now, was spinning uproariously between the present and the past. It would be an exaggeration to say that sometimes I didn't know when or where I was, but there had been moments when the long dammed-up memories—of New

York in the early '60s, then the move to L.A., and all the while of the Annas, the bouffanted, exotic-eyed, hip-swaying girl group I'd written hit songs for, tunes like *He's So Bad (I Love Him!)*, *Lost Memories*, and the one at the center of my life now, *Love Will Cut You Like a Knife*—sent my head whirling into places I hadn't let it for decades.

SilverTone Studio was my destination. Once I got to L.A. and rented a car, I took the 401 north, then got off at Sunset and turned east toward Hollywood. I hadn't been back to Los Angeles in over 30 years, living my quiet music teacher's life in Scottsdale, Arizona; and even though it was after midnight here, and for me on East Coast time, after 3 a.m., I was way too jazzed to stop.

A few miles along Sunset the curvy, tree-lined road straightened and I hit the Strip, still full of glitzy boutiques and record company offices, where in my day Dean Martin's rat-pack boîte, Dino's, held sway. SilverTone Studio was nowhere near them. It was on the flats east of Highland, a low-slung, nondescript building between a car wash and a Spiffies coffee shop on the nonglamorous part of Sunset. But I always liked this beat-down Hollywood better than sleek West L.A.; it had always felt like home. I used to joke to Punky about how I could drive from my apartment in the Hollywood Hills down here blindfolded, every turn of the wheel so deeply imbedded in my shoulders.

Now it all looked quite different to me. This section of Sunset was being built up, and there were chain-link fences around construction areas everywhere. I kept my eyes open for the Spiffies that had been our hangout, but I never saw it. Likewise the car wash. Then I'd driven so far I was certain I'd passed SilverTone.

I could see it so well, though. The studio door was scuffed, battered wood adorned with brass numbers for the five-digit address (two of them missing). Inside was a wait-ing room, of peeling-up linoleum, brown Naugahyde chairs, and rusty floor-standing chrome ashtrays, that was even smaller and more austere than the one next door at the car wash. No one would ever be in there waiting, though. Then through another plain door and . . . you were into the womb itself.

As I turned the rental car around, it all came rushing back to me, everything about that room where we'd recorded thirty-some years back. The high sky of stippled white acoustic tile, the gray baffles crashing like waves, the wobbly little wooden chairs the players would squinch into, the boom mikes swaying like lost cranes, the control room (where I'd always be) lined with polished aluminum-plated outboard equipment and the huge Neve console—grander and more complex than an airplane cockpit. Rich Armour would be in their twiddling dials; Punky, too, feet up on the console, his blond goatee tilted onto his cupped hands, his preternatural blue eyes glowing, a thin black Nat Sherman cigarette skirling smoke . . . all ears. It was one stroke of Punky Solomon's genius that he could suck out notes from inside other notes, hear overtones that dogs would miss, feel chord changes bars ahead just like a chess grandmaster; and there he'd be, leaping out into the studio to move a mike just so, reaching over the bass player Karen DeWilder's shoulder to show her a double-stop run he wanted leading to the bridge, whistling a riff to the horn guys, Jimmy, Kirk, and Steve, or walking straight to the singer on the session and going up on the tiptoes of his Italian Beatle boots, tearing into their face like a drill sergeant on Parris Island. Barney Fredericks the guitar player called Punky Napoleon behind his back, and one day Punky heard him. From then on, when things in a session were going well, we'd see him standing there, listening, *listening*, with the fourth button on his hand-made pirate shirt undone and his right hand slipped inside; and none of us could ever tell if he was doing it as a quiet goof on us or out of his pure subconscious.

In truth, though I worked with Punky Solomon for five years, our work starting in New York City, just up around the Brill Building, at 1650 Broadway, or in the rat- and prostitute-infested firetrap in the West 30s in which Punky had his first studio built for him, the true music we made was right here in Hollywood. When he called me out to L.A. to do that final Annas session, Anna Dubower's hair was down from its famous teased-high beehive and the girl-group sound was close to dead. But only close to. . . . *Love Will Cut You Like a Knife* was going to keep it all going, be the greatest song ever, Punky's greatest production (that was why Punky and that gangster Manny Green slipped their names onto it). As Punky put it at the time, "You and Princess wrote me a song, Dink, that's gonna kick open the gates of fuckin' heaven."

And it did. Punky pulled out everything he had, celestas, trumpets, French horns, cymbals, and tympanis all churning and bucking like God's own tempest, and the Annas' voices cracking through the sonic storm like lightning flashes. It was rock 'n' roll first, but it was the *Ride of the Valkeries*, too. When the tune was finally mixed and Punky had airmailed me the first pressing in New York, I was blown away. Punky had taken our simple piano-voice demo and blown it up till it rang like Yahweh's cymbals at the end of the world. And yet, there was no question it was Princess's and my song, no one else's—and I'm going to prove that if it takes the last damn breath I have.

There it was. I was sure of it. I pulled up across Sunset in the rental car and fixed the location from the air pumps that had been at the car wash, the only part of the block not yet knocked flat. All I could see were heaps of broken concrete, steel cable, and—now that I could focus better—chunks of what had been the persimmon-red tile roof on SilverTone Studio.

I wasn't there the month they recorded *Knife*. I was back in New York. (Punky's and Manny's lawyers were planning to use that against me now, though Manny evidently wasn't at the session either.) But my heart was in that studio. And more. My grandmother's ring.

I was moving too fast to bother to lock the car, and I jay-walked across Sunset. There was a chain-link fence around the whole block, and it was topped with razor wire that caught the light from two floodlights at the corners of the lot. Nobody was inside, as far as I could see. Just the rubble.

It was the ring I wanted; for 30 years it had been the ring that I've wanted. It was Grandma Helene's. Nothing fancy, just a plain gold band with a small but elegant diamond. A Tiffany setting. Her engagement ring.

I looked for a way into the sealed-off construction site. On the side street off Sunset was a wide gate, locked with two padlocks, and when I stood in front of it, I could see the razor wire had been pushed aside atop the gate. Not very far, but there was a good two-and-a-half-foot opening.

The jump down to the other side jarred my old knees, but I landed clean. The two bright floodlights beamed down, and cars were running steadily along Sunset, but nobody seemed to have seen me vault the fence, or cared. I crouched low though, just in case.

Around me were waves of detritus, seeming to buck and toss under the floodlights. I gingerly walked over a large con-crete wall, now splayed on its side, only to find more blocks of concrete everywhere I looked. Did I have a hope in hell of finding in this sea of rubble the ring I gave to Anna Dubower?

Can I stop here and tell you a little about Anna? For those of you new to her legend?

Anna Dubower was a true soul of America. Her father, jazz musician Gerry Dubower, was descended from fighters in the American Revolution; on her mother's side she was a mix of black, Native American, and Cuban. She'd spent her first six years in Greenwich, Connecticut; then, after her father's death, moved with her mother and sister to East Harlem. (Quite a tumble, and far from the middle-class Kew Gardens where Princess and I grew up.)

From 1963 to 1965 the Annas (Anna singing lead, with her sister, Trudy, and cousin Doris (Sweet) McClain on back-up) had five Top 5 records, two going all the way to Number 1. When the group toured England in the fall of 1963, they were, next to the Beach Boys, the biggest act going. That year, right before the British Invasion, Anna, with her long legs and wild hairdo, found herself the toast of young, mod England. On that trip Anna slept with John Lennon (and fended off Mick Jagger).

Think about it: This fact is far more significant than wagging tongues now would have it. The Beatles and the Stones were beginning their magnificent alchemy, turning scratchy, imported American rhythm and blues records into performances so vital kids around the world would explode in hysterics before them. The two groups were making records so intense that even now, over thirty years on, you put them on the CD player and the room jumps. They were prescient, too. While we in America were listening to white-bread music (and God knows, Princess and I wrote our share of pop drivel), the young Brits were going straight to the source: Muddy Waters, Chuck Berry, Arthur Alexander, Smokey Robinson, Little Richard. They were searching for the soul of American music, and sure Anna Dubower was an exotic, mixed-race hottie, and sure she was already a star whose records John, Paul, George, and Ringo covered in north-of-England tours, but both John and Mick went at her, I'm certain, because for them she was it: the haunted-eyed, raven-haired incarnation of the true church of rock 'n' roll.

Look at her pictures. They're easy to find on the Web, in the plentiful tribute sites; or perhaps you still have the famous poster up on your wall: Anna in that slinky gold-sequin dress, with her wild bangs, dangly earrings, with her cat's eyes and pouty pink lips, radiating the absolute certainty that she can see just what you want—and show you how to get it.

Millions loved her back then. Many cherish her memory even now. I . . . I know I still do.

Of course it's the image, the sound, the transporting magic that the Annas still have—in the harmonies of their voices, the brazenness of their performances, the way Anna *devoured* the air around her—that is timeless. And certainly anything I felt then or feel now is caught up in that; how could it not be?

But yet, of all of us who worshipped this glorious, distant host of the true church, I'm the only one I know who took it further; who loved the real Anna Dubower, the *natural* woman, as our pal Carole put it so well. Even now I can remember her warm, swirling scent; that heady mix of hibiscus, rose, and tangerine off her pale brown skin. Even now I close my eyes and feel her touch along my arm, my hand, my fingers. . . .

And though for years I hung back, writing their songs, doing my job, revering her from afar, on one star-bright night, with Anna trembling before me on that New York rooftop, I was the one who stepped up and did what was right: I fell to my knees and gave her my grandmother's ring, with nothing but love and devotion—and as I tell myself to this day, a true vision of a life together—in my heart.

Anna's answer? She kissed me and loved me but needed time to think. So much was going on. A week after my proposal, she flew back to the Coast for the final *Knife* sessions, promising me an answer when the recording was done.

I never got one. From what I'd heard, when Anna arrived, she'd shown off the ring with pride and enthusiasm. Then something happened; I've never known what. By the end of the *Knife* sessions Anna had left the ring behind on a shelf in SilverTone's small, shared bathroom.

Rather than a cleaning lady take it away, Punky took the ring and put it in a box in the control room. Later I heard he'd been saving it for me, next time I was in L.A. That's where it stayed, I presume. Three months later Anna Dubower was dead. And when I was back that one last time, for her funeral, the ring, and all the furious promise it held, was more than I could deal with.

I was lifting chunks of concrete now, looking for a spectral glint. Did I have any real hope? I found broken reels of Ampeg tape, found whole sections of the pin-point-pierced acoustic tile. A cracked plastic knob caught my eye: This could be where the control room had been.

I started digging at the concrete. I caught the side of my hand on a particularly jagged piece, and blood flowed. Still I pushed on. O.K., I knew it was probably futile—maybe the ring wasn't even there, and if it was, how could I find it?—but I at least wanted, after all these years, to give it my all.

I should have come for the ring earlier, but I couldn't. I couldn't easily face what happened in the three months after the *Knife* sessions. I was devastated by Anna's death, and all the death around me, and that, coupled with the resounding failure of *Love Will Cut You Like a Knife*, spun my life like a diabolical merry-go-round. I quit New York, left the music biz, wandered for a while, then ended up in Scottsdale, where I've lived all the years since, teaching music at Porter Graves High School and carrying on the on-again, off-again, not quite ever settled relationship with my wonderfully patient fellow teacher, Misty Warren.

I knew I wasn't going to find the ring, but I kept looking . . . looked until I did find half a 45 record, black wax with Punky's distinctive San Remo label. I picked it up carefully and peered closely at it under the yellow sulfur lights. When I made out the few telling words, LOVE WILL CUT YOU, my heart jumped.

God, how I'd loved this record. Even if the session

meant I'd lost Anna for myself, at least there was this disc. The record should have stormed to the top of the charts; should have been the Annas' third Number 1. Two years earlier it would have. (And now, thirty years later, in a resurrection unimaginable at the time, *Knife* was all over commercials and movie soundtracks.) But by 1966 everything had changed. Irony of ironies: The Beatles and the Stones, our British acolytes, had driven our own music from the charts— the music they'd worshipped, loved, and emulated.

I turned the record so its flat-black wax caught the light. This was it: The first official pressing of my last produced song. I had the left side of the record, and there was the blue and yellow San Remo label, with the dainty drawing of the lighthouse and its thin-line beams of light shining forth. I also made out the record's timing: a crazy-long for 1966 three minutes, fifty-two seconds. (And even that was a lie by Punky of about forty seconds.) My gaze traced the fine grooves, tripped over the cracked edge. Broken, never playable again. I held the thin plastic for another minute as my head lightened and a swirling roar crashed through my thoughts, then I let it fall back into that wasted concrete sea.

Chapter Two

I WAS BACK IN New York on Monday, back in the court-room on Centre Street, and though it was bright and beautiful outside, the sun laving the downtown buildings with a creamy yellow and glinting gold off windows, I was stuck in this boxy, plain courtroom. It was 9:30 and Sandy Kovall, my young, whip-smart lawyer, was introducing evidence, mainly a sheaf of notes to songs that Princess and I had written, including, of course, *Love Will Cut You Like a Knife*.

The trial business was pretty pro forma, and I took the time to look around the courtroom. At the defendants table were Punky Solomon and Manny Gold. It hadn't escaped my notice that each day they'd taken seats at the edge of the long table, their attorneys between them, and that not many words had been exchanged. Neither of them, of course, wanted to be here; and as far as I knew, Punky and Manny hadn't had anything much to do with each other since the *Knife* session days—and they hadn't always liked each other then.

In the first row behind the defense table each day Moe Grushensky, the old record man who had given us all our starts, showed up, and I kept thinking: Manny, Moe, and Punky—what were they, the Pep Boys? But that would of course be selling these men very short.

Manny, with his thick, fleshy features, the fur rising pelt-like out of the open collar of his white shirt, and a helmet of black (probably by now Hair Club for Men) hair, still sported his gold-chain goombah look, though he was paunchy and double-chinned where thirty years back he'd been tight, tough, rock hard. His florid cologne hadn't changed, though; even from the defense table I could smell it. And he still had that immediate thug vibe, that underboil of violence, where the moment you saw him you thought: That guy's trouble. Smart would be simply to cross the street.

Moe Grushensky, on the other hand, was a tall stick of a man (though an inch shorter than me) with a high forehead, bald as a billiard ball even then. He was a calmer man whose silence always felt like a force; stand next to him even now and get pulled into his old-style, 52nd Street hipster orbit.

Manny Gold had initially come to the rock 'n' roll party as Moe's date. Starting in the early '50s, Moe Grushensky had run half a dozen record companies in New York, including Black Dog, Topper, Way Out, and one he called Holy S, which shipped the truly crazy stuff. Start an independent record label, and you need money as much as—probably more than—talent, and Manny was his money man, backing him in projects, funding deals, paying musicians, settling bills at studios, keeping the race to the next hit going top speed. It's said that there was a time pre-Beatles when Gold had a finger (or at least a nail) in a third of the top 40 records in *Billboard*. He and his cohorts ensured that new records got airplay then found their way to the stores, from Korvettes to Woolworths, where America's "jungle music" loving teens could drop 89 cents on the music that drove their parents bonkers. Manny was also the guy who shipped boxes out the backdoor as well as the front, brought along a couple of huge dudes known as Spic and Span to clean up any irregular payments, who made sure well-placed deejays always drove the latest Lincoln or Caddie. Essentially Manny Gold stuck his hands into the golden rock 'n' roll stream and diverted as much of it as he wanted into his and his friends' well-hidden pools.

Then there was Punky Solomon. Punky had toned down his act since his palmy days. His hair, though dyed blond as in the old days, was cut short and spiky, a cut common on twentysomething actors and in truth not awkward on his well-lined face. He had that perpetual L.A. tan, which set off a vivid white scar on his left cheek, and had taken to wearing Hawaiian shirts—the vintage, thousands-of-dollars kind—even here in the New York courtroom. Punky was always a mix of crazy, spritzing, in-your-face energy and absolute, imperious remoteness; in his seat now he fidgeted constantly, tapping a pencil on the well-worn wooden table or unbending and rebending paper clips, and yet his mien was wholly undisclosing—amused, patient, respectful, yet giving away nothing. At times he even seemed to be enjoying himself. Anna, who in the group's heyday worked as closely with Punky as anyone, had said in an interview in *Hits-a-Poppin'!* magazine that "Mr. Solomon—I always call him that—has at least *eight* layers of personality." She said she'd personally gotten as far as four or five.

Why were we all here? Here's how the label for our song, initially a flop but now in seemingly every fifth movie and at least one commercial an hour, read:

LOVE WILL CUT YOU LIKE A KNIFE

(SOLOMON, GOLD, STEPHENSON, DIAMOND)

THE ANNAS

That second line on the label was of course a lie. I was here simply to set things right.

✳ ✳ ✳ ✳ ✳

I WAS HERE WITHOUT Princess Diamond, though. It had been at least twenty years since I'd last talked to her, and she didn't seem very happy to hear from me when I called from my home in Scottsdale. It took a number of calls to get her number—she clearly liked to hold on to the trappings of her celebrity—and I had to get by two gofers before she finally answered herself.

"Dink Stephenson," she said in a voice that, even with polish and money, still carried subtle traces of her Queens honk. "Well, well, well."

"Hey, pardner," I said. That was how we used to call each other, even from the beginning: *Pardner*, as if we were cowpokes riding the Western range rather than Queens kids trying to climb the granite buildings of Manhattan.

Princess was silent for a moment, perhaps turning the old salutation over. "So, what's up?"

"I'm calling—" I'd decided to come right out with it. "Calling about *Like a Knife*. It's been burning me, the way it's getting played all over the place, and we still have to share credit on it."

"I've noticed that," she said after a moment. "That it seems to be catching on. I wonder why?"

"Because it's a damn good song—damn good record, too. Gotta give Punky credit for that."

"It was—is." Princess spoke softly, with noticeable hesitance. Although our songs had got her going, she'd dropped the Princess and was now Michelle Diamond, Broadway composer; no small move, the way rock 'n' roll had fared on the Great White Way. Her first show, *Angel's Trumpet*, was opening in a couple months.

"And I just want to get what's right for us."

"Dink, what're you doing now?" Princess asked after a moment.

"Same thing." I shrugged over the phone. "Living out here in the desert. Teaching."

"Right. So what're you proposing?"

"A suit. Against Manny Gold and Punky Solomon. Get our names back. Our royalties—"

"Do you need the money that much?"

"Do I—" I shook my head on the other end. This wasn't going exactly the easy way I'd thought. "No, it's not the money ... well, not just ... I mean, I hate to see those crooks getting our dough and all, but it's more than that. We wuz robbed!" By now I'd fallen back into a full-blown Queens accent; it surprised me no end to hear it. "I just want what's right."

"Have you consulted a lawyer on this?"

"Better. He's consulted me." I winked, though of course Princess couldn't see that over the phone. "He, um, found me. Young man named Sandy Kovall. New York boy, Upper West Side. Loves the old music. He approached me. He's handling the case just for a cut, not even a retainer."

"So you have nothing to lose."

"Not that I can see."

"You're not concerned about—"

"What, Manny? He's an old man now."

There was a long, hollow pause on Princess's end. I wondered, not for the first time, if I was too confident about that. Then: "What do you want from me?"

"The obvious. Join the suit with me. Get the credit to *Knife* back where it belongs—you and me in that little room at 1650."

There was a long pause, then Princess said, "Can I think about it?"

"I think it's a no-brainer, but sure." How could she not step up to get her—*our*—honor back?

"I'll get back to you then." Another pause. "See you, Dink."

Two days later her phone message said she wasn't going to be able to join me in the suit. She also said she didn't think it was necessary and would rather I didn't do it. When I tried to call her back to find out more what she was thinking, the two secretaries made it clear that she would not be available at all.

I immediately called Sandy to tell him Princess wasn't aboard, but he didn't seem too concerned.

"What we need to prove," he told me, "is exactly how the song was written. If we need testimony from Miss Diamond, we can subpoena her. She'll testify to everything you've told me, right?"

I took a deep breath, lifted my hands in a slight shrug even though I was on the phone. "I don't know why she wouldn't."

"Then off we go!" This was Sandy's favorite phrase. He

said it with a lift, as if the words themselves were up on the balls of their feet, ready to run down the road. Hearing them always made me feel better.

"Off we go," I said softly as I hung up.

✳ ✳ ✳ ✳ ✳

WHILE I SAT IN the Centre Street courtroom the past whispered and rustled around me at every moment. I'd never really thought—certainly never admitted—that I'd moved to Arizona to put my past behind me; it just made a lot of sense at the time. After *Knife* bombed—well into the British Invasion, and with the scratchy-voiced, long-winded Bob Dylan (it took me awhile to admit what a genius he was) and all his folk-rock acolytes atop the charts with songs like *Mr. Tambourine Man* and *Like a Rolling Stone*—I knew our well-crafted girl-group pop truly had been swept by. No huge sadness: We'd had our day, I told myself, and a damn good run. I was getting reasonable royalties on a couple dozen songs, even the ones split with no-accounts like Manny Gold (and *Knife* was far from the only one so encumbered). There had been too much death, and after Anna's, I was in numb shock—on the far side of all those bombs exploding—and I just couldn't be in L.A. or New York any longer; I hit the road and, well, with my asthma Scottsdale made a lot of sense. When it became apparent that I needed something to do, I thought about teaching music; I'd always liked kids and loved thinking about the nuts and bolts of music theory. I came to believe I wasn't running from anything but toward a useful, less complicated, patently transparent life. After ten years I finally stopped renting, bought my ranch house in the hills, caught the eye of the cute, blonde-bobbed chemistry teacher, moved Misty in, moved Misty out, moved her back in, and back out, baked in the sun over 300 days a year, turned high school kids on to the joys of harmony; and for thirty years, that was my life.

Did I know when I let Sandy talk me into the suit how

much it would stir up the past—memories floating like white wisps of teasing fog? I didn't really think about it; just wanted to right the injustices. But as I sat here at the oak table, Manny and Punky across from me, the whole saga reared back and started snapping.

It all started, I believe, in Princess's bedroom. I was 16, Princess 15, and it was the fall of 1957. Rock 'n' roll had taken off a year or so before, and now it was all anyone at Forest Hills High could think about. I'd never been that musical—what, I'm going to learn the ukulele (my father played it, before he died), I'm going to take up the accordion just like Lawrence Welk?—but now I was taking guitar lessons, and not just anywhere but on 48th Street in Manhattan, a glorious F train ride away from Kew Gardens. Princess, a grade behind me in school, lived a few blocks over; I wasn't really aware of her, though after we got together, I did remember her sitting out on the stoop in front of her house with her older brother and sisters watching *The Honeymooners* on the black-and-white console TV they dragged to the street with an endless extension cord. Her brown eyes were huge, her nose bigger than it was later. She had a curious flip to her hair then, more exaggerated than the other girls in her class, and she parted her bangs just an inch more to the side; it was subtle but hinted inexorably, at least to me, of something dangerous and wanton.

Turned out, the truly wild Princess was in her piano playing. She'd been studying since she was, like, three, her mother, Millie Diamond, prophesying performances at Carnegie Hall. She could ripple off Bach and Haydn like running water, and when I met her, she was being schooled in the Spaniards: Albeniz, Granados, de Falla. But just as the little extra flip of her hair cut through the air like an indomitable corsair, the piano playing of her soul—Little Richard–style, Johnnie Johnson–style—charged ahead and took no prisoners.

I'd started talking to her one afternoon when she turned up across from me on the F train. She was carrying a patent-leather 45 box with high-kicking poodle-skirted dancers on it in pink and black, and after I'd racked my brain trying to figure out where she was going in the City with that, I just got up and stepped across the car and asked her.

"Do I know you?" she immediately said in her forward, buzz-saw-cutting voice.

"We're at Forest Hills High together. I'm a grade up."

She pinched her brow then, her unplucked eyebrows coming together, and said, "Larry Stephenson."

I stuck out a hand. "Friends call me Dink."

"That's a funny name," she said.

"It started out Dunk, 'cuz of me on the basketball court." I put my hands together, mimed a shot. "Then it became Dink—you know, when you sink a drop shot."

"You got the height," she said with half interest. "You any good?"

I shrugged. "Not too bad."

She didn't seem particularly impressed. We were silent, then finally I asked where she was going.

"To the Upper West Side. Gonna hang out with my cousin Betty. Catch up, play some discs—"

"You like music?"

She looked guarded. "Um, pretty much, yeah—"

" 'Cuz I'm on my way to my weekly guitar lesson."

Her eyebrows lifted. Then she looked skeptical. "Where's your guitar?"

"Um, I use one of theirs." My mother, who had saved up special to buy me my first Silvertone, was afraid someone would steal it from me on the subway, so I used one from the music store.

She bore in. "And who do you play like?"

"Well—" This was a tough question. There were no lessons offered in rock 'n' roll guitar at Sam Ash then, it was all theory, scales, and jazz chords. But at home I followed my heart. "Cliff Gallup."

"Gene Vincent's guitar player," Princess said. She reached into her 45 pack and pulled out a disc with a turquoise label. *"Twenty-flight Rock."*

"I love that song."

She kept her demure face, then pulled out another one. "Can you tell who this is just from the label?" That was my first question ever on *Princess Diamond's $64,000 Question* show. I took a quick glance at the orangish label, then nailed it.

"Buddy Holly. Coral Records, 'cuz you wouldn't be carrying Teresa Brewer or Guy Mitchell."

"What song?"

"I'm guessing—no, not *Peggy Sue*. How about *Words of Love*?"

"Close," Princess said. *"Rave On."* She held it up closer to me, and I made out the black lettering. "I like the beat. Just like—"

"Bo Diddley."

Princess nodded then, and that was the moment our partnership began, though it didn't really get going till two weeks later, when she finally invited me over to her house after school.

"Princess, darn you, don't play that jungle music!" was the first thing I heard when we were in her room. It was painted pink, with huge stuffed animals everywhere, and pictures of Elvis, Buddy, even the Drifters and the Moonbeams on her walls.

"Ma, stop yelling," she shouted down the hall.

"I said it, Princess!"

She was sitting at the spinet piano, which butted up against her bed; she could literally roll off the mattress and onto the piano seat. Later I'd found it had been a family piano in the sitting room that one day Princess had all by herself shouldered through the door to her room. She banged out a cascade of major chords, trilling her fingers over the sixths and sevenths.

"Darn you, Princess. At least shut the darn door!"

"O.K., Ma. But I gotta tell you, I got a boy in here."

"A . . . what?" And a second later the long-faced, fine-eyebrowed Mrs. Diamond was looking in at us.

"Ma, this is Larry. He likes to be called Dink, but I'm gonna call him Larry."

"Hi, ma'am." I stood and shook her hand.

"How're his manners?" Mrs. Diamond asked, past me; then she turned to me. "How're your manners?"

"I try," I said. I was trying not to laugh.

"Well, let's just keep that door open, shall we. And try to keep that jungle music down in there."

As soon as her mother left, Princess started playing *Good Golly, Miss Molly*, and it was as loud as an oncoming train.

It took us three months of after-school piano-guitar jams, high-holler harmony shouts, into-the-evening Elvis–to–Wanda Jackson–to–Frankie Lymon and the Teenagers rave ups, before we tried to write a song. By then Mrs. Diamond had accepted me, often inviting me for dinner. Mr. Diamond, I found out, had died when Princess was nine, a few years before my father. They didn't have much money but they owned their duplex home. Mrs. Diamond worked at a high school across town, managing the cafeteria. That got her out after the lunch break, and thus home before us. Not that there was anything of note to chaperone.

One afternoon Princess was twiddling around with a Platters song, *The Great Pretender*, when she threw more of a backbeat kick into it. Then she rose a fourth up from the main chord, then back down with a sixth, and like that started humming another melody.

"Hey, what's that?" I said. I was lying on her bed. It was a Diamond house rule that you took your shoes off before you came in. Seemed strange to me, but Mrs. Diamond said she'd read in *Ladies Home Journal* that that's how they did it in Japan. So I was lounging back there, a couple pillows squinched up behind me, my white socks kicking a volley-ball back and forth between my feet.

Princess didn't answer, just kept humming along as variations on *Great Pretender* flew out from her fingers; and then the tune didn't sound like anything I'd ever heard before. It swooped and soared off from the steady, rhythmic *shoop-shoop* of the Platters tune.

"That's cool," I said. She glanced over at me then, her cow-brown eyes glinting from under her bangs.

"Give me some words."

"Some—"

"Words," she repeated. "First ones that pop into your head." She was fully turned toward me, though she still rippled the new tune out of the piano.

"*I got a girl who—*" I started to mumble, then: "No, *I want a girl with fire, want a girl so nice. Girl who can melt my heart of ice.*"

Princess winked. "You got a heart of ice?"

I pulled back slightly. I was getting into the story here, the character, this guy who everyone thinks is distant and cold, but inside he's just dying for some high-temperature chick to turn him on. "*Girl who can see me the way I really am. Love me and need me and make me a man.*"

"You need some lady to *make* you a man?" Princess snickered.

"Not me," I said, flustered. "The guy in the song. Guy who sings the song. Like the guy in the Crew Cuts—"

Princess was right back at me. "That's who we're writing this for? Lame-o white-boy group like that?"

I pursed my forehead. "Hey, I don't know. I'm just making it up."

"Think Negro," she said. "Think black guys on a street corner, like over on Jefferson Street. What do they want?"

A guffaw exploded out of me. *"Girl who can walk it and talk it and shake like jam | Girl who knows just what kind of man I am."*

"Bing, bing, bing," Princess cried. She boosted the beat so it was rollicking, like Frankie Lymon, like the Clovers, and she hollered, *"Walk it and talk it and shake like jam."* The song was starting to kick.

"O.K.," she called out, fingers trilling in a holding pattern on a major chord, "think chorus. What's the song come down to?"

"What every song comes down to," I smarted off. *"I want you, and you want me—whoopee, doopee, doopee, dee!"*

"Larry! Come on, serious here." Princess leaned back, lightly fluttering her fingers over the keys as she knitted her brow. "O.K., I got it, *Like a man, like a man—the man I really am."* Her voice soared in plangent tones; she sounded like the girl she was, of course, but for just a second there I could imagine her as a moon-faced black dude in a plaid suit whooping it up before a silver microphone.

"Sweet!" I cried. I started singing along, adding, *"The man, the man, the man I really am.* That's what it's called, *The Man I Really Am?"*

Princess was still banging at the piano, going over the chorus, fine-tuning the filigree notes over the basic chords. "For now," she said. "Good enough for now." Ripple of notes; Fats Waller would've been proud. "Yeah, this is a good start. Now how about a bridge."

"A . . . bridge."

"You know."

By now I'd dropped the volleyball and was sitting up on the edge of her bed. "I don't," I said. "What's a bridge?"

She frowned. "What do you think it is?" That was always the Princess Diamond way, then and forever: Quiz you, make you think, challenge you, pull you out of yourself.

"How the fuck do I know?" just burst out of me.

"Larry!"

"Sorry," I mumbled. Princess had a real thing against coarse language; All Things Refined, was her motto, as well as her mother's. "O.K., I gotta play this game. A bridge is . . . something that goes over a river."

"Or a roadway. Or train tracks." She was still playing the tonic chord, *Bb* in this case. Running enough variations on it so it wasn't boring. "So a bridge does . . . what?"

"Princess!"

"Larry, come on."

"O.K.," I said. I closed my eyes, thought of the lovely, light-bejeweled arc of the Whitestone Bridge not far from us. "A bridge . . . takes you from one side of things to the other."

"Hah!" Princess exploded. "And so. . . ."

"O.K., Professor Einstein, a bridge in a song takes you from here to there."

And like that she sang our chorus again, *"Like a man, like a man—the man I really am,"* then jumped the chord up a fourth, to *Eb.* "Words, Larry, *words.*"

"O.K., all right, give me a second." My head was empty, a dark, vacant space. I heard Princess feather that *Eb* chord, waiting for me, and as if they were bright planets swinging by in orbit, words turned up. I sang in an almost falsetto, *"Only she sees it / Only she believes it / She's my true-blue girl."*

"Good," Princess cried. "I don't like that *'true-blue girl,'* though. That's banal."

"Banal?"

"Boring, Larry, *boring*!" She hung on a *C minor* chord for a minute, then said, "I think we can just pull in the title again, hammer it home." She sang, *"Only she sees it / Only she believes it / The man—the man I truly am."* I caught the change there, from *really* to *truly.*

And, damn! It worked.

We left the song there for the afternoon, though I scribbled down the lyrics we'd come up with, and Princess in her prize-winning script penciled in the chords above the words, then flicked off the accompaniment on the staff paper she kept by her bed. The next day after school I couldn't wait to get back to her house and work some more on our song. I waited for Princess underneath the school flagpole, where we usually met to walk home together. But she didn't show.

I called her that night at home.

"Oh," she said, "we were going to work?"

"I thought so, yeah," I said. I was in the kitchen after dinner, using the new wall phone. Behind me my mother was washing dishes. I had to cup my hand over my ear to hear Princess. "So where were you?"

"Oh, I was out skating."

"Skating."

"With a . . . friend."

"Who?"

"Greg."

"Who's that?"

"Oh, a friend." Was she smiling on her end of the phone? Smirking? Or just blank-faced? I couldn't tell.

"How come I don't know him?"

"You don't know everything about me, Larry Stephenson." She paused. "I actually don't think you know *anything* about me."

What was going on here? Was she trying to make me jealous? That didn't seem likely. There had never been anything like that between us. I mean, I liked Princess amazingly, but I was hung up on this girl in my class, Mandy Pappadapolous, which I think Princess had sort of sussed out. And even if she hadn't, I'd never given any indication of *liking* Princess. She really wasn't my type at all. For one, she was so pushy; and for another, she had a long, rectangular face that, even though she tried to hide it with her curls, was just a little too long, too boxy. Her eyes were wide and brown, wonderful, true enough, but to me they looked too far apart. Her chin was solid—no, stolid.

Princess was attractive enough, though, mainly through her energy, her vibrancy. I did love to be around her. And of course I didn't think I was any great shakes in the looks department, at least back then. My hair was in a crew cut, which made my slightly large ears pop out like Howdy Doody. I was also so tall, well over six feet, and had a pretty good build, I guess, because I liked to work out with my pals Sandy Aronson and Pete Crown, but of course I had my asthma, and sucking on my aspirator was no turn on, believe me. Still, I guess some parts of me must've worked, because I'd been getting secret notes passed to me since I was in elementary school, and in high school I noticed clusters of girls would sometimes fall ripely silent as I walked past on my way to the gym.

Still, what was Princess getting at?

"Well, what about our song?" I said.

"Let's get to work on it."

"When?"

"*Now!*" Bang, there was that Princess Diamond burst of energy. "Why don't you just run on over?"

"I'm pretty much—well, I got some homework to do."

"Well, yeah, Larry, and I gotta wash my hair—"

"Princess, it's true. This damn geometry."

She didn't say anything for a while, then said, "All right, tomorrow, after school. The flagpole?"

"Of course the flagpole." I was suddenly breathing furiously. "Hell, I'd still be there if I hadn't wised up."

She let my carping go by. "I'll be there tomorrow, I promise."

"All right," I finally said to her. Then we hung up.

It took us a couple more afternoons to finish up *The Man I Truly Am*, and we hammered it down tight like a well-built house; blew a storm of criticism at it, and it still stood. Along the way we started on another tune, called *Drop Kick*; it was a little contrived, high school football as a metaphor for love, but the rhymes snapped and the wit shone through. At the end of the week we were psyched at how well we worked together. We were sure we were on our way.

Of course the last thing the record business wanted then was a couple of young teenagers from Queens peddling rock 'n' roll songs. We recorded demos of our two tunes on Princess's uncle's reel-to-reel, then she dragged me through the tiny offices along Broadway. Everywhere the response was the same: *Whatta ya kids want? You think this is* Romper Room? *You want me to listen to your . . . tape? All you got's a tape? You ever hear of acetates?* Pointing to the record player on the desk. *Now get outta here!*

Princess found a place that converted our tape into a disc, and said we had to go back. I kept thinking of all the cigar smoke—just a minute in one of those offices and my asthma was kicking in; I was trying not to double over wheezing—and the guys with the cauliflower noses barking at us, and I told her I couldn't. No, not possible!

That stop Princess? Of course not. And she even got a couple listens to our demo, and at least one word of encouragement. I quote: "Come back when you grow up, little girl."

Princess spit the sentence out with contempt. "I am grown up. Look at me." She was standing in all her five-foot-eleven glory. "Pigs! We'll show 'em."

"What do you mean?"

"We'll find our own singers."

"Our own. . . . Where we going to find them?"

Princess gave me a look as if she couldn't believe me. "Larry, New York's full of 'em—every darn street corner. Queens has them. But . . . think about the Bronx! Brooklyn! *Manhattan!*"

That's how we first saw the Annas. For the next couple of years Princess dragged me to every talent show, after-school dance, church-basement sing-off she could find. She got really into surveying the talent, and so we were lying low now; not pushing our songs on anyone (though we kept writing them), not venturing into Brill Building territory, not doing anything more than putting the best eye we could on what was out there.

The girls called themselves the Meringues, and we found them at a Friday-night talent show at a high school in Upper Manhattan. This was 1959, and though the girl-group sound wouldn't take off for another few years, there'd already been one timeless girl-group hit, the Chantels' *Maybe* in '58, as well as a couple charting singles by the Shirelles. (Their first Number 1, written by our 1650 neighbors and competitors Carole King and Gerry Goffin, the great *Will You Love Me Tomorrow?*, wouldn't hit for well over another year.) The Meringues didn't have any clear models for what they'd come up with, and we didn't have anything in our heads for what we'd see. So when I saw those leggy girls, in their tight black leotards and pink angora sweaters, hair teased up tall as baker's toques, sassy smiles winking perfect white teeth, the three of them on that low wooden stage in the school auditorium, with the terrible acoustics and a desultory audience perched on wobbly chairs with swaths of punk initials switch-bladed into the wooden armrests, I was shaken to my 18-year-old soul.

Here's what Princess and I discovered: Three girls, the oldest, Trudy Dubower, 16; the other two, her sister, Anna, and cousin Sweet McClain, only 15—all of them easily going on 21, hell, 25. They were dressed identically, and in that year when all girls still wore dresses or at least skirts, they were in those tight, thigh-hugging leotards and fuzzy angora sweaters. I right away noticed the lovely swell under Anna's baby-blankie top. The name, the Meringues, I found out later, came initially from pies that Mrs. Dubower loved to bake in their East Harlem kitchen—when I came to know her, I met a round, sweet, bubbly woman who always seemed to have a pie cooling outside their fifth-floor window—but by now the name evidently referred to the way they'd done their hair: swept up, then tumbling higher and higher in a towering calculus of improbable flips and waves.

On the stage was a professional backup band—CORSAIRS, it read on the bass drum head—five guys in shiny red-and-gold vests and tight pegged black slacks, with pompadours flying high. The Corsairs hit a solid beat, the snare drum popped, and the three girls moved in step to the front of the stage, Anna out front, Trudy and Sweet flanking her. Anna leaned into the silver microphone, almost kissing it. And then the girls started singing. They weren't doing original songs, just covers of current groups like the Spiders, the Teenagers, the Chantels, but they made the tunes jump. The first thing I could tell about Anna's voice was that it was big enough—almost as big as her hair—but unformed; she blasted forth with uncommon passion and fury, but didn't hit every note spot on and occasionally stumbled over her breathing.

At least that's what later I remembered having seen, after Punky, Princess, and I had worked with the girls and polished them to professional standards. What I was sure I saw that night was the hottest, wildest chickie ever.

Anna had this fascinating coloring, a faint mocha under soap white, and her skin was smoother than any I'd ever seen. Even from the audience she picked up all the light around and just glowed. Her hair then was a deep burnished brunette with mahogany tones, and though most of it did its curling thing above her forehead, she had a straight-cut sheath of bangs that she kept brushing aside in nervous but dear flicks as she stood there and sang. Each time she did, she rolled her eyes—*Oh, that darn hair!*—and yet they were always wonderfully expressive eyes, with a catlike sweep at their corners; timeless, Egyptian eyes. Anna in her tight leotard had the curves, too. Trudy and Sweet were fine lookers, but if either of them had been singing lead, no way you'd think anything but, How come that girl over *there* isn't carrying it?

How did they sound? They had *me* with every note, though to this day I don't know if it was their performance or just the way Anna held the stage. I'd crept forward in my chair till I was on the edge of it. Next to me Princess had folded her arms over her chest and lifted her chin. It was hard to know what she was thinking about the Meringues, the fifth of ten groups on the bill that night. Maybe nothing. Or maybe she was reading my interest. Not that that should have mattered.

The girls sang their three songs, and then on came the Harlequins, four black girls in pink pinafores who twirled and spun in tight choreography and hit harmonies far richer than the Meringues; they did everything great, and I wasn't surprised to see Princess moving to the edge of her seat.

After the show we compared notes.

"I think we could work with them," Princess said. We were in the trophy-case-filled lobby to the high school auditorium. There was this hideous over-bright light above us, and Princess looked washed out, even though excitement beamed off her face.

"They're a little rough," I said. "But I see the talent there."

"I thought they were smooth as a milk shake—"

"Hey, should I jot that down? *He walked into the room, smooth as a shake / I found myself caught doing a . . . a double take. . . .*"

"No, how about, '*Right then I thought my heart would break—*' " Princess snapped her fingers, added her usual kick to my stirrings of a melody. "Sure, make a note of it. But really, we should go talk to them, right?"

"Sure!" I said. I was still half-distracted with my new

lyrics, teasing a little more lift out of the melody and beginning to imagine the lovely girl I'd just seen on the stage singing it.

Princess charged ahead of me backstage. All of the acts were bunched about, chattering up a storm. The winner of the talent show had been announced, and the prize had gone to a solo act—a guy with Presley looks and Little Richard moves. Second had gone to a guy group singing pure doo-wop. Third had gone to the Harlequins. Now all the other performers were carping noisily over the choices while packing up.

I saw the three Meringues in a corner, in front of a floor-length mirror, all alone except for a couple older women. I was heading right to them when I realized Princess wasn't with me. I stopped, looked around. She was far off to my right, waving at me. *Come on, come on*, I could see her lips saying. She was of course standing right next to the Harlequins. My head jolted back.

The Harlequins' leader was Renee Montgomery, a pie-faced cutie compared with the Meringues, a demure one-wave flip and well-polished dark-java skin.

"I was just telling the girls how much we liked them," Princess said. She was smiling a big, canary-eating smile.

Renee held out her slim, fingernail-painted hand, and I shook it, followed by those of her backup singers, Jackie, Marsha, and Sharleen. I could tell they were all very polite and well-mannered. "You guys were great," I said.

"And I was just about to tell them that we're interested in producing them," Princess said. I started to say something like, Are we ready to produce anybody?—we don't even have a studio or any experience, when Princess shot me a look. She turned to Renee. "We can get to you next week, if you're free."

Renee turned to her groupmates; they all threw curious eye storms back and forth, the months if not years of basement rehearsals, going over and over harmonies till they were clear as glass, in each eyebrow flutter. A moment later Renee stepped over and shook my hand. "Yes, Mr. Stephenson, we'd love to come work with you. Do we need to sign a contract now?"

Princess reached over and took Renee's hand from mine, then vigorously shook it. "No, no," she said. "We'll start working on some material informally. When the time is right, we'll go to our lawyers and get everything drawn up perfect." She stepped back with a huge smile on her face. "Welcome to P&L Records!"

Chapter Three

OF COURSE THERE wasn't any P&L Records (nor L&P or *D*&P, as I'd have had it), and there never was. Didn't matter a whit. There was Princess and our backlog of songs, and after about a year of steady work we'd cut three discs on the Harlequins and put the last of them—*The Herald of the Morning*—in the Top 40.

We'd also connected with Moe Grushensky and Manny Gold. I looked over at Manny, with Moe behind him, now. This was Tuesday morning, and more motions were being presented to Judge MacIntire. I was told this first week might be nothing but legal wrangling; Sandy planned to start calling witnesses on Monday. Frankly, I was surprised the two guys were still going. Moe had had a constant cigar stuck in the corner of his liver-colored lips from the day I met him, and even now, during each break, he'd take the elevator downstairs and light up on the street. And Manny! Though sleek and cool in the '60s, the years had made him beefy in the jowls and chin, and his belly swelled under his monogrammed shirts. He at least tried to pretend he'd kept his hair. He'd also been a huge drinker and three-pack-a-day smoker till a couple heart attacks and a quintuple bypass threw the fear into him; during the trial, though I've seen him munch on carrot sticks in the hallway, I can tell what dances before his eyes is a two-inch Porterhouse.

But there they are; and there they both were back in 1960 when Princess and I and the Harlequins went looking for a record deal.

We had the Harlequins polished to a fire-engine-chrome brightness. They sang beautifully, moved with small but perfect gestures, and on the stage looked like they were born there. They were only singing songs by us then, a few we'd written before we'd hooked up with them, but most tailored just for them. The lesson? Princess and I fired on all pistons when we had specific singers to write for. Our work, in truth, wasn't about *our* self-expression; it was telling the stories our singers would sing if *they* could write. That was the case then, and that was the case, certainly, with the Annas.

I hadn't forgotten the exotic chick singer with the big voice stepping wild before her two backup girls in that high school auditorium, but I didn't do anything further to contact them. Our time was full with the Harlequins, and Princess had made it clear she wasn't interested in white girls in bulging angora sweaters. For Princess and me it was all about the music; and in our hands those four black girls were as vibrant and responsive as a beautiful Stradivarius or a racing Lamborghini.

Moe Grushensky owned Bel-Air Studios, this airless place in the Bronx (named after hoity-toity Bel-Air, California, where Moe's cousin Morris had moved after making a pile helping establish the L.A. rag trade). Bel-Air Studios was off Fordham Road, behind a candy store that ran numbers. It was just a nine-foot-by-twelve-foot room, with a small closet next to it with a hole knocked into it—the control booth. Moe recorded onto a two-track Studer. He'd set the place up to capture the local street-corner-singing talent, and he'd already had years of hits under a number of self-owned (then self-lost) labels. Back in the late '50s, Moe was the quintessential record man; he could wave his finger in the air and pull out a hit, as simple as if he were wrapping cotton candy around it.

Manny Gold was the quintessential character, hustler, *gonif*—and Moe's partner. Well, sort of. Manny was partners with anybody he shook hands with, if he wanted to be; he'd partner up with the sun and the moon if he could've gotten them on the vig. We didn't use the word *mafia* then, or *cosa nostra*, or any of those terms that moved copies of *Look* magazine. We didn't say anything. We just knew that Manny was the money guy—if you were so dumb as to actually need money to pay for musicians and studio time and record-pressing plants.

Manny was the brother-in-law of Dante Sylvestri, who worked in the Sylvestri family trades of gambling, truck hijackings, and shakedowns. Dante had married Pitzi Golderstern, and the family was none too happy about that. (I saw Pitzi a few times; even over 40 she was one of the hottest women I'd ever seen—whistlebait in toreador pants.) Was there a job for Pitzi's younger brother? Well, there was the little religion problem, and though he was tall enough, he sure wasn't made of muscle; still, the story goes that Dante saw some crazy fire in his eyes, and after a couple of tryouts way up in the Bronx (barely whispered about to this day), Manny was in.

Manny knew money, and after an apprenticeship in the family's loan-shark program, the Sylvestris set him up as angel to the whole early R&B group scene. Manny's one great asset? He actually *liked* Negroes, and more important Negro music. None of that Mario Lanza or Johnny Roselli shit for him. Manny started paying twenty-five bucks for a haircut, bought suits at Brooks Brothers, and legally changed his name to Gold; said it gave him class, like he'd gone through a down-town banking program. After that he plastered his name over everything he could: publishing contracts, songwriter credits, production credits—anywhere he could get a slice of the pie.

So those were our pals. The funny thing was, Moe and Manny made the best music. Princess used to say that if Mitch Miller of Columbia Records took the subway out to Queens and knocked politely at her door—and if he had the whole blooming Martin Luboff Choir hanging back there, trampling the rhododendrons and crowding up the sidewalk—and ol' Mitch got down on his knees and begged her to let him sign the Harlequins, Princess would simply tell him to take his little goatee back across the East River.

"White bread" we all called that corporate *scheiss* when we were being polite, and all we ever wanted to eat was pumpernickel and dark-seeded rye.

Moe and Manny's approach to business? *These are bums off the street we're dealing with, why do they deserve anything?* So the deal they signed us to was of course extortionate—I think we'd see about half a cent on a 45, and then only if they paid us—but Moe was going to let Princess and me produce the girls, and that we did. The only catch: We had to stick their names on the records as cowriters. Who'da believed the writing team of Diamond, Stephenson, Grushensky, and Gold—but there we all were, even from the earliest days, right under the title on those first Harlequins records.

Princess and I talked about it. We both knew it was either sign on or don't record. Either play along or . . . well, there were the occasional record guys who mysteriously— and possibly luckily—turned up on crutches. *Stairs—yeah, that's the deal. See, I'm so, so stupid. I just tripped and, yeah, fell down this flight of stairs. . . .*

Was all that in the back of Princess's head when I told her about my lawsuit? Sure, Manny was an old, belly-swollen guy now, but there was no reason to think he was any less connected or that he'd stopped packing. (Though of course he couldn't smuggle a gun through the metal detectors at the courthouse.) Word was, the music biz wasn't that different, even if old-fashioned payola was now being called "independent promotion" and CDs fell off the backs of trucks instead of records. Was I at risk going up against Manny Gold now? I glanced across the courtroom at him and Punky, then took a deep breath. I liked to think all the publicity my suit was getting—this was the famous Punky Solomon in the docket, and the fabled Anna Dubower being mentioned in every other breath—would keep me safe. But in truth I just didn't know. Did I have second thoughts? Daily. *Hourly.*

Would anything get me to withdraw my suit? Another deep sigh. Nothing I'd been able yet to imagine.

And so far everything had proceeded in an upright, straight-forward, *legal* manner. Still . . . let's just say I planned to keep watching my back.

✳ ✳ ✳ ✳ ✳

IT WAS IN EARLY 1962 that Punky Solomon turned up, and it was just when we needed him.

Princess and I had our songwriting chops down. With the small success of the Harlequins, we'd moved down to Tin Pan Alley, renting an office the size of a walk-in refrigerator at 1650 Broadway, just up from the Brill Building, with nothing in it but a castoff steel desk, a couch with feathers floating out of it, and a scarred upright piano. Windows? Well, our neighbors were lucky; they looked out on an airshaft. But we loved the place, worked it like a job. We'd show up about 10 a.m., Princess always with a bagel, me with an egg-and-bacon sandwich; coffee would be available down the hall for a nickel; and we'd settle in, Princess at the piano, me lying on the couch, and we'd riff on our lives.

"What happened to you yesterday?" Princess would say.

"Not much."

"Well, something had to have happened." She'd squinch up her nose.

"I don't know, I went to the dentist—"

"You went to the—"

"Yeah."

"And?"

I started singing, a tune I'd giggled through on the subway in.

> *I went to the dentist, to have a tooth pulled*
> *The dentist stood over me, he was such a scold*
> *He said, "You've been eating way too many sweets"*
> *I said, "Since my baby left me, that's all I want to eat."*

"Are you kidding?" Princess said when I was done, though she kept her fingers crackling on the ivories.

I shushed her with a finger before my lips.

"What're you gonna call this sucker?" She banged a particularly loud chord. "*Cavities of Love?*"

"I'm working on it," I said. "I think I got it. Just keep playing."

She did, and I went on:

> *He said, "You gotta get some new love in your diet*
> *"Or else your teeth are gonna buy it.*
> *"You need love floss to beat . . . those cavities."*
> *Love floss—clean 'em right up. . . .*

"*Love Floss?*" Princess made a face. "Larry, are you nuts?" But she was smiling, too.

"*Love floss*. . . . Damn, I need a rhyme for *up*."

"*Love floss*," Princess sang to the tune, "*O.K., you can spit now in the cup.*"

"Yeccch! That's sure Top 40!" But I was starting to crack up, too.

"*Love floss, love floss, love floss—I think I've had eeee-nough*," she sang over her laughter. When she finally stopped playing and we looked at each other, trying to keep a straight face, I said, "All right, so what happened to *you* yesterday."

But inspiration struck often enough, and when we'd finish off a tune, we'd head up to Bel-Air Studios and work to record the song in Moe Grushensky's back room.

Recording was simple. We'd bring in our hired musicians, drums, electric bass, guitar, piano, maybe a couple of strings, set 'em up around two microphones, then turn on the Studer. It was a raw sound, though that wasn't anything we were consciously going for; really, it was all we knew how to do. We didn't care that much about levels, and the only way to change anything anyway was to move one of the mikes away from the drums and closer to the piano, say. But then you had to have a whole new track, and though the

Harlequins were good—as were the other groups Princess had dug up for us, the El Coronas, the Majesties—they'd wear out if we had to do too many takes.

Of course the records only had to play well out of juke boxes and car radios and small, tinny disc players, and we thought we were doing fine until we heard Millie Strong singing *Wading in the River of Love*. Good fuckin' God! That record, Punky Solomon's first chart production, sounded like you were standing waist deep in that river of love, and it was wide as the Mississippi, and rain was falling, thunder bellowing, lightning snapping—the very heavens had just cracked wide open. All there in two and a half minutes of music. By the end of the tune you weren't wading in that glorious river, you were swimming for dear life.

Wading in the River of Love had come out of L.A., SilverTone Studios to be exact, and Punky Solomon had produced it. The record debuted on the Hot 100 at Number 12, leaped to Number 3 the second week, then held down Number 1 for three weeks after that. You couldn't turn on your transistor without hearing it; and even for pros like Princess and me, you couldn't turn on your transistor without *hoping* you'd hear it. It was the first single that got church and opera and some shanty down in Mississippi all into the same groove. You went into the song with your heart and soul knocking; you came out of it cleansed, baptized, redeemed.

The stories about Punky Solomon came east before he did. He'd evidently grown up in a small coastal Northern California town, San Remo, which he later used as the name of his record company; but how a Jewish kid started out there, we never knew. One story had Punky's parents escaping the Nazis, not penniless so they ended up in Brooklyn but instead absconding with Nazi gold; the other tale going around had his father, like Manny, being "connected" back East but pulling his chips off the table and hiding out in a castle overlooking the sea. Punky, it was rumored, had grown up a pampered prince, world domination his birthright. None of this was ever spoken of in Punky's presence; none of it was documented in any way.

But what we heard—and knew beyond doubt—was that Punky Solomon had hit the L.A. music scene unlike anyone before him, with furious, unstoppable ambition and, true coin of the realm in our biz, astonishing ears.

When we heard that Punky was moving east—in rock 'n' roll, L.A. was still nowhere in 1962—we all wanted to meet him. Up and down Tin Pan Alley the word was out: The L.A. boy genius producer was coming to town.

Somehow Manny Gold got him. Had they done business on the Coast? Was there some truth to the tales about Punky's father? Had Punky heard that Manny was the guy in town who made things happen and sought him out himself? Or was there more to their getting together than I ever knew? You could certainly believe the latter, but when Punky first turned up on Broadway, Manny in his high pompadour and Eddie Fisher glamour turned up next to him, his arm around Punky's shoulders, showing him the ropes.

We met Punky at Manny and Moe's invite at the Edison coffee shop, in a back booth already replete with kasha and scrambled eggs. Punky was at the center of the table, and we had to reach over the food to shake his hand. His handshake—that was the first thing I knew about him, and I've never forgotten it. It was light, not really limp, but with no I'm-a-tough-guy affectation; his hands were smooth, and the handshake had a silky, gossamer-wings quality to it—his hand hung there, lighter than air, and it was as if you were shaking an object existing beyond willfulness or even gravity. A little disconcerting, especially the first time; but that handshake was not the only quality that made Punky such an original and now well-known character. There was his voice, of course, a little higher pitched than usual but with a curious bass rumble to it, too, as if he were two instruments—flute and bassoon, say—at once. There were his tattoos, way ahead of his time: curvy sea-maidens along his forearms, a wreath of thorns around his left wrist. And then there was that brilliant paintbrush goatee I always loved. Was it Punky's influence that got me to grow my own goatee a couple months later, along with half the guys we ended up playing with in L.A.? Well, I'll never admit it.

And whatever the truth to Punky's background, it was all a mystery; indeed, the mystery was one of the things that made Punky Punky. Though there was one interview with him in the teen mag *Hits-a-Poppin'!* that I came upon a couple years later where he seemed to let a little something out. The interviewer asked what Punky's first inspirations were, and instead of him saying the obvious, Elvis, Frankie Lymon, the Chantels, he answered like this:

"You know, it was a painting—a picture of a painting."

"For real?"

"Yeah, it was that Botticelli thing, the honey in the half shell. In a book at the library. I don't know, there was just something about that painting, the blonde chick standing there, really mysterious, and that hair—dig, her hair flew up in the air, but also fell all the way to her, well, her secret place. Man, I loved that hair, and that sense of freedom, and the way the angels flew around her. The whole thing was just so magical."

"I don't really—"

"No, you see, I used to go down to the beach after school every day when I was a kid and just sit there. I didn't have a lot of—well, I just went every day and sat there alone. And I looked out at the sea."

"You looked out and—"

"And I saw things and heard things. Deep rumbles. Rhythms. And . . . well, that's why I loved that painting."

"You saw girls floating on clam shells?"

"I *saw* things, man. And heard them. Let's just leave

it at that. Things that made me who I am. That's all I can say."

When we sat down, Punky turned immediately to Princess. Now I have no doubts that in our partnership she and I ultimately were equals; we both polished off our share of chorus hooks and swooping falsetto bridges that kicked our songs home. But it was also true to both of us that Princess was the serious motor here, in terms of getting our stuff out, of fulfilling our ambitions. It was equally true that whenever we met someone for the first time they'd usually talk to me first. She was the girl, I was the man. Simple as that. And they all only trusted the man.

Not Punky. He was all over Princess. "I love your stuff, you guys," he said, his voice breathy, his baby-blue eyes right at Princess's calf-brown ones. "I love your street sense. When I hear a Harlequins tune, I see jack hammers, I see subway exhaust blowing out of those rubber cones, I'm right here in the middle of the big, wondrous city."

Princess gave a slight nod, said, "Thanks."

"Yeah, but it's more than that." Punky leaned forward. "You know what kind of shit they put out around here." He waved his well-manicured hand. I noticed for the first time a gold ring with a huge black garnet stone in it. "*I love you, you love me, shooby, dooby, dooby, whee.* They could be manufacturing it in an oven—throw in some flour, some sugar, some almond extract—voilà, there's your next hit for the little girls and the little boys—the teen-ag-ers." He pounded the table, so hard the cups and saucers jumped.

"Teen hits! I can't believe it." Punky's mouth was moving fast, his fine hands flicking the air before him, quick as a humming bird's wings. "Teen this, juvenile that. Anybody who says that doesn't hear it—doesn't hear the fuckin', the fuckin' . . . stuff."

Punky winced, his fine, plucked eyebrows bowing over his fierce blue eyes. He was never that articulate, and usually he didn't bother to try to get the words right. I remember session after session when all he'd tell the players was something like, "I want it to sound more like . . . more like. . . ." A wave of his arms. "More like . . . *that*!" And the magic was, they'd always get it—just what he wanted.

"I hate fuckin' teenagers," he went on. His fingers were scampering over the table, strangely as if he were playing boogie-woogie piano. "And yet—the kids get it." Up flew his hands: crescendo! "So we gotta go for them. The fuckin' teenagers." Punky himself was only twenty-two then; I was just twenty-one; Princess twenty. "You know?"

I wasn't sure what exactly he was getting at, but even with all his cursing, which Princess purported to hate, he had her mesmerized, and she just nodded away.

"But the—the fuckin' cake bakers, they just throw in their vanilla, their marzipan—" Punky's eyes flickered then, a gesture I understood; he'd used a cool word and was storing it away. And sure enough *marzipan* turned up in a song a year later: *All our plans / Sweet as marzipan.* "And then they laugh with, with . . . contempt!

"But you guys—" now his eyes glanced at me "—you don't got any contempt. You don't look *down* at your songs, you look up at 'em. Me too. We're puttin' truth, the astonishing truth, in those tunes, man. You know? We're . . . we're . . . we're. . . ."

Punky's hands churned like helicopter blades, but he'd run out of words. The table was quiet for a minute, everyone contemplative in the wake of Punky's word-flurry, then Moe Grushensky called out to our waiter, "Hymie, more coffee." Then to all of us: "Come on, eat up. The kasha is getting cold!"

Later I thought about what Punky was trying to say. He was saying that we weren't writing symphonies or operas, or epic, epochal poems like Eliot's *The Waste Land* or Pound's *Pisan Cantos*, but nonetheless we were no less serious about our art. We just had tight definition, like a sonnet, a Schubert art song. Two to three minutes. (You went longer at your peril, as we all later found out.) Verses, choruses, one or two bridges. A hook that would immediately pull you in when you were cruising along in your Chevy. Words flowing straight from the Philco transistor up by your ear to your immediate soul while you walked from the school parking lot to first-period homeroom. Rhythm sweeping in with such vivid yet subtle force that your feet had to start moving, as involuntarily as breath. Simple, compressed passion exploding with enough fury to change your life.

Punky saw that we were trying to get to this place of masterpiece, our little bites of heaven; and God knows he was, too. By the end of that breakfast it was decided we would all work together.

But not in the Bronx. Punky didn't even have to see Moe's Bel-Air Studios to know they'd be too small, too cheap to work for him. He'd need a big room, and he wanted it in Midtown. Manny shrugged, said we could lease some place, no problem, but Punky said that he'd love his own studio, just the way he needed it. Moe glanced up, to the god of his bank balance, and said, "We can do it. Might take a little time, though."

"I want to come out with a huge bang." Punky gave out his thin, devilish smile. His blond bangs fell over his forehead. "Like the fuckin' A-bomb." His hands scooped out a mushroom cloud, then he lowered his hands before him and leaned forward conspiratorily. "Some new songs, maybe even some new singers." Then he uttered the words that forever changed my life. "Wouldn't it be great to get some *white* girls who could do what the Harlequins, the Shirelles are doing?"

✳ ✳ ✳ ✳ ✳

IT WASN'T THAT the Meringues and their vivid lead singer were merely a distant, floating vision to me in my just-before-sleep bed; I'd started looking out for them. The group just never seemed to be anywhere. Remember, this was the very early '60s: There was no *Time Out* magazine, *The New Yorker* only covered Broadway. Except for the huge Alan Freed Brooklyn Fox galas, rock 'n' roll was a furtive, adolescent pursuit; there was no rag that covered small sock hops, talent shows, battles of the bands. And there were a million groups. I always kept an eye open for the Meringues, but I just never found them.

That was going to change. Punky's statement sat with me. Of course I knew about Sam Phillips down at Sun Records: "Get me a white boy with the Negro sound and I could sell a million records." Phillips had found Elvis and sold a gazillion. But that color line had long been breached. The Shirelles sold a million records now.

No, I think Punky was after something else—a widening of the palette. There'd be black songs to be sung, then there'd be white ones. (This was a year before Berry Gordy at Motown packaged Mary Wells and the Supremes as any old girls next door.) And, yes, someone like Anna Dubower, who certainly when you first saw her looked mostly Anglo, could be an easy eyeful for white boys, brown boys, black boys, any ol' kind of boy . . . hell, *this* boy. In any event, after Punky's words, I became obsessed with finding the Meringues.

I didn't tell Princess, though. I set out on weekends cruising clubs, schools, anywhere the music would be played. I asked around. "The Meringues—what, they a spic group?" This scenester, in front of a car wash, had a waterfall that'd give Niagara pause, and pimples.

"No, like lemon meringue pie. White, frothy."

"You're making me hungry, man. But I don't know no group named that."

Nobody knew no group like that.

I'd describe the girls, and my voice would flute up into winsome wishfulness.

"I knew three girls like that, sisters, a cousin I think."
This from a girl with a Breck hair flip and pleated skirt, stick-
ing up a flyer for a rock 'n' roll show on a plywood building-
site fence in Upper Manhattan.

"Oh?"

"They were really good. What was that name again?
Macaroons?"

"Meringues."

"Yeah, I think that was it. Tight black pants, tight pink
sweaters." She pursed her pretty brow. "But that was last
year. Something—something tells me they changed their
name."

I leaned forward. "To what?"

"The. . . ." She shook her head. "Something like clothing. The Poodle Skirts? No. The Cameos? The Peter Pan
Collars? No, not any of that." She gave her head another
shake. "I'm sorry, Mister, just can't think of it."

I kept looking. Then one Sunday I was driving my mom
and my sister, Nancie, out Sunrise Highway to our cousins
on Long Island, and when we passed a white-pilastered supper club called the Stardust Lounge, I saw a sign that said,
SATURDAY NIGHT: THE PENNY LOAFERS. Right above it
was a photo, and as we drove by I could just barely make out
three girls with cats' eyes and hair piled high.

Could that be them? Saturday night, right? I closed my
eyes and saw them up on the stage of the Stardust Lounge
. . . last night. My heart fell.

On the way home I told my mom I wanted to pull over.

"What for?"

"Um, work."

"You don't have any work." Mom, dreaming of a doc-
tor/lawyer/Indian chief, never saw my songwriting as real
employment.

"I'm not gonna talk about that now."

"It's all the way over across the highway."

"It's important, Mom. We could just swing around the next turnoff and—"

"I gotta go to the bathroom."

"Mom!"

"Nancie, you want to stop for Larry's silliness—"

"If Dink wants to, Ma, I don't see the—" my sister said from the backseat.

"But I gotta go to the—"

"All right, all right," I said, throwing up my hands. I just drove on, straight back to Kew Gardens.

But that night I was more and more sure that the Penny Loafers were them. I thought I could head out on my own to the Stardust Lounge the next Saturday night—if they were playing one Saturday, might not they be on the next?—but it turned out I couldn't wait till the next week. The next morning I woke up lit bright by my vision of the girls; I borrowed the car and drove back out to Long Island.

The Stardust Lounge had that look all nightclubs do during the day, quiet, unearthly still, somnolent—like Sleeping Beauty in her bed, waiting for that nighttime-is-the-right-time kiss. I felt out of place till I saw the poster I'd seen from the road. There my three girls were, hair high, eye-shadowed eyes wide, smiles saucy, knowing; the only thing different was how they were dressed, in pastel dresses, and posed: sitting on straight-back chairs, their ankles demurely crossed like country club girls.

There was no sign of life, but I pounded on the tight-shut metal door with the little peep window, and finally a short guy with a big forehead and a tiny mustache peeked through the window, then opened the door.

"Hey, buddy, whattaya think, we're closed."

"I know," I said. I looked at the guy for a second: It was only 11 a.m. "I'm looking to find The Penny Loafers."

The guy shrugged. "They'll be back next week, man."

"This really can't wait." I pulled out one of the cards that

Princess insisted we have made up: P&L RECORDS, LARRY (DINK) STEPHENSON, VICE PRESIDENT A&R and handed it over. "I'm trying to contact the girls. Might have a—"

Up went the mustached guy's eyebrows. "You thinking of signing 'em?"

"Well, just an audition for—"

"Hey, you sign 'em, I oughta get a finder's fee, right, buddy?"

I didn't know what to say for a second, then thinking of what Princess would do, I told him, "Absolutely. I find them, we'll have our lawyers call you right up."

The guy led me back to his cluttered office, walls hung with black-and-white promo pictures of dozens of groups, desk piled high with carbon copies of invoices. He rooted around in a metal box jammed tight with three-by-five cards, then pulled one out. He pursed his mouth, his mustache bowing like a crow's wings. "I don't have a number, just an address we put on the checks."

"No phone number?"

He shrugged again. "I remember right, the girls don't have a phone."

That seemed odd, but back in the early '60s not everyone did. "O.K., the address'll be great."

He held back the card. "You're not gonna stiff me now, are you?"

I smiled. "I'll talk to our lawyers." I gave my head a shake. "Not a chance."

The address was on East 120th Street, pretty far over— Spanish Harlem. That was unexpected. The girls had looked pretty much Anglo to me.

I headed back to town, crossed over the Triborough, then out 125th. The building was four stories, built of yellow limestone with a stoop at the entrance. The apartment number I'd written down was 4B. There was no buzzer by the heavy black-metal door, and when I tried it, it wasn't locked.

Up four flights of crooked, wobbly stairs. I heard music blaring from a front apartment, a rhythmic Cuban *son*, that caught my feet and put an involuntary bump in my hips, but when I approached that door, I saw it was 4A. 4B was in the back.

The door opened onto a tall, high-foreheaded woman with thick, curly black hair. She was holding a feather duster, and she looked happy. There was a welcoming smile in her eyes.

"Hello," I said. I held out one of those business cards. "I'm Larry Stephenson of P&L Records, and I'm here looking for the, um, the Penny Loafers. Are they—"

The woman interrupted me with a shake of her head. "I don't like the name either, but it gets them work." The tall woman gave me a wink. "And that's what it's all about, right, Mr.—" She turned my card in her hands. I saw her fingers were long, slender, and well-callused. "Stephenson."

"Um, yes, ma'am."

I didn't know who this woman could be. She had high, regal cheekbones, sharp green eyes, and bright-red painted lips, but her skin was dark—the color of well-worn leather— yet exceptionally smooth. I caught what I thought was a trace of the lead singer in the woman's thin nose, her half-moon cat's eyes, but her skin was so much toned with brown and black.

"And you're wondering who I am?"

I felt my eyebrows pinch. "I was told this was where they—" I started to say again.

"Well, come on in," she said. She held out her fine hand. "I'm Ramona Sanchez Dubower." She gripped my hand tightly, then let it go and let me follow her in.

"And you are?" I finally got up the courage to say.

"Oh, I'm the girls' mother." She threw her head back, opened her fiery lips. "Well, Anna's and Trudy's." Her gaze bore in at me. I heard a whisper of an accent. "And I just bet you're dying to know how *that* miracle came to take place."

She loved to talk, Anna's mother did. She also, it turned out, had a bit of the stage mother in her: She loved nothing more than to brag on her daughters. She poured me a tall glass of a teeth-meltingly sweet fruit punch, swirled a fresh lemon slice into it, then sat me on the plastic-wrapped striped couch and told me more than I ever hoped to know.

The part I found most interesting was about her own background. Ramona Sanchez had been a big-band singer when she'd met Gerald Dubower, trombonist with the Peg-Leg Murray Band; Dubower was, on his mother's side, from Mayflower stock (and his father's, a more suspicious Isle of Man family), raised in Connecticut, now the Dubowers' black sheep as he toured the country blowing hot jazz. Ramona's father was Cuban, her mother a half-black, half-Choctaw woman from Mississippi; she'd grown up in Greenwood, Miss., but her family moved to New York City when she was twelve. She started singing all around Harlem, and that's where she got hired by Peg-Leg and fell hard for the black-eyed horn player.

Marriage, two kids—both girls, Anna and Trudy—a move to Greenwich, Connecticut, and then thirteen years back, Gerald Dubower was killed in a bus accident outside Kansas City. The family was devastated, Anna in particular. "Her father loved her special," Ramona told me, "and sometimes I wonder if she's ever even half got over him." She raised her eyes.

"What'd you do?" I asked. I was pretty drawn in to the story, interesting in its own right, but of course the history of this girl I'd been having my hypercharged fantasies over. I kept seeing the younger, paler version of this woman in my mind's eye. Both Ramona herself and the vision in her of Anna held me enrapt.

"Well, you know," she said, "times got tough real fast. We got no insurance, no help from the—the Dubowers, and so, well, we moved down here. It's only a couple buildings away from my sister." She swept out her arms. "Not a wonderful place for children, but I made sure the girls made the best of it."

She had decided that nothing—"*Nada*, nothing," she insisted—would keep them from becoming musicians like her and their father, from being stars. She started recounting all the girls' lessons, practices, early gigs—their dedication, Ramona's sacrifices—and I guess she was starting to see me getting a little impatient when she said simply, "So, Mr. Stephenson, what if I tell you that P&L Records might be a little too late?"

That snapped me up. "Too—"

"Well, you know—" big smile "—the girls are off right now at an audition."

I rose up on my seat; could hear the plastic covering crackle behind me. "What do you mean, they're at a—"

Mrs. Dubower smiled. "Oh, yes, there's a lot of interest in my girls." She pursed her lips. "But I can tell that you and—" she held up my card "this P&L Records, well, that you're *quite* interested in them—"

"I—"

"Yes, not everyone sits here and lets me just go on and on." She laughed again. "So I'll put in a good word for you when Anna and Trudy get back." She folded her hands before her. "That is, if they don't waltz in here waving a freshly signed contract."

"Do you know who they're auditioning with?" I asked.

She held her head to the side in a sharp, peculiar way, and I saw a glimpse of her innate shrewdness. "Now how wise do you think that would be?" She waved her thin fingers through the sunlit air.

"I understand you—that you don't have a telephone?"

"Oh, that's not a bother," she said, her nose up a little. "We can make calls very easily from the corner, or from my sister's place," she said making sure I knew this was no big deal. "My sister Cheryl has a phone. I can give you that number—that works out for the girls very well." She leaned toward me. "You can try her later . . . if it's not too late."

Did she enjoy torturing me? Or was it just the way my fingers were snapping involuntarily, my shirt was clinging to my back? Damn! Of course the second I heard about their audition I wanted the girls more than ever.

I found Princess at our office, and was about to tell her all about my morning when she said, "Forget the coffee."

I was stirring some cream into my cup. "No, Princess, this is important. I think I've—"

"No, no," she said, pulling the coffee cup out of my hand and dragging me toward the door. "This is *more* important."

I gave my head a shake. "What's up?"

"Punky's found a new girl group—he's really pumped."

"And?"

"They're auditioning this morning. He wants us there."

I shook my head, involuntarily.

"Larry, this is good."

I couldn't believe it. I was thinking about Mrs. Dubower and the girls and how we had to—

"No, it is," Princess said, interrupting my revery. "You'll see. This is really, really good."

$$* * * * *$$

"GUYS, THESE ARE the Penny Loafers," a beaming Punky Solomon said. "Manny Gold told me about 'em— found 'em out on the Island. What do you two think?"

Princess didn't say or do anything; I don't think she recognized them. After I pulled up my dropped jaw, I simply smiled and said, "They look good to me."

"Girls, these are two of the finest young writers in the biz. This is Princess Diamond, that's Dink Stephenson. You might know their work with the Harlequins."

Bright recognition on all three faces; then as one they all

curtsied, as if they were meeting the blinkin' Queen of England. I gave my head a quick shake. The girls had spiffed themselves all up; makeup was subtle, their dresses were wide-skirted flowery prints, and their shoes—yes, they were penny loafers.

"Well, we got the boys here," Punky said, nodding to a clutch of session guys in the new studio. "So why don't we just get started."

Moe Grushensky had gotten to work fast. He'd taken a dumpy old building on far West 38th Street he happened to own, then got some of Manny's family friends to come in, tear out walls in the back space, and build up this capacious, white-tiled room. Punky moved through it all like it was his own sandbox. He was clearly taking these girls seriously. He situated Anna at a center mike, Trudy and Sweet to either side, got the band tuned up—"Walter, that *B* string is a little flat," he called to the electric guitarist; Walter looked appalled, shook his head fast, said, "No way, boss," then plunked the second string; we all hung our ears on it, and though it sounded solid to me, Walter scowled and gave his tuning peg an almost infinitesimal twist—then led Princess and me into the wide control room.

"O.K., let's take one," Punky called into the P.A. The girls fluffed themselves before the mikes, brushing back their hair, straightening their collars. "What is it you're singing?"

"One of the songs from our club dates, Mr. Solomon," Trudy said. She had the lowest, widest voice; she usually came in under Anna and thickened her somewhat breathless, girlish soprano.

And like that they were off in a half-standard, half-bebop version of *When the Red Red Robin Goes Bob Bob Bobbin' Along*.

It wasn't . . . bad. And it was certainly more polished than what Princess and I had seen in the school auditorium the year before. Trudy and Sweet cut behind Anna in precision uptown footwork; Anna swept up to the mike, her dress noticeably rustling, and touched it gently, caressed it with her long fingers, brought her lips up close to it and . . . sang about birds.

But I could see the sexiness there, it was so deep within Anna that even this supper-club performance in their on-the-way-to-church clothes couldn't ruin it. It was in the way she breathed, just a hemibeat longer than normal. It was in the way she unfolded her fingers, slow and fluid, like flower petals in a gentle wind; in the way her hips never stopped moving, even when she was standing stock-still before the mike. It was also in the way she faced her imagined audience, straight on, saucy but in control, provocative but giving nothing away, hot but . . . cool, too. There was almost no beat to this benighted tune, but her hips rocked to a beat anyway—a rhythm outside the music that only she could hear. Move she did, catching the air, pumping against it, swaying in fine, rumbly curves as if she just couldn't help herself.

"Whaddya think?" Punky said to Princess and me in the control room.

"They're . . . nice," Princess said.

"Yeah, I know." Punky stared through the glass at the girls as they threw themselves into the standard. I could still hear in Anna's voice the power I'd felt when she was leading the Meringues, but it was muted, brought way down in their new guise. *"Nice."*

"I like 'em," I said.

"You like anything in skirts," Princess said.

I shot her a look.

"Are you hearing something we're not?" Punky turned to me. A frown cut across his thin lips. " 'Cuz I ain't hearin' it, man."

"I think I am," I said. Punky hung his gaze on me. "I think they didn't know they were supposed to sing rock 'n' roll."

"And you think it'd be different if you told them?"

The memory of the three Meringues rose in me, in their tight, black, curve-hugging leotards and provocatively rising pink angora sweaters, their sky-topping 'dos and saucily made-up mouths, their balls-on step, slide, step toward the mikes; with half a squint I could see them just like that again. The girls weren't really that far away from how they'd been; it was just a trick of the eye.

"I do, yeah."

Punky looked at Princess. "You want to let Dink have a shot?"

Princess stood back, brought a slender finger up to her wide chin. Remembering her reaction to the Meringues, I was purposefully not saying anything about our having seen them before. "I think it's a waste of time," she said.

Punky turned, lifted his goatee.

"You're the one who wants the white girl group to do R&B," I said. Punky nodded. "Well, who do they got as models? The Lennon Sisters? The Fleetwoods? Connie Francis?" Punky was paying attention to me. "Didn't you say they were working at some white supper club—on Long Island?" My voice rose.

Now both Punky and Princess shot me a look. I realized that nobody had mentioned the Stardust Lounge gig. I quickly plunged ahead.

"So what do you expect? Here, give me a week with 'em, I think I can come up with something closer to what we all want."

Punky glanced at Princess again, who was noncommittal, then said, "Sure, Dink. Whatta we got to lose?"

✳ ✳ ✳ ✳ ✳

SO THAT'S HOW I first came to know Anna Dubower: as a coach, a songwriter, a respected member of the Punky Solomon team. It would take years to shake being pigeon-holed like that.

Of course, I was all business when we got together in the
Bronx the next day. I wanted us at Bel-Air Studios; wanted
the way the walls there dripped soulful harmonies and irre-
pressible rhythms, thick as an oft-burned candle. I'd told the
girls not to dress special for the rehearsal, just wear something
comfortable. I wanted to see what that would be. And there
they came, Anna with her long black hair pulled back in a
pony tail beneath a lilac scarf, more lilac in an Orlon sweater
with ten buttons (the top four undone) and pink pedal pushers that hugged her curvy hips. The lilac set off her lovely
eyes and her creamy dark complexion. A swatch of the palest
pink lipstick mellowed her mouth, a mouth I have to admit I
felt the sharpest desire to kiss right then and there.

The backup girls were dressed similarly, Trudy in a
wide-blue-striped broadcloth shirt and longer twill pants,
Sweet in a tangerine Dacron top and robin's-egg-blue pedal
pushers—not so close to Anna it looked planned, but a natural harmony: three girls who simply fit. They'd come in jab-
bering and laughing among themselves, sharing a clear and
private joy.

I was encouraged. It wasn't the harder-edged back-alley
look I'd seen in the high school auditorium, but it was
young, fresh, and full of bright teenage life. A good start. I'd
have to keep the freshness but get them back to the bad-girl
flash that I just knew Punky would fall for.

I'd decided to come right out and tell them what was
what.

"The nightclub act, the Lennon Sisters stuff, that's *not*
what we're looking for." I was sitting on a wooden stool; the
three girls were on lower chairs in front of me. They gazed
up with silent attention. This close to Anna, I kept noticing
her eyes. I found them distinctly distracting: subtle green-
brown irises with multitudes of tiny gold flashes in a milky-
white setting. These were *not* quiet eyes. They were eyes of
power and focus; eyes that made you look at them, and kept

your gaze. More than that, eyes that seemed to cast a clear, delicious cocoon—of yearning, of desire—around you.

Simply, they were the eyes of a star: able to bring the whole world down to just you and her . . . no, to just you and your *dreams* of her. As with any true star, that's where you loved her: in places so private it would be an embarrassment to acknowledge them, to do anything but let the flow of wanting carry you along.

I grabbed a deep breath, gathered back my wits. "You know, I saw you girls perform last year once, it was at a high school talent show—I can't remember which one—and you had a totally different look. You were much. . . ." I fumbled for the right word.

"Sexier?" This was Anna, with both a pout and a smirk in the corner of her mouth.

"Sure." I looked up and away from her, couldn't hold her intense gaze. "But I was going to say something like 'tougher,' like you were. . . ."

"Bad girls." This was Anna's sister, Trudy. "Yeah, it's a thing we used to play around with."

"Used to—"

"It didn't get us any work," Trudy said, and I knew then that she was the businesswoman in the group. "Promoters thought we were . . . I don't know . . . criminals or something."

"Like JDs," Anna said, using the shorthand for juvenile delinquent.

"Are you?"

Anna laughed, glanced at her sister and cousin, then winkingly said, "Maybe, Mr. Stephenson."

I let that dig go by. What was I, maybe a couple years older than Anna? But right there and then, I was the grown-up.

"Well, I think that's much more what Punky and Princess and I are looking for. A new look like that. New kind of girl group."

"That's what you brought us all the way up here to tell us?" Trudy said. "You said something last week, we could've given you that then."

"I want to get it right."

"Why?" Anna said.

I wasn't sure what she was asking; I thought the answer self-evident. But maybe there was more to her question. Maybe her eyes that could reduce the whole world to me and her were looking so deeply into me that that simple question of *why* could mean anything, could ask for everything. Some grown-up! "Because we—Punky, Princess and me—we see a new sound coming, a new look. And we want the right group to get there with."

"We're going to get a record deal?" Trudy said point-blank.

"I think . . . yes, if we can nail down what I saw last year . . . that should just be a formality." I was looking right at Trudy. She was pretty, no question about it, but she didn't have her sister's preternatural grace.

"Wow!" the second backup singer, Sweet, said, her eyes round. *"Girls!"*

"Well, we'll believe that when we see it, Mr. Stephenson." Trudy had her jaw out there.

I gave her and her cousin a smile to suggest they had nothing to worry about. "Call me Dink, please." I kept my eyes on the two backup singers.

It was Anna who said back, soft as a whisper, "Dink." I looked over at her. The light that fell from her eyes was a shower of gold.

✳ ✳ ✳ ✳ ✳

THE RECORD DEAL *was* just a formality. The girls and I worked hard the rest of that week. I handled the music, teaching them four of my and Princess's songs, as well as better arranging their earlier, pre–supper club repertoire. Sweet, it turned out, although she didn't say much, was a master of mascara, eyeliner, and rouge. With a large cast-off mirror I found on the street and dragged into Bel-Air Studios, Sweet, Trudy, and Anna set to work getting back to the look I'd seen the year before, but refining it. I guess I'd been in the business just a little too long even then, because I kept speaking in terms of "the look," "the makeup"—the theatricality of the whole thing. But the longer Sweet worked with them, the more I felt their true selves coming out. I recognized this in a naturalness, a simple comfort yet a daring in their presence. To my great joy we weren't turning the Penny Loafers into something new, we were letting them simply become themselves.

I knew the name Penny Loafers would have to go, and none of us were that crazy about calling them the Meringues again. We tried on some names we came up with: The Eyelashes. The Satineers. Lady and the Tramps. But none seemed right.

It was Punky who came up with the Annas. "It's simple, straightforward. It has a good sound—I like the way it dances on my lips. *Annnn-naaaaas.*"

"It's got that good symmetry," Princess said. "Same thing coming and going. Like a palindrome."

"A what?" Punky said, raising the brows over his blue eyes. "What kind of pal you talking about? *Pal Joey?*" He laughed. "Doesn't sound like no pal of mine."

Princess rolled her eyes. We were all of us at Punky's studio on 38th Street, where we'd been the week before. The girls—the Annas?—were in tight rayon sheaths, their hair beehived up, spit curls curving along their ears. They looked *bad*, like trouble, like anything they sang was going to take you to the wrong side of town, throw you up against a wall, then dump you there. And yet it wasn't all scary; at the same moment they held their innocence, like kids just digging deep into the closet playing dress-up.

The girls chattered nervously among themselves in their

private way—that tight little family band I came to know so well—while we checked them out. Princess still wasn't sold. But I knew from the look in Punky's eyes the second the girls walked in, thighs working against the tight fabric, breasts cantalouped beneath the rayon, hair scraping the sky, that he was in. I found out later that Punky had an older sister, called Corky, who'd turned him on to black R&B years back, slipping into his bedroom at night to dial in the fugitive sounds from the Big X out of Tijuana, then bop-dancing with him to *American Bandstand* after school. Corky had bona fides: She'd even done a stint in reform school for shoplifting makeup and costume jewelry. She was a grade school teacher now not far from where they grew up in San Remo, California, but kept her proto-punk spirit. Punky worshipped Corky, and no doubt saw her incarnated in the girls before him now.

"Besides," Punky went on, "your new name celebrates our lead singer here—our *star*." A quick glance to Trudy and Sweet. "You girls O.K. with that?"

What were they going to say? This was Punky Solomon. They nod yes and Punky'd have a disc out on 'em next week—and with Manny Gold attached, it would get guaranteed airplay. They say no, and . . . back to the Stardust Lounge.

"So here's to the Annas." Punky went over and took Anna's hand, cupped it in his own as if it were a small, furry rabbit, pawed it mercilessly. *"Annas rule!"*

Chapter Four

THE ANNAS' FIRST RECORD! And ... Punky Solomon's debut in New York City.

The song was Princess's and my *Perfect Dreams*, the sessions grueling and intense, Punky's goatee flying, Anna's hair starting piled high but quickly coming undone and streaming wildly down her back, Trudy's and Sweet's voices soaring, Punky driving everyone through take after take—"This fuckin' record's gonna debut at Number 1!" he'd keep crying—and each time through, the record getting bigger and bigger; our four-note intro, cellos, bass, timpanis, and trumpets blaring forth, the girls *shushing* in with their gentle-wind harmonies, then Anna stepping up, singing, *"Heaven's in your mind / And in your perfect dreams / The more you chase them / The more they come to mean"*— well, it wasn't Keats or Shelley, but in Anna's voice, rich and full but ... not good enough. "More," Punky cried, waving his hands before Anna's unflinching face. "More, more, more!" So ... another take, the orchestra churning, the girls building to a bigger roar, and Anna shouting down the final crescendo, *"Oh, Ohhhh, Ohhhhhhhh"* over the girls chanting, *"Dreams, dreams, dre-eee-eams. . . ."*

Weeks later the record was done. Moe had had a test pressing—an acetate—made up, and we all crowded into the control room to hear its first playback. *Bang!* The record ripped out of its four-note hook and never let up. They'd mixed Anna so she whispered and cooed through the first two verses, then lifted like a jet taking off through the bridge, third verse, and that *Oooh-oooooh* endless coda. Trudy and Sweet sang like demons behind her. The musicians played like madding geniuses beckoning hellfire. And Punky, Punky had filled every single second with towering sound.

When the record came out, it was like nothing anybody had heard—girl-group pop married to that old liquor peddler, Beethoven, and his devil's kindred, Maurice Ravel. It was the biggest, most diabolical rock 'n' roll noise yet to leap out of our tiny transistor radios.

And it went straight to ... Number 2. Punky was dismayed, even though two weeks later *Perfect Dreams* hit Number 1 and stayed there for three weeks. "We gotta do better with the next record," he cried, pacing back and forth in front of Princess and me as if it were all *our* fault. "Number 1 right off the fuckin' bat!"

✳ ✳ ✳ ✳ ✳

HOW DID *Perfect Dreams*' success change the Annas? How didn't it?

The first thing Punky did was to send the girls out on tour, one of those package deals with ten or so acts. On that first tour were Lloyd Price, Bobby Vee, Leslie Gore, the Drifters, the Marcels, Linda Scott, and a couple up-and-coming Fleur-de-Lys Records artists out of Detroit, the Daisies and the Cravattes. The Annas started fifth in the order, but by the end of the tour they'd been moved to first billing—their song was atop the charts, and they were what the kids wanted.

Reports came back from the tour. Words had come up between Anna and Trudy. Sibling rivalry, for sure, probably perfectly natural, but they still weren't talking to each other. Was Trudy jealous of how the group was now called the Annas, her sister so out front? I don't think that was it; she'd always been the backup singer, and that hadn't changed. Probably it was just the stress of being on the road. In any event, next thing I knew Punky was flying out, I think it was to St. Louis, to try to straighten things out.

Punky stayed with the tour for a week, then flew back to New York for business, then returned while the tour went up and down the West Coast. Reports were that things were now fine between the girls, and we didn't know why Punky was spending so much time with them. Princess joked that it was Punky's idea of a vacation, being on a rock 'n' roll bus tour. The tour ended in L.A., and word came back that the blond genius wanted us out there; wanted to go into SilverTone Studios and nail the girls' follow-up hit.

This was my first trip to L.A., though Princess had gone out there a couple of times before. Back in 1963 flying seemed a rare adventure; we settled into our plush seats, ate a good meal, and hours later got off at LAX. Punky had sent his Bentley for us, with his fake English/Cajun chauffeur, John Ed, and that afternoon we sloshed champagne in the back seat as we curved along Sunset Boulevard.

SilverTone was in its heyday. It only ran two tracks, which was all anybody had then. (A few years later, when the number of tracks went to four, then eight, then leaped to 32, SilverTone always lagged behind.) But SilverTone was a very alive room that all the top L.A. players knew as home.

When we walked in, a little lit up from the champagne, all the great L.A. players were there: Barney Frederick, Eldred Smith, Karen DeWilder, Jimmy Sanborn, a half dozen others, and Rich Armour behind the mixing desk. Princess had met them before, and they gleefully called out her name, crying, "Princess, Princess, where's your crown? Where's your scepter?" She laughed and cracked back, "Where're your fuckin' manners?" I was surprised at her curse, but Punky stood at his podium and joyfully clapped and clapped.

I shook a host of hands, then noticed the Annas off in a corner. I gave them all a hello wink, but only Trudy waved back.

"O.K.," Punky said, "excitement's over. Back to work."

The song was *He's So Bad (I Love Him!)*, and it was . . . well, the best phrase I heard for it was "more obvious" than

Perfect Dreams. This was truly teen pop, but orchestrated in Punky's trademark big way; behind Anna, Trudy and Sweet kept singing, *"He's so bad,"* over and over, as Anna belted out, *"But I love him, yeah, I love him. . . ."* That was pretty much the song, but it right off conjured up dark clouds of musical sound, shot the chords through with silver light, swirled countermelodies mercilessly, and brought the whole extravaganza to a thunderous close behind Anna's gut-tearing cries of *"I love him, I love him, I love him . . . so!"*

Throughout the recording that day Anna kept on a pair of Jackie Kennedy sunglasses, large, curvy, eye-concealing shields. She wore a hot-pink blouse and black stretch pants so tight they looked painted on. She kept her blouse open at the top—at least *five* buttons now—and I kept grabbing provocative glimpses of her soft olive skin. I hadn't seen Anna since the *Perfect Dreams* sessions ended, and still I was surprised when Princess leaned over during one vocal take and whapped me across the cheek with rolled-up sheet music. "Jesus, Larry," she said, "down, boy."

"What?"

"She's just a fantasy, kiddo." Princess held her solid chin out. "And worse, she's Punky's fantasy now."

I shook my head. "What're you getting at?"

"Look at her," Princess said. I did, trying to see Anna through her eyes. To me she didn't look that different from the vision I'd found that first night at the talent show, just a little more regal, more self-enclosed. Or maybe it was just the black, impenetrable sunglasses. "She thinks she's a star now."

"She *is* a star," I told her.

"Well, yeah, we'll see."

"You don't think they're nailing *He's So Bad*?"

"Oh, it's going right to the top." Princess stepped back. "But *you're* not going with her."

"Who said anything about—" I started to say, flustered.

"Oh, jeez, Larry, all I'm saying is don't be so ob-vi-ous."

I didn't know what to say, so I said nothing. But I did wonder why Princess always got so touchy around Anna. The thought came to me that she damn well needed a boyfriend, and quick.

Then she got one. His name was Salvatore Phillip Bono, Sonny to all of us, this brown-haired, pudgy-cheeked eager little beaver around SilverTone Studios whom Punky had taken under his skinny-armed wing. The kid—I always thought of him that way, as the kid, even years later when he'd become, well, Sonny—was eager and helpful, to a fault. He was the kind of kid who, you sent him out for coffee, brought back cups of tea, too, just in case anybody had forgotten to order it.

I'm not sure what Princess saw in him . . . well, actually, I am. Sonny worshipped her; in those days before Cher, he worshipped *anyone* actually making the music—or at least gave a damn good impression of that. Sonny literally followed Princess around the studio; she made a gesture that she was ready to sit down—and once she got the hang of Sonny, she was always throwing glances out as if she was looking for a chair—and there the kid would be with one for her to drop into.

I was surprised by Princess and Sonny, but I was more surprised that I got a girlfriend, too: Trudy Dubower.

I hadn't had that much to do with Trudy before. She was the older of the two sisters, and the one with her head most on her shoulders. She was certainly attractive, with high cheekbones and devilish black hair, but I'd never seen her with anything like Anna's mysterious glamour, her charisma; Trudy was simply and truly the backup singer. But from all our encounters, I'd found her to have a basically pretty cheerful demeanor, to be very straight-up; at the least, someone who could become a good pal.

It was at the end of a long session, and Trudy and I were

the last ones in the studio. It was around 11, and Punky and Anna and the musicians had taken off, and Sonny had just driven Princess away, when Trudy said, "Hey, Dink, looks like it's just you and me—want to get a bite?"

I was caught off-guard; but I was famished and said, "Sure. What do you have in mind?"

"Heard about this good diner—wait, they don't call 'em diners in L.A.; I mean coffee shop—but it's really fun. Out in the Valley."

"Sounds good." She led me out to the now empty parking lot, to the '59 Ford Fairlane Trudy had rented for her and her sister. (Most of the musicians drove 'Vettes, but Trudy later told me she didn't want Anna learning to drive in a car like that.)

I settled in the passenger seat, and when we were heading north, Trudy said, "I don't know if I ever really thanked you for your work with us last winter. The way you took us and got us ready for Punky. And . . . the way you stood up for us."

I blushed a little. "I think you did."

She half turned to me, smiling; and this close up, and directed at me, it was a smile that warmed me. "No, I mean really thank you—as in, I don't know if we'd be here without your help."

I smiled back. "That's generous."

"Yeah, well." And the sweetest little flash of light caught her brown eyes then. It threw me. As I said, Trudy always was fine-looking on stage, but she and Sweet were the setting to Anna's jewel. This was the first time I'd seen her sparkle on her own.

"You like L.A.?" I said to change the subject. We were on Cahuenga, heading over the hill next to the freeway.

"Some," she said. "Anna loves it—loves the sunshine, the trees everywhere, the . . . well, that it's so close to Hollywood." She lifted her chin. "I miss New York, though."

"Yeah, me, too."

"I do love the sunshine," Trudy said, "though we hardly get to see it."

"Yeah, all this sunshine. I don't know, sometimes I wonder if it does something to you." I paused for a moment, then added, "Maybe it gets in and steals your soul."

"Pretty heavy, mister." Trudy was smiling.

"Well, it's my first trip out here." I shrugged. "We'll see."

I leaned back in the Naugahyde seat. I was feeling more and more comfortable here with Trudy driving along. The oven-hot air blew over my face, and I closed my eyes. I felt a strange but not unwelcome bloom of contentment.

"So what makes this dine—this coffee shop special?"

"You'll see." Trudy smiled, and the even, smooth, subtle glow that came off her then surprised me, too.

I closed my eyes again. Then Trudy said, "Have you heard about Anna's love life?"

"Have I—" I started. I hadn't heard anything about anything. Anna had turned out to be notoriously private, and, in truth, I had more than once taken a turn in the other direction away from whatever gossip was floating around—I just didn't want to know. "What do you mean? Haven't you guys been on tour?" I was speaking fast, just throwing words out. "When would she have time?"

"Well, perhaps those aren't the right words. There isn't any love, or even a helluva lot of life." Trudy laughed.

My upper teeth bit my lower lip. "What are you getting at?"

"Manny Gold."

I nearly spit. "Manny . . . Gold! What the hell?"

"Oh, Dink, it's so funny. Ever since *Dreams* got to Number 1, Manny's developed this terrible crush on my sister. He's calling her from New York like every night—sometimes two or three times. We're sharing a room, and I can't stand it, the way the phone keeps—"

"This is for real?" Though I tried to keep the tone even, I could hear my voice go up.

"Sure is."

"But the way you put it, I mean—" I felt myself swallow "—Anna hasn't, um—"

"Reciprocated?"

I nodded.

Trudy gave out a light laugh. "Something's up with her, I think—though with my sister I'm never really sure." She shrugged her shoulders. "She's so private, even from me. But I don't think it's Manny."

"That's good."

"What do you mean?"

"Well, Manny, he's awfully—"

"Sleazy?"

I smiled. "I didn't want to use *that* word."

Trudy laughed, and right then her laugh was the most perfect thing. "Why? Afraid he'll kill you?"

"Um—"

"Or more likely, have you killed."

"I'm not going to say anything."

"How'd you like a gangster coming after *you*?" she said. We'd gotten over the hill, and Trudy turned toward Toluca Lake.

"Don't have to worry much about that."

"You have *anybody* coming after you?" Her voice had softened, and I thought she might be asking a whole other question.

"Why do you ask?" I was a little surprised.

"Tit for tat."

I shook my head. "Not really—at least no one I know about. Who'd bother? I'm no star, just the songwriter—"

"Oh, Dink, don't sell yourself short," she said quickly. "I think—well, we talk, all the girls, and all of us think you're, well—" and then her voice fluted up, mock breathy, like she was just a teenager with one of those new Princess phones pressed to her mouth "—we all think you're really, really dreamy."

So I didn't know if she was kidding or not. Did she think this about me—did Anna? My forehead was hot, and I winced and looked down. Even if she meant even a little of it, I never took compliments like that well; back then they made me totally self-conscious.

Trudy was clearly waiting for me to say something back, but I just shrugged, and she suddenly looked uncomfortable, too. I finally looked over at her, but she'd turned her attention to the driving.

A short while later Trudy pulled into a drive-in restaurant with a towering sign that read SQUEAKY'S, then hit her brakes as a tight-topped, short-skirted woman flew by on roller skates, a tray heaped with burgers and malteds in her hand. She gingerly pulled the Fairlane into a bay. Another miniskirted roller-skate waitress zoomed up to the window. She leaned in, close enough to nearly kiss me, then said through a starlet smile, "What'll it be, champ?"

"What do you say now, Dink?" Trudy said after we'd ordered. "Like L.A. a little better?"

✳ ✳ ✳ ✳

THAT'S HOW IT STARTED. The drive-in was fun, the roller-skate girls zippy, the burger juicy and delicious; and the next thing I knew, we were back in my hotel room. We danced awhile to standards on the radio, cheek to cheek, as Fred Astaire would have it, then started kissing, slowly, happily. After awhile Trudy took a step back. Her eyes, though not as huge or feline as her sister's, were large, ready. Her hip dipped, she shook her shoulders, then she did what only a classic bad girl can do: She reached behind her and undid some pins, and her sky-high beehive came tumbling down.

What I remember most about Trudy Dubower then was

how modest she was. She kept her clothes on for as long as possible, then put her bra and panties back on right away and found my bathrobe hanging on a hook next to the toilet. She had a long, thin body that fit fine next to mine, though she had angles—elbows and knees that for a while there collided with me as I moved around and over her. I remember, too, what I have to call a hungry mouth; once passion had taken us over, she used it to pull at my skin, actually lifting patches of it off my bones.

Trudy always had this vivid clean smell, warm and promising, like something fresh-baked. When we were finished, and she'd wrapped herself in my robe, she curled up next to me and we talked.

You can think the worst of me if you have to, but while I was with Trudy, I kept thinking of her sister. These were involuntary flashes; I couldn't help myself. I just wondered what Anna's breasts would feel like in my hands. I wondered what path her fingernails would take down my back. I wondered what sounds would burst like tiny bubbles from *her* mouth as she clutched her thighs tight to mine.

Anna wasn't far from Trudy's thoughts, either. When we were settled, the first thing she said was, "I have to tell you, Dink, I'm so amazed by what's happening to us—the records and all."

"You guys are great," I said.

"Thanks." She kissed my ear. "You know, I was just thinking how we used to play, when we were kids, Anna and me, about being singing stars. The funny thing is, it was *my* favorite game. We'd have the radio on, Rosemary Clooney or the Fontane Sisters, and I'd take a broomstick and pretend it was a microphone." Her voice was breathy, a little wistful, but sweet. "I was that year older than Anna, so she looked up to me. I'd be there singing along to the radio, and she'd be my audience. Sometimes Sweet would be over, too, and she'd also be in the audience."

"I bet you were good."

"Oh, I could shake that *Mambo Italiano*." Trudy dropped into a wide Italian accent, adding, *"That's a nice!"* She laughed. "But what I remember from then was Anna's eyes, like a hungry pussycat's, watching me flounce around with that broomstick. She was a good girl—never fought me for it or grabbed at it. But I could see her looking—watching."

"The star-in-waiting."

Trudy let out a long sigh then. "Do you think I'm jealous of her?"

This surprised me, out of the blue like that. I said, "Are you?"

"I—I honestly don't know. Sometimes I think I may be a little ... other times I just thank God that she's got what she's got." Trudy raised herself on her arm then, turned over just a bit, then set her chin on her banded fists. "You know, that star thing—"

"I don't know if she could do it without you—you and your cousin." Even as I said this, I wasn't sure I believed it.

Trudy didn't either. "That's nice of you to say. I don't think Punky feels that way, though. Punky seems only to have eyes for Anna."

I shook my head. "No, Punky can do anything with anybody—he could get good tracks off of fire hydrants, he put enough strings and echo behind 'em." Trudy gave a laugh. I touched her hand. "And, you know, even if he doesn't seem to need you, I know Anna does. And Princess and I think you guys make the group."

"You *are* sweet!" Trudy leaned over and kissed me, and at that moment, really for the first time, I realized that I had just gone to bed with Anna Dubower's sister; and that she was close to falling asleep in my arms. This led to the strangest sensation. I was confused for a moment, as if everything were truly, deeply wrong; as if I'd violated a secret trust I had with Anna herself. Of course that was nuts, but I still pulled back a microinch from Trudy, which of course she noticed. I turned my eyes away from her. The sense of being in some place I didn't belong seared through me; I felt my forehead get hot. It was like . . . like I'd taken a turn I hadn't planned and was in a whole new world I didn't understand.

"You're thinking about her, aren't you?" Trudy whispered.

Did I flinch? How much *did* I flinch?

"It's O.K. I sort of figured that might happen."

"You—"

Right then she reached out with her long, cool leg and rubbed the ball of her foot up and down my thighs. My hairs bristled back and forth. The panic receded as quickly as it had come.

I was kind of scrambling when I said, "That thing about Manny Gold—I had no idea."

Trudy's eyes brightened. "It's funny, isn't it. There Manny is—he's stuck in New York, some goombah thing, a guy out here who has it in for him—and since my sister's here, he's going nuts."

"Sounds like it—"

"Oh, you don't know the half of it!" Trudy let out a pealing laugh. "Manny's got this idea Anna's taking up with Elvis—"

"What?" That's the first I'd heard of anything like that.

"It's not true—I don't even know if Presley knows who she is. But to Manny, well, Anna's the queen of rock 'n' roll, and so why wouldn't the King want her?"

I leaned back, then laughed, too. "Makes sense."

"Oh, you should hear my sister. Most of the time when Manny calls she just has me say she's not around—a lot of the time she *isn't* around—but sometimes she'll take the phone. God, you should be there. 'Oh, Manny,' she'll go. 'I'm all alone out here, and I need somebody to *love me tender*. If I just had *a little teddy bear* to play with.' " I chuckled, and Trudy started giggling so hard she made the bed shake. " 'Oh, Manny,' " she went on, " 'this damn fleabag joint, it's *a heartbreak hotel.* Manny, Manny, it's just *tooooooo much.*' "

"That's really funny." My whole upper body was shaking, too.

"That's my sister. Can't keep her down."

I nodded, sharply quiet, suddenly lost to my own thoughts.

Trudy was silent a moment, then she said softly, "But I understand, Dink." The high laughter was gone; her voice was calm, serious, almost somber. "We can take this slow—really slow. I know it doesn't seem like it tonight—" her eyes sparkled a second "—but that's my way anyway." She was gazing straight at me, and finally I looked back into her eyes. "O.K.?"

I gave a quick nod. "There's nothing wrong."

"Don't worry, Dink." Her eyes were light, hot. "I mean it."

I almost said thanks, but that would immediately mean that she knew me better than I thought she should; and that I was good with that. Instead, I reached out and lightly brushed her shoulder.

"What do you think Anna will say?" Even I could hear the feigned nonchalance in my voice.

"About us?"

"Yeah." I noticed I was holding my breath.

"I'm sure she'll be happy."

As much as I didn't want it to, my heart dipped. I softly closed my eyes again.

"Dink?"

I didn't speak.

"Dink?"

I still kept silent.

"She wouldn't be good for you," Trudy said then.

That roused me. "What do you mean?"

"My sister." Trudy gave her head a shake. "She really wouldn't. I know Anna at least *that* well, and I—"

"I don't know what you're talking about," I said, interrupting her.

It took Trudy a long moment to give me a half nod. "It's all right." She lay back, looking up at the ceiling. "That was the thing, you know. There I was, parading around with my broomstick, singing my heart out, and I kept seeing Anna's huge, brilliant hazel eyes in front of me. I know what they can do to you. Even *I* wanted to look into those eyes. Even *I* thought they were there only for me." She gave a snort, rising from deep inside her. "And she's my damn sister."

I didn't say anything, my head a vise of tense, undifferentiated thoughts. Trudy, ever sensitive, picked right up on it. She leaned over, kissed me on the mouth—roused me—then said, "I'm going to go." I halfheartedly reached out to stop her, but she shook her head. "No," she went on, "I think the best thing might be to just keep this our little secret."

"You mean, not tell—"

"Dink, this was great. I'd been thinking about it for—" She smiled, then brought her finger to my lips. "But let's just keep it to ourselves for now, O.K.?"

Not sure what I wanted, I simply nodded. I was getting a headache, I noticed.

"See you," she said after she'd pulled her dress back on.

"Trudy," I said when she was at the door.

She turned, whip-fast.

But whatever I could have—or should have—said then just wasn't there. "I'll see you tomorrow."

She nodded, then she was gone; not just her, but that delightful fresh-baked, anything-is-possible scent, too.

The next day I wanted Trudy Dubower again—fiercely, driven. I wanted my hands up her skirt and her hands down my pants. And she came to me, as if there'd been no tension the night before, nothing more than glorious, loin-snapping sex. And that's how we kept it. Each night she'd steal down the hotel stairs, the three floors to my room; I'd let her in, and we'd devour each other. Each morning I'd look for some indication that Anna knew what was up, but she was all work with Punky and never gave me a sign that she noticed—or cared.

He's So Bad (I Love Him!) was finally in the can, Punky's obsessive, detail-ridden production over. The record was more astonishing than *Perfect Dreams* and did debut at Number 1, just as we all hoped—and Punky had prophesied. By then we were back in New York City, and things were changing. With two back-to-back Number 1s, the Annas were the hottest group in the country. It was early November of 1963. The Annas were booked for their first tour outside the U.S. They were on their way to England.

Chapter Five

THEY SAY EVERYBODY remembers where they were when they heard that John F. Kennedy was shot. I certainly do. Actually, what I remember most was the night before we all heard: We were in London, at dinner at the Carriage House: Punky, Princess, and me; the three Annas; our English tour manager, Dirk Scolderring; Brian Epstein, the Beatles manager; and next to Anna at our large round table, a tipsy and getting tipsier John Lennon.

I have to set the scene. This was November 1963, and the Beatles, while the rage in England, were three months from coming to America, appearing on *The Ed Sullivan Show*, selling a gazillion records, and beginning the British Invasion that almost overnight shouldered our kind of music off the charts. In England that November, the Annas, next to the Beatles, were the biggest thing going. *Perfect Dreams* had gone to Number 1 the third week it was out over there, and *He's So Bad* got to Number 3. The girls' hair was up, teased high, and their clothes were tighter than ever; and it was safe to say nobody in England had seen birds, as Lennon kept putting it, looking quite like them. There were even days when we'd be getting ready for our show in a smallish town when a walk down High Street would literally stop traffic.

As the white-shirted maître d' led us to the table, John Lennon had put his hands together as if he were praying— or begging—and said, "Please, Miss Anna, Miss Anna, please, please, please, let me sit next to you."

Anna laughed. John Lennon that night was an importunate pup; he bounced on his winkle boots and shook his bangy Beatles hair. I have to say, up close seeing a man with that bowl-cut, bangs-on-the-forehead hairdo (Lennon's hair was a rich, cured-leather brown with gingery undertones) was disarming; literally nobody else but the Mop Tops (except for maybe the Three Stooges) had a cut like that, though of course almost all of us did within a couple of years. Lennon batted his bright blues eyes . . . and Anna laughed.

"In America, we say, 'This is a free country.' What do you say here?" she said to Lennon before she sat down.

"We say 'God bless the Queen, mum.' " He winked. "Then we say pass the fookin' ammunition."

So there he was next to Anna. Punky was sitting next to Epstein, then Princess, then me, then Trudy and Sweet, then Scolderring and Anna, who was next to John, who was again next to Punky. We had mounds of Yorkshire pudding and those radioactive British peas on the table, though Lennon said when the food arrived, "I'd be happy just with a jam buttie, but here in England they make us eat this royal crap."

"Looks good to me," Anna, who could always pack it in, said.

"That's because, darling, you *are* royalty." Lennon took her hand. "You're the fookin' queen of rock 'n' roll."

The table laughed, but we all knew it was true. And through the meal he made a constant joke out of buttering Anna's bread for her, showing her how to eat British style (knife pressed against back of fork, then quick to the mouth), refilling her wine glass—being the perfect courtier.

"So when are you all coming to America?" Punky asked at one point.

"We're hoping for next year," Brian Epstein said. He was a small, refined man, with a soft up-country accent to Lennon's broader, rougher one. "There are contracts to work out—always contracts." He took a sip of his wine, then set his glass down. "Tell me," he said softly, addressing the table. "Do you think there's any chance in hell anyone in America will care about a British rock 'n' roll group?"

At this point in the States, *She Loves You* and *Love Me Do* had been released on, respectively, Swan and Vee Jay records, both tiny black-owned labels that had not been able to break the tunes at all. Now we'd gone to see the group play a few nights before in a cinema in Lancashire, and we'd been astounded. The level of audience hysteria, the screaming, hair-tearing, hand-clawing—the girls in the audience convulsing as if in epileptic fits—was truly nothing we'd ever seen . . . or even imagined. Kids had erupted at the rock 'n' roll shows at the Brooklyn Paramount, but it had never gone much further than dancing in the aisles. These girls around us were having fits, breakdowns, in the presence of the lads. Still, I remember thinking right then that, Yes, sure the girls were undone, but they're English girls, and it's still a British band—what can they know about rock 'n' roll?

Punky surprised me. He let Epstein's question settle gently on the table, everyone leaning forward, waiting for somebody to say something; then Punky set down his fork and said, in the tones of almost an afterthought, "You're gonna be the biggest thing that's ever happened in America." Then he softly touched Epstein's shoulder.

"Bloody hell!" Lennon cried.

Epstein lifted his left eyebrow. He looked at Princess. "And you, darling?"

Princess didn't speak for a moment. Later she told me she could feel it already, a threat from the Beatles, and she always wondered whether, had she said something different that night, Epstein might have felt a little stutter, a slight hesitation about the charge he was to lead against the former colonies. I always told her, No, no, the lads were unstoppable. It really was the biggest thing anyone would ever see.

Princess didn't answer Epstein but turned instead to Lennon. All she said was, "Want to put one of our songs on your next record?"

"Bloody hell!" Lennon cried again. He'd been drinking Scotch and Coke since we'd sat down, and I'd lost count of how many he'd ordered. "You know, we had a song on our

first LP called *Anna*, by this bloke Arthur Alexander." He winked at Anna. "Was I singing that about you, darling?"

Anna held his gaze, calm, undisclosing.

Lennon turned to Princess and me. "But we'll never be better than you guys. Jeez, you wrote *He's So Bad*! Macca and me, we're just . . . just playing catch-up."

Punky smiled. "Treat us kindly, Mr. Lennon."

Anna fidgeted in her seat then; she looked uncomfortable.

"What's the matter, Your Highness?" Lennon said, eyebrows raised.

She ignored her seatmate. "Punky, do you really believe that?"

I leaned forward. As I said, I was dubious, too.

"Someday, dear heart, you'll tell your grandchildren you sat next to this man at dinner."

Anna set her chin in a way that made her look profoundly unpersuaded.

"Indeed, anything that happens tonight—*anything*—you'll be remembering for a long, long time."

This seemed a curious thing to say. Anna looked like she had a plethora of responses and couldn't settle on any of them. Lennon, though, wasted no time; he reached right over and took her hand. "Hear that, love, you and me, we're gonna be memorable." His voice sloshed a little. "The great Punky Solomon said so. Maybe he'll put us both in a song. Punky, you want to do a tune with me and Anna?"

Though Lennon still held her hand, she held it out only diffidently.

"I think you two can make beautiful music together, yes I do." Punky folded his hands together over his chest, leaned back. His baby blues shone, his goatee lifted.

Anna raised a brow over her milk-silver eyes. The rest of us were silent. There was something awkward, unsettled on the table now.

"So how's Cynthia, John?" Dirk Scolderring said, straight-faced.

Lennon, still holding Anna's hand, said, "You mean my fookin' bride?" He shot a dagger across the table. "She's home with my fookin' son."

Everyone went up in their seats. Eyes turned subtly toward Brian Epstein, who rose to the occasion.

"You know, since we've been down in London, I've been asked to join a number of private clubs," Epstein said, discretely changing the subject. "One of them just recently started letting ladies in." He raised his eyebrows. "What say we give the old duffers there a thrill—let 'em have a gander at the cream of American womanhood."

Punky loved this, you could tell. A real English private club! He'd seemed to immediately hit it off with Brian Epstein; two Jews from the hinterlands conquering the brave new world of pop. "Let's go," he said. Then he fought Epstein for the check and won—unbelievable, since Punky *never* picked up checks. Princess and I gave surprised glances across the table.

On the way out Trudy came up and put her hand on my back. Things between us had cooled in the weeks before we'd left for England, and on the tour here hadn't picked up. I still wanted to sleep with her, but we just never seemed to. Like you'd say, we were too busy, I guess, though nobody ever really is.

"Want to go off and see more of London?" she said.

"Like what?" I was surprised to hear this, but it wasn't that unwelcome. Unlike Punky, I had no great desire to go hang with a bunch of stuffy British lords.

Trudy leaned in close and said, "George and Ringo told me about this dance club—said they were going to be there later. We should stop by."

"Sounds like more fun to me. Sure."

"Less embarrassing, too," Trudy said, in little more than a whisper.

We were standing on the sidewalk in Mayfair when we told the group we were going to head off on our own.

"Where you going?" Punky said.

"Oh, just off, see some sights," Trudy said. "Nothing that interesting." Then she turned to her sister, with quiet entreatment in her voice: "Anna, you want to come?"

How close was she to joining us? I'll never know. She looked at Punky, who held her gaze with his blue eyes, and then glanced over at Lennon, who was walking up and down the sidewalk twisting his elbows out and stepping tall with his feet. He looked like a kid playing Buckingham Palace guard.

"Not tonight, sis. You two have fun."

A big black cab pulled up, and Brian Epstein held the door as Punky, Scolderring, Sweet, Anna, and, finally, John Lennon got in. As it pulled away, Trudy said, "I don't know why he was doing that back there."

"Who?"

"Punky."

"What do you mean?"

She gave me a sharp look. "You saw him."

I let out a long breath. "I don't know." I was trying to tell her that I didn't want to talk about it, and she finally got it.

"So, O.K., let's go dancing."

I hailed a cab, and we were quiet on the way to the basement club in Soho. When we got there, George Harrison and Ringo Starr were already there. Harrison came right up, bowed deeply, and said, "Madam, can I have the honor of this dance?"

Trudy laughed. Now it was her time to have a Beatle at her service. "I'd be honored," she said, as if this were a junior cotillion; and then the two of them hit the cramped dance floor and frugged and Watusi'd through the night.

I sat watching them for a while. Harrison was wearing one of those early Beatles suits, gray moleskin sans collar, and under it a black turtleneck. Trudy had on a pink sheath dress that accentuated the curves of the body my hands had come to know so well. All the Annas were teasing their hair like crazy over here in Britain, just to stand out more, and Trudy's was piled up what looked like a couple feet above her bangs. She and George made a cute couple shaking their hips and bouncing against each other: the very picture of the new fun-loving, anything-goes youthful energy we were charging into the world with. And it was damn persuasive.

I'd thought to try Lennon's drink, and so I had a Scotch and Coca-Cola in front of me. It was goofy: like a kid playing at being grown-up. Of course back then that's all any of us were actually doing.

I watched George and Trudy awhile longer. She kept smiling, giggling, throwing her hands up in abandon, then sliding up and hip-bumping the tall Beatle; and finally, when my drink was done, I knew that I wasn't needed there any longer. I waved a goodbye to her from my seat, but I wasn't sure she noticed. I went over and tapped her on the shoulder; she spun around, said, "Oh, Dink, I'm having *such* a good time!" George flashed me a crooked-teeth smile. I smiled back, tapped Trudy's shoulder again, gave her a little wave goodbye, then turned and left.

We didn't hear the news until the next morning.

I got up early. I'd had a lousy night, tossing and turning, and popped my eyes open early and couldn't fall back asleep. I was strangely anxious. I went down to the hotel lobby, looking for a cup of tea, and out the front door heard a newsboy crying, "Assassination! Assassination!" I saw the hand-scrawled news placard triangled on the sidewalk:

KENNEDY, U.S. PRESIDENT, SHOT IN DALLAS

DIES ON OPERATING TABLE

JOHNSON SWORN IN AS 36TH PRESIDENT

My heart clutched in my throat. I couldn't believe this. I bought three papers and ran back to my room. After I'd devoured them, I went up and down the hotel, rousing people. I dug up Punky, who immediately got very white and very very quiet. He took a paper from me and went back into his suite. I knocked on Trudy's door and got no answer. Then Anna's.

It was John Lennon who answered the door, with a hotel towel around his waist, and nothing else.

"Is Anna here?"

He tossed his head to his right over his shoulder. His hair was tousled; he yawned.

"I'm here to tell her that Kennedy was shot."

Lennon snapped to clarity. "Your president?"

"He's been killed—assassinated."

"Bloody hell!" he said. He looked stricken. "Buggers, that's terrible."

"Yeah, I—I don't know what to think. Here—here are some papers." I held out the two Punky had left me.

Anna appeared then. She was wearing a blue-terry cotton robe. Her hair was mussed in a way I'd never been allowed to see it. It was still half teased up, but the other half had collapsed to her shoulders. Wisps flew out every which way, though it still framed her face beautifully. There was lipstick smeared off her mouth, and sleep in her eyes.

"Dink, what is it?" she said breathlessly.

"Your president, my dear, he's been killed," John said.

"My—what?"

Lennon held out the paper, headline clear. Anna took it in, and just as Punky had, she went white. Her breathing got rough, noisy. "I don't believe it—"

"I just found out," I said.

"We gotta—. Shit, we don't have a TV in our room. Dink, do you have a television?"

I shook my head no.

"Maybe in the lobby?"

"I'm sure somewhere," Lennon said. He moved back in

the room, dropped the towel and pulled on his pants. (I can't forget that: pulled them on over nothing but skin.) Anna excused herself, took some clothes into the bathroom, then came out dressed. She combed her hair fast in front of a mirror. Then we all took the elevator down to the lobby.

Even with this amazingly sad news draping the nation, unsettling all the world, Lennon sitting there in the hotel's café watching TV caused a stir around us. Waiters pointed, hotel guests whispered words behind cupped hands. Anna's being there—I'm not sure anyone noticed.

We were all in total shock. I have to admit, we weren't the most conventionally political people then, pretty much ignoring elections; we'd write our rousing teenage anthems, then go off to frug away the night. But Kennedy's death wrenched us into a different world. We agreed we didn't wholly trust Lyndon Johnson, and we knew that a true bright flame of possibility had been snuffed out.

We also were unsettled about what we'd find back home. Punky, on the TWA flight, put it best. This was almost a week after the assassination. We were all in first class. Punky went from seat to seat and said, "I want you to know, I think everything's going to change now. I don't know how, don't know what's coming along, and I don't know what we can do but just what we do now—make the best records we can.

"But I want you all warned. I don't think anything is going to be quite the same from now on."

Chapter Six

BOY, WAS PUNKY RIGHT.

Paul McCartney has famously said that it was the Beatles' plan not to come to America until they had a Number 1 hit, and, well, they did: *I Want to Hold Your Hand*, blaring feverishly out of every transistor radio in the States. There we were, at Punky's hotel suite in New York (he'd flown in to wish his pal Brian Epstein well), hunkered down like the rest of the nation on that famous Sunday night in February 1964, watching the "realllleeee beeeeg sheeeeeeew." The excitement, the screaming, the winsome, winning lads . . . Punky called it halfway through their third song, *She Loves You*: "You're a young kid, you see 'em, you want to be 'em. They make it look so easy, so damn natural." He craned his head back at all of us and said, "We are totally fucked."

It's really simple, cruel math: There can only be ten songs in the Top Ten, forty in the Top Forty; and when half of them suddenly pop up from England (Beatles, Stones, Dave Clark Five, Herman's Hermits), and a quarter more start flowing out of Detroit (Miracles, Mary Wells, Essmay, the Supremes), well, there're only so many places for your own magnificent efforts.

Punky's response? Dig in, focus, work harder. He whipped Princess and me and the girls into the studio and, fast for him, came up with *So Alive*, which he pressed up and got out in April '64; it was a driven tune, with the trademark Punky Solomon sound, Anna singing it powerfully and passionately, Trudy and Sweet following her through every turn, and it . . . got to Number 27. Then in the fall came *Lost Memories*, a ballad that Princess and I wrote out of our sense that things were slipping away; that tune charted at Number 38.

Punky paced, ranted, ripped into his blond hair, cursed, volubly started dealing with the devil, right in front of us, but finally fell back on the tried and true: Work harder, more songs, more records, and . . . get the girls out there on the road.

He sent the Annas on a two-month-long bus tour, eight or ten groups all jammed together, and I have to say, I was kind of glad to see them off. Since England things hadn't been great with Trudy. We didn't break up, exactly (as we'd never officially been going out), but after that night in London I'd left her frugging with George Harrison, there had been hesitant moments, times when she'd say something and I'd say, "I don't quite understand," or I'd say something and get the same from her; and those less frequent times when we were alone together, my legs stretched along her cool skin, and as much as I continued to desire her, I didn't quite trust her. Nothing got past Trudy, of course, and soon she was quieter, cooler to me; then simply not there.

After that Christmas of 1963, more often than not we just kept missing each other. If the girls were in New York, I was in L.A.; if L.A., well, I was visiting my mom and sister, Nancie, back home. Punky kept scheduling record dates, and I made every one I could, but they had less of the sky-shooting thrill of our first sessions; now making songs that we all tacitly knew had only a rare hope of streaking to Number 1 was a far more workmanlike business. The studio musicians would roar up like always in the 'Vettes that Punky's records had paid for, but in the studio the electricity—the finger sparks that snapped off every note, the dog-ears-only magical hum that we knew floated beatifically above us, the genial confidence that the next two and a half minutes of twirling Ampex tape was going to change the world—none of that was there. And once their vocals were laid down, neither were the Annas.

I heard stories, about Anna in particular. It was 1965, and with no hits in sight, she was taking the drop down the charts hard. *Perfect Dreams* had bought her a bungalow in the Hills here in L.A., but more often than not, she was back home at her mother's place in Spanish Harlem, where the rumors were she stayed curled up in her own bed. There was also talk that she was drinking, and the glimpses I did catch of her, she looked different. Anna was still gorgeous—to me, more so than ever—but she'd tamed her 'do, all the girls had, teasing their hair less and letting it fall in gentle flips to their shoulders, and she'd filled out, too. The woman I saw was much more a lioness in full bloom than the panther teen that had stalked the charts a couple years back. But she also looked a little more teetery, less sure of herself, overall less together.

I tried to keep tabs on her private life, but I never heard much. What I saw of Trudy, she as usual said she didn't have a clue. Anna was still famous enough that rumors occasionally flew by, but they were rarely credible. I did hear that Manny Gold was still in the overall Cinemascope, hovering, glowering, but from all I could tell, he wasn't doing any better with Anna than he had when she was topping the charts. Lately even the make-it-up gossip sheets had stopped mentioning her so often, no longer linking her with whatever Hollywood publicist's darling, Tommy Sands, say, or Sal Mineo or Ricky Nelson, could use an extra few lines of ink.

What was I up to? Well, I never hurt for women, and whether I was in L.A. or New York, I always could find someone to step out on my arm. In New York we'd hit the Copa, take a cabriolet through the park, crack a magnum of champagne; in L.A., hop into my red MG and run Mulholland, then watch the lights spread before us glitter like diamonds—that is, do all the stuff eligible young men were supposed to do. But it wasn't lost on me that my companion's eyes would always go widest when the talk turned to how I'd met the Beatles. And though my eruptive needs were almost always met, I found it felt like work to shovel the girls home the next morning; and my eyes would glaze when I sat a day or two later looking down at the paper with their phone number on it. Yeah, most of the time one fabulous night out was enough.

In our songwriting Princess and I branched out, too, turning out tunes for other groups—even some of the British Invasion bands; songs that charted far better than any of the girl groups were doing—but the sad truth always hit me: If we weren't writing a song for Anna and the girls, it was just a job.

There were always diversions—it was that time in the mid-'60s when, um, diversions began to be widespread, big business—and I tried my share. I think I spent a lot of 1965 toked up on weed, and my "medicine cabinet" (the brown leather shoulder bag I sported, over my Mexican shirt, along with my new, reddish-brown beard) always held a rainbow array of pills: some that made me larger, some that made me smaller, and some that, well, after a while no longer seemed to do anything at all.

Somehow the days always got filled up. They say that if you can remember the Sixties, you weren't there; well, I *was* there. I can also say that though I didn't always know what Anna was doing—didn't always know what *I* was doing—there was never a time I stopped thinking about her; no time in my most private, lucid moments that I stopped nurturing my own perfect, perfervid dreams.

Then one afternoon I caught a break. It was the late summer of 1966, and I was in SilverTone Studios with Punky going over a mix of a new song called *All We Do Is Run*. It was a different take on the group, Anna not singing lead at all, but the three girls doing the whole song in harmony. It was just me, Punky, and the engineer Larry Dobell listening over and over to the recording, trying to get their voices to blend perfectly, when the phone rang and Punky took it.

He immediately frowned, then sighed. He said, "We're really busy here, babe. Can't you just take a taxi?"

He listened silently, then said, "I know, I know—no, I'm sure there's nothing to worry about. Really, Anna."

My ears perked up. Then Punky said, "O.K., I'll see what I can do."

"What is it?" I said when he hung up the black phone.

"Oh, Anna—she went off on her own, and she seems to have gotten lost."

"Where is she?"

"Somewhere in the Valley—at a shopping mall. She said some people have recognized her, and she's a little spooked."

"Fans?"

Punky shrugged. "You wouldn't think *that* would bother her, but Anna's been acting a little, oh, skittish lately."

I nodded; I'd seen that, too. "So what are you gonna do?"

"*Me?*" Punky's goatee dropped down. "I'm not doing anything."

"But—"

"You wanna go get her?"

I quickly said, "Sure."

"Larry, we can spare Dink, right?"

Our engineer gave a genial shrug, Why not?

"O.K., she's at some place in the Valley called Fashion Square. Some fancy-shmantzy shopping center."

I told Punky that I knew where the mall was, Princess had made me go shopping with her there one Sunday afternoon. Then I got in my MG and drove as fast as was sane over the hill.

I couldn't find Anna right away. I tore into stores, scouted the open-air mall. I was worried either something had happened to her, or she'd taken Punky's suggestion and gotten a taxi—though I knew that procuring a cab in L.A. could be a long, involved effort. Then I saw a restaurant at the edge of the mall, the Jolly Roger, and went in there.

The place was remarkably dark, a midnight-blue carpet, blood-red banquettes, muted lighting. There was a dark wood bar with glittery glasses, but Anna wasn't there. I gave a quick wave past the woman seating people and walked to the back of the restaurant. My hunch was right: There Anna was, alone, a scarf hastily pulled over her high hair, and over her eyes heart-shaped sunglasses that took a wild flare at her temples.

She didn't see me at first, and I took a long look at her. Her jaw was slack, her shoulders slumped. She had a drink in front of her; it was lemony-yellow, with a plastic pink parasol floating in it. Over it she looked quiet, sad, almost morose. Finally I waved, and she beckoned me over.

"Jesus, Dink, what're *you* doing here?" Her voice was breathy, high.

"Punky told me you called."

She gave a pointed glower then, her mouth turning down. "And what did *Punky* say?"

"Just that you needed some help."

"And, what, he couldn't be bothered to—"

"He was . . . well, I volunteered. We were just mixing *All We Do Is Run*. It wasn't so necessary that I was there."

"What was he doing, taking my voice out of the mix?"

Her tone was unexpectedly sharp. I shook my head. "No, no, just getting the blend right. Punky and Larry—you know, they got the ears. I wasn't really needed."

She paused then, and I saw some thought—couldn't read it—flit through her lovely head. Then she lowered her Lolita sunglasses so I could finally see her eyes. She smiled. "Well, *I* need you." She beckoned for me to take a seat, right next to her on the burgundy banquette.

As I slid in, I said, "So, Anna, what's going on?"

"Oh, Dink, it was a disaster. I took a taxi out here just to do a little quiet shopping—Princess said I'd like it—but when I got here, people just started coming up to me, following me around."

"Fans?"

A pause. "Probably."

"How many were there?"

She looked up at the ceiling, then shrugged.

"So a bunch of fans started, what, chasing after you?" The way things had been going, I found that a little hard to believe.

She took a long second, then gave me a nod.

"Why didn't you just give them autographs?" A waitress had come over, and I turned to her and said, "Coffee—black."

"Dink?" Anna went.

"I don't understand why you didn't just—"

Anna had just taken a sip of her drink, then set it down and said, "It's a little more complicated."

"Anna?"

She faced me straight on. "Dink!"

I pulled back an inch. "O.K., why don't you tell me everything. Where were you?"

She gave me a sharp look, then said sweetly, "It was in the big store down there, it's called Bullocks." She leaned back, then cranked out the word "Bollocks!" mimicking a British dockworker. Her eyes brightened. "So I was in *Bollocks*, and the next thing you know, I was being followed—"

"That's strange. I—"

"Yeah, it was really strange. It was this huge woman, with big black glasses—" she leaned toward me, confidingly "—in a hideous plaid dress. She reminded me of Miss Masterson back in grade school. She was one of my teachers. In class she'd call on me, saying, 'O.K., let's ask the half-breed.'" She winced. "Miss Masterson even used the n word about me and Trudy—"

"Jesus."

"Yeah, it was horrible." Anna pouted.

"But what about the woman in the store. What did she want?"

"What do you mean?"

I held her eyes. She was being evasive. "It wasn't just an autograph, was it?"

She inhaled deeply. "She said she thought I was going to steal something."

"Were you?" I was thinking of the Annas' bad-girl thing, and the words just came out of me.

Anna turned on me with an abrupt suspicion. "Dink, whose side are you *on*?"

I just looked at her.

"No, of course not, but it was like I was a kid again, down at Macy's or Gimbels. You walk in with your hair a certain way, you feel the creepy eyes on you, right away. They're *sure* you're a criminal." She gave her head a shake. "I thought they were more, I don't know, liberal out here in L.A."

"You sure she wasn't just a fan?" Something wasn't quite adding up, and I guess I simply wanted that to be the case.

"That woman was a Patti Page fan, Dink. This was a woman still wanting to know how much that fuckin' doggie in the window was."

I chuckled then, an eruptive snicker, just couldn't help it. "It doesn't sound too bad. They didn't arrest you or anything, right?"

Anna was dead silent.

"Right?"

"Well, there was a little . . . moment." She winced.

I reached out and put a hand on her shoulder, gently, totally concerned now. "What happened?"

"The woman—she had a name tag, said her name was McGillicudy. Wasn't that the name Lucy used to use when she was trying to pass herself off as somebody else?"

I kept my gaze straight on her, quiet but steady; rubbed her shoulder.

"Well, she brought over a security guard. And he—he talked to me."

"Did either of them know who you are?"

"I don't think so." She dropped her elbow onto the table with a thud. "They don't know their rock 'n' roll at *all*!"

"And?"

"Well, it was really mortifying, Dink. The guard took me out of the store. Just dropped me in front of it and said that I should never come back!" A low growl came out of her. "I was—I was so *humiliated*! I mean, I'm Anna Dubower!"

My head was spinning a little, but finally I gave her a comforting nod. Funny, but I think she was waiting for it.

She nodded. "That's when I called Punky—goddamn Punky! That man is such a—" She hmmphed, then said, "Thank God you were there!" She twitched her fine nose. "I didn't know what to do. So I came in here to cool out, you know. And then . . . then you came in to save me." She lowered her sunglasses again and smiled at me with her eyes.

That was the warmest, most beautiful, most enticing smile I'd ever gotten . . . and it turned my heart. But still I didn't know what to think about what I'd just heard. Whatever had happened back there in the department store, I was glad Anna hadn't been arrested—I could see the headlines now, FADING ROCK 'N' ROLL STAR HELD IN SHOPLIFTING ARREST. I figured I never would know exactly what had gone down. But what I did want to know was what could have driven Anna to do whatever it was she would not admit she'd been doing.

"You're fine now," I said soothingly. "I have my MG, I can give you a ride back to your place."

Anna sipped her drink, then made a face, her jaw tight, her nose crinkling. She shook her head. "I—no, I don't want to go back there." She paused a second, then stood up. "I have a great idea, Dink. Let's take a drive. Let's go to the beach!"

That's what we did. Along the way I looked for an opening to talk more about what was going on with her, but I couldn't find it. She'd said, "What a great little car!" but then once I was on the freeway, she tilted her head back against the seat rest, pulled her scarf down over her forehead, kept her sunglasses on, and just sat there as I zoomed along. In truth it was hard to talk over the engine and the wind whooshing through the open car.

I took us out the Ventura Freeway to Topanga, then over to Pacific Coast Highway.

"Should we stop?"

"I like just driving with you," she said. "The wind, the sun, the. . . ." Her voice trailed off. "It makes me feel safe."

I smiled to myself at that.

A ways up the coast I saw a restaurant on a pier, and I turned in. It was getting to be dinner time, and I wanted to stop.

"Boy, I love fried seafood," Anna said as we looked at the heavy laminated menu. "Reminds me of City Island. You ever go out there?"

"All the time as a kid, cruising, yeah." I smiled at the recollection of such innocence.

"Boy, I loved that place. That was freedom for me, City Island. Like it was the end of the universe, know what I mean?"

"It's a lot more beautiful here." We were in Ventura, and our seat in the restaurant flat-out faced an orange and gold sunset that blanketed the sea with shimmering ripples.

"It is, isn't it?" Anna ordered fried abalone—said she'd never even heard of it and wanted to be adventurous—then settled back in her chair. She looked a lot more relaxed. "This is lovely, Dink." She smiled toward me again. "What a nice day this has turned into."

Walking back to my car after dinner, Anna took my arm,

leaned in to me. "You know," she said slowly, stretching her long legs into the MG's front seat, "we've never spent this much time together before, just you and me. I feel—well, it's great."

My whole body hummed, but I didn't say anything, just climbed into the driver's seat.

"Yeah, this has become the best day I've had in ages." Anna looked at me then, something cloudy in her eyes; then shook her head, shook it away. "Thank you, Dink. I'll never, never forget it!"

I was turning the key in the ignition when she gave me the strangest look. Her gaze had dropped from my eyes to my chest. Then she reached over and did something I'll never forget. She'd been fumbling in her bag and pulled out a small, snubnose pair of scissors, and she reached over and grasped a thread flying off my jacket. "Do you mind?" she said.

"What?" I said, half-startled.

"You have a . . . a thread there." Her smile to me was heartbreakingly sweet. "Just thought it'd be better to get rid of it." She deftly snipped it away.

Then she kissed me.

Out on the road we were silent for the longest time. I was kind of speechless, not sure what to say to her. Anna put on her Jackie K dark glasses and simply sat there with a wide, generous smile on her face.

"You know," she said—and I had to lean over to hear her—"I just love this car."

"It's a beaut, isn't it?"

We were on the Ventura freeway, somewhere northwest of the city. It was nine at night, and I was cruising fast enough the lines on the road flew by just like dots.

"Sure beats Trudy's damn Ford . . . or Punky's phony-baloney Bentley."

I glanced over. She was looking straight ahead. "Wait'll

you see this." I punched the accelerator then, fiercely, putting all my weight against it as if I could drive the pedal not just to the bottom of the floorboard but into the engine itself; I wrenched the car into overdrive and kept it floored. The MG took off like a rocket.

"Wheeeeee!" Anna went. She threw her hands up in the air, as you would on a roller coaster. She'd kicked off her sandals when we'd gotten into the car, and now she raised her legs, setting her bare feet on the edge of the seat. As the car sped down the road, her knees spread open. The wind pushed back her light, open skirt, stretching the yellow cotton tight against her thighs. There was a boxy Plymouth ahead of me in the fast lane, and I swooped right to swing around it, not losing any speed. The speedometer pushed 85, 88, 95. . . . Anna's knees were up under her chin. She had this thrilled, amazed look on her face—a girl getting her first look at Christmas morning.

The yellow skirt climbed her thighs. I kept stealing glances over; couldn't not. The skin up there was smooth and perfectly tanned. Her knees fell farther apart. The dress stayed skin-tight. Then I caught a flash of her underwear. For a second I caught a shadow and thought the underwear was black, which unexpectedly upset me. But then I saw pure white cloth.

If she'd stripped off all her clothing right then and threw herself at me, it couldn't have struck me harder than that secret glimpse. The underwear was wide, prim, and far less revealing than any kind of swimming suit; and yet there it was, high up under her skirt, open to the wind—to me.

I did my best to keep my eyes on the road. I slowed the car some. *Some*. Like that Anna's hands went back to her side; she grasped her skirt and tugged it down over her knees.

"Whooooaaaaa!" she let out. "This . . . this car is *really* something."

I smiled at her. "Glad you like it."

"Oh, Dink, it's *amazing*!" She was flushed, her face bright, her breathing loud and panting. I kept the car at a steady 72, zippy but nowhere near where we'd just been.

"Anna, listen, I'll take you out in this baby anytime you want."

"Really? That'd be fabulous, Dink."

"How about tomorrow?"

She answered me right away. "You got it, Mister." Then she nodded to herself, smiling, and leaned across the gear shift and kissed my cheek.

"This really has been the best day! I can't believe it. It started out so . . . but then you came and saved it." Another kiss, sweet and light against my night-stubbled skin.

But I didn't see Anna the next day. While I'd been out of the studio a call had come in from Brian Epstein: The Beatles wanted the Annas to open for them on the second half of their fall '65 East Coast tour. Punky initially said uh-uh, no way, the girls were too big for that. Remember London, 1963? Remember *Perfect Dreams*? Remember *He's So Bad (I Love Him!)*.

Epstein knew Punky. He simply sat there on the line, waiting, the man holding all the right cards.

The next morning the girls flew east to rehearse.

I still remember published photos from that tour. The Annas in their tight white suits and high white go-go boots, up on the lip of the stage, waving like flowers before the stamenlike mikes. The hair tumbling loose from their smaller but still-there beehive hairdos. Legs kicking high, wide, stadium-engulfing smiles on their faces. And that ol' satyr John Lennon leering from the wings.

The girls were gone for only a month, but it felt like forever. And though I never forgot our drive that night, when I next spent any time with Anna Dubower, it was all business. Punky had heard good reports from the tour; the cheers were there, the shouts, the adulation. Maybe things hadn't changed that much. We had to give it one more shot; give it our all.

We were starting work on *Love Will Cut You Like a Knife*.

Part Two

Chapter Seven

SOMETHING HAD HAPPENED in court. We had finished with opening statements and were about to start testimony. The subway downtown had held me up, and when I finally got to the courtroom, I walked in at the tail end of an altercation—some kind of shoving match between Punky and Manny.

"What's going on?" I asked Sandy Kovall. A bailiff had Manny Gold's arms pinned behind him; another two were standing between Punky and his fellow suitmate. Judge MacIntire was pounding her gavel, sharp slaps ricocheting off the courtroom walls.

"I want this courtroom calm," the judge cried. "We cannot proceed until it's calm."

"I'm not sure," Sandy whispered to me. We both looked over at the two men. "We were all just sitting here. Then, I think, Manny said something to Punky, and Punky said something back." Sandy's eyes widened. "Then Manny just jumped at him, his fists out—"

"Jesus."

"Yeah, the judge had just walked in. She's pissed. Good thing the bailiff grabbed Manny so fast."

"I mean it." Judge MacIntire gave her gavel a couple more whaps. "O.K., that's better." Then she looked straight at me. "And glad you finally got here, Mr. Stephenson."

"Um, Your Honor, I'm—" I started to say, but Sandy took my arm, and Judge MacIntire looked past me.

"O.K., now that everyone's here, and calm, we have a lot of business ahead of us." The judge lifted her eyebrows.

"But I tell you, gentlemen, one more disruption from either of you, and I'll throw you both in jail so quick, you won't know what hit you. Got it?"

All eyes on Punky and Manny. The bailiff had let Manny's arms go, and Punky had taken his seat at the defense table; but there was still fire in both their eyes.

"I mean it, gentlemen." The judge leaned back. "O.K., Mr. Kovall, are you ready to proceed?"

✳ ✳ ✳ ✳ ✳

THAT'S WHEN the trial began in earnest. Our gambit was simple: prove that Princess and I had written *Love Will Cut You Like a Knife*, then demonstrate that the defendants didn't have a lick of evidence that they'd contributed anything. We'd bring up witnesses who made it clear they hadn't ever written any songs—at least Manny Gold—and that there was a pattern of their forcing their names onto writing credits, going back to the '50s. It would be, Sandy insisted, a slam dunk. We didn't have a jury, just Judge MacIntire, who was all business.

The only fly in our sticky ointment: Princess's refusal to have anything to do with the suit. But Sandy explained that she was necessarily "joined" to the suit, since she was a cowriter, and that if she refused to testify, she could be coerced to appear.

"Coerced?"

"The judge will sign a subpoena for her."

"*Will* subpoena her?"

"I think she will, yes. Any trial, but this in particular, is a fact-finding enterprise above all. She'll want all the facts she can. So she'll bring in your cowriter." Sandy paused. "We don't have anything to worry about with Princess Diamond, do we?"

I shook my head. "We wrote the song, just the two of us, and you have my envelope." This was a phone bill envelope that I'd grabbed quickly to write the first sketch of the lyrics to *Knife*. Princess had worked up the next draft, including chords, and I didn't know if she still had paper on that, though I remember her as never throwing anything away. "I'm not sure why she isn't here. I think it's because she's about to be the big Broadway tune-meister and doesn't need the money or want the aggravation."

"Well," Sandy said, shrugging, "it won't matter. If Judge MacIntire finds that she's a material party—and of course she is—then she'll get her here. Or if the defense thinks they need her, though I don't know why they would."

That'll be interesting, I said to myself. I noticed I was standing a little straighter, tighter. I hadn't seen Princess since right after Anna died in January 1967, and she hadn't even answered me personally when I felt her out about the lawsuit now, thirty years later. Of course I knew what she looked like—or at least what New York's best photographers could make her look like—but the real woman herself. . . . I'm not sure why, but it made me a little anxious to think about seeing her again. Probably just high-school-reunion-type nerves.

"But that's down the line," Sandy said. "And I don't think *we* need her. We'll do fine with just you up there."

"Thanks," I said.

"No, I mean it." Sandy gave me his cocky smile. "Just tell the judge how it all went down, and we're home free."

So there I was, this Tuesday morning after the long Memorial Day weekend, the courtroom still buzzing with whatever had gone down between Punky and Manny, when Sandy called me to the stand.

I told them my name, Lawrence Stephenson, my address in Scottsdale, and my occupation, high school music teacher. Sandy led me through my early history, bringing out our early hits with the Harlequins and the Annas. He had me run through my general writing practices with Princess, and then he asked me if there had been other occasions when the defendants had put their names onto songs we'd composed.

That drew an objection from Punky's lawyer, seconded by Manny Gold's, and it was sustained. So I didn't answer, just sat there quietly, waiting.

Sandy moved out from behind our table. "O.K., let's go right to the issue at hand, the song *Love Will Cut You Like a Knife*. We're going to go through it slowly, punctiliously, how it came to be written and recorded. Along the way we'll place into evidence documents proving authorship—the only documents, I might add, that have been submitted in this case."

Another objection, but this one overridden.

"Well, it's true," I said in answer to Sandy's first question—we'd decided to get this fact out ourselves, knowing that Punky's lawyer would make as much hay out of it as he could, "that the idea for a certain kind of song came from Mr. Solomon."

"What did he say to you?"

"He said he wanted us to write a new song—"

"And was this the first time he told you he wanted a new song from you?"

"No, of course not. We were the songwriters for the Annas. Punky was always after us to work up new material."

"So this was simply a request that you get to work."

"Basically," I said.

"Basically? What more was there?"

"Well, we were all under some pressure because of the Beatles, the way they'd taken over the charts. Punky said he wanted something big—"

"Something big?"

I smiled. "The words he used were, something 'just . . . fuckin' . . . big!'"

All eyes in the courtroom toward Punky. He was silent, unmoving at the defense table.

"But that was it?"

"I asked him what it should be about—"

"Because?"

"Because sometimes Punky would, well, give us some ideas."

"But not in this case?"

"He said, 'You'll work it out.' He just wanted something killer—a song that would shake up the radio."

"And that was your assignment—"

"Yes—"

"To write a great song." Sandy was standing right in front of me. "A *really* great song—"

"A big song—"

"One that would make Number 1?"

I nodded. "Yes."

"And that made this . . . this not-yet-written-at-all song, well, different—"

I shook my head this time.

The judge leaned over and said, "You have to give a verbal response."

"Um, not really. We were—there seemed to be more at stake—but Punky, all of us, we *always* wanted a Number 1 song. That was the whole point."

"And every song you wrote went to Number 1?" Sandy said.

"Of course not."

"And why not?"

"Because—" I paused a moment. "Because, well, we'd write them the best we could, then Punky would produce the hell out of 'em, and the Annas would sing 'em for all they were worth . . . and then still it was totally up to everyone who heard it on the radio, whether they'd request it, buy it— the kids made the hits, ultimately, you know."

"And was *Love Will Cut You Like a Knife* a hit?"

I shook my head.

"Mr. Stephenson."

"No, Your Honor," I said. "Not then. Not then at all."

"But my understanding is that now your song is more popular, that's it being played on TV, in the movies, that the licensing—"

"That's true." I nodded.

"So that's one of the reasons we're here now, isn't it? That there's more money—

I half shook my head. "That's part of it," I said, "but it's not everything—"

"Then we're here because—"

"Because there were only two people who wrote *Love Will Cut You Like a Knife*, and there are four people who have their names on it," I said. My jaw was tight. "I only want—"

"You only want?"

There was an objection, but before the judge said anything, I got out, "I only want what's fair—what's ours."

✴ ✴ ✴ ✴ ✴

A FEW MOMENTS later Sandy said, "All right, now I want to walk you through how you and Princess Diamond wrote *Love Will Cut You Like a Knife*—"

The judge interrupted. "It's not escaped our notice that Miss Diamond, the alleged cowriter, isn't here. Mr. Kovall—"

"She requested not to be here, Your Honor, and we don't believe we need her for our case. But if *you* believe that you— or the defense—do need her, we'll welcome her participation."

The judge nodded. "That'll be fine. Proceed."

"So you told the court that the idea for *a* song—'a really big song'—came from Mr. Solomon. But the idea for the song itself, where did that come from?"

"Well," I said, "Princess and I had our ways of working. If we already had an idea for a song, we'd try to flesh it out. But if we didn't—if we were under assignment to come up with something new—then we'd simply put ourselves in our office, with our piano, and start riffing."

"Riffing?" Sandy lifted his chin. "Is that the technical term?"

Judge MacIntire gave a little laugh, then said, "Mr. Stephenson?"

I looked up at her. "Um, yes it is, Your Honor. We would do what we call 'riff.' " I smiled, too.

"And that is?" Sandy said.

"It's how you do it. You . . . well, somebody gets a word or a phrase, or a musical hook, and then the other person runs with it. You pass the idea back and forth, move it along, make it better. You *riff* on it."

"Got it," Sandy said. "And what happened with the song in question, *Love Will Cut You Like a Knife.*"

"A little of both."

Sandy lifted an eyebrow. "A little of both of what?"

"Well, I had the initial idea, and I'd jotted some words down on the back of my phone bill. I was on the F train heading to Midtown—I remember it like it was yesterday—"

"Objection," went Manny Gold's lawyer. "The plaintiff is under oath. It's expected that he remembers everything he testifies to, correct?"

"Sustained. Strike that last phrase. Mr. Stephenson, you're on the subway, and you're suddenly struck with an idea—"

"Your Honor!" Manny's lawyer cried.

Judge MacIntire flushed, just for a moment, and her cheeks reddened. "All right, Mr. Kovall, you may proceed."

Sandy gave me a wink. "So, you're on the subway, then what happened?"

I closed my eyes a moment. It was true, no matter what the correct jurisprudence, I *could* remember it as if it were yesterday. I'd been back in New York for a couple of weeks, staying as I always did with my mom and sis. Punky had sent Princess and me back here to come up with our new song— the song that would save the Annas, Punky, the whole girl-group sound. Princess and I were meeting every afternoon in our dilapidated office at 1650 Broadway, and so far we'd come up with zip.

We knew it was the pressure, and we weren't sure what to do about it. We started turning up punctually at one, Princess each day in a dress and a smart hat, and I even taking to wearing a tie—I think we were hoping that, we make it like a real, grown-up job, we could get something going—but the whole idea of writing a song that had to beat back the tides had us paralyzed. Any idea we had—even the kind of good, gritty, cool-cat ideas we'd turned into hits before—seemed puny and insubstantial. At one point Princess came in with a lyric whose chorus went, "Take that, God!" I called it the *Yahweh Blues*.

We'd almost decided we weren't going to get anywhere, which made us even more nuts. We always showed up exactly at 1 p.m. That is, we'd wait outside on Broadway until our watches clicked straight up, then we'd head to the rickety elevator to take us up to our seventh-floor office. Office on seven—that must be lucky, right? The last time we'd written a good song there, our last Annas song, *The Truth Is in the Air*, I'd had a fried egg sandwich while we wrote it. (The song took half an hour, warbled out between greasy bites.) So I started buying a fried egg each day before we started in. The result? Princess came in one afternoon crooning, *"My belly's growing, and I don't know why / Hope it's just egg sandwiches, and not a baby boy."*

"Cute," I said between bites, my lips glazed with yellow yolk. Then, mostly joking, I said, "Hey, that's an idea: a song about an abortion."

"A—" Princess gave me a dark look.

"No, really, nobody's ever done that before that I can think of." I was still just having a go at her. "We can start it all big and portentous, have the girls talking over the opening, like the Shangri-las with *Leader of the Pack*. You know, 'So, how's Jimmy.' 'He's good.' 'What's wrong, Anna?' 'Well, maybe he's a little too good.' 'What do you mean?' 'He's given me a . . . little gift.' "

"*Larry!*"

"You have a better idea?"

Princess simply shook her head. "Come on, finish your sandwich. Let's get to work."

"Right. And get right on all the ideas *you* have?"

Well, that's how it was going. We'd been at it for weeks. And where were the Annas all this time? They'd gotten off the Beatles tour months back, in the fall of '65, but Punky wanted to keep them busy, so here we were in spring '66, and they were out touring again, in a package show with the Shirelles, the Marcels, Don and Dewey, and a host of others. The show felt like an oldies tour and didn't do that well. Punky made a couple of records with the girls that Princess and I didn't write, pulled them off of demos sent west by Donnie Kirshner, then didn't release them. I was never sure why. Maybe he just didn't hear that kernel of *hit* in them; maybe he was worrying that he could no longer hear a hit as well as he could before.

In truth, I didn't know what was going on with Punky then; reports came from California that he was getting a little strange. His hair was growing out, touching his shoulders; his goatee was longer, too, and Barney Fredericks started calling him Fu. He made the chauffeur of his Bentley wear a top hat at all times. And he started spending every weekend in Vegas. Word was he surrounded himself with showgirls and dropped unimaginable amounts of dollars; one rumor I never confirmed had him outside Elvis's dressing room, drunk and insisting he be let in to see the King; and the Memphis boys not knowing who Punky was and threatening to call the cops.

An ugly picture. All of which made it all the more imperative we write the world-changing song to save us all—the song that had us stopped cold.

✳ ✳ ✳ ✳ ✳

"I WAS ON THE SUBWAY," I said from my perch in the witness chair, "sitting there, looking around—for a writer, the subway's great material. All of New York—all of humanity—spread out before you, and you can just . . . woolgather—"

"Objection! Witness is digressing."

"Overruled," Judge MacIntire said. "He's just telling his story, his way. Go on, Mr. Stephenson."

Sandy said, perhaps a little too tauntingly, "Please, Mr. Stephenson, just tell your story—in your own way."

"Well," I said, "I got an idea. It wasn't the first I had on the subway, nor the last. Just a line for a song. I turned it over in my head, then wrote it down on an envelope."

"Your Honor, I want to put into evidence—" Sandy consulted a clipboard "—plaintiff's exhibit number 5." He handed the smudged envelope scrap up to the judge, who looked at it, then said, "So entered, plaintiff's number 5."

"So, let me back you up," Sandy said. "You're sitting on the subway when you get this idea. What *was* the idea, and how come you got it?"

"Well, it was a song idea. That's words that fall together just right—words that sound like they'll make the hook of a song, that will lead to more words."

Sandy said, "I'm not sure I'm—"

"It was just an idea. Love will—" I paused. "Love will do something. Love will smell like a rose. Yeah, right. I wasn't in that good a mood either. Love will make you see the light. Pretty if it were true, right? But that didn't suit my mood. What I was feeling was, well, Love will hurt you." I took a deep breath. "But you always want to be as specific as possible, so I came up with: Love will cut you . . . cut you like a knife." I raised my eyebrows. "You see, you *feel* it. The words are . . . sharp. *Love will . . . cut . . . you . . . like a . . . knife.* You feel them right across your skin!"

"And that's what you're looking for, right?"

"Of course. Something the listener will feel right off—viscerally."

I noticed Judge MacIntire smile at me; guess she liked that word.

"But, tell me, it wasn't just an *academic* exercise, was it? You weren't just playing with words? There was something going on with you that made you think that, right?"

I sighed. Sandy and I had discussed this endlessly. I didn't want to talk about *why* I wrote the song, just how, but he said that revealing my personal reasons—my personal life—would give the suit more credibility. Just let Punky Solomon get up there and let all the world see *his* personal life. Not to mention Manny Gold's.

"Um," I dithered on the stand, "I have emotions, um, like anyone else, and I . . . I was feeling sort of, you might say, the pain of love—"

"The pain of love?"

"Well, yeah." I winced.

Even now I could remember that day. I'd found out the night before that Manny Gold was planning to propose to Anna. *Manny Gold!* Wasn't he just this goombah gnat buzzing around the whole scene, money bags and brass knuckles at the ready? I knew, of course, of his long-standing thing for Anna; but I had no reason to think he was ever going to get anywhere with it. But Princess had told me that he'd persuaded her to take a boat trip with him—Bahamas, if I remember right—and that he had a whole plan: get her out there on the water, isolated from everything, and then work on her till she agreed to marry him.

"I don't believe it," I had said, truly incredulous. Princess and I were having drinks after another day of fruitless songwriting. "How do you even *know* this?" Princess's eyes lit up. Then she sang, to an interesting melody, *"I thought it was just the weather / Till I put two and two together."*

I lifted an eyebrow. "You're making this into a *song?*

She tilted her head to the side, that way she had, then shrugged. "Punky told me Manny was away on a cruise." She smiled; seemed to be enjoying this. "Then Trudy said the same thing about Anna."

I put my hand to my chest. "Are you sure?"

"Well, I did a little more digging around."

"And?"

"It's true, far as I can tell." She took a long minute, then shook her head.

"What's that mean?" I shook my head, too, in imitation of her.

"You're going to ask me what she's going to say—"

"Yeah, I am."

"And I'm going to say I don't know." She hooked her eyes at me, lifted her wide chin.

"You don't—"

"They're out there now." She leaned back, then said, "You know, you seem awfully put out, Larry. Are *you* still hung up on her?"

I caught myself. "I don't know what you mean."

"Right, Larry." Princess snorted, then sipped her martini. "You know, maybe you should ask her to marry *you*." She laughed, and it was like a stab to my heart. "That is, if she's not already hitched." She lifted her eyes. "Then again, you might want to avoid the humiliation."

I knew our work was going bad, but I was shocked by what Princess had just said—*everything* she'd said. My head spun for another minute, then I simply got up and went home.

I didn't sleep well that night, ending up watching the *Late Late Show* on TV—I remember it well: *Double Indemnity*, Barbara Stanwick and Fred MacMurray, with its astonishing tangles of lying and duplicity—then just kicking up sheets nearly till dawn. I finally fell out; woke up sweaty and disoriented. *Anna . . . Anna and Manny Gold?* For a moment I felt the room list and thought that *I* was on a ship.

On the F train into Manhattan I stayed lost to my thoughts. There were a couple of cute Spanish girls, fifteen-year-olds, playing a tag game up and down the car. One of them looked a little like Anna, same dark hair, wide mouth, bright eyes. And each time I saw her, I felt burned across my skin . . . no I felt like acid was eating at me . . . no, I felt cut by the sharpest, most deadly blade. . . .

I always carried a ball point pen in my shirt pocket and I pulled it out, reached in my jacket, where I found the telephone bill envelope, and on the back I wrote, *"Love can beat you / Love can defeat you / Love can take your life / Love can slice you / Love can dice you / Love can cut you . . . like a knife."*

I sat back on the rocking and rolling subway train and looked at those words, and I felt better. Writing can do that. The right words can come in and staunch the bleeding. Words can wrap themselves around you like a poultice. Words can ease you on down.

When I got to our studio Princess said, "Listen, about last night, I don't know what got into me. I'm sorry."

Her admission startled me; it wasn't in her nature to apologize. "You are?"

"I was—well, a little cruel, Larry." Princess was wearing slacks and a V-necked cashmere sweater that showed off her deeply tanned chest. "I really don't know what I was thinking. Maybe I was just worried that whatever happens on that boat would upset everything—as if we're not flummoxed enough."

"Sit down," I said.

"Sit—?"

"Down. Now. At the piano. I got a chorus, got the words, maybe even a beginning of a melody. Here, listen." And I held my envelope in front of me and sang to her, *"Love can beat you / Love can defeat you / Love can take your life / Love can slice you / Love can dice you / Love can cut you . . . like a knife."*

"Hey!" she said. Her fingers were finding chords that

cadenced powerfully. "Hey, hey, hey!" She moved up the scale, then down, then around, and my hint of a melody got strong and moving. "Boy," she shouted over the pounding piano, "maybe I should be cruel to you more often."

I gave her a look then. "It wasn't you," I said, but soft, mostly to myself.

"What was that?"

I shook my head. "Nothing."

She shrugged. She was moving the song along now, the tune for the chorus finished, attacking the verse. "You got more words?"

"Give me a melody, let me see."

We didn't finish the song that afternoon, but we got pretty far. After that we took our time, moving slowly through it, refining it, building it up in the chorus, cooling it off in the verse; making it as big with just Princess's and my voice and her piano as we could. When we finally felt we'd nailed the tune, we ran it off on a two-track tape, called up Punky, and told him we'd get it to him as soon as we could.

"The pain of love," Sandy reminded me, pulling me from my reverie. "I'm sure we all know it, but what was it specifically that led to that morning on the subway with your writing the lyrics on that phone bill?"

"It was a . . . a girl."

"I know this is hard for you, Mr. Stephenson, but it's important that the court understand that these were true emotions you put into your song, and that they were *your* emotions."

"A girl I loved from afar. I was young, and—" I shrugged. "I'd just been told that somebody else I knew had proposed to her. I was . . . was afraid I'd lost her forever—lost any hope of having her."

"And that was—"

"It was horrible." I tried to get a smile out, make it sound light, just one of those things. I doubt I succeeded.

"By the way, did you lose the girl?"

Now I could smile, genuinely but wanly. "Not then. She actually turned down the other man's proposal." I looked out to the defendant's table, caught Manny's eyes. He glared back at me.

I turned to Sandy. "Later, well, later I proposed to her myself—"

"And?"

I thought back to that night in L.A. a few weeks earlier, combing the rubble for my grandmother's ring. "I never got an answer," I said softly.

"You never—"

"Before I could, she . . . she was dead."

Sandy looked at the judge then, to make sure that she'd heard me. She had. Her eyes looked troubled.

"Your Honor," Sandy said, "I suggest we—"

Judge MacIntire anticipated him. She rapped down her gavel. "The court is adjourned until 9:30 a.m. tomorrow." The judge turned her eyes, now sympathetic, on me. "Mr. Stephenson, you're excused."

Chapter Eight

"THAT WAS GOOD up there," Sandy said in the hallway. "I think we made some points."

I stood there looking down at him. For a moment I was too angry to speak. Then I got out, "Don't ever make me do that again. That's not why we're here."

Sandy took a step toward me. "We're here, Dink, to prove that you and Princess wrote the song—that's it." His voice was harsh, then it lightened. "But trials are funny. You gotta use every edge you can."

I was still glaring at him. "Sandy, I mean it. Don't do that again."

"Hey, don't worry." He did a little foot shuffle then, holding his briefcase. "Tomorrow we're taking you into SilverTone Studios. You'll tell the court how you and Princess finished writing the song, and then how it was recorded. That Punky was there, sure, but no trace of Manny Gold." Sandy winked. "Piece of cake."

The next morning I was back on the stand. Judge MacIntire greeted me warmly. Sandy and I had gotten to the court early. Punky was already there, but Manny rushed in just half a minute before 9:30.

Sandy started right in. "Let's pick up from where we were yesterday. Now you said you got the first idea for *Love Will Cut You Like a Knife* on the subway, and that you and your cowriter worked over the lyrics for the next few weeks. Then what did you do?"

"When we were finished?"

"Yes."

"Well, we made a demo tape, just Princess and me, with her on the piano."

"A demo—that's a recording of the song?"

"A simple recording, just to get the tune and lyrics across."

"Do you still have that demo tape?"

I felt the interest in the court tighten. At the defendants' table everyone leaned forward.

But I had to shake my head.

"Your answer?"

"Um, no, I don't."

"Does it exist?"

"I don't think so."

"But you don't know?"

"We did it on tape, which was erased, but before that, we took it like we always did to Dick Charles around the corner. He pressed it up as an acetate—that's like a record but only on one side—and then we sent it off to California—"

"To Mr. Solomon."

"Yes."

"And Mr. Stephenson, as far as you know there was only the one acetate of the song?"

"It was just to give Punky—Mr. Solomon—a heads-up. We were scheduled to fly out to the Coast the next week, and we'd be working on our song then."

"So just the one copy."

"As far as I'm aware, yes." What I didn't say was that I hadn't taken the tape to get made into an acetate, Princess had, and she said she'd sent the disc off to L.A. airmail. And that was that.

"Well, it's a shame we can't hear the original demo, compare it with the released record." Sandy took a couple steps toward me. "If that were the case, I'm sure we wouldn't even be here at tri—"

"Objection!"

"Sustained. Mr. Kovall, just the facts."

"Well, we do have early recordings that Mr. Solomon made, when the song was new to him and the group the Annas were first working on the song. They'll be put into evidence shortly. But first I want you, Mr. Stephenson, to tell the court more about what happened when you and your writing partner got to L.A."

"It was—it was just like the old days." Then I laughed, a loud, inappropriate guffaw.

"Sir?"

"I'm sorry." I fought to get myself under control. "It's just that that was over thirty years ago, but the old days I was referring to were less than eighteen months before."

"I see. Things had changed?"

"*Everything* had changed—and, oddly, nothing had. We were all back, me, Princess, Punky, the three Annas, and Punky's regular crew of musicians."

"So you were all back in a kind of, what, comfort zone," Sandy said. "You all knew what your places were?"

"That's true. It felt good to be there, too. Good to feel the old energy."

"So let's talk about *Love Will Cut You Like a Knife*. When did the defendants first hear it?"

"Objection—calls for speculation."

"Sustained. Mr. Kovall—"

"I'm sorry Your Honor. Let me rephrase it. When did you first *play* the song for the defendants?"

"Well, I never played the song for Mr. Gold. He wasn't even at the studio when we got started. And Punky—he had the acetate we'd sent him."

"Did you see it?"

"Casually, yes. It was on a shelf in the control room."

"How did you know it was your demo?"

"It had the title written on it."

"In?"

"In Princess's handwriting. Acetates were usually just white labels, nothing fancy. On it she'd written LOVE WILL CUT KNIFE. I noticed it because there were those three words missing."

"O.K., so Punky had received the demo disc—"

"Objection!"

"All right, all right. The demo disc was in the same room where Punky Solomon was making a record, the same song that was on the disc, right?"

"Yes, sir."

"But nonetheless you and your writing partner played the song for Mr. Solomon."

"As soon as we got there. We'd had a couple new ideas a few days later, and we played the new version for him. Princess played it on the piano, we both sang."

"Just like on the demo."

"Exactly as we did on the demo."

"And—" Sandy was right up in front of me now. His voice was large, firm, rising. "The demo you sent Mr. Solomon, *and* the demo you played for him that first day in the studio—they were the song, lock, stock, and barrel, that was released by the Annas four months later under the same title that you wrote it under, *Love Will Cut You Like a Knife*, and that's the same song we are here to ascertain its true authorship."

I waited a moment before I spoke, in the same spirit that we'd sometimes put a pause into the build from a verse to a chorus; you wanted the listener to be with you all the way, and stopping the music and letting him or her hang with you till the beat kicked back in would do it every time. We called it the "*Billboard* moment," after that emotional swell we'd work into a song that would simply flutter your heart-strings—and send the record to the top of the charts. "Yes," I said, then I paused again. I could feel interest grow. Beat, beat, beat. Then: "It was the same song, yes."

"Exactly the same song?"

"Basically the same song."

"Basically?" Sandy raised an eyebrow, discretely so the judge could see. "Not exactly?"

"A song—any song—can change while it's being recorded. A singer can't always hit a note, you get a new idea—things can happen."

"So, Mr. Stephenson, how much changed from your demo to the final record?"

Another pause, again everyone's ears hanging on me. "Not much."

"Can you tell us . . . exactly?"

"I can tell you as well as I can remember."

"And that is?"

"I know we changed some words in the second verse. I think in the second half of the bridge Princess rewrote the music." I leaned forward. "But that was it. The chorus stayed the same, the opening—most all of the song."

"And what you just said, 'We changed some words,' 'Princess rewrote the music,' the two of you songwriters were there at the sessions. When there was a problem, you stepped in to fix it. It was still your song . . . lock, stock, and barrel?"

"Objection—counsel is drawing conclusions."

"Overruled," Judge MacIntire said. "You may answer."

"For as long as I was there, yes, it was still our song."

"Thank you." Sandy turned then, and walked back to the plaintiff's table. He poured himself a glass of water. I reached over and did the same. Sandy said, "Your Honor, I'm about to embark on a line of questioning that will cover in more detail the work in the studio. I want the court to understand how these youthful geniuses worked together. It could be a—"

"Yes, Mr. Kovall, O.K., let's take a fifteen-minute break. We'll readjourn at 10:45." And Judge MacIntire brought her gavel down.

✳ ✳ ✳ ✳ ✳

"BRILLIANT!" SANDY CROWED. "Right in the pocket."

I smiled. *In the pocket*, meaning tight and in the groove.

Well, Sandy fancied himself a hipster of sorts; wasn't everyone these days?

"You made it go smoothly."

"Yeah, so what I want to do is have you give a flavor of what it was like in the studio, you, Princess, Punky, the musicians, and the three girls. How, for one, Manny Gold wasn't even around—"

"For most of it."

"As far as you know, he was never even *at* the studio."

I nodded. Actually, Manny Gold had followed Anna to L.A. and was in town the whole time; it was just that while I was there, Punky wouldn't let him into SilverTone. It was only when it was time to put the disc out that Manny somehow shoehorned his name onto the writing credits.

"And for two, you guys and Punky had a great working relationship—"

"Most of the time."

"*Enough* of the time."

I shrugged.

"And that while he did all kinds of amazing things to make the record what it was, he did not *write* anything on the song."

"That's our case," I said deadpan.

"And the truth—"

"And the truth."

"I'm looking forward to this," Sandy said, clicking his heels together the way he did. "This is going to be a great morning. Then—hey—I'll take you to Nha Trang, this amazing Vietnamese place I know behind the courthouse."

When I was back on the stand, Sandy said, "Now as I said before the break, I want to take you back to the studio while you were recording *Love Will Cut You Like a Knife*. How far along was the production when you arrived from New York?"

"It was just getting going."

"And this was going to be a long session?"

I nodded. "Punky always took as long as he needed on a record, but I had an intuition this was going to be longer than usual."

"And it was—"

"The whole thing took over three months. The longest date before that was four weeks."

"When did the session start?"

"July of 1966."

"And it lasted until. . . ?"

"September.

"What took so long?"

I leaned forward. "Well, while I was there, he was just—just moving very slowly. He was trying for something nobody had done before, this big song produced in a huge way. It can take years for someone to write a symphony." I shrugged. "Punky was shooting for that."

"A symphony?"

"Music with complexity, breadth, and power. You can call it what you like."

"I think we get it. What actually did you witness while you were there?"

"Well, Punky spent the first week working on the drums—"

"Just the . . . drums?"

I nodded. "He had two kits going—he always liked that; deep, pounding rhythm—then he added timpanis, marimbas, claves, tambourines, bells . . . on and on. Our percussionists brought their full kits to a Punky Solomon session; when in doubt he had guys on call from the L.A. Philharmonic. As I said, he spent that first week on the rhythm, recorded it, then tore it all up and started again."

"Nobody was singing yet?"

"Oh, no."

"But . . . it was still the song you wrote."

I nodded again, then quickly said, "He was just laying the foundation. Some of the rhythms changed, this and that, but the chords weren't affected, and the words weren't even addressed yet."

"And that's pretty much how things stayed?"

"As long as I was there."

Sandy nodded. We'd agreed we wouldn't go into why I left the sessions. Sandy told me that the other lawyers would probably bring it up on cross, and he wanted to wait till they began to attack me before I divulged to the court why I had to leave L.A. and return to New York. I wasn't looking forward to talking about that at all, so I agreed.

"So let me jump ahead then. When did you first hear the finished recording?"

"October."

"How did that happen?"

"I was still in New York. Princess sent me an acetate."

"A new acetate?"

"Yes."

"And where were you when you played it."

"At my—at the house I grew up in. In Queens."

Sandy smiled at Judge MacIntire. She'd grown up in Queens, too, he'd told me. Far Rockaway.

"And tell me about that day."

I shifted in my seat. "Well, I had the black acetate, and I put it on my record player—"

"Were you excited?"

"Objection!"

"Overruled," Judge MacIntire said. "The witness can describe what he heard on the, um, acetate, and how he felt about it. Proceed."

I nodded at the judge. "I was excited, yes. Nervous. I wanted to see how Punky had produced our song."

"And?"

"I was blown away. It hit me immediately. The

percussion—the timpanis, the triangles—I was caught right up in it." I closed my eyes. "Then I heard Anna Dubower's voice singing our words to our tune. It was . . . breathtaking."

"You thought it was a great record?"

I'd been holding my breath a moment and let out a stream of air. "I did, yes. I was bowled over."

"And you *still* think it's a great record?"

"I—I admire it, yes. I also think that overall Punky mixed the voices a little too low."

"Is that why it wasn't a hit?"

I shook my head. "I don't know why it wasn't a hit." I shrugged. "It's a hit in its way now, though. Everybody knows *Love Will Cut You Like a Knife* now."

"Indeed, they do. And, please, one more time. The record everyone knows and loves—that song is, what, well over ninety percent the *song* that you and Princess Diamond—you two alone—wrote."

"Absolutely."

Sandy nodded to the judge, then toward the defense table. "Your witness."

✳ ✳ ✳ ✳ ✳

PUNKY'S LAWYER was named Donald Furtie, and he was a red-faced, silver-haired, pink-bow-tied fellow, late thirties, wearing the most expensive shoes I'd ever seen. He strode right up to me and said, "Mr. Stephenson, I'm going to go over everything you've told us—all the true evidence of what you contributed to *Love Will Cut You Like a Knife*—but I want to start with the recording session. You said you were at the actual sessions for only a short while—"

I nodded.

"Sir?"

"Yes, that's true."

"And how long were you there?"

"Three weeks."

"Three . . . weeks?" Furtie rolled his eyes.

"Yes."

"And—remind me—how long was the whole *Knife* session?"

"Three months."

"Three . . . *months*?" Furtie said. I didn't respond. "Was this usual?"

"What do you mean?"

"Wouldn't you normally be at the whole session?"

"In and out, I suppose."

"But you left this session only three *weeks* into it?"

"Yes, sir."

"So in truth you don't know what happened to the song you and Princess Diamond sketched out for Mr. Solomon."

"Objection!" Sandy said, jumping up. "He's badgering the witness."

The judge raised an eyebrow. "Overruled," she said.

I glanced at Sandy, who lifted his chin. All part of the plan.

"Thank you, Your Honor." Furtie gave a self-satisfied smile, then turned back to me. "Mr. Stephenson, the simple truth is you were not there."

"Only for three weeks."

"And why did you leave?" Furtie leaned toward me, his eyes bright.

I swallowed, my mouth so dry I made a noise I was sure ricocheted through the courtroom. "Because I had to go back to New York."

"You had to . . . go back to New York? Right in the middle of the session for the biggest song of your life?"

"I had to, yes."

"Why?"

I glanced at Sandy, who gave me a quick, encouraging nod. Then I said, "Because my mother was murdered."

I could feel it, a sudden silence in the courtroom followed by a subtle flow of sympathy from Judge MacIntire. Donald Furtie looked startled—this hadn't come up in his deposing of me—and he looked as if he was unsure what to do next. He must have decided he couldn't simply walk away from it, so he said, "She was . . . murdered?"

"In a convenience store a few blocks from our home in Kew Gardens. She was there during a robbery, and she got shot."

"I see. Well, that would be a, um, a reasonable reason not to be at the session." Furtie looked like he was trying to think fast on his feet. "But . . . you never went back. Why was that?"

"Because of my sister—"

Now Furtie got it. I could see he didn't want to go there, but Judge MacIntire leaned over and said, "Mr. Stephenson, what happened with your sister?"

"She had, Your Honor, when she was a kid, she had polio—before the vaccine." I heard myself swallow. I'd been fifteen, and the diagnosis had floored us. The next thing I knew, Nancie could no longer walk. "She's in a wheelchair. When my mother . . . when she died, the only support for my sister was taken away. I . . . I had to find out a way to take care of her. Make sure she got care."

"I see." The judge looked at Furtie, who just stood there for a moment.

Finally he said, "Well, I'm sure it was a tragedy, sir, and you have my deepest condolences. But . . . the fact remains that you weren't at the recording session for *Love Will Cut You Like a Knife*, so you can't possibly know what contributions my client, Mr. Solomon, made to the final record. Isn't that true, sir?"

I didn't answer.

"Sir?"

I still didn't answer, and after a minute Furtie backed up

and said, "O.K., I want to go back to how you said you and Ms. Diamond wrote the song."

Furtie led me back over ground we'd covered, but I wasn't there. Those last six months of 1966 were the worst (and yet, later, the most hopeful) period of my life. To put it simply, my mother's death devastated me. I immediately felt as if I were underwater; everything but dealing with the aftermath of the shock took place in a murky, distant world that the day before I'd been part of and then could no longer find my way back to. Even now that time spooks me; in part I moved to Arizona to put myself as far away from everything that went down as I could. But now I was right there again.

I got the call about my mother from my Aunt Josie. It had come half a minute after I walked into my Hollywood Hills apartment after a day in the studio. Punky had gotten unhappy with the drums again, and all day he moved engineer Larry Dobell and his mikes around the drum kits and the percussion. Larry would place a bullet-shaped mike, the prime drummer, Eldred Smith, would go *thonk, thonk*, Punky would stick his curled finger under his goatee, then shake his head . . . and Larry would move the mike half an inch to the side. *Thonk, thonk, thonk*. This was the only thing going on. The rest of us were dying, but the musicians were on the clock, and I was expected to be there, so that was that.

When I picked up the phone my aunt was sobbing. I didn't recognize her at first; had the first startled thought that this was Anna Dubower, in some new scrape, calling me up. I wasn't sure I said it, but I thought it loudly: *Anna? Are you all right?*

"It's your Aunt Josie, Larry. I have . . . bad . . . news."

"What is it?"

"Are you sitting down?"

I wasn't, but I grunted a sort of yes. "Aunt Josie, what is it?"

"It's your mother—"

"Mom—"

"She's . . . she's been shot."

"She's . . . what?" The word *shot* didn't compute.

"It's a terrible tragedy. You better be sitting down? Are you?"

O.K., I sat, in the chair next to the telephone table. The black receiver was pressed tight to my ear. Long distance reception was never great back then, but I was hearing Aunt Josie clearly.

"I'm sitting, I'm sitting."

"Well, she was in Pawlinski's, you know, the convenience store on Queens Boulevard. There was—" she was sobbing again "—a robbery. It . . . it went . . . wrong. Your mother, she was there buying some milk. But she . . . she must've gotten in the way somehow. Oh, Larry!" And this horrific cry leaped over the phone.

I was on a plane first thing the next morning. There had been two robbers, both wearing bandannas pulled down below their eyes (just the way we played cops and robbers as kids), with slicked-back black hair—the police said they were thinking Puerto Ricans. One of them was seen to have a limp. But that was all they had to go on. This was before the days of video cameras in stores, and there were just a few eyewitnesses: one in the store, another from across the street.

The woman in the store said that one of the robbers shot old Mr. Pawlinski, and my mother started hitting at him with a rolled-up newspaper. It was the second robber who shot her, twice, once to the head, the other to the heart. She was dead immediately.

My sister, Nancie, was home alone in her wheelchair.

I was in shock. I'd been close to my mother, calling her at least twice a week whenever I was in California and always staying with her in New York, and I loved my younger sister. She was an 18-year-old spunk. Even with her polio, she went to school, loved music, played piano, had a boyfriend. But she couldn't take care of herself. In a second I forgot everything about Punky Solomon, *Love Can Cut You Like a Knife*, and moving that mike another half an inch off axis. . . .

At first dealing with the funeral and all Mom's friends and the estate kept me busy, but when that died down, I kind of got obsessed about the investigation. I could hardly sleep at night, imagining my poor mother innocently buying her milk in the near empty convenience store, swatting at the murderous robber like he was just some misbehaving kid, then jolted back by the .22-caliber slugs. The whole picture made me shudder—worse each day. I started spending mornings wandering by the local police station, then popping in, trying to keep pressure up, not be too obnoxious, but who knows how careful I actually was. The *Daily News* had run the killings on the front page, along with sketches of the robbers, but so far the police had no actual suspects. In my night ruminations they flitted across the edges of my vision and ran and ran, and I ran after them, tackling them, pummeling them brutally with my fists. But they weren't caught . . . and I felt my life was simply on hold till they were.

I had moved back into my old bedroom. My mother's room, we kept the door shut. I was taking care of Nancie, who needless to say was at least as grieving and distraught as I was. There were times during that first month when only she bucked up my spirits. She also said that we had to work something else out; she didn't want me to do nothing but take care of her. I was silent. I didn't *want* to do anything else. And whatever was going on in L.A., well, Princess called often to check up on me, tell me that the recording was proceeding (Punky even more insane day by day), but she never said they needed or even wanted me out there; and even as the initial shock passed, I found I just wasn't thinking about any of it: *Knife* or music or Punky or Princess or even Anna Dubower.

Till one evening she called. We'd just finished the TV dinners that were Nancie's and my common repast and were getting ready to watch a Yankees game when the phone rang.

"Dink?" she said. Nobody in Queens was calling me by my nickname, not Nancie or Aunt Josie or the cops or anyone else in the family. Just hearing that snapped me into a new head.

"Who is it?"

"Dink, it's Anna."

My heart jumped, the first spark since I'd come home. "Where are you?" I think I asked this because I didn't hear much hiss on the line.

"I'm . . . I'm in New York."

"Really?"

She must've thought I said something like *What*, because she repeated, "New York City."

"At your mother's?"

"Yes."

"What're you . . . aren't you . . . isn't the recording still going on in L.A.?"

"Um, I'm taking a break from it."

"A break?" That sounded curious. I couldn't imagine Punky allowing that. "That's fine with Punky?"

A long silence. "Dink, I was hoping to see you."

"Yeah, sure," I said quickly. My forehead was hot. "Anytime."

"Sooner the better."

That gave me pause. My head was clanging from being wrenched from my simple Queens world back into memories of all the complicated desires and hopes of my other life. "Tonight?" I said. "Is that what you mean? I'm—I'm just here in Kew Gardens with my sister. We're about to watch the Yankees game—"

"Do you want to meet me?"

I looked over at Nancie. She was watching me with

intense curiosity. There was now a fine sheen of sweat on my forehead, and more marks on my polo shirt. She evidently could read enough that something was going on, and she gave me an encouraging nod.

"Sure. Where do you want to get together?"

"Do you have a car?"

"My mother's, yeah—"

"Oh, Dink, I'm so sorry about what happened to her. Did you get my card?"

I shook my head, and it was like she heard me.

"You didn't? Damn that post office. Well, I want to tell you that we were all devastated. Just *deee*-stroyed!"

"Thanks," I said quietly.

"So, why don't you come pick me up. We'll go for a drive. I've been thinking about that time you came and rescued me in the Valley. In your MG—"

I let out a tiny chuckle. "You might be disappointed. My mother's car is a Chevy Bel-Air—"

A pause, then she said, "Oh, Dink, I don't care. I—I really, really, *really* want to see you."

"Are you all right?"

Another short pause. "It'll be good. We can talk."

"O.K., good, fine. I'm on my way. Just give me your address . . . wait, no, I remember where it is. East 120th, right?"

"Near Second Avenue. Tell you what, how long do you think you'll be?"

"Half an hour?" I said, giving my best guess.

"Well, no reason to disturb my mother. Say, I'll meet you on the corner of 120—no, make that 122nd—and Second Avenue in half an hour."

"Got it," I said.

When I hung up, Nancie said just two words: "Anna Dubower?"

"How'd you know?"

"Larry, go to her, I'll be fine."

"I love you, babe," I said. I grabbed a windbreaker, went out back, and hopped into my mother's rattly old car.

Anna was waiting on the corner just as she said she'd be. She was standing under a street lamp that cast down a thick glow that fell like a languid waterfall. The tumbling yellow-ish milky light nearly washed out her features. She stood with her arm hooked against her side, a long leg extended. She wore flowing black pants and a tight-cut white blouse; a fine gold strand glinted below her neck. Her hair—that wonderful, trademark beehive—was down, brushed straight with a slight flip at the bottom, like the actress Natalie Wood. She wore a scarf over it that as I got closer I saw was blood-red.

She ran up to the passenger door when she saw me pull up, and tugged it open. She shot me a glance—*Can I just jump in?*—and I said, "Come on, it's good." Then, when she'd settled, I said, "Where do you want to go?"

She seemed a little breathless and didn't answer right away. She shook her head. "It doesn't matter."

"How about Ventura Beach?" I said blithely.

"If only—" She gave me a pale smile.

"How 'bout a club—you want to go dancing or something?"

She shook her head. I noticed that she sat very still next to me on the front seat, her hands wrapped together over her tummy. "Just some place quiet, Dink." Her voice was not much above a whisper. "Any place we can just sit. All right?"

"Got it," I said. I took us to the park beneath the Throgs-Neck Bridge, where I used to go with girls years back. I knew it would be quiet and nobody would bother us. We could talk, if that's what Anna wanted—*needed*—to do.

We pulled up in a half-lit part by the water. There were a couple cars in the lot but far away from us. The ramp up to the bridge loomed above us. A faint light rose off the water.

And we sat. I had no idea what was worrying Anna and wasn't sure I could just come out and ask; and she didn't say anything. Just looked straight ahead.

Finally she spoke, and what she said surprised me. "You smell good."

I lifted my chin. "Thanks, I guess."

"No, you just smell . . . clean." She nodded. "Like a good, clean man." Her gold necklace caught the faint light.

I didn't say anything back. We kept sitting there silently.

Finally, it was too much for me. "Anna, what happened?"

She turned, her full lips pursed. She brushed a few strands of hair from her eyes. "What do you mean?"

"Why are you here—in New York."

She seemed to hold her breath, then let out a long sigh. "Like I told you, I'm taking a break from L.A.—"

"But why?" I was facing her straight on. It wasn't just her hair that was different from when I'd seen her and the girls in L.A. Almost all of her performance makeup was gone, and without it her pale olive features under the blood-red scarf looked both softer and more delicate than usual, her hazel eyes less catlike. As I looked closer I did see a blush of lipstick, but it was less vermillion and more a natural pink-red; altogether sweeter, more approachable.

A long inhalation. "Can we just sit here, Dink. I—it feels really good just sitting here. It's so . . . quiet."

"Sure." There was a light whoosh of traffic falling from the bridge overhead, and an occasional bleat of a distant foghorn, but that was it. The night pressed against the car, you could really feel it.

As we sat there in silence I kept turning over the reasons why she could be here. Some hitch in the recording? But Punky liked his artists nearby, even if he was just moving drum mikes around. A fight with someone? But that didn't seem like Anna, and who would it be with, and over what? Maybe a problem at home? But with all my troubles, wouldn't she tell me about any problem with her mother right off? No, nothing made much sense.

A couple minutes later I said, "Maybe too quiet. You want the radio on?"

She shook her head. "No, please, no music."

"No . . . music?" I didn't get that. "Anna, are you sure you're all right?"

"I just need—Dink, this is great here—" She waved a hand "—this is just what I need. This . . . quiet. You don't know—you just don't know."

I reached over and touched her elbow, gently. I didn't move my hand, just cupped her arm. "Anna, what was it? What happened to you?"

She turned to face me. She didn't speak for the longest time. I think I heard every twig snap and pigeon squawk for miles, but I heard nothing. She took my hand. "Please, Dink," she said, her voice breathy like a girl's, "please don't ask me that."

I felt funny then, really odd, like I'd just walked into some kind of fright show at a carnival, where you get the willies and you're not even sure why. The tone of her voice, the way she pressed my hand—it all felt like damp leaves had run down my back, an eerie, horrific whistle had raised the hairs on the back of my neck. And yet I didn't have any idea why.

I tried a couple more times to ask what was bothering her, but she simply shook her head and repeated that she just needed to be quiet. Still and quiet. So we sat there, for at least two more hours. We didn't speak. After a while I held her arm, and she took my hand, and then an unknowable time later she moved across the Bel Air's front seat, her skirt catching on the Naugahyde and riding up. She was right next to me. I raised my arm, and she folded herself into me, her soft, fallen hair light on my shoulder. I could feel her breathing slow and steady on the bare skin of my upper arm.

That's how we were, for all that time. I was hearing everything, and then I was truly hearing nothing—nothing but her soft breathing and the beating of my own heart. I saw the long span bridge, the blue-black night, the glow off the water, and then I saw nothing—nothing but this beautiful woman next to me, whom I took in with every breath through my skin. I was enveloped in her perfume, different from before; subtler, richer, a tempting blend of hibiscus, rose, and tangerine. All that while Anna never dozed off, but she didn't move either; and then she finally stirred. She didn't have to say anything. The way she moved up and a little away from me was loud and clear. I turned over the key, fired up the engine, and drove her home.

On the street in front of her apartment building she leaned over and kissed me, fully, deeply, and with our mouths wide. It was just like that day in Ventura, but different, too. She felt smaller, more fragile, and yet hungrier with her mouth. My desire was different also. All the horror of my mother's murder, and my deepest fears that the crazy numbness I felt was all I was ever going to feel . . . all that dissipated, at least for the moment, in that one kiss.

Then Anna was gone.

When I got home to my mother's, Nancie said with a wink, "How'd it go?" She'd been waiting for me near the front door, reading a *Life* magazine.

"Um, fine." I wasn't looking at her. "We drove around some." A shrug. "Nothing special." I smiled. "How'd the Yankees do?"

She looked at me long and hard, that way Nancie had that let me know that she always—*always*—saw right through me. I saw her eyes read how worked up I was.

But, sweet girl, all she said was, "Mantle homered in the ninth." A blithe shrug. "They won."

✳ ✳ ✳ ✳ ✳

MY FIRST THOUGHT the next morning was not of my mother but of Anna. I called her right after breakfast.

Her own mother answered. "Dink Stephenson, haven't seen you in a dog's age." I heard a hint of her accent; sensed she was smiling.

"And how long is that, Mrs. Dubower?"

She paused a second, then laughed and said, "Too long, Dink, way too long."

She put Anna on.

"I woke up worried about you," I told her.

"That's so sweet!" Her voice surprised me. It was morning bright; I heard a lilting joy in it, as if she'd just been sharing a joke with her mother. It was so different from the night before. "You know, I woke up, well, not worrying, but *thinking* about you. I want to thank you for last night. Oh, Dink, you were so great." A pause, then her voice darkened a shade. "It was just what I needed."

"Glad to, um, you know—" I was a bit surprised by her. "Um, be, um, useful—"

"So when am I going to see you again?" she said, interrupting me.

"Oh, anytime you want. I'm really not doing that—"

"How about tonight?"

I felt my head jerk back. "Sure. You want to go out for another drive, or maybe—"

"Uh-uh," she said, and I saw her in my mind's eye, shaking her head, her eyes lambent, her black hair dancing over her fine-boned shoulders. "I'm going to come to you. I've been thinking I'd *love* to see where you grew up, meet your sister and all."

"You want to—"

"Yeah, it'd be great to have dinner with you. Just some burgers or something."

"Um, just a second, let me ask Nancie." I cupped the

phone, then called out, "It's Anna Dubower, she wants to come here for dinner."

My sister looked at me as if I'd just seen a ghost. She said, "Fine by me."

"Nancie says it's good by her," I said into the receiver. "But . . . it's not so easy to get here. Why don't I drive in and pick you up—"

"Dink, don't be silly. I'm a . . . well, I was . . . but I'm still a city girl. And, really, people don't recognize me so much anymore." I felt her smile to herself at that. "So I'll just take the subway. What line is it again?"

I told her, we set the time for 6:30, and then I hung up.

"You *do* look like you've seen a ghost," Nancie said, setting down her book. I told you she could read my mind.

"I'm—I'm—" Then I shook my head and made a "Whhffffhhhhhhhh" noise through my lips.

"We better get to the store," she said. "Come on, I'll go with you. We'll get something good."

"Anna said hamburgers would be fine—"

"Trust me, she wants a home-cooked meal. I can tell. I'll do it. It'll be great."

And it was. Anna swept in, a glowing ball of light. All the gloom and secrets of the night before seemed blown away. I don't know if I'd seen her so happy in years. And just that boundless cheerfulness tore shreds through the gray, leaden cloud that had surrounded me for weeks.

Nancie had spent all day on a roast chicken, spring vegetables (but it's September, I protested), stuffing, mashed potatoes, biscuits, and dessert—it was stick-to-your-ribs, trencherman food, and Anna went right at it.

She and Nancie hit it off great. She kept saying, "Nancie, nobody cooks like this—even *mi madre* doesn't cook like this. This chicken is so rich!"

I don't remember her speaking any Spanish before, and couldn't understand why she was now, since she was only one part Hispanic, unless it was being back in East Harlem with her family.

"How is your mother?" Nancie asked.

Anna immediately reached along the table and took her arm. "Nancie, Dink, you know how *sorry* I am about what happened to your mother. I can't imagine such a—a shock. Are you any better about it at all?"

"It's tough," Nancie said. "Really tough on Dink, though he doesn't say that much." A glance at me.

It's not true I didn't talk about it, but if it was, well, I still didn't say anything.

"How are you going to deal with it?"

"You mean?"

"Well, Dink's taking care of you for now, right? Dink, how long are you planning to be here?"

And now Anna's large milk-white eyes were full on me. I'd been noticing it all evening, a way she looked at me that was different from before: with more intensity, more search-ingly, with some mysterious question hovering behind her luminous cat's eyes.

"I don't know yet." A look at Nancie, who must have wanted to ask that question, but hadn't yet. "It depends."

"On what?" Anna was leaning over her plate.

"Well, things that I'm not, um, talking about." A shot from Nancie. "O.K., well, till everything is straightened out—"

"What Larry isn't saying is that we don't know what to do with me yet. We're all still too upset about Mom to see the future clearly. And I—I really can't take care of myself, at least he thinks that—and it's true I never have—so we're not sure where I'll go."

"Are there any possibilities?"

"We're talking to our Aunt Josie," I said. "It might work out with her."

"Josie isn't keen on it," Nancie told Anna. "But she's willing, if she has to. But if you ask me—"

Anna interrupted with a light laugh: "Nancie, what would *you* like to do?"

"Well, Miss Dubower, I'd like to live here by myself. I think I could do that. With a little help."

"Larry?" This was Anna, calling me by my real name for the first time.

"It would be a huge change for her. As she said, she's never been alone—at all. Even if it would be smart, it'll take a long time to work out." I glanced from Anna, to Nancie, then back again. "Wouldn't it?"

"A part of me right here and now would love to move in with you guys, help you get over all this," Anna said. She was bubbling with enthusiasm. I hardly believed it.

"You're kidding," Nancie said.

"No, no, I'm not." She turned her round eyes from my sister to me. "I feel so . . . so *right* here. Like it's just where I belong." She suddenly brought a hand to her mouth. "God, I can't believe I'm saying this. Isn't this just too, *too* presumptuous?"

Neither Nancie or I knew what to say, I could tell. We just looked at Anna, lead singer on two Number 1 songs, singer in the middle of recording the song of her life right now in Hollywood—except that she wasn't there; she was here in Kew Gardens with us—and we didn't know what to think.

Anna went on quietly. "I didn't mean to shock you. I only want to help, really. I know what I'm saying is crazy, but I mean it—I really do." She was blushing now. "If you could see my life, I mean, being here with you would be helping me as much as I'd be helping you." She stopped speaking, then was stone still. She stared straight ahead, and I had no idea what she was seeing. A flurry of emotions stormed across her face, then were as quickly gone. "I'm sorry," she went on, softer now, though with no less of the yearning, eruptive need than had just been there. "That was crazy. I—I don't know what I was thinking. Will you forgive me?"

"For what?" Nancie said.

"For—well, speaking about something I should only have thought."

"But it'd be great," my sister said, lighting up. "I can't think of anything I'd love more than having the two of you living here with me. Dink?"

Now I was blushing, though not as much as Anna. I was silent a long while, then I said, honestly, "I don't know what to say."

"Don't say anything." Anna reached over and touched my arm gently. "Don't say a word. It's fine. It's all going to be all right." She spoke those last words with anything but conviction, and I couldn't help but worry again about what had happened to her in L.A.

The wild wind that had just swept along our sails died now. A moment later Nancie wheeled back from the table to the refrigerator, then said, "You guys got room for dessert?"

"What is it, darling?" Anna said.

"Boston cream pie."

Her hand flew to her throat. "Oh, my God!" she cried. "Do I love Boston cream pie! That's the one food I remember from growing up in Connecticut. How'd you know?"

"I didn't."

"If you promised me Boston cream pie, I would, I really would just stop everything and move in with you guys. God, I'd love that. Eat like this every night and blow up like a house." A pealing laugh. "Larry, would you still love me if I was as big as a house?"

That stopped me cold. *Still love me?* I didn't know what to say.

But my sister saved me. "What kind of house?"

"What do you mean?"

"A duplex, like they got a block over? Or a stand-alone?

Or how about like we got, four-story apartment building? Big as our place?"

"Oh, my, pie like this every ol' night, I'd be as big as—as big as that bridge you took me to last night, the one we parked under."

"You guys were parking under a bridge last night?" Nancie turned her sharp eyes on me. "You didn't say anything like that to me."

"It was innocent," I said.

"Oh, I bet!"

"Don't believe a word of it, sugar," Anna said. "This brother of yours lured me to his favorite ol' parking place—where he took all his chickies in high school. Under this huge wonderful bridge and this huge wonderful orange moon. He's a slick one, aren't you, Dink?"

"Larry, you didn't say a word!"

"Bet you he also didn't tell you how much I love him." Anna's voice sparkled, and it seemed clear to me that she was just having a goof now.

"Well, he might not tell me *that*," my sister said. "And he hasn't said a word about how much he loves *you*." She winked at me. This was some game they were playing, the two of them. "Of course, he didn't have to."

"Isn't that just like a man!" Anna erupted. "Boy, all this rich, good food—this Boston cream pie!—it's going right to my head. I feel—Nancie, you didn't put any liquor in that pie, did you?"

"Only two quarts of bourbon."

"Well, then I *am* drunk." Anna stood up then and spun around, arms out, hands scooping the air. "And wild. And . . . ready for anything!"

I stood up then, too, saying, "Well, I'm going to start cleaning up. I'm going to wash the—"

And Anna threw herself on me. She seemed so small, and she fit so well, her arms went around my neck, and her breasts swelled against my chest, and she slid her body in with mine. She had her twirling energy, and she sent me spinning, too. I lifted her then ... she seemed lighter than air ... and spun her feet-off-the-ground around the room.

We stopped finally, breathless, Anna collapsing into me. Nancie said, "Don't worry, you guys, I'll clean up. You just go off and have some fun." I looked at my sister, a look both heart-warm and unsettled. "I mean it. Larry, you haven't had a drop of fun since you've been here. I'll take care of every-thing. I can, you know."

"She can, you know," Anna said. She danced around me, as if she actually were drunk. It was the most amazing thing. Then she said, with a logic that though it astonished me, seemed absolutely right; yet later what happened next opened up all the questions that transformed my life. This—this was the moment on which my whole life turned. "Come on, Larry, I want to see it." My eyes answered: *See what?* "Your room, the room you grew up in." Anna grasped at my hand, clenched it tight. "Come on, show it to me right now."

"I'll be in the kitchen, you guys. Don't worry a *thing* about me."

In all the years I'd lived here, in all the nights I'd slept alone in my narrow bed, conscious of girls, desiring girls, dreaming of girls, getting sweaty and letting my hands steal low to where my hands should not have gone, I'd never—never—actually brought a girl home to my room. My moth-er or sister had always been there, there were plenty of other places to go, and it just seemed not right to me. But when I pushed open the door to my small room down our long hall-way, there Anna was, right behind me.

"Oh, wow, look at that," Anna said, from around my shoulder. She was looking at my model car collection, three rows of meticulously painted and customized hot rods I'd worked up when I was eight, nine, ten, lined up on glass shelves. "Oh, you like baseball, too." She'd seen my

Yankees pennants from those winning days in the early '50s, splendid championship felts I'd picked up outside the stadium. "And look at all those records—Jeez!" I had a whole wall filled with stacks of 45s and 78s; after baseball cards, they were my first after-school purchases. Anna turned to me. "What a wonderful bedroom. Incredible! I feel like, like I'm a girl again. Like nothing—nothing bad has *ever* happened to me."

She fell into me then, her body full against me, just pressing me and letting me hold her, as we'd been the night before under the bridge. Then she pulled back to look around again. "It's like an amazing time warp. Nothing's changed, has it?"

"Nothing," I said. I was a little self-conscious, though. It seemed odd to me that a grown-up man would be living here with all his boyhood trophies. "When Princess and I started writing stuff, I was still a kid and too busy to change things, and then I got my place in L.A.—"

"Oh, you don't have to explain anything. This—this is priceless. You don't know how ... how really good I feel right now." She lifted up on her toes. "This is one of the things I love about you, Dink, that you're so ... oh, unchanged."

I heard the word again, *love*, now for the second time; but I also heard the word *unchanged*.

"No, don't look like that, that's not what I mean—at least I don't mean anything bad by it. It's ... you have this deep, gentle, honest quality. It's sort of like a boy's—innocent, trustworthy, just so all-American. It's just like this room—this wonderful room. I—it just makes me feel, well, just really solid. Really good and...."

Her mouth was only a couple inches from mine, and I could feel the warm breath that trailed her words. Her citrusy, flowery scent was all around me. I also felt the words begin to fall away, and that's when I kissed her—kissed her

full on her mouth, with both of us standing, our hands beginning to touch each other's sides, our knees a little weak, and
our heads growing light. I was sure of that lightness, for Anna
wobbled a second, as if she'd gotten dizzy, and I reached out
and held her up—tightly, strongly, *solidly*.

"Oh, Dink, I need you so," she hissed into my ear as she
held on to me. "Don't ever let me go."

Can I admit how I felt? How as I was rampant with
desire for this warm, sweet, eager woman in my arms, I also
couldn't forget she was Anna Dubower, who'd moved me
with her wondrous voice and wild-girl image as she had so
many young men around the world. But then I was so much
closer to her: She'd sung *my* songs, and with such passion and
conviction that it was as if she were inside my head. But
even with all that, even with the real Anna in my arms, the
true essence of Anna Dubower—the conjured vision of
her—couldn't help but eternally float as distant from me as a
song on a transistor radio playing houses away.

"I'm afraid, Dink," she said, and those words startled
me; brought me back to myself. Forget every word in the
previous paragraph.

"You're—" I shook my head. "There's nothing to—"

"It's not you, I've told you, it's just . . . that. . . ."

"It's all right," I whispered. I held her up, my hands firm
on her shoulders. I could feel thoughts furiously whipping
through her head. "Just be here with me. Just with me."

"I wish—I want—"

"It'll be fine," I continued, soothingly. There's a way,
when you're with a woman for the first time and a moment
comes and it's decided you'll sleep together; and I knew that
moment had come even before she'd said she needed me.
But I was also a little surprised that Anna could seem so vul-
nerable. This didn't seem like her, or at least how I expected her to be.

We'd been moving over to my bed, and now I sat down.

Anna waited a moment, her fingers fluttering against mine, then she sat next to me. She was trembling, like a cold, wet kitten would if held in your hand. I knew now that something terrible had hurt her, and that it was my role—my duty—to carry her past that.

"Do you want to just talk?" I said.

She stiffened, then shook her head.

"You're sure?"

"Dink, I want this too," she said in a firm, low voice. "I *want* this."

"O.K., just trust me. We'll go slow. I'll be easy—"

But she didn't want to go slow, and she wasn't easy. It was like a final restraint had burst and she threw herself at me. She pulled out my shirt, unbuckled my pants. She lifted her ass as I slid her own capris down her legs.

I was inside her when she tightened, then whispered, "It hurts."

I stopped moving. "Is that—"

"It's all right," she said quickly. She was blushing. "Don't stop."

"But are you—"

"No, it's all right, it's good. If I hurt, I hurt. It's just—" And she let out a sob.

That stopped me cold.

"No, no, please, Dink, keep going, love me, hurt me, hurt me, love me. . . ." She was breathing wildly in and out. She faced me straight up, her lovely eyes wide open. She kept looking and looking, and I wasn't sure what she was seeing, if she saw anything at all; and then I shut my own eyes, my urgency driving me deeper into her. When I was close, I tried to pull back and out—I had no protection on— but her arms were wrapped tight around me, pinning me to her naked chest; and when I sputtered home, I was still half inside her.

She was crying softly as I lowered myself off her. Her

body grabbed tight against mine, her lower hairs scratchy against my leg, and as she sobbed—deep, wrenching tears— she twisted and jolted against me, like a car whose carburetor troubles keep the engine hiccuping.

I held her, and as much as I'd wanted and needed to be inside her, it was this, the quiet closeness, that moved me. I know one can get sad, and I've been in bed with women after sex when I was torpedoed by the worst blue funk, but there was none of this here; this was light and buoyant and simply right. I felt that *so* strongly. I hoped Anna felt it, too.

She licked my ear lobe, then turned a warm smile on me. "This is what I wanted to get to, darling," she said.

Had she read my thoughts again? "What?" I said, teasingly, though of course I knew. I just wanted to hear her say it.

"This."

"This *what?*" I pressed. I was already deep into a new idea . . . no, more than an idea, a plan . . . no, God no, not a plan but an obsessive, all-consuming, lifetime desire. Though I hadn't articulated it to myself, I'd felt it for months. I was seeing the rest of my life as clear as day.

"I'm not going to say anything more," Anna said, and out came a laugh. "I'm not here to *flatter* you."

"Do you know what you *are* here for?"

She giggled. I was startled, but pleased at how quickly she'd brightened. "Do *you?*"

"I have an idea," I said, and I was brightening, too. All night it had felt as if we'd known what the other was thinking, was going to say. "Come on, let's get dressed."

"Why?"

"I want to take you up on the roof."

"Up on the . . . roof?" she gently chirped. "God, I love that song." She was referring to the Drifters' quintessential New York ballad *Up on the Roof*, that paean to sanctuary in the midst of the oppressive city—the only place, as Rudy

Lewis sings it, where you can escape the trials of the day, where wishes have half a chance of coming true.

"Come on," I told her. I was already up and pulling on my shirt and pants. "Let's do it." Anna was right with me. She slipped back on her bra and panties, then her capris and white blouse. "Wait here just a second," I said. "O.K.?"

She gave me a curious nod, but I was already halfway down the hall. I slipped into my mother's room. I'd avoided it since the first few days after I'd been back, but now I had a mission and went right in. The first thing that hit me was how much it still smelled of her; her perfume, always a little heavy with gardenia, hung in the air, off her silk blouses and from the uncapped bottle on her dresser. I felt a wave of dismay and pulled up. Was I rushing things too much? What was Anna going to say? But I knew I couldn't back away now, had to pursue this full-tilt. We needed it, Nancie and I—no, *I* needed it.

I went to my mother's dresser and fumbled through the top drawer till I found the well-creased envelope with the words "Grandmother's ring" written in my mother's indelible pencil on it. I slipped the whole crumpled envelope into my pocket.

The way you got to the roof was by climbing two flights up the inner staircase, then jimmying open the wedged-shut iron door. I had to throw my shoulder against it to get it to finally pop open, but, I thought, that's good—probably nobody will be there.

And, thank God, we were alone. It wasn't a great rooftop, only six stories tall, and cluttered with a noisy boiler fan and a small water tank, but the buildings around us weren't any higher, and so we could see all the way to the Triborough Bridge, and of course the whole sky was star-spattered above us.

The Drifters had it right: This was another world up here, cool, quiet above the chatter of the street and the babbling TV noise coming out of windows, just dark enough, and . . . magical. As soon as the door swung shut behind us I took Anna's hand and drew her to me, her eyes melting, her chin strong, her lips pulsing. She folded her head against my neck, then twisted over to kiss me.

"This is wonderful." She ran a finger over the top of my ear.

"It is, isn't it?"

"A million, billion, *gazillion* miles away."

I hugged her. "That's the point, right?"

She turned then and faced me straight on. "So what are we doing here?"

I let out a light smile. The envelope in my front pocket burned through the cloth of my chinos to my skin. "Enjoying the night?"

"I've been 'enjoying the night' since your sister's roast chicken."

"Well," I said, "there's more to come."

Her eyes danced, then her hand went down and cupped my balls. I stiffened through my pants.

"Up here?" I said, drawing in a stiff breath.

"*In a second!*" Anna laughed. "But you've got something on your mind." She kept her hand where it was, but the gesture wasn't at that moment particularly erotic, just a comfortable way of declaring what she touched was hers—all hers. I let her hold me.

"Um, I do."

"Out with it, fair prince!" She laughed, then took a step back, giving me plenty of room. Did she know what I was about to do? Could she read my mind that well?

But when I pulled out the envelope, then lowered myself to my knees, she sucked in a sharp breath. I could feel it, like a gust of wind. Her elbows pulled tight against her side. "Dink?" she whispered.

"I know it's wild," I said. "I *know* it's crazy." Was this the way to go about it? I knew I wasn't thinking straight. "Really, really crazy. But—"

She held out a hand, her palm . . . no, I couldn't read her gesture. Her palm was more up than held out protectively; she wasn't, I was sure, warding me off. Was her extended hand beckoning me on? It wouldn't have mattered, though later that was how I chose to take her motion.

"Anna, I don't know if you were just joking earlier, but I want you. . . . I . . . want you . . . want you to be part of my family, my sister and. . . ." I shook my head. This wasn't sounding quite right either. "I want to make your life perfect." The rough tar paper on the roof bit my knee. I gave my head a shake. "I want you to marry me." There it was. I looked down, unfolding the ancient envelope, and pulled out my grandmother's engagement ring. It was a pure yellow-gold band with a Tiffany diamond that glinted in the distant city light.

Anna was silent for a while, her eyes round and huge and silvery like the moon glowing above us. She looked excited to me, happy and excited. My heart flushed warm.

"I don't know what to say." Her eyes were locked on mine, and I could tell she truly meant her words.

"It's easy. Say yes."

"I—" She closed her eyes then, and drew in the night air as if it were a lovely bouquet. "Oh, you don't know how much I'd love to—"

"Well, then—"

"But Dink—" she reached out and took my hand; the hand without the ring in it. "I . . . I can't say yes tonight." She closed her eyes again, and I could see an unspoken thought burden her, twist her features. She faintly shook her head, then said, "I just—it's not real here, up on this roof. I wish it were. But it's not. You know that—"

"I'm not asking you to live with me here on the *roof*. I'm asking you—seriously asking you—to be my wife."

She thought for a moment, then said softly, "I know."

I waited.

"Here, let me have it."

Idiot me, I didn't know what she meant. "Have—" Oh, fool, the ring. She wants the ring. I held it out.

She took it and held it between her thumb and middle finger, turned it under the light. "It's lovely," she said. I waited. She didn't slip it on.

Then she sighed. "Dink, I meant it, everything I said, everything we did tonight—I *meant* it. You're my—you've always been—my . . . my safe place." She looked around; her eyes sparkled. "My *rooftop*." A light smile. "So I'll keep your ring for now, but I can't put it on yet. Not till I'm sure—and I can't be sure tonight. There's too much—"

"Like what?" All those unanswered questions about what had happened in L.A. flooded back.

Just the faintest shake of her head. "Let me do what I have to do. Please?"

"And that is?"

A sigh. There was a hint of irritation in her voice; I hoped it wasn't from me. "Please, trust me, Dink. I have strong— huge!—feelings for you, and I need you, too, probably more than you need me. But . . . you just have to let me do what I have to do."

Now I drew in a deep, noisy breath. "For how long?"

"Oh, I know this is hard, darling—I *know* it. You just have to trust me. Really, trust me." She took my grandmother's ring and put it away in her pocket. "For as long as I need to."

I was . . . what was I feeling? Hopefulness and excitement and the dark fingers of utter discouragement; faith and dismay; love and furious joy and an icy wind nipping at my toes as they hung out over the edge of a gangplank my desire had drawn me out onto . . . and the shadows of circling sharks below.

But I believed she was giving me the best she could. "All right," I said.

"You mean it?"

"I love you more than I could ever . . . ever tell you," I said. "I loved you before I even met you. That was . . . you and the girls at that talent show. I've—I've written song after song for you." I swallowed. "I guess I can wait a little longer."

"I won't keep you hanging," she said. "I mean it."

"I know you won't."

"Just till I'm certain. Till . . . till I—" I leaned forward. I felt she was going to say something more, about what was weighing on her. I was both desperate and yet terrified to hear it. But she caught herself. "Till things are—well, till I absolutely know for sure."

She let out a long, hard laugh then. "Hey, come on, get on up. You've been down on your knee long enough."

I took the hand she offered me and let her pull me in to her. Her hand went right back to where I wanted it. I traced the tops of her breasts with the tips of my fingers, kissed her earlobe. And then we made love again, right there up on the roof.

At dawn, as we were climbing out of my bed, she took out the ring and held it out, into the creamy yellow morning light. "It's beautiful," she said. "It was your grandmother's?" I nodded. "Which one?"

"My mother's mother."

She pressed my hand. "Then I'll cherish it all the more."

At the door I kissed her long and hard. I'd offered to drive her home, but she insisted on taking the subway back, just the way she came.

Over the next week I saw Anna as often as I could. She kept riding the F train out to my place, letting me take her on long heel-scuffing walks through the late summer air, then settling in for dinner and the night. It was tight in my narrow single bed, but we fit so well; and I have to admit, all day long I simply seemed to be waiting for that moment when Anna, chastely arrayed in a floor-length pink nightgown, slipped under the covers with me and let me hold her—and held me back. The mattress was too narrow for us to do much else but clutch each other tightly; and for that alone I've always held that bed sacred in my memory.

I hadn't really lost that heavy, gray, underwater feeling from Mom's murder. I was still spending a lot of time at the police station but to no avail; they simply had no real leads yet, though they wouldn't admit that. Sometimes I saw life as I used to see it, quicksilver, all-possible, a bounty of color; but then the horror of my loss would come down hard and I'd catch my breath, as if I were being strangled.

Then I'd come home to find Anna already there, sitting in the kitchen with Nancie, gabbing away. She'd have a glass of Coke in her hand, ice cubes clinking against the sides; and when I came in, she'd give me that great Anna Dubower smile—demure yet passionate. She'd ask about Mother and get so sad when I said there was nothing new. I'd give her a Well, what can you do? smile. She'd catch it, wink, give me the same fatalistic grin back, then to Nancie's increasing amusement, we'd excuse ourselves and disappear into my bedroom.

This lasted a week. My grandmother's ring wasn't mentioned, and Anna never wore it, but all the while she settled in at our apartment I had the feeling that she was working at getting used to me—to us, to being part of a family with me and my sister. And each day got better.

Yet I was nervous about her, too. Why wouldn't she simply agree to marry me? Was this just her careful way? And what about everything I didn't know about?

Then on Sunday night she didn't come over, didn't call, didn't say a word. Nancie and I picked at the roast she'd cooked, stumbled through small talk, sat mutely through *Ed Sullivan*. All the time I was asking myself where Anna was, what she was hiding, what didn't I know about what was going on.

She turned up as usual on Monday, as if nothing had happened. I probably should have let it be, but I couldn't.

"Where were you last night?" I said. We were at the kitchen table, Anna sipping her favorite Coke, me working a Rheingold beer.

Anna pulled back her head. "Nothing special—just doing stuff."

"Like what?"

"Dink, what're you asking?"

"I'm—" What was I asking? I took a deep breath. "I'm asking what's going on—"

"You know what's going on."

I leaned toward her. "And that is?"

She took a moment to answer, then her eyes brightened and she said, "We're almost living together." A light shrug. "We're . . . working things out."

I sighed, couldn't help myself. "But . . . I mean, there's so much I don't know. I still don't know why you left Los Angeles, why you're here, what you're doing with me—"

"Oh, that's easy." A small, sly smile bloomed. "I love you."

My heart almost stopped. I think that was the first time she'd said it like that, so direct, so certain.

"But the rest of it, darling, we agreed I just have to be able to keep some things to myself for now."

The look I gave her was half adoring, half glaring.

"I know, I know," she said, reaching out and taking my hand. "But I'm here with you now." A nod. "That's what counts, isn't it?"

It took me a long minute, but I finally nodded back.

The next morning, we got up early, as always, did our ablutions like any old couple, had our usual bowl of cornflakes with Nancie in the breakfast nook, and then I walked her, as always, to the subway.

That was it, the last time I saw her. The picture is forever in my mind's eye: Anna Dubower, in her sleek tangerine capris and elegant, grown-up silk blouse, her fluted nose and fiery eyes, her generous black hair on her shoulders, her lips pursed and eager. . . . Just that: Anna skipping down the sidewalk to the F train entrance, then pirouetting as if on a stage before blowing me one last kiss.

Chapter Nine

ON THE STAND I answered Donald Furtie as best I could. No, I said over again, I wasn't at the session. Yes, it was hard getting my sister situated. She finally ended up just where she was, at home, but it wasn't easy. There were developments with my mother's murder and I had to stay in New York City. By then the sessions for *Love Will Cut You Like a Knife* were over, and as I'd said, the next thing I heard was Punky's acetate of the final record. "Yes, it was very much like the song Princess and I wrote."

Furtie went over and picked up the phone bill envelope I'd first scribbled the lyrics on. "O.K., here we have your *first* lyrics." He conspicuously read out, *"Love can beat you, love can defeat you, love can take your life / Love can slice you / Love can dice you / Love can cut you . . . like a knife.* Tell me, how much is that like the *final* lyrics?"

"Well, they changed."

"Would you say they changed a lot?"

"You were reading my first ideas. There were some pretty dumb lines: *Love can slice you / Love can dice you.* I mean, it sounds like a jingle for a late-night TV ad. But we worked on it."

"You and Princess Diamond?"

"Yes, sir."

"Can we see evidence of *how* you worked on it?" Furtie took a couple steps toward me.

I leaned forward to meet him. "You can look at the song itself."

"You're referring to the completed song?"

"Yes."

Now Furtie took a few steps back. "But if I were to ask you for evidence of the song between this . . . envelope—" He held it with two fingers and waved it as if it were a greasy, foul piece of trash "—and the song as we now all know it, what would—"

"Objection! Calling for a hypothetical."

"Sustained. Can you rephrase, Mr. Furtie?"

"O.K., Mr. Stephenson, I'll ask you directly." He leaned in again. "Where's the evidence—the *physical* evidence—for how your first scribbled lyrics changed to become the final song."

I didn't answer right away. I wasn't sure what the right answer was.

"*Sir?*"

"Um, there was the, um, the demo disc that Princess and I sent to Punky—our first acetate." I turned my head and glanced toward Judge MacIntire. "That was very close to the song itself."

"Yes, the demo." Furtie pursed his brow. He walked over to the evidence table and moved his hands above it. "Did I *miss* something? Was I out of the room at any—"

"Objection!" Sandy called again.

"Sustained," the judge said. "Mr. Furtie, no grandstanding. You only have to impress me, not a jury. Understood?"

"Yes, Your Honor." Furtie turned to me. "But it's true, isn't it, that this demo acetate you made has not been put into evidence."

"That's true."

"And that's because it doesn't exist?"

I shrugged. "I don't know."

"It may also be because, well, if it did exist, hmmnn, it might show that the song that Mr. Solomon began to work with still sounded like, how did you put it, a Ronco TV commercial?"

"*Objection!*"

"Sustained. Mr. Furtie, please rephrase your question."

"With pleasure, Your Honor." Furtie walked right up to me. "Tell me, Mr. Stephenson, how can you prove, short of your word against my client's, that what you gave to Mr. Solomon was anything like the final recording of *Love Will Cut You Like a Knife*?"

I didn't move. How could I answer this? Was there an answer? Not one that I had.

"Your Honor, the witness isn't responding."

"Mr. Stephenson, please—"

I shook my head. "It just doesn't work that way."

"What way is that?" Furtie lifted his chin and nose into the air.

"We just, well, we just work on the song, change things, we don't need to write them down—"

"Convenient, Mr. Stephenson," Furtie interrupted. "But the truth is that there is no actual evidence that you can provide this court to demonstrate any interim states between your scrawled idea on the back of this envelope—" another shake of the dank thing "—and the final record. Isn't that true?"

It felt like the whole court was holding its breath. My own breathing was a racket between my ears. I didn't see any way out. Finally, I said, "That's true, as far as I know, but—"

"Thank you. I'm finished with this witness for now."

The judge looked toward the defense table, where Manny Gold's double-chinned lawyer, Chuck Potawski, sat with a big smile on his face. He gave a genial wave and said, "I'll waive my cross for now, Your Honor."

"Then we'll take a recess for lunch. Everyone back here at 1:45."

✳ ✳ ✳ ✳ ✳

WE WENT TO Sandy's Vietnamese noodle joint behind the courthouse and had some amazing food, but that did little to lift his or my spirits.

Over his fried spring roll Sandy sighed. "Well, the worst is that it's going to be your word versus theirs. Punky and

Gold will no doubt tell different stories, but MacIntire's a smart cookie, and I don't think they can hoodwink her."

"I hope not."

"No, you're going to be the more credible." Sandy bit down on the spring roll. The scents rising off the food were fragrant, exotic. "It just makes more sense that you wrote the song—you guys were the writers, for God's sake." He was bucking up his enthusiasm. I wasn't so sure. There're lots of ways songs come about, and once you're in the studio, it's like a pressure cooker: You throw all the ingredients in and boil and steam the hell out of 'em, and out comes a record. A case could be made that the person cooking the raw ingredients was the real chef. It wasn't true in the case of *Knife*, but I knew that Furtie and Potawski were going to push that angle for all it was worth.

"I'll do my best."

"You did fine. Good as you could." Sandy's plastic chopsticks clicked against each other nervously. "Too bad we don't have that damn demo acetate. You sure it's lost?"

I gave a big shrug. "I never had anything to do with it."

"But we haven't looked hard for it, have we?"

"It went to Punky Solomon. Like I said, I saw it there in the studio, at least those couple weeks I was there. But after that—" I made a *whfft* sound through my lips.

"Solomon could have it!"

"But didn't you ask him about the acetate in discovery?"

"He could've lied." Sandy sipped from his tea. "Or *did* lie."

I shrugged. "It's possible. But this was over thirty years ago. It was just a plastic disc. And once the song was being worked on, once all the musicians knew it, the demo wouldn't be very important."

"But you can't say for sure it's gone?"

"I don't have a clue." I took a bite of the crisp spring roll.

"But if we did have it, it would nail our case tight, right?"

I nodded, swallowed. "You play the acetate Princess and I made side by side with the released record, yeah, it'd sound virtually the same—without all the effects, that huge Punky Solomon sound, of course."

"Fuck the Punky Solomon sound." Sandy's eyes were flashing. "We got to get that disc."

"I don't know—"

"I'm going to do it," Sandy interrupted me. "We have to." He gave his head a couple of determined shakes. "Yeah, no way around it now."

"What?" I said, but I knew what he was thinking. Princess Diamond. I sighed. I guess I was hoping to avoid seeing her, but I understood his point. Calling my ol' pard Princess to the stand could go a long way to corroborate everything I'd testified to. And . . . she was there at the *Knife* sessions till the end. It was a long shot, but I read what Sandy was thinking: Maybe *she* had an idea where that demo acetate had gone.

＊ ＊ ＊ ＊ ＊

AFTER LUNCH Sandy left to confer with Judge MacIntire in chambers, with Furtie and Potawski, and the judge readily agreed that Princess should testify; she wrote out a subpoena for the next morning, then adjourned court for the day. I told Sandy that it'd be better if he let me try to get hold of Princess, rather than hearing from an officer of the court, and he communicated that to the judge.

I knew Princess was in New York City. Indeed, there'd been a picture of her on Page Six of the *Post* the day before: Her musical, *Angel's Trumpet*, was opening in a week, and New York was buzzing over the leap of a pop songwriter to Broadway. There'd also been a long piece on Princess in last Sunday's *Times*, on the way her show was challenging Broadway orthodoxy. The writer's take: Was it even possible for someone best known for rock songs thirty years ago to compose a successful Broadway musical? Leiber and Stoller hadn't yet been able to. Paul Simon's *Capeman* had been knocked on its ass by critics and deemed a failure. And though it was anyone's guess what dreams lurked in the hearts of our competitors such as Jeff Barry and Ellie Greenwich, Gerry Goffin and Carole King, and Barry Mann and Cynthia Weil, who with Jerry Leiber and Mike Stoller, had actually written the timeless song *On Broadway*, so far the only one bold enough to actually mount a Broadway musical was my Princess. In effect the piece said the knives were out for her.

Which meant, I was sure, that my cowriter would be even less happy to hear from me now than she had been before.

But there was no way around it. I called her office, they said of course she was hopelessly busy, I explained carefully who I was (the twentysomething assistant didn't immediately know my name; so much for our own timeless work), and then explained again that I was simply trying to give Princess a heads-up; that she *was* going to be subpoenaed by the court, which meant that she would have to show up whether she wanted to or not—or risk going to jail.

"*Jail?*" the assistant cried. "*Angel's Trumpet* is opening on Tuesday!"

I was quiet, patient on the phone, and the assistant hung up.

Five minutes later the phone rang. It was Princess herself.

"Dink, what the fuck is this!" she shouted into my ear. "Don't you know about *Angel's Trumpet*?"

"It sounds great, Princess."

"It *is* great, Dink. So why are you torturing me? I told you I didn't want any part of your goddamn lawsuit."

This was how I'd decided to play it: quiet, patient, forbearing. "You have to be a witness."

"I don't have to do fuck!"

I hung fire for a long moment, that swelling silence before the hook comes back in. Then I said, "Well, yes, you do. The judge is subpoenaing you."

"When?"

"Tomorrow. You're in town, and it's tomorrow."

She was silent for at least a minute, maybe longer. Then I could hear her fold. "How long is it going to take?"

"Probably just the morning. My lawyer needs you to tell the court about what happened when Punky was recording *Knife*. That it remained the same song you and I wrote."

"Well, it did."

"That's all you have to do, Princess, tell 'em that."

She sighed, a gust of breath like static over the phone. "That's it?"

"I'm sure you'll be back to your play by the afternoon."

"What about the press?"

I was quiet a moment, then said, "Hey, long as they spell your name right, eh?"

A pause, then: "All right, you bastard. But I'm not going to forgive you."

"Ever?" I'd heard a hint of amusement in her tone. Just a trace.

Another Princess pause. She knew how to work the beats, too. "We'll see."

"It'll be good to see you again," I said.

"Yeah, right. All the grayhairs hanging around the high school reunion."

I let that go by. "By the way, do you—is there any chance you know where that demo for *Knife* went to? That acetate you made for Punky."

Another pause, though this one didn't feel purposeful. Then Princess said, "I'll see you tomorrow morning, you shit. Let me put my assistant Bonnie back on, you can tell her where and when."

✳ ✳ ✳ ✳ ✳

WHEN ANNA DUBOWER walked waving down the steps at the Kew Gardens subway stop, I expected to see her the next day. Although we'd made no specific plans, I had no reason not to expect her to show up as usual. Instead I got a phone call that afternoon.

"Dink, sweetie, I have bad news."

My heart jumped.

"No, not *that* kind of bad news." She gave a blithe laugh. "I have to go back to Los Angeles."

"You have to—"

"Well, I sort of want to, too." I didn't say anything. "Let me explain." I waited. She let the silence hang; like the rest of us, she loved those dramatic pauses. "No, I just gotta go record again, and—darling, here's the *good* news—I feel like I can do it again because of you—"

"Me?"

"You, dear. And our wonderful week together."

I didn't say anything. I heard her swallow. "Well, Punky called—he insists I come back to finish up *your* song. I—well, I feel like I'm ready to go back there now."

"You never did tell me why you left L.A. in the first place."

A pause. "I didn't?"

"You know you didn't."

"Well, I feel so much better about it all now," she said. "Thanks to you."

Another long pause. I was a little pissed, and I didn't know what she was really saying, so I waited again.

"I'll call soon, dear." Another pause, this one more purposeful, I was certain. "And . . . Dink, I haven't forgotten. I'm sure I'll have something to tell you real soon."

In my mind's eye I saw her then. She was holding out her left hand with my grandmother's ring on her finger, sparkling in the late-summer Upper Manhattan sunlight.

"And Dink, I'm getting excited about it again. I want to make the record great."

I sighed, but silently. "I'm sure you will."

"I especially want to make you proud."

Was this overkill? Or was I just angry and frustrated that she was leaving me? I said again, "I'm sure you will." Then: "Have a good flight."

"I'll call," she said.

That was the second to last time I talked to her.

Her leaving right then made me a little crazy. I immediately wanted to follow her out to the Coast, but I couldn't: I had to stay and work things out with Nancie. Continue settling up my mother's affairs. Do what I could with the police. Try to shake my enduring funk. And . . . and I know this now, I was a little anxious about seeing Anna back in our other world. It was my boyhood bedroom where I'd been sleeping with her; it was our roof world where we'd made our troth; it was our breakfast nook where we slurped our cornflakes; all these safe places so close to me—and *only* these safe places—where the fact of Anna and I existed. Hell, yes, I was nervous—I didn't know what would happen when she showed up in L.A., in the lair of Punky Solomon and Manny Gold, away from any influence from me.

It was Manny I most worried about. He'd never relented in his quest for Anna. I'd never gotten a good answer about their ship voyage to the Bahamas, just that his proposal had been turned down. From what I heard, even that hadn't stopped him from pursuing her. I also still didn't have a clue why she'd left L.A. in the first place, and Anna wasn't telling me. Now that she was 3,000 miles away, that made me worried, too.

With Anna not there, the heavy grayness bombed down again. I did my best to get things settled in New York. Nancie wasn't that enthusiastic about leaving the apartment, but I didn't know what else to do, so I explored with Social

Services possible places for her to live; went out to look at a few group homes. This was grim business. And of course all day long every day I burned with the need for the man who murdered my mother to be caught.

Still, I couldn't let Anna go. Every night I lay in my old, now sadly sagging bed and tried to imagine what was going on in L.A.—but I didn't know. I wanted desperately to fly out there, just drop everything and go get my love, but those were thoughts that only made sense when I was awake at four in the morning; when I got up the next day, all my responsibilities in New York would slam my head back into the pillow.

I did talk to Princess, who said they were all working hard on *Knife*; that Punky was being a pain in the ass, as usual, but that she could see the lines of a final, fully produced record; and that the Annas were, as usual, keeping mostly to themselves. I did ask specifically about Anna, had she said anything about her time in New York, how did she seem, was she all right?

Princess was silent a moment.

"Princess?"

"She seemed really happy when she got back from New York."

"Really—"

"Yeah, happy, Dink." Was Princess smiling? Did Anna say anything about my proposal? Princess was always a keep-it-tight-to-the-vest girl, and she didn't elaborate on that. "And then—well, it's been mostly work."

"That sounds O.K."

"Yeah, I—I think she's fine, Dink." A pause. "I'm not too worried."

I sucked in a breath. "Not too *worried*? About what?"

"Dink, I don't really know everything about how she is." Another pause. "I think she's doing as well as she can." Then, brighter: "She's singing great. Best I've ever heard her."

"Princess?" I said, half imploring, but her end of the phone went quiet, and I knew that was all I was going to get out of her. I did take some relief in hearing that Anna was singing *Knife* so well; singing it, as she'd said, for me.

What made me most crazy was that Anna still hadn't called. The day after I talked to Princess, in mid-September, I decided I had to speak to her. I'd left messages before, at the studio, but this day I decided I'd just call her where she was living really early or really late and insist that she come on the phone. I stayed up till 2:30 one night, calling her at 11:30 her time, but got no answer. The next morning I woke up at nine and called her bungalow right away. It was 6:00 a.m., and she answered the phone sleepily, crankily.

"Who is it?" she said.

"It's me," I said softly. I can't tell you how much I wanted her voice to change: to soften, to reply sweetly, *Dink?*

"Manny," she said, "is that you?"

Oh, shit.

She went on, "I told you not to call me at home—ever. You fuckin' prick."

"Anna, it's me," I said firmly. "It's Dink."

Her voice *did* change. I'll always remember that. "Oh," she said. "Oh, Dink, you surprised me—"

"I thought—I was thinking—we have to talk."

"Yes, talk." I heard her yawn; more, I *saw* her yawn. Her wild raven hair tumbling to her shoulders. Her dreamy milky eyes. Her skin with that first-of-the-morning blush I'd come to know so well. "Of course."

"How come you didn't ever call me back. I left lots of messages—"

"It's—I've—" She faltered. "Oh, Dink, I have been thinking about you."

"And I've been thinking about you—"

"And about New York, what happened. I haven't forgotten—"

"I hope not."

"Oh, no! How could I? It was—it was the one good thing to happen to me in—"

"But you haven't wanted to talk to me?"

A long, whistling sigh. "Dink, I—I just." A pause. "There are things here I have to, um, work out."

"Like what?"

"Dink, listen, these are things that I have to go through. Just me. I'm really sorry—"

"What about Manny? You thought I was—"

"There's nothing with Manny."

Could I believe this? "Anna—"

"Dink, nothing." And I saw her then, finally woken up, her pink nightgown straightened, her hair pulled back off her forehead, her large almond eyes shaking off sleep at last. "I want you to know one thing, darling. I think of you every night—*every* night. It's—it's knowing you're there for me that keeps me going. Really. Sometimes I think it's all that's keeping me going—"

"Then we should at least talk—"

"I know. I know it. But—it's just so far away here—"

"I see—"

"Let's— We'll try. O.K. But, Dink, this is real. There *are* things here that I just have to get through. A lot of things I just have to—"

"Anna, tell me. You *have* to tell me. I'll do whatever I can. I—I still want you to marry me—"

"I know." I saw her sparkle. "I think about that all the time. I love the ring—"

"Are you wearing it?"

A pause, and I could see her look down at her finger. Was the engagement ring there? This time in my mind's eye I couldn't see her that well.

"I'm keeping it safe, darling." Then: "Listen, I have to go."

"Anna, listen to me, I'm here for you. Things—well, things aren't great here. The cops still don't even have any suspects, and Nancie, well, it's been hard to get things set up right with her. But I'm plugging along. I'll get out there to be with you as soon as I can—"

"I know you will."

"And you want me to come?"

"Darling, I want what's best. Just what's best. So . . . let's talk again. I'll call you soon." Another beat, then she whispered, "Oh, I do miss you, darling—I do."

To this day I hold those words to my heart. Then the line clicked, and she was gone—gone for good.

✳ ✳ ✳ ✳ ✳

PRINCESS DIAMOND BLEW into the courthouse wearing a pale-green linen pants suit, her hair in an expensive, highlighted wave, and a pair of $500 shoes I knew she didn't buy at a place like Alexanders, where we'd both shopped when we were first starting out. I recognized her, of course, but in a way I didn't. She'd never been frumpy before, but she'd been—well, with her brown cow eyes and thick jaw, she'd never turned heads. And certainly back then our work had come first, and glamour was for the onstage performers, the Meringues and the Annas. Princess favored bulky sweaters and tight-creased miracle-fiber pedal pushers. But before me now was Princess Diamond, Broadway composer—and all-around gal about town. And, you know, she didn't look bad at all.

I was in the hallway waiting for the trial to commence when I saw her striding down the hall directly toward me. Right there she was in my face.

"O.K., Larry, I hope you know what the fuck you're doing. This is not—*not*—" She stamped her foot for emphasis "—my idea of a good time."

"I'm having a ball," I said straight-faced.

That pulled her up. "You're—"

"Having a ball."

And like that it was the old Princess. I could see her wheels start turning, that *What's Dink throwing at me?* look in her face, the frantic but fun scramble for a comeback . . . hell, I could see her go deep into herself and think, *Having a ball . . . is there a song in that? Maybe that solves that problem I'm having in the third act. . . .*

I reached over and gave her a hug. She smelled of lilacs and hay. After a second she hugged me back.

"O.K., I give up," she said. "What's fun about being in court here?"

"Justice."

She was looking into my eyes to see if I was goofing. She saw, I'm sure, that I wasn't. "You really want to win this, don't you?"

"It's our song. And it's a fuckin' great song at that. I just want the correct credit." I held her gaze. "Question is, why don't you care that much?"

She shrugged. "I don't know. I suppose I'm distracted." She lifted her shoulders. "I guess the song'll bring in more money, we get rid of those two poseurs—"

"Should do that."

She put a hand on my shoulder. "Maybe part of me, also, you know, doesn't really want to go back to that time. At least not to . . . *Knife*." She winced slightly. "You know?"

I heard real feeling in her voice, and so I told her the truth: "It's all been coming back to me. *Everything*." I glanced down. "I thought it was worth it. I still do . . . but some of it's been hard."

"Do you—" She turned her brown eyes away, then slowly back at me. "Do you still miss her?"

"You mean, is there maybe a good reason I've never married?"

She took a step back. "Larry, I'm not that presumptuous."

I gave my head a shake. "I'm sorry. Yes, I do think of Anna—often. I've been thinking of her a whole lot *more* than often these last weeks."

She touched my shoulder, then nodded to the courtroom door, just opened by the bailiff. "If this will help any, I'll do the best I can."

I gave her a tight nod.

Sandy put her right up on the stand. She stated her name, her occupation—"Um, writer of musicals for Broadway"—then Sandy asked Princess to start from the beginning, and she pretty much told the court the story the way I had, up to the time I left the sessions for New York. "But you stayed on in Los Angeles, yes?"

"Yes."

"For how long?"

"The rest of the recording session." Princess brushed back a few strands of her bronze-tinted hair. "I was there even when the record was released."

"Let's get the chronology right."

"If I can remember—"

"I'll tell you what we've heard the timeline is—"

"Objection!"

"Sustained. Mr. Kovall. Just ask Miss Diamond what happened."

Sandy nodded, then said, "We're in August 1966, and Mr. Stephenson has just left to attend to his mother's murder and care for his crippled sister—"

"Your Honor!" Furtie cried. "Objection!"

"Sustained." Judge MacIntire brought down her gavel. "Mr. Kovall—"

"Your Honor, I just want to make sure we're all clear what was going on."

"Yes, but you know you can't lead the witness. And, besides, I'm fully cognizant of Mr. Stephenson's troubles."

"Yes, Your Honor." Back to Princess, waiting patiently. "Mr. Stephenson left in August, right?"

"It was a couple weeks into the session, and we started in—" Princess pursed her brow "—early August. So, yes."

"And how long did the session last?"

"October, I think."

"And that was because—" Sandy swept his hand out.

"Because Punky back then was a punctilious craftsman." Princess looked over toward Punky, the first time I'd caught her, and gave him a sharp, ironic, but somehow caring look. For his part, Punky raised a fine blond eyebrow and winked back. "He would spend a day, hell, two days just getting a kick drum sound. You've heard about life on a movie set, how boring it really is? Well, back then a Punky Solomon session was pretty darn slow."

"What did you do while he was setting up microphones?"

"When I was there? We used to have an ongoing poker game, with the musicians." Princess closed her eyes, gave out a light smile. "It was over in a corner, a table set up on top of a couple speaker cabinets. One of those old felt ones, with eight sides. Barney Fredericks brought it in. We'd have to lift it off the amps when they were actually playing."

"You and all the guys?"

"Karen would play, too. Karen DeWilder. She was our great bass player." Another secret smile. "She could out-bluff 'em all."

"The point was, you were there."

Princess nodded. "I was there."

"So even though Punky Solomon was clearly involved in every aspect of the recording, every detail, tell me, did he change the song much?"

Princess sat silent a moment, then shook her head again slowly and said clearly, "No, not much really."

"How much?" I could see Judge MacIntire lean forward.

"There were, I think—it was a long time ago." Princess pursed her brow. She was looking straight at Sandy, not a glance now toward the defense table. "I think Punky wanted some different words in the second verse." She brightened. "So I gave them to him."

"You wrote new words to the second verse?"

A glance at me. "Well, Dink wasn't there, and it was only two lines. I just made up some stuff on the spot, and Punky liked it."

"So Punky was—"

"Like an editor . . . or a director."

"And you were the writer."

"Oh, yes."

"How about musically? You know, did Punky rewrite any of the music while he was moving his microphones around—"

"Objection!"

"Sustained. Mr. Kovall, rephrase the question, please."

Sandy paced back and forth. "All right, Miss Diamond, did Punky Solomon write any of the music?"

"There was—it's coming back to me now." Princess put a finger to her forehead. "There was a problem in the bridge, we went into it fine, but it didn't resolve quite right for the third verse."

"So Mr. Solomon changed it?"

"Oh, no. He simply pointed it out. I sat down at the piano and played some chords. He liked one in particular, and I ran with that."

"And that's it?" Sandy was right in front of Princess, pushing.

"That's what?"

"All Mr. Solomon did—suggest there was a problem. . . ."

"Objection."

"Mr. Kovall, let the witness answer, please."

"He asked me to change the music, and he helped me find the right chord. That was all."

Sandy stepped back, then nodded.

"So, simply put, is it accurate to say that Mr. Stephenson and you were the sole writers of *Love Will Cut You Like a Knife*, and that even when Mr. Stephenson wasn't there, you personally made all the changes?"

Princess flashed her eyes. "That's safe to say."

"And that the record that was released in October 1966 was in *all* ways the song that you and Mr. Stephenson composed."

"Almost all ways, yes." Now she was looking straight toward Punky.

"Almost all—"

"Well, there was editing, shaping, but that is what a producer does—what he gets paid for. Dink and I wrote the song, lock, stock, and barrel."

Sandy nodded deeply. *Bravo!* She'd even used that same phrase Sandy and I had used before. Like minds thinking. . . .

"I have one more question, Miss Diamond, then we'll let you get back to the preparations for your musical, *Angel's Trumpet*. You testified that you sent a demo—an acetate—to Los Angeles."

"Yes."

"Do you, Miss Diamond, know what happened to that demo disc?"

Princess took her time answering. "Well, Dink asked me about that." She shrugged. "I didn't have anything to tell him."

"But you're under oath now. The court needs to know. Can you try a little harder?"

Princess took a moment, lifted her thick chin. "All right. I remember taking the tape to Dick Charles on Broadway, who made the acetate. Then . . . the tape got reused. But I sent the disc to Hollywood. . . ." Princess gave her head a quiet shake, then a second later smiled. "I remember seeing it in the studio with Punky. Then we—"

I leaned forward. I could see a new thought come to her. My hopes rose.

"Yeah," Princess said, then nodded to herself. "We gave it to Anna Dubower." Another nod, and we all could see her remembering this at just this moment. "Right, that was it. We gave it to Anna when she went back to New York after she'd gotten pregnant. She could keep working on the song that way." Princess shook her head. "But now I'm sure we never saw the disc again, even when she came back."

It took a while to hit me. I'd heard the word *pregnant*, but it was a classic double-take—I sped right past it, then turned around, and it walloped me in the jaw. My head was actually thrown back. My hands gripped the oak table. *Anna went to New York because she was pregnant?*

Sandy had heard it too. I'd never said anything to him because I'd never known it. Even in my shock I could see him thinking: Anna Dubower was *pregnant* during the *Knife* sessions? I didn't know that. Could that be germane? I can't see it, but it's something new, and I don't want anything new. . . .

"Thank you, Miss Diamond," Sandy said quickly. A turn toward Furtie and Potawski. "Your witness."

"After a break," Judge MacIntire said, lowering her gavel. "We'll see you back on the stand, Miss Diamond, in twenty minutes." A glance to the defense table. "And I still hope we can get you back to your musical before lunch."

✳ ✳ ✳ ✳ ✳

"PRINCESS," I CALLED to her in the hallway outside the courtroom. She was walking away from me. "Just a—"

She turned. "Dink, let me go to the restroom. I'll be back in a second."

Sandy was at my side. "What was that?"

I shook my head. "I don't have a clue."

"It's news to you?"

"News to the world, I'd say. Have you ever heard anything about Anna Dubower being . . . pregnant?"

He shook his head.

"I wonder if Princess knows what she's done?" Sandy said.

"I'm going to ask her."

"Where is she?"

"Bathroom."

"Get to the bottom of it, Dink. I—I can't see how it'll affect anything. It's just the song we're concerned with. But . . . but I hate surprises, and that was a whopper."

"Yeah, you could say—" I muttered. I'd purposefully made it over to a window bank, leaning against it. I looked out into the sparkling New York morning. Then I glanced at my watch. Judge MacIntire had said twenty minutes, and eight had already gone by, with no sign of Princess.

I was clacking my fingernails against the radiator grill. Anna pregnant? *Before* she went to New York? Meaning, before I was with her? She'd said nothing about that, not even hinted—had she? I racked my brain. And who could have been the father. . . ?

There was Princess, walking swiftly in her expensive shoes. "We have to talk," I said.

"Larry, they expect me back in the courtroom. The judge—"

I stepped in front of her. "No. Right now. What you said—"

"Dink, it's the truth, I don't know where that stupid acetate is. I gave it to Anna, just like I testified—"

"Who was . . . pregnant?"

Princess froze in front of me. "You didn't know?"

"No."

"You didn't?" Princess's arced eyes widened. "Even when she was back here with you—"

"She never breathed a word about it."

"But when she came back to SilverTone, she said you'd asked her to marry you. I'm remembering that right, aren't I?"

It took me awhile to nod faintly, yes. I thought of that conversation I'd had with Princess those thirty years ago, when she'd been cryptic about Anna's happiness.

"And I was sure that was because she'd got you, to, well—"

"Go on," I said.

Princess half-shrugged, half-winced. "Make an honest woman of her."

My forehead was hot, my breathing strained. I noticed I was clenching and unclenching my fist. "It wasn't about that at all."

"I guess not." Princess reached over and touched my arm tenderly. "Oh, Dink, I'm so sorry."

Sandy came out into the hallway and waved at us. "Hey, come on, you guys. It's starting up. Princess, you're on again."

"Later," she said, looking seearcingly into my eyes. What did she see? I couldn't say. Then she gave my arm a squeeze and went back into the courtroom.

✳ ✳ ✳ ✳ ✳

I FOUND IT HARD to pay close attention to Princess's cross examination; I was still totally hung up on Anna's being pregnant. I tried to puzzle it through. She had to be at least a month, probably two, when she left L.A. for New York City. She showed up in late August, which meant she must've been impregnated in, say, early July. I was still in L.A. then, though I had no idea who Anna could have been with. She died on January 6, 1967, which would have made her—I counted on my fingers—six or seven months pregnant at her death. Her death had been ruled an accident by the Los Angeles medical examiner, and pills and a high alcohol level in her blood were mentioned in the press. But I'd never known Anna to take pills—she wasn't a Marilyn Monroe in that way. The ruling had seemed suspicious to me, and to the dozens who wrote pieces examining the tragedy, but nobody had ever produced any hard evidence to the contrary, as far as I knew. But . . . I also knew that nobody had written that Anna Dubower was pregnant at the time of her death. Could the medical examiner have covered that up? But why would he? And what had happened to her child? And . . . why did she die?

My head was whirling with all these questions; questions I'd never let myself consider before. I'd been shaken by losing touch with Anna, by being flummoxed by my duties in New York when all I wanted was to go to L.A. for her; and then the news of her death just stopped me cold. It was too much like what I'd just gone through with my mother; not worse but overwhelming in a whole other way. I was becoming a connoisseur of grief and devastation. For a while there it was damn hard to hold myself together and keep going each day. I did make it to her funeral, one more lonely man in black at Forest Lawn on that gorgeous sunny L.A. day, but then I simply turned away from it all. But this news blew the gates open wide. I sat in the courtroom trying to keep as still and quiet as possible, but inside I was erupting.

I'd only been half hearing what was going on with Princess, but then her voice rose. Donald Furtie had been hammering at how everything the court had heard so far about the composition of *Knife* was coming from the plaintiffs, and Princess, emphatically, said, "But I'm not a plaintiff."

The rise in tone caught my ear. Furtie said, "That's true, isn't it?"

Princess disdainfully: "Yes."

Furtie took a few steps toward the stand. I could feel a change, his focusing on her, boring in. "But you *were* approached by Mr. Stephenson to take part in this suit, correct?"

A quick flicker of light in Princess's eyes: "Yes."

"And you declined."

"Yes."

"You were dragged here kicking and squirming."

"I was subpoenaed, if that's what you mean."

Furtie tilted his head back. "And wasn't that because in truth you know the case has no merit?

"Objection!" Sandy burst out.

"Sustained!"

Furtie gave a small smile. "All right, of course, you'll never admit that, even if you didn't see any good reason to join the suit—"

"Mr. Furtie." The judge's eyes were hooded.

"Yes, Your Honor, all right, I'm almost done." A flick of his bow tie, a wide toothy smile at the judge, then he turned back to Princess. "O.K., one last thing, the *alleged* recording of the demo tape. Don't you find it peculiar that nobody saved the acetate of what was going to be one of the greatest records in rock 'n' roll history?"

"I don't—"

Furtie pressed in, interrupting Princess. "And don't you find it a little strange that we keep hearing about this *essential* piece of evidence, evidence that, if it were produced, would change the course of this trial, from nothing but 'He said, she said' to actual, demonstrable evidence?"

"I couldn't—"

"And isn't it also true that—"

"Objection!" Sandy jumped up. "He's not allowing the witness to answer."

"Sustained. Mr. Furtie, why don't you give Miss Diamond the chance to respond."

"Yes, Your Honor." Furtie backpedaled a couple steps. "Isn't it true that if you could produce the tape—"

"It's an acetate," Princess interrupted. "A wax *disc*—"

"The . . . acetate. If you could produce it, or if Mr. Stephenson could, wouldn't that be the best thing you could do for your case?"

"Objection. Argumentative."

"Overruled," the judge said. "Witness may respond."

"Your Honor," Sandy cried, but the judge just held up her hand.

"Well, I suppose it would help," Princess admitted. "But there really isn't any reason to—"

"Thank you, Miss Diamond," Furtie interrupted. He turned around and faced the defense table. "Mr. Potawski, do you have any questions?"

I looked over at Sandy, made a gesture that said, *Do you think that hurt?* Sandy took a minute, then shrugged. He still looked confident, but I was feeling that Furtie was successfully pointing toward what looked like the biggest hole in our case, the lack of confirming evidence: the acetate itself. That was hammered home with the one salient thing Potawski said: "We've heard from Mr. Stephenson, who is one of the names on the record as writer, and now we've heard from you, Miss Diamond, one of the other names on the record as writer. You do under-stand that soon we'll be hearing from the *other two names on the record*—those who have an *equal* claim to be the writers."

Princess didn't answer; there was no real question there.

"No answer to that, eh? No problem. We'll be clearing this all up soon enough. Your Honor, I'm done."

✳ ✳ ✳ ✳ ✳

THE JUDGE EXCUSED Princess from the stand, and I went up to her. "We have to talk," I said.

She glanced at her watch. "I have a tech rehearsal in half an hour. Even if I get a cab right away, I don't think I'll make it."

"Princess, we *have to talk*." I spoke as firmly as I could. I was also standing right in front of her. I had to know everything she knew about Anna's pregnancy, about the last months of her life.

"It's about Anna, right?"

I didn't feel I needed to answer.

"O.K., I guess I owe you that. You want to ride uptown with me. You'll probably have to skip lunch, since they'll need you back here. But you're welcome."

Fortunately, we got a cab right away, and the traffic wasn't too bad, so Princess was able to relax in the back of the taxi. I sat perched on the edge of the seat, turned toward her.

"You really didn't know?" Princess said as the taxi ran east to the FDR.

"Princess, I don't think anybody knew. She never breathed a word to me, and I've never read anything since. Are you sure? How'd you find out?"

"Remember that tiny bathroom at SilverTone?" she said. I nodded. "Well, I walked in there once on Anna. She was on the toilet, crying. I asked her what was wrong, and she shook her head. She was . . . well, she was very emotional after she got back from New York, and she'd fall into tears pretty often—especially when Punky was pushing her on her vocals. But then she flushed red and turned away from me, facing the toilet, and. . . ." Princess quickly brought her hand to her mouth, gagged a little, then shook her head. "Right away I said, 'Are you pregnant?' You know me, I just blurted it out. She wouldn't admit it at first. Then finally she did—"

"Did she ever tell you—"

Princess interrupted my question with a swift shake of her head. "No, Dink. Never."

"You know what I was going to ask?"

"She never told me who the father was. As I said, for a while I thought it had to be you."

I let that go by. "She really told you all about me?"

"Finally, yeah. Hell, she was wearing your ring—"

"Wearing it openly?"

Princess nodded. "Yeah. At one of the sessions right after she got back Punky said, 'Hey, Doll—' Remember how he loved to talk Damon Runyon? He said, 'Hey, Doll, nice rock. What's up?'"

"What'd she say?"

"She just smiled and said it was her little secret."

" 'What,' Punky pressed, 'you meet some oil man there in the Apple?' 'No, silly,' Anna said. She looked pretty damn happy, though. And you know Punky, he wouldn't leave it alone. Finally, he got her to admit it was a ring from you—your mother's, right?"

"My grandmother's."

"Yeah, that's it. She had it right there on her finger." A light smile. "Her ring finger."

"Did she say anything more?"

"Punky went at her, of course." Princess rolled her eyes. "He was here, he was there—you know. Scratching, scratching. He got the whole story—"

"Which was?"

"That you'd proposed to her, and that she hadn't yet said yes or no."

"What did Punky say to that?"

Princess leaned away from me. "I'd rather not say."

"I bet!" My next thought: I'm glad I'm suing his ass.

"But she seemed happy, Anna did. Truly happy. Of course, I didn't know she was pregnant then—"

"Did anybody else know?" I interrupted.

She shook her head. "I don't think so—but I don't know. She never said another word that I heard."

"It wasn't me," I told her. "Couldn't have been."

Princess gave her head a quick shake. "Then I don't have any idea."

"*Princess?*" The question was of course burning up my thoughts.

A wider shake. "I really don't, Dink. She wouldn't say, and I think the whole thing with Anna and you made Punky a little nervous, so he let it go. We just had a record to make, that was it."

I leaned back. I believed her, that she didn't know who had gotten Anna pregnant, and yet the fact that she was already impregnated—I was thinking in these formal words; this was my Anna, I couldn't use even to myself a phrase like *knocked up*—that fact was making me crazy. After all these years. Of course, I wasn't the first to sleep with her, I mean, John Lennon and who knows who else beat me to that, but that she'd been carrying somebody else's child that night on the roof . . . I don't know, it just turned everything around.

"I really don't think anybody but Anna knew then," Princess said. "I . . . I never saw anyone else around, at least those last few months—"

"But before?"

She shook her head. "Our Anna was always *sooo* secretive. You remember—"

"What about Manny Gold?"

Another quick shake. "He wasn't there. Punky had banished him from the studio, and I never saw him—"

"Waiting for Anna, say, after a session?"

She shook her head. "I never saw him."

I let out a huge sigh. Princess gave me a small smile. The taxi had left the FDR and was pretty far west along 42nd Street.

"We're almost at the theater," she said.

I nodded. There was one more thing—just one more thing I had to ask. "Do you . . . do you have any idea what happened to her that . . . that night."

"You mean?"

I nodded again.

She was silent a moment, then she looked away from me, half out the window. "I hadn't seen her since the *Knife* sessions ended. We were both in L.A., but I just didn't run across her. I . . . no, nothing till I got the call."

"Who called you?"

"Punky. He'd gone and ID'd the body."

"*Punky?* I didn't know that. Not Trudy?"

"I don't know. Maybe she was there, too. But Punky, he told me himself that he was the last one to see her—that there at the morgue. . . ." She let her voice trail off. "Oh, excuse me," she said to the driver, "go up Eighth Avenue, then let me off at 45th Street."

"Do you think," I said, "that it was like they say. An accident?"

Princess took a while to answer. The cab made its turn, then pulled to the curb. Princess finally leaned over and took my hand, held it gently. "I never thought much about it." She was sort of looking at me, but not quite. "I mean, she was dead. *Knife* was a flop. It just looked like—well, even *I* got really depressed. It felt like everything was over. We weren't going to put the Annas back together, and that was—"

"I know," I said softly, remembering it all again. I don't know how well I kept the pain out of my voice. "I know—"

"You—"

"Yeah, I fell apart, too," I admitted. "I never. . . . I couldn't. . . . Oh, even when I was out there for the funeral, I didn't even try to go and get my grandmother's ring. I just—"

"I didn't see it, you know, at her service," Princess said. I'd totally blocked out that day from my thoughts, sitting in the back row of the church, trying to decide whether I could bear to walk up and look at the coffin—to see her one more time. I'm embarrassed to say I couldn't.

"You didn't?"

"It wasn't on her finger in the casket." Princess winced.

"I know. I—well—" I gave a sad snort.

The cab was idling at the curb, but Princess still held my hand. "Dink, she really was thrilled you'd proposed to her. I'm sure—sure she would have said yes sooner or later. It was probably her . . . condition. She seemed so distracted, emotionally distraught. I'm sure that—"

"Thanks," I said softly. A tear had formed in the corner of my eye. Princess saw it and reached up to brush it away.

"Dink, she *did* really care for you—she did. I saw it in her eyes."

I started speaking then, my voice in a monotone, sounding numb even to me. "She left the ring on the bathroom shelf at SilverTone," I told my former partner. "Punky just told me that. He said he found it and put it in the control room." I sighed. "It's gone now."

"It wouldn't make any difference anyway."

"I know. You're right."

Princess sighed. "God, that was so long ago. Seems like just yesterday—"

"Like things sort of froze."

A thin smile. "Sort of."

Now I pressed her hand back. There was nothing more to say. I rubbed my eyes, but no more tears were coming. "Hey," I said, trying to sound brighter, "good luck with your show. Can I—can you get me tickets?"

Princess gave a little laugh. "Well, I *hope* it's an immediate sell-out, but, sure, I'll have a ticket for you for opening night next week." She opened the taxi's door.

"Great," I said. "And Princess, thanks."

"Hope you win the case—"

"Hey, hope *we* win."

She smiled with her crinkly brown eyes. "Yep. Hope we win." Then she was out of the cab and lost to the bustle of midtown New York.

Part Three

Chapter Ten

SANDY SAID THAT we're in trouble. He shook me with that assessment at lunch today, Friday. This was two days after Princess left the stand and Sandy wrapped up our portion of the trial. The defense had put Punky on the stand, dressed seriously now in a light-as-a-cloud Italian linen suit, a pale-gray silk shirt (no Hawaiians today), his old-fashioned, now-graying hipster goatee, expensively trimmed; and Punky had turned the staid courtroom into charm school. He used his subtle blue eyes on Judge MacIntire (and there I thought she was sort of smitten with *me*), and told the story his way. He loved working with Princess and me, we were so damn talented, and yes, with some of our songs we did bring in all the parts of the song—and weren't there plenty of records we'd all made in which the writers' credit was just Stephenson/Diamond?—but that's not what happened with *Love Will Cut You Like a Knife*. It was true, he said, that I had the original idea, but he swore that that's all Princess and I brought to L.A. Furtie asked him pointedly about Princess's demo acetate, and Punky said he'd never heard anything like that. That when we'd come to Los Angeles, we'd all gathered at Punky's house and wrote the song on his piano, just like the old days. He also said Manny Gold had been staying with him then, and that while Manny hadn't been actively involved in the full construction of *Knife*, he had been in the room at a crucial time and came up with quite a bit of the bridge and some of the chorus.

"I remember it like it was yesterday," Punky said, smiling. "We were all in the studio I built inside my house, with this old, beat-up upright from 1619 Broadway I'd had shipped out from New York—it cost a fortune, but I'm in many ways a sentimentalist—and Princess and I took turns playing it. Dink and Manny threw out lyrics to us, and after a couple days' work we had the song." He lifted his shoulders. "Lock, stock—and barrel, too."

"And of course it was refined further in the studio," Furtie said.

"Oh, sure. As I always did."

"And the other writers weren't always there?"

"The song was pretty much done when we went into SilverTone to teach it to the musicians, but, yes, as we've heard, Dink was in New York, I don't know where Manny Gold was, and Princess was hanging out at the studio, but if I remember right, she was pretty bored. The song was done; she didn't have very much to do. She and Anna, the lead singer, Anna Dubower—" I wasn't sure why Punky stressed this right then "—and she spent a lot of time together while I was—" a shrug "—tinkering with the drum mikes." Another genial lift of his shoulders. "Girl talk time."

"So everything we've heard before—"

"Well, it was a long time ago," Punky said. "And there were a number of songs where Princess or Dink did give me an acetate. They're probably just remembering it wrong." A shrug. "I'm sure that's all it amounts to."

"Your witness," Furtie said, tipping his hat to Sandy.

As I sat there fuming, Sandy went at Punky's fabrication but couldn't shake him. It was a simple case of his version versus ours, just what we'd feared. And my lawyer couldn't break him down.

"Maybe you'll have better luck with Manny Gold," I said. We were having lunch again at that Vietnamese place on Baxter. I was dipping a spring roll into the golden, carrot-flecked sauce.

"I don't think they're going to put Manny on the stand."

"They won't?"

"He's not Punky, that suave, I mean. And I guess they figure that if the judge has to do nothing but choose between your version and Punky's, well, she'll decide she can't decide, and that'll be that."

I was alarmed now. "But it's a total lie. We never even worked at Punky's house."

"How can we prove that?"

"Bring Princess back?" That morning's *Daily News* had had a good feature on her forthcoming play that should've put her in a good mood.

"But she's not a disinterested party." Sandy held his chopsticks before him. "Think, Dink, who could back up your story?"

"The musicians? A lot of them are dead, but . . . I think Karen DeWilder could help—"

"Do you know where she is?"

"Still in Hollywood? *USA Today* did a piece on her and what's left of Punky's crew a few years back—"

"And what would she say?"

I leaned back. "I guess that Punky taught them the song we sent to him."

"Would Punky have shown her the acetate?"

"I don't know. Princess says she saw it in the studio and that Punky gave it to Anna—of course, if he was planning his robbery of our credit even then, he might have—"

"That's what I'd think," Sandy said, interrupting. "I'd think he'd have it all set up ahead of time, or at least not do anything too obvious. And . . . I would even doubt that Princess did see the demo at the studio. She might've mis-remembered that."

I shrugged. "I don't know."

"We could try the musicians, but if all they can say is that Punky taught them the song at SilverTone, that doesn't help at all." Sandy frowned. "What else?"

"Princess says that Anna had the demo. If only she

were—" I started to say. Sandy raised an eyebrow. "I know,"
I said. "You're going to say, *Don't get ridiculous.*"

Right then Sandy leaned forward. "O.K., Dink, there
was this plastic acetate disc with your song on it. No question
about that, right?" I nodded: No question. "And if Punky
gave it to Anna, and she took it with her to—"

"But she's . . . dead. Over thirty years ago. I don't see
how—"

"What about her sister?"

"Trudy?" Sandy gave a swift nod. "But she was in L.A.
when Anna took the acetate to New York."

"Have you asked her about it?"

"I haven't—haven't seen or spoken to Trudy Dubower
since Anna's funeral."

Sandy leaned back, a shrimp at the end of his chopsticks.
"Worth a shot, Dink, don't you think?"

✳ ✳ ✳ ✳ ✳

THAT NIGHT FOR the first time I truly rued my decision
to go ahead with the lawsuit. It was sinking me deeper into
the past than I'd ever expected to go.

There were also good reasons why I didn't want to see
Trudy Dubower again.

I don't know what Anna had told her sister about my
proposal, but she must have said something. The last time I
saw Trudy was at Anna's funeral, and I was astonished to
find that she seemed to blame *me* for her sister's death. She
was in black lace at the funeral, set up by Punky Solomon;
her hair was down, and she was without makeup—clearly no
longer an Anna in any way. Her eyes were red and ringed
from tears.

"Trudy, I—" I started to say.

She was standing by a pew in the Forest Lawn chapel;
Anna herself was in her open casket in the front of the room.
"You don't know what to say, right?"

There was a touch of hostility in her voice. "I don't, yes. I don't at all. This was such a complete—"

"*Shock?*"

"Trudy," I said, stepping toward her. "What is it?"

"Where were *you?*"

I shook my head. "What do you mean, where was I?"

"These last months."

"I was in New York—you know that. Dealing with my mother's death, my sister—"

"But not your fiancée."

I'd jerked back then. I was still under the notion that what had happened with Anna was our secret—the secret up on the roof. It startled me that anyone else would know. "Your sister wasn't my fiancée. At least not officially. She never accepted my proposal."

"But that doesn't change anything."

"Doesn't change what?"

"That you simply weren't *there* for her. She needed you. Needed you more than you'll ever know—"

There was more to her tone than just her words, I was thinking. I hadn't forgotten that Trudy and I had once been lovers. "But, Trude, she only called once. She didn't return *my* calls—"

"And look what happened!" She gestured toward the gold casket; hugely expensive, I understood. Punky's doing, too.

"Trudy, you don't think—"

She shook her head, then whispered something under her breath. I didn't hear her, just a low and angry tone.

"Trudy, what?"

She fixed me with her sad, furious eyes. This time I heard every word. "You failed her, Dink." She gave her head a half shake. "You disgust me." She turned and walked away then, and except when we stood at the grave site, that was the last contact I'd had with her.

Now I wouldn't even know where to begin to find her again.

It was at Anna's funeral, I believe, that I gave up the music business. It wasn't just the shock of losing her or losing my mom, or the fury I'd found in her sister; it was also something that had been building for a while. As I've said, the business was changing, our kind of music turning out of style, and I knew that even before the total failure of *Love Will Cut You Like a Knife*.

The record came out in late October 1966, and then . . . nothing. It wasn't getting more than token play—no KHJ Boss Pick to Click, no KFWB Good Guys Can't-Miss choice—no, you could drive around L.A. or New York that fall and go a whole day without hearing *Knife*, though you'd hear the Beatles' *Yellow Submarine*, the Monkees' *Last Train to Clarksville*, ? and the Mysterians' *96 Tears*, even the Spanish group Los Bravos' hit, *Black Is Black*, at least once every couple of hours. *Knife* did chart that first week: Number 76. No bullet. The next week it climbed to 63. It moved up to 59, then started falling; two weeks later it was off the Hot 100.

There were lots of explanations bandied about. For one, word was that Punky wasn't doing any of the stuff he did at the beginning of his career to help a hit along. He'd spent so much time in the studio that he was worn out by it, plus he'd thrown so much into the record that when it came time to promote the disc, he let his arrogance get the better of him. One New York program director told me that the attitude coming off of *Knife* was: *I'm a genius, this is my greatest work, of course everybody will fall down and worship before it.* The PD's response: "The little fucker never even showed up in town offering to take me to dinner. And I'm gonna play his fuckin' genius record? Record was a piece of muddled shit anyway. What happened to the clarity of *Perfect Dreams*, of *So Alive*?"

Which gets us to the disc itself. I've never actually been convinced that music could be "ahead of its time," but what can you say about a record that flops in the day then becomes such a huge megillah over thirty years later? Still, I've always thought Punky went too far with overdubs and burying Anna's voice—what you hear most of all in *Knife* is Punky's production, the technicolor scope and Wagnerian ambition of it . . . all in a four-and-a-half-minute pop record. (The 3:52 was printed on the label; in truth, the record clocked in another forty seconds longer, but no deejay wanted to play a more than four-minute song.) I think Punky was trying to prove something, and I don't know if he did or not, but whatever he was trying to work out within himself infected the record.

Then there are those cynics who say Punky just didn't cough up enough payola to give the record a bullet.

Number 59 . . . then pow. And as with Wile E. Coyote, when you go off the cliff with a 45, it's a long, long way down.

Punky, as if his neck were chained to the record, flew off the cliff with it. Even in New York I heard about crazy behavior, fights in restaurants, weeks when nobody could find him, rantings that he'd never make another record for such an ungrateful world, full days spent in bed followed by nights driving aimlessly on the L.A. freeways—Punky's legendary meltdown. And then Anna died in January 1967.

After Anna's funeral Punky disappeared for over a year. Rumors placed him in Greece or South America. It was widely understood he wasn't in L.A., though it was certainly possible he could have hidden in his mansion for all that time. I didn't know, and I didn't really care.

After the devastation of Anna's funeral, and my words with her sister, I flew immediately back to New York. My sister had been accepted in a group home in Rockaway and had moved in on January 2, and it was only a week later that I had to drop everything and fly to L.A. Now I wanted to check up on her, then put our mother's apartment up for sale. But when I got to New York, Nancie said that she hated the place and wanted to go home. I told her I didn't know how we could manage that, and she said she didn't care, she just wanted to live in the only home she knew and loved. She was adamant, so I took her out of the group home and moved us both back in to the apartment we grew up in.

But now I knew I couldn't stay there. I didn't mind taking care of Nancie, but fortunately it turned out it was possible to bring in enough help to keep her going. We had carpenters in, building ramps and hanging railings; we made deals with the local merchants; we filled out all the paperwork with Social Services. All this took time.

All the while I was itching for a new start. I needed—I *had*—to put everything behind me. My sister, bless her heart, understood; she could tell I was miserable in Queens and knew I couldn't go back to L.A.

"So where's it going to be, Larry?"

I shook my head.

"Don't you have *any* idea?" We were in my mother's sitting room, me in my usual chair, Nancie in her wheelchair.

"All I know is New York and L.A., and I don't want either of them."

"Too many memories, right?"

I nodded.

She leaned forward. "And you just want to forget everything?"

This was sort of an odd question, but I guess I did, and so I nodded again. She nodded, too, as if I'd answered a large question she had, though I didn't have a clue what it could be. I simply shrugged. "It could be anywhere. That's what's throwing me, I think."

"What do you want to do?" Her voice was a little softer, more compassionate.

"I don't know that either."

"Oh, Larry." Nancie rolled over to me. "I can't believe you've lost Mama and Anna so close together."

I had nothing to say to that. I was at a pretty low ebb then, needless to say.

"O.K., here's what I think. You take some of Mom's insurance money, buy one of those Volkswagen vans, like kids are doing, and you just take off—"

"Where?"

"Start with the Queensboro Bridge, then just keep going." She smiled. " '*So long, New York. Howdy, East Orange—*' "

I shook my head. "That sounds so—"

"Irresponsible?"

"Well, yeah." I'd been so focused on the songwriting, the business, for years now, since I was a teenager. I couldn't remember Princess or me ever actually taking a vacation.

"All the more reason. Listen, from what I read, it's a great time to get out into the country. There's all kinds of stuff out there. If I weren't stuck here in this damn wheelchair, I'd be out hitchhiking somewhere right now."

"Yeah, right."

She wheeled a few more feet toward me, took my arm. "Larry, I mean it. I understand that you have to put everything that happened behind you, I do. This is the moment. You just have to throw yourself out there. You'll find it—I know you will."

I didn't have that faith; didn't have anything. But my sister kept after me, and pretty soon I owned a robin's-egg blue VW van with silver trim, outfitted for camping. I called it Meteor. And there I was, tootling over the Queensboro Bridge, through Midtown, the Lincoln Tunnel, and out the other end into . . . America.

I could fill another book with that trip, the endless miles, the cheap motels, trying to find something other than country music on the radio. I became a connoisseur of cheeseburgers (best bet: Cincinatti). Other highlights: the R&B band I sat in with in Jackson, Miss.; the sloe-eyed waitress in

Tuscaloosa with the Airstream trailer out back; the gospel service I attended in Memphis; the bridge I slept under in Chicago; the Arapaho man I picked up in Wyoming who took me to a sweat lodge that actually began to bake the grief out of me; the hitchhiker who turned me on to hashish outside of Jackson Hole; my first glimpse of the diamond peaks of the Phoenix Mountains. By the time I got to Arizona my beard was Gabby Hayes full; I was road weary and pretty much feeling like anybody but the old Dink Stephenson. I moved into a motel outside town, fell into talking with a man in a straw hat in a coffee shop who told me that the area was booming and that they needed teachers like crazy, and then I woke up one morning thinking, That could work.

It did. I got hired by the Scottsdale system as an itinerant music teacher; I'd show up at a junior or senior high school, turn kids on to rhythm and harmony, then head back to the decent apartment I'd found off Camelback Road. I took up golf. Went out with a succession of women I met, usually in bars, often sweet-natured, some sour, till things sort of stuck with another teacher, Misty Warren. She's short—everyone notes the contrast to my height—red-haired, with a round face and eyes that bubble like a glass of ginger ale. We've been, well, together now over eighteen years; and if I never married her, it wasn't because she didn't want me to. I cared for her, and treated her as well as I could, but somehow it never seemed right to take that final step. But lately, well, things had been . . . what're the words people use? *Strained? Difficult? Troubled?* Or maybe just: *Tired.*

Or all of the above.

Misty wasn't keen on my lawsuit. If she'd resigned herself to my never popping the question, she certainly didn't want our comfortable, Wednesday-night-at-her-apartment, Saturday-night-at-mine life disrupted. Before I left for New York, we'd sort of broken up, not for the first time, and though I was surprised I didn't miss her that much, we both knew that by my going back to my past the way I was, I might not come out the other end the same person. If after all this I simply returned to Scottsdale, well, I had the feeling she might not be there for me. But more and more I couldn't see myself going back. That life in Scottsdale simply looked too comfortable, too safe—too *known*.

The truth was that I'd launched my lawsuit against Punky and Manny Gold in the same spirit I'd set off in Meteor those thirty years before: *Goodbye Queens, hello East Orange*. . . . And I had no idea where I was going to land when it was all over.

✳ ✳ ✳ ✳ ✳

IF IT EVER *was* over. I let out a long sigh. Sandy was right: If I was serious about my suit, it was time to find Trudy Dubower.

Sandy told me this is how it would work: If I could get something that would suggest the demo acetate existed, he could go to the judge and ask for a continuance based on the possibility of new evidence. Judge MacIntire would want some strong proof that a grant of time would bring forth this evidence, and that the evidence would be persuasive.

"She'll be asking, 'Why didn't you get this disc before the trial began,'" Sandy said. "'You knew it'd be important.'"

"And what's our answer?"

"That's one more thing you're going to have to come up with," he said. "You have all weekend. If we can't get something solid by Monday morning, I can't go to her. Got it?"

I did. It was 4:30 Friday afternoon, early April, the streets wet from a brief shower. I was feeling this itch to make something happen, and yet I hardly knew where to begin. I wasn't a detective; and even if I were, the case was over thirty years old. I remembered how good I'd been at tracking down the Penny Loafers all those years earlier. I wandered south through a mist to the subway next to City Hall. There were a lot of trains there, but by the time I bustled down the steps I knew where I was going.

The thing with Harlem is that compared with the rest of Manhattan, it seems low; four-, five-story buildings, if that. I took the 5 train up to 125th Street and walked out into what felt like another city. The clouds had parted and the sky swept away above me. I hadn't been up in this neighborhood since that night I picked up Anna and brought her to my mother's in Queens, and yet it looked exactly the same. There were kids playing double-dutch jump rope on the sidewalk; there was a bodega offering candles and *carne*. I could almost hear the Shirelles and the Annas coming out of transistor radios, but actually the music playing out of windows was hip-hop and merengue.

All I had was the Dubowers' old address, from when I'd tracked down her mother, and when I walked down 120th, I went right up to her building. The yellow limestone place didn't look at all different, though other buildings on the block had been knocked down, leaving vacant lots surrounded with wire fencing. At first I couldn't remember the apartment number—it was in the back, I remembered, but was it the third floor or the fourth?—and when I got up to the buzzer, I didn't find the name DUBOWER on the raised-letter tape list. I stepped back, looked at the metal door with the foot-square hole filled with wire-meshed glass. I was about to hit a random buzzer and try to talk my way in when a small, creased-skinned Hispanic guy came up behind me, so silent and quick I just turned and he was there.

"Looking for Mrs. Dubower, right?"

He was short, with big ears and a tiny gray mustache, and he seemed to hop on his thick black boots.

"Excuse me?" I'd heard him, but wasn't sure I had.

"Mrs. Dubower. She don't live here no more."

"She doesn't—" My head spun. "How did you—"

"You're newspaper, right?"

"Newspaper?"

"*Periodista?*"

I shook my head. I got it now. "No, I'm not a reporter." I looked tight into his brown eyes. "Why do you think that?"

"Lots of newspaper here." He glanced up at the building, toward I thought the fourth floor. "Lots."

"For the Dubowers?"

"Señora Dubower." The little man shook his head. "She *muerto*."

"She's dead?" I'd only met Anna's mother a few times, but I'd liked her, especially her energy, and the thick black hair and full red lips she'd passed on to Anna. "When?"

"Many years. Many many years."

"But you say—by the way, who are you?"

"Ramón." He stuck out a shrunken, wizened hand, and I shook it. "*Estoy el super.*"

I nodded. "And you say . . . newspaper reporters were here? Why?"

"They want to ask about Anna." Just the one name. As if alive to him.

"Did they say why?"

"She's . . . *embarazada.*" I shook my head. That was a word I didn't understand, though as he moved his hands out over his stomach as if caressing a ball, I got it. So Princess's slip—if it was a slip—had been caught. I hadn't seen any stories yet, but something must have gotten out.

"I'm not a reporter—not a *periodista*," I said quickly. "I'm an old friend of hers."

"What's your name?" Ramón was peering closely into my face, reading it.

"Dink." I shook his hand again. "Dink Stephenson."

His face went light. "I remember you. *Sí.* You make the songs."

"Yeah. I wrote her songs."

"Big trial." He pointed in a southerly direction.

I nodded. "That's me, yeah." So what I was up to had even gotten up this far. I looked Ramón right in the eyes and said, "It's important that I find somebody who knew Anna. Knew Señora Dubower—"

A thought, rabbit-quick, then another thought ran behind Ramón's eyes. *"Vamos,"* he said, and took me by the hand. His fingertips were rough, scraping over my palm like ink erasers.

We went down the street three buildings, then Ramón leaned on a doorbell, spoke quickly in Spanish, then stood back as the door buzzed open. We climbed three flights of almost buckling stairs, then Ramón rapped on a door. After a long minute it cracked open slightly, and I could see someone peeking out. More rapid Spanish, and this time I heard my name mentioned—twice.

Finally the door swept back, and there was a short, dark-haired woman with wide eyes and full lips. She took a long look at me, then threw herself forward, hugging me tightly to her. "Dink, it is you," she said with only a light accent. "Jesus, it's like all those glorious days are coming back to me."

I still wasn't sure who ... no, of course, it was Anna's aunt, Sweet's mother. I'd met her a couple of times back when we were first working with the girls. She, like Anna's mother, had married an Anglo, taking his name, and she, too, was so light-skinned you were never sure of her background.

"Mrs. McClain," I said, smiling.

"Call me Cheryl. Come in, come in." She kept a wide smile on me, but her eyes glanced around her apartment. "Can you believe I'm still here? After everything?"

"It's a nice place." It was, too. Clean, well-lit, nicely furnished if a little old-fashioned.

She seemed like she read my mind. "Well, the chair, the sofa, it's all from back in the day when the girls were singing.

Doris bought me a whole set with one of her first big checks. One of her *last* big checks, too." A sudden sharp glance. I didn't know what to say, so I just kept silent. "I've been reading about your trial downtown," Mrs. McClain went on. "I hope you stick it to those bastards."

Her sudden fury surprised me. "Punky and Manny Gold?"

"Those thieves!" More fire, but like that it was doused. "Come on, take a seat. Would you like something to drink?"

"Sure," I said. She pointed to a deep-seated burgundy arm chair, and I dropped into it. A minute later she was back with a glass filled with soda.

"Coca-Cola O.K.?"

"Fine." I took a sip. "I bet you're wondering why I'm here."

"I heard what that woman said about Anna—said it right there in the court so everybody could hear. It's not true, is it?"

I shrugged. Wouldn't Sweet's mother have known? But why would she? Anna told almost no one and, I guessed, certainly hadn't told her family. I was wondering, too, if she'd told them anything about me—about us. "I don't know," I said truthfully, though I didn't doubt Princess. "I just know what I heard, too."

"I think it's a lie!" she cried. "Anna was a *good* girl." Her voice rose. "I know, I know, she *pretended* to be a bad girl, everybody pretended she was a bad girl, but she wasn't. She was my niece. I *know* my own niece."

"I'm—"

"Is the Coca-Cola all right?" she interrupted me, like that, calm again.

"It's fine, Mrs. McClain."

"Cheryl!"

"Got it," I half mumbled. "So, I'm here because—" I started to measure my words, then gave my head a quick shake. "I'm surprised to hear about Anna's mother—I didn't know. I'm very sorry."

Mrs. McClain nodded. "Ten years ago." She touched her chest. "Her heart. She—she never moved either."

I shrugged in commiseration. "Well, the reason why I'm here, it's not at all about what they said about Anna, I'm really looking for an acetate, a demo ... a record—" Mrs. McClain cut me off with a nod; of course she knew what an acetate was "—that Anna probably had with her when she came back to New York—in August, before she died—"

"A record of that *Knife Cut* song—that last song the girls did."

I leaned forward. "That's it, yes."

A slow, tumbling nod. "I remember it, yes. Anna was playing it over and over when she was staying with her mother. Trying it out. Working on each syllable."

"Really?"

"Each syllable, yes. She was a perfectionist. Everybody talks about that Punky Solomon, like it was all him." She pursed her lips, made a face. "But that's all a lie, too."

"Mrs. McClain, what I'm trying to do is see if I can find that—"

"For your trial—"

"Yeah. It would be a—"

But she was already shaking her head. "That was ... it was over thirty years ago." A longer shake. "I don't have any idea where—"

"Did Anna take it with her when she went back to Los Angeles?"

A long moment while Mrs. McClain pursed her brow. "I—I don't know. She was—she was working on it, and then she wasn't anymore ... and then she was gone." One final shake. "I'm sorry, Dink, but I just don't know."

"And all Mrs. Dubower's things?—"

"I took what I thought was important." She shook her head. "But I never saw that disc. No, never."

"You didn't . . . see it. It wasn't left at her mother's house then, you're sure of that?"

She nodded. "I would have remembered. That was . . . that was an important record. It was Anna's last." A shake. "I don't think it was the girls' best, but it was their last. I would've kept the record if I'd seen it." She looked me in the eyes. "Sorry."

"No, no, this is great. I mean, not—well, it helps. She had the acetate here, she took it seriously, and yet it wasn't left at her house." I was thinking out loud. "Is Trudy—do you know where—"

Mrs. McClain gave her head a quick shake, meaning, I don't know where Trudy is. I went on. "How about Sweet, is Doris—" And then Mrs. McClain rolled her eyes, stopping me. I pulled my head back.

"You want to see my daughter?"

"Um, do you think—would she know something?"

Mrs. McClain was silent for a long moment. "This would help?"

"It might mean everything."

She swallowed deeply, her Adam's apple visibly bobbing on her throat, then said, "I don't see her so much."

"I'm sorry to—"

"No, she's too good for her old mother. She's got a fancy life now. She lives in Connecticut." She half spit out the final syllable of the state.

"It would be a huge—"

Mrs. McClain fixed me with a vivid stare. "She cared a lot about you, Anna did. I was there when she told her mother. She told her mother *everything*, and she said that you had been sooooo kind to her—" I'd looked down then, and she stopped speaking.

"I loved her," I said softly. The words just came out of

me. I looked up, straight into Mrs. McClain's eyes. "I think I always did. Always." I shook my head. "But I just couldn't save—"

Sweet's mother held up her hand, interrupting me. "There were bad people around her," she said. Her gaze was distant, and I couldn't tell what she was seeing. "*Bad* people." She stood up, with dispatch. "O.K., Larry, listen, I'll give you her address in Connecticut, you go see my Doris. Make her tell you what she knows. Maybe *she* can help you."

A thousand emotions were flying through me. All I could say was "Thanks."

✳ ✳ ✳ ✳ ✳

THE DRIVEWAY was long, and as I headed up it in the car I'd rented, I caught shimmering blue-green glimpses of Long Island Sound. The house when I pulled up to it had a wide porch, white porticoes, and an easy charm. It looked like somebody's—anybody's—dream house.

I'd called ahead, and after a minute of hesitation, Sweet had agreed to see me. She was waiting on the porch in a pure-white pants suit, a thin gold chain around her neck. She looked younger than I would have thought, with an untraced forehead and thick auburn hair—certainly younger than I felt—and seemed to have picked up Connecticut charms that erased all of East Harlem—not to mention bad-girl rock 'n' roll.

"Dink, this is amazing!" she said, holding out a hand. "I heard about your trial, but I never thought I'd see you."

"Thanks for letting me come up here." She was smiling, and I smiled back. "This is quite a spread."

"Thanks," she said. There was a beaming pride on her face. "We like it."

"You're married?"

She nodded, then said, "With three grown-up kids. Can you believe it. My husband's a doctor—a radiologist."

"That's good." I nodded back.

She gave me only a light smile that I took to mean, *See!*

Sweet led me around the back of the porch to an enclosed area, to get us out of the April wind but to still let us see the expanse of the house's grounds. Sweet showed me to a white wicker seat next to a white wicker table, and after I'd taken it, a Dominican maid came up and set down a pitcher of lemonade.

"I am *sooooo* ready for summer this time of year," Sweet said. "I'm outside all I can be."

"Thanks," I said to the maid, who went back into the house. "This is a sweet place," I added, for my host.

She raised an eyebrow. "You're making a pun, Mr. Songwriter Man?"

I shook my head slightly.

Sweet smiled. "Nobody's called me that—" she shook her head "—I can't remember."

"It seems at least as long to me."

"What've you been up to?" she asked.

"I live—well, I've been living in Scottsdale, Arizona—"

"Oh, we love it there. Jay likes to golf, and we try to go each winter. I never knew—"

"I keep a low profile." I shrugged. "I teach music in the public school system. Done that for over twenty years."

"And now?"

"Well, the trial. I'm taking a leave—" I raised an eyebrow, meaning, that's all there was to say.

"And how's it going—downtown?"

I leaned forward. "That's why I'm here, Sweet." She pulled her head back at my actually calling her by her nickname a second time; seemed to turn the word around. Then she nodded, as if for just this one afternoon it was all right to call her that. "I'm looking for something—"

She shook her head. "I'm sure *I* don't have it." It seemed odd she'd respond so quickly, before I even said what it was. "I don't have *anything* from back then."

"I guess you wouldn't." My gaze took in her house and garden again. "This is more of a maybe you know where it is. I'm looking for that demo that Princess and I did of *Love Will Cut You Like a Knife*. Do you—"

"I remember that, yeah." She pursed her brow. "Punky—God, hadn't much thought of Punky Solomon in years either—Punky had it in L.A. He played it for us. And . . . didn't Anna take it with her to New York?"

"That's what I've heard. Do you remember seeing it after she returned to L.A.?"

Sweet brought her hand to her chin, tilted her head a certain way . . . and I was seeing her again, just as she'd been when singing backup to her cousin in 1964. Sweet always had the straight-up cutest face in the group, if not the sexiest. Her face had been heart-shaped with dimples, and though it was longer and thinner now, I caught a glimpse of the ripe heart shape now—that young girl sashaying and harmonizing behind my true love.

"I don't, Dink. I don't think it ever came back with her. The demo was there for her to learn the song, and she had it nailed when she got back to L.A." Sweet's eyes closed for a second, and then she said softly, "You know, I still miss her."

"Me, too." That came out too fast, involuntarily.

"I bet." Her eyes brightened.

That emboldened me, and I said, "Did you hear about what Princess said at the trial. That . . . that Anna was pregnant?"

Sweet swallowed. "Yes. I heard that."

"Did you know that she was?" She shook her head. "Your mother said it's not true—"

Sweet shook her head more furiously. "My mother is still back in *1956*. Nothing's changed for her—nothing ever will."

"She seemed—"

"Oh, she's *soooooo* stubborn. Look, over there. See that white cabin? That's where she should be living, not down on

East 120th Street." Sweet made a whinnying sound. "Sometimes she makes me *sooooooo* mad!"

I gave her a minute to calm herself, then said, "About Anna—"

"Oh, yes, Dink. Sorry." She reached out—it was a stretch—but she touched me gently on my arm. "No, I didn't know she was pregnant back then, but I'm not surprised—"

"Not—"

"Surprised." A wag of her head. "Nope, not surprised."

"Do you have any idea—"

Sweet raised an eyebrow. "It wasn't you, was it?"

It made me feel very odd to hear her say that. I simply shook my head.

"What about Manny Gold?"

I tilted my head. "Are you . . . guessing?"

A nod. "With Anna—she was so private."

"But you knew about that cruise they went on. Where was it to, the Bahamas?"

"Bermuda."

"Oh, O.K." I leaned toward her a little. "What was that about?"

Sweet leaned back in her wicker chair; she fingered her necklace, then let out a long sigh. "I really don't know why Anna did it. She knew Manny was crazy about her, and she'd always put him off. I—" she gave her head a shake "—I'm certain she didn't have a sudden change of heart about him." Another shake. "No, that trip was always a puzzle."

"But they were on a ship, or in Bermuda, for a whole week together."

"But when Anna got back, she told me—she swore— that nothing had happened between them." She looked right at me. "Nothing."

"Manny proposed—"

"He wanted to, that was his plan. But my cousin didn't let him do it." Sweet lifted her head back, seemed to pull a thought out of the clear blue air. "I remember, she told me, 'Dorie, he actually started to get down on his knee, but I started laughing—' "

"Laughing?"

Sweet brightened. "She said, 'I made that crazy boy stand up and put his little box away—and it never came out again.' She winked when she said this, too."

"So she didn't—"

"My cousin didn't agree to marry him, that's for sure. Anything else happen on that boat for a week?" Sweet shrugged. "But she did swear to me she wouldn't let him touch her. Though, you know Anna—"

"Anything in L.A.?"

Sweet closed her eyes a second. "Well, you know, Punky banished Manny from the studio, but . . . I think I saw her go off with Manny at least a couple of times in his little sports car."

"Just a ride—"

"A late-night ride."

"To where?"

Sweet shrugged. "Just away from the studio."

"That's not much—" She nodded, and I asked, "Do you know anything about why Manny was banned from SilverTone? What was that about?"

She looked into the distance for a moment, then shook her head. "There were specific instructions to keep Manny out, I remember that, but I never knew the full reasons why."

"Was there ever any—"

"Gossip?"

I nodded.

"I heard they had some kind of business going, some stuff on the side—"

"Punky and Manny?" My eyebrows went up.

"Yes. That was the story. But I never knew what it was." Sweet rolled her eyes. "You remember me back then. I was such a ditz!" She let out a bright little chirp. "I was the original out-of-it girl. God, I can't believe anybody was ever so naive. My daughter Schuyler stopped being that naive when she was *five*."

"You know," I said, "I wasn't there for the end of the sessions—or for when the record came out, or when Anna—"

"Died?"

I nodded, then leaned forward. "Was it an accident? What do you think?"

"I never saw her abusing pills, or even drinking, but I know she was pretty stressed out there toward the end. Was there stuff I simply didn't see?" Sweet tightened her forehead. "There could've been. Did the pills and booze kill her, like the coroner wrote?" Sweet waggled her head. "It's like Marilyn Monroe, you know. Accident, suicide, something worse. . . ."

"Something worse?"

"No, I meant Marilyn Monroe. Not my cousin Anna. With Anna—Dink, I've always thought it was an accident, just as the coroner reported. It was the simplest—"

"But you're not sure?"

"I'm—" She went quiet, then gave me a faint smile. "I'm sorry, I'm no help at all, am I? And all this talk—really, all you want is the demo record, right?"

In truth, I didn't know what I wanted. Probably just that: the truth. If I could find it.

"I think what I really need," I said, "is Trudy. Your mother didn't know where she was. And I haven't talked to her since Anna's—"

She held up her hand. "She was furious at you, Dink."

I felt my shoulders sag. "I know."

"I always said there was nothing you could have done."

My eyes lightened: thanks. "But I don't know whether she'll see you."

"You know where she is?"

She nodded once, quickly. "I love Trudy. I loved Anna, too. They were my true sisters—the only ones I really had. My whole family. . . ." She looked out the porch window, to the seemingly boundless grounds around her house. "You know, Trudy's had some—" Sweet started to go on, but then stopped herself.

"Sweet?"

She shook her head, then said, "Nothing." But I'd heard her tone: The way she'd said "Trudy's had some . . ." it sounded as if the next words would be of trouble. "Dink," she went on, "let me talk to Trudy. I can do that. Can I call you—"

"I have to . . . well, my lawyer says that I need something definite by Monday morning. About the demo disc."

"I'll call you tonight. I promise," she said, animated again.

"I'm at the Edison Hotel. I won't budge."

"Good." Sweet stood up. "Well, it's been . . . amazing." She held out her hand. "Dink Stephenson. I never would have—"

I leaned in then and embraced her. She was thin, and I felt her shoulder blades through her white jacket; and the thing that got to me was that she felt like Anna—*just* like her. I took a step back, shaken.

"You know, Dink," Sweet said, "there's one thing I hadn't thought of. Did you know Anna kept a diary?"

"A di—" My head went suddenly light.

Sweet brightened. "God, what must be in that. John Lennon! Do you remember that night in London? And Mick Jagger—did you know Mick Jagger was after Anna, too? I don't think he ever got anywhere, though—"

"She kept a . . . *diary*?" I was still unable to process this. *A diary?* A daily record of . . . all Anna's secrets? . . . "How often?"

"You mean, like, what, how often did she write in it?" I nodded. "I think at least three, four times a week."

"*Jesus!*"

"There might be something in that about the demo recording, what she did with it." Sweet brightened. "Might also be more about you and Princess writing the full song yourselves, right? I can't believe I didn't think of it sooner—"

"Do you have any idea," I said, speaking very slowly and carefully, "where Anna's diary might be?"

She half-shook her head. "I never heard anything more about it, not word one." She pursed her brow. "Unless Trudy has it. She was the one who gathered up all of Anna's things."

"Trudy?"

"Yeah, want me to ask her?"

A sudden flash of caution. "Sweet, could you just see if she'll see me. Maybe it'd be better if you didn't mention the actual diary. All right?"

"Sure." She reached out and touched my shoulder. "And, Dink, you'll let me know what you find out, won't you?"

✳ ✳ ✳ ✳ ✳

ANNA'S DIARY. My heart actually sped up when I thought about it. What would it be like? I knew Anna liked to read, mostly popular novels, and she always seemed to care about the words that Princess and I wrote. So would her diary simply be: *Had a nice day. Sunny. Sang some. Ate fish for dinner. . . .*

Or would it divulge the deepest secrets of her heart?

And if that, how much of them could I bear to know?

I was unable to settle down after I left Sweet. I drove my rented car back to Manhattan, checked it in, then headed to my hotel. The bill on the place was growing, and though Sandy Kovall wasn't charging me anything (yet), this trial was working deeply into my life savings. I had to—*had to*—find that demo disc.

In my room I began pacing, couldn't stop. I kept glancing at the phone. I hadn't eaten since breakfast but my stomach felt too jumpy for food, and yet I was also getting lightheaded from not eating. Room service? I hated to pay it, and also that meant these four walls would just keep pressing in. I'd told Sweet I'd be in all evening for when she called. But my best guess was that Sweet would be home all night herself, and when she did call, the hotel could take a message and I could call her right back.

So I hit the street. The Edison Hotel is on 47th Street off of Broadway, and I easily dropped into the crowd out in the theater district this Saturday evening. I still couldn't think what I wanted for food, but it was a relief being outside on the street, and I just let myself go; I drifted. I headed west to Ninth Avenue, then north to 57th Street, then back down on Broadway. I don't think any of this was on purpose, but now I was walking past the heart of Tin Pan Alley, those buildings holding the warrens of offices where Carole and Gerry, Jeff and Ellie, and Princess and I wrote our songs. Then I was in front of the Brill Building itself, 1619 Broadway, its brass fixtures polished to gleaming, looking like the richest, most wonderful office building you could imagine. I stood outside it for a moment, and then I pushed in through the rotating doors.

There was a uniformed guard behind a podium. "Can I help you, sir?" he said. He was a round-faced African-American in his thirties, a policelike cap tilted on his head.

"It's all right," I said. I gave him a friendly nod.

He tilted back his head. "I'm sorry, sir. It's Saturday night. Nobody's here."

"No problem. I used to work in here some. I just want to go up and look around." I headed to the elevators, patterned in their sunburst brass.

He held out an arm, right in front of me. "I'm sorry, sir, but nobody but tenants with passes are allowed in."

"I'm harmless." I shrugged. "As I said, I used to work here—"

"When was that?"

"Um, a while back."

"Well, if you don't have any current relationship with one of our tenants—and more than that, if you don't have a pass—then I'm sorry, but I can't let you in."

"I used to work with Punky Solomon," I said.

"Who?"

"Punky Solomon. You know, *Perfect Dreams*? *He's so Bad (I Love Him!)*?"

"I don't know those songs, sir."

"They play them all the time on WCBS. You mean, you work here in the Brill Building and you don't know Punky Solomon's records?" My voice rose.

The guard was simply shaking his head; less a direct no, I realized, than simple indifference. "I'm sorry, sir. I'm enjoying talking to you and all, but I can't let you in." He touched a nightstick hanging behind his podium. "That's the rules."

I shrugged. Well, nothing I could do about that. I felt chastened, though, and a little lost. The past . . . it really is a landscape. It can challenge you with mountains and towering cliffs; it can also open right in front of you like a pale, endless desert.

There was an old record and sheet music store at the corner of 49th, under the Brill Building, called Colony Records. It was the joint that got the first pressings of our new songs; they'd play 'em out the front, then put Princess's and my sheet music in the window. At least nobody tried to stop me when I turned in to the shop.

They were pushing karaoke tapes in a big way, but once I got past the front counter, I was in a store with bins of old LPs next to the compact discs, tons of sheet music in the back, and—a new development to me—large glass-covered cases full of artist memorabilia for sale. I saw a case marked BEATLES, with lunch boxes, bobble-head dolls, headbands, combs, record cases, and trading cards, all with images of the four Mop Tops. Another case featured Elvis memorabilia. Then I saw a case that said GIRL GROUPS.

Mostly there were LPs and 45 picture sleeves, from the Shirelles, the Orlons, the Shangri-las, the Harlequins. There were also some tickets to package shows of the groups at places like the Brooklyn Fox. Girl groups were never marketed as big as Elvis or the Beatles; I don't know if any of them, even the Annas, ever had a lunch pail or a bobble-head doll.

Still, it was fascinating to see this stuff again. They had two Annas 45 sleeves: one for *Perfect Dreams*, the other for *He's so Bad (I Love Him!)*. (I wanted to drag the guard next door in to see them.) There the three girls were, in shimmery sequined dresses, their hair puffed high as heaven, their lips full, dark bows, their mascara gleaming even in the faded art on the yellowing sleeve. I looked at the price tags: *Perfect Dreams* was going for $250; *He's so Bad* for $175. Good God, could prices for this old stuff be that high?

Something in the back of the case caught my eye. It was just a black 45 disc with a white label with handwriting printed on it, hard to make out from here. I got down on my knees and peered through the protective glass. It was clearly an acetate, but I still couldn't make out what was on it. For a fiery second I thought I saw the words *cut* and *knife*, but then I made out the smudges and saw they read *Give Him a Great Big Kiss*—a Shangri-las release from Christmastime 1964.

Next to the disc was a white card that stated the price was $2,500. Beneath that in smaller letters it said:

ORIGINAL DEMO RECORDING, SHANGRI-LAS
GEORGE (SHADOW) MORTON
RED BIRD SINGLE, DEC. 1964

I kept looking at the disc, then I had a crackling idea. I went up to the front desk and said, "I'm interested in one of the records in a case over there." I pointed to where I'd been. "The Shangri-las demo disc."

"Yes, sir, that's $2,500," said the clerk, who was a guy half my age with a short, combed-forward haircut and big brown eyes. "A bargain, I think. That's an original acetate."

"I know." I leaned forward. "Listen, I'm wondering if you might have any other demo discs on girl groups. Like the Annas. . . ."

"I don't think so. Probably anything we have would be out there."

"Or know where to get one?"

"I'm sorry, I don't handle that stuff."

"Is the guy who does around?"

The clerk shook his head. "He's not in till Monday."

I bit my lip. "This is important. I . . . I really need to see if he can help me find an old demo acetate for *Love Will Cut You Like a Knife*. You remember it?"

"Of course. Punky Solomon. The Annas—their last record." To work in this place the guy was obviously a fan, and indeed, he started looking at me a little differently. His eyes brightened. Now how he knew what I looked like, back then or now, I wouldn't know; I was just the nondescript writer. But a moment later the guy held out his hand and shook mine. "It's an honor, sir. That was . . . that's a great song."

"Thanks," I said. I felt myself blush. This was probably the best surprise I'd had in months. There was a wide, warm light in the guy's eyes.

"This is a real honor, Mr. Stephenson. I'm Skip." He pumped my hand again. "Hey, I've been following your trial. How's it going?"

"That's why I'm looking for the acetate. I—"

"Then you need to talk to Jimmy Devine," he interrupted. "Jimmy handles all our oldies memorabilia. He's pretty plugged in."

"Jimmy . . . Devine? The Divine Jimmy Devine?"

"You knew him?"

"Just by rep," I said. Jesus, that was 1963. "He was program director at WMAC, right?"

"That's the man." The kid was smiling. In the day Devine was a big shot; now he was handling trinkets for a music store. And I . . . I was trying to teach high school kids harmony when all they really wanted was to drop beats and samples.

"Could I—"

Skip took a pause for a second, then said, "Tell you what, Mr. Stephenson, I'll call him for you, tell him you're here. He's a little cranky sometimes, but I think he'll talk to you."

I said that would be great, and Skip left the counter, then disappeared behind a nondescript door. He came out a minute later with a portable phone to his ear. "Um, Jimmy's out hosting a show tonight. I got his daughter. You can leave a message with her if you want."

"Great." I took the phone, talked to what sounded like a hyped-up teenage girl, and gave her the number of the hotel. She promised—double promised—to give her father the message as soon as he got home. I told her he could call me at any time.

I have to say, that made me feel a lot better. I picked up a couple hot dogs on the way back to the hotel, ate them as I walked, then went up to the front desk. No messages. I stood there, said softly, "None?" The clerk shook his head.

I lasted ten minutes in my room when I broke down and called up Sweet in Connecticut. The phone rang for a while, and I was about to hang up when finally she came on the line.

"Oh, Dink, Jesus! You'll never . . . I have Trudy *now* on call waiting."

"You—"

"I've been talking to her for the last thirty minutes. I was just about to call you—"

"Where is she?"

"Home."

"And home is—"

"Just a second, Dink. Hold on." I heard the phone click, then nothing. I waited, my heart loud in my chest. Finally, Sweet was back. "She'll meet you tomorrow morning in the city. You just tell her where."

Chapter Eleven

THAT NIGHT I DREAMED of Anna. She was the same age as when I proposed to her, but she was dressed like women today. The way the dream started, she was right there sitting on my lap. Her hair, gently waved, feathered my shoulders, my cheeks, my hands. She was close to me. Her breathing pillowed against my cheek. Her hands hung on my shoulders. Even in the dream I smelled her perfume, and it was overwhelming.

She was so close to me. She had on a low-scooped blouse, and a half inch of black lacy bra—like something from Victoria's Secret—kept showing over the rise of her pale olive-skinned breasts. She moved closer.

What I remember most was the swell and pulse of desire in me. It was a twenty-five-year-old's yearning, rising out of the deepest part of me like clouds of heat. Anna's cat's eyes sparkled. Her fingers played with my hair.

Oddly, there was a soundtrack to this dream, Bruce Springsteen's short, febrile song, *I'm on Fire*. I kept hearing his whispery voice: *Oh, oh, oh, I'm on fire. . . .*

For all of the dream Anna and I just sat there, she on my lap, closer and closer, and me more astonished, even disturbed. I couldn't remember a dream racking me with such emotion.

Then she leaned over and whispered in my ear; two words, over and over, "Find me. Find me, Dink, find me, find me, *find me. . . .*"

When I woke up I was trembling.

✳ ✳ ✳ ✳ ✳

TO MEET TRUDY I'd chosen the Edison coffee shop since it was 1) right downstairs, and 2) one of our main hangouts from the early '60s. There wasn't much around

Midtown that was unchanged from that time, but the Edison was: the same shuffling gray-haired lifer waiters, same gefilte fish and matzoh ball soup on hand-drawn menu boards, same bas-relief salmon-colored walls. I was sitting right next to a large impression of a vase; above me were carved figures of beautiful young women and men disporting in games. The whole thing reminded me of Keats's urn: *unravished brides of quietness . . . fair youths . . . forever piping songs forever new. . . .* I was there at 11 a.m. this Sunday, in a salmon-colored booth, sipping a cup of tea with lemon. I kept scanning the entrance, figuring I'd recognize Trudy as soon as she walked in. I was wrong. I was still looking toward the door when a woman in a gold scarf sat down across from me.

"Dink," she said, "you look exactly the same." A flicker of a smile as her gaze ran up my body. "Still tall as ever, I see." A wink. "Cute, too."

"Trudy?" Maybe it was the scarf, pulled tight to her head and leaving the small oval of face that remained looking a little pale and not quite natural; maybe I was expecting the high breaking waves of her early-'60s 'do, but I really didn't recognize her.

"I know, Dink," she said. She leaned over then and kissed my cheek. Her smell, of clean soap and a trace of perfume, was the same; and memories of her flooded back. I hadn't ever met a woman I'd slept with all those years ago in the present, and it was a strange sensation: immediacy and distance at once, nothing changed . . . and everything. "It's good to see you."

"You're not—"

"Mad at you?" Trudy shrugged. "I have a lot better things to be mad at than you, darling."

There was something I was seeing then, a thinness, paperiness to her skin; and a way it pulled tight over her cheekbones. The pale gray skin tone set off her lips and eyes, almost like chiaroscuro. The Trudy Dubower I remembered had ripe, fulsome skin underneath her fabulous hair. Trudy now . . . well, I could see that she was still a striking woman, but with the concealing scarf and translucent skin— she was very different, and it was taking me awhile to get used to that.

"How've you been?"

She fixed me with a tight look, then shrugged. "Been better." Quick: "How're *you*? Doris tells me that you've been living in Arizona all this time."

"True."

"Do you like it?"

"It's been all right." I gave a weak smile. I guess we had to go through these pleasantries. "I've been teaching high school—music. But I'm not sure I'm going back."

"Oh!" Trudy bowed her darkened lips. "A little life-changing adventure, eh?"

"I guess." I wasn't feeling that comfortable here, not as I had with Sweet, and I wasn't sure why. It's like something— *everything*—was not being said. "You've heard about my lawsuit, I suppose."

"Of course." Trudy beckoned over a waiter and ordered a bagel and tea. "That's why we're here, right?" She fixed me with a vivid look.

"I, well, I do have some things to ask you."

She kept looking at me, and it was an intense, searching glare. It made me feel creepy. I wasn't sure what she was looking for, or what she could be finding. There was a . . . well, Trudy had always been the most serious of the Annas, but I didn't remember her being as preternaturally focused as this.

Then she turned it all around. "You know, Dink, seeing you again—and you do look really good, you kept that yummy hair and all—" her eyes brightened "—it brings those days back to me a little. But I have to tell you, I really don't think of that time at all." She started to butter her bagel. "I know it sounds weird, but there are times I'm not sure Anna ever existed. It's just so—"

"Really?"

"Well, no. She's my—she was my sister, my whole life in a way. Maybe what I can't believe is that she's dead." Trudy's eyes were oddly beseeching. "Does that make any sense?"

"Not really," I said softly.

"I know." She gave a little shiver. "Like I said, I really don't think about it much. It's . . . it's just like it all happened to someone else." A shrug. "I guess."

I reached over and put a hand on her lower arm. "Trudy, what is it?"

"What is what?" Sharp—sharper than she needed to be.

"Please."

She didn't answer for a long time, just took nibbles of her bagel, and washed it down with tea. I waited. I understood that what it was she couldn't yet tell me was all that really mattered here and now at the table, and that I just had to wait her out. I was right. Finally her eyes shut and she said, soft as tears, "I'm going to die, Dink."

"You're—"

"Soon." Her eyes opened, thin slits. "Sooner than anybody would want."

"I—"

"You don't have to say anything. It hasn't been easy, needless to say." A small laugh. "I have lymphoma, Dink. I'm undergoing treatment. It's not working all that well." A powerful wince. "And that's it."

"I'm so sorry."

"Thanks." She let out a long breath then, more air it seemed than she could have been holding inside her. "So, O.K., that's out." She brightened under her gold scarf. "Now what can I do to help you."

"No, no, tell me," I said. "I want to hear more about you. What've you been doing all these years?"

Trudy didn't believe I really wanted to know this, so it took some cajoling, but finally she gave me a sketch of her life. After the Annas she'd tried to get on as a singer, but it was clear that if she wanted more than gigs at the occasional Holiday Inn, it wasn't going to happen. So she went to school, becoming a psychologist, setting up practice in Brooklyn, where she lived in Park Slope. She was divorced and had a couple of grown kids.

"You live alone now?"

"With three cats." She rolled her eyes. "Can you believe that?"

"It doesn't sound like that bad a life. Kids, a real career—"

"And now sick to death."

"Is it? Are you?" I fumbled for the right way to put this. "Are they sure?"

"They're not, actually. And I—I gotta stop being the drama queen. That was Anna's role, wasn't it? I was always down-to-earth Trudy. And I really don't believe it, that I'm going to die—well, not all the time, at least. Maybe this morning. Maybe not tonight." That wan smile.

"Trudy, I'm really—"

"It's all right, Dink." She touched my hand across the table. "O.K., now for what we're here for. What do you need from me?"

"It doesn't seem so—"

"Oh, don't be silly. Besides, I know what you want. Doris told me." Her face was Kabuki cryptic. I waited. Then she shook her head. "I don't have it."

"The acetate?" I wanted to make sure we meant the same thing. She nodded. "But you do remember it?"

"Anna took it with her back East." She shrugged. "That's the last I saw of it, too."

"You know how great it'd be if I could find it—"

She nodded. "I'm sorry, Dink." A pause, then a subtle wink. "Is that it?"

"How much else did Sweet tell you?"

"Well, she told me that . . . that it wasn't *you*." She kept her undisclosing expression, but her eyes lit up; it was like the old Trudy for a second there, the clever, witty one.

"It wasn't." I shook my head. "No way."

Trudy leaned back. "And here for all these years I was sure it was." She gave her head a small, sweet shake. "When I heard Anna was pregnant, and that you'd offered to marry her, well, it made sense to me—"

"That's why you were—you were so furious at me?" I said this half holding my breath.

Her gaze speared my own eyes then, and I understood that whatever answer she gave would only be part of the truth. "Part of it," she finally told me. She looked down. "A big part of it."

"I—I didn't have a clue," I said, fumbling. "I just thought that—hell, I don't know what I thought."

"It seemed logical," Trudy said. "And I guess I was ready to believe that—" there, in her eyes, that glimpse of boundless white desolation "—believe the worst."

I was startled. Had she been that jealous of me and her sister; and hurt by us, too? Was that what she meant?

"I'm sorry," I half-whispered.

That startled her. "For what?"

No, it wouldn't be good to push it further, to articulate it. It wouldn't be good, I knew, to say anything else about this at all. I changed the subject. "Sweet thinks it could be Manny."

Trudy abruptly shook her head. "Anna hated Manny Gold. She saw him for just what he was, a punk gangster."

"What about that cruise they took together, Anna and Manny. To the—"

"Bahamas."

"No, it was Bermuda, I heard."

Trudy shook her head: *What difference?* "That was just a . . . a lark."

"What do you mean? Didn't Manny propose to her?"

"Manny propose? Who'd you hear that from?"

"Princess."

Trudy shook her head. "I don't know. Anna went, but just for a change of scene. That's what she told me. I told her it was crazy to go anywhere with Manny Gold—like waving a red flag in front of a bull. And you know what she said to me then?" I shook my head. "She said, '*Exactly.*'"

"Meaning?"

Beneath Trudy's tight-drawn scarf, her forehead creased, she looked pained. "I truly don't know."

"But you're—you feel certain she didn't sleep with Manny on that trip? I was thinking the time could work out."

But Trudy seemed to be remembering things better. "I don't think so." She shook her head, but she sounded less than certain.

"Sweet also mentioned that Manny gave her a few rides home from SilverTone when you were recording *Knife*—"

"But Manny was banned from the studio. Punky simply banished him."

"Sweet says they met up outside."

"But I always drove Anna back to her house."

"Always?"

Trudy closed her eyes, then opened them slowly. The look in them was disturbed, abashed. "Something happened—I'm remembering it now. Yes, there *was* something with Manny Gold." She pinched her forehead. "Damn! What was it?"

"He never stopped pursuing her, from what I heard—"

"He was crazy about her—*crazy*!" Trudy winced. "Do you remember that? It was embarrassing. Anna was embarrassed by him—"

"Then what—"

She grimaced. "I just can't remember. O.K., wait, there was one night. Late." Her brow pursed tighter. "I was at my sister's bungalow, waiting for her—and she came in all flustered. I mean . . . God, I can see her face that night . . . *flustered*'s not the right word. Her hair was a mess, there were tears, her lip was cut—"

"Her lip was—"

"Yeah, there was blood. She wasn't good, Dink. I was all shaken. God, I really blanked this out, but it's coming back to me now. I got her into the bathroom and helped her off with her clothes, and she was bruised—I remember now, she had marks on her, blue-black marks, all over her thighs, inside—"

"Good God!"

"How could I have blanked this out?" Trudy looked distant.

"What did Anna say? Did she say what happened?"

"She said—yeah, she said she'd been out hiking and she tripped. She fell down. 'At night?' I said. This was about midnight, at least. She said, 'It was such a beautiful night, and I just went out into the hills. The moon—' 'Were you alone?' I asked."

"And?" I was shaking my head.

"It took her a minute to answer. She was pretty spaced out. Then she nodded. I didn't really believe her, but I didn't know who it could have been, and I—I didn't think she was lying to me. She was always really honest, Anna was. She might hide everything about her life, but if you asked her direct, she was truthful—if she answered you. Even when we were girls. She'd be in playing with my dolls, I'd find a mess, I'd confront her about it, and she'd say, 'Yep, it was me'—and she'd help me pick them up."

"So—"

"So I thought that maybe she *had* been hiking, like she said, just with somebody new she'd met and didn't want to tell me about."

"But now?" When she didn't answer right away, I said, "When was this?"

"Before the *Knife* sessions got started—"

"That was July—"

"Right. This must've been June."

"And I—I saw her again in New York in late August. And she told Princess she was pregnant in September—"

"Three months—"

"Plenty of time, right, to know—"

"Dink, do you think?"

"Remember Manny was banned from the studio? When was that?"

"I remember that. It was—right after the sessions started. Punky simply wouldn't let him in."

"And yet he got his name on the record as a cowriter."

Neither of us spoke for a moment. Then Trudy shook her head. "You were gone, and I was busy helping record Punky's 'masterpiece'" —she flicked two fingers on each hand through the air— "but it was clear something unusual was going on between Punky and Manny. I wasn't sure what, but—"

"Could Anna have told Punky—"

Trudy half nodded, half shook her head. "They were close, sure, but I always thought it was just in the studio. Still, if Manny had—well, done what we're thinking—and then he came to the studio and Anna got upset, well, yeah, Punky could've gotten it out of her."

That bastard! Anger flew up inside me like a sharp-clawed bird. I was even more furious at that smug little shit than during the trial. How could he—

"But we don't know Manny raped her," Trudy said, as if she were reading my mind. "There's not even a beginning of proof, of evidence—"

"Her diary—"

"Her—?" Trudy jerked her head back.

"Sweet told me that Anna kept a diary. Did you know that?"

"Of course." Trudy nodded. "Since she was about

twelve. All kinds of fascinating things. Like: *I fell down today on my roller skates. . . . I think Billy Santiago in home room likes me. . . . Someday I'm going to be a star. . . .*"

"But she kept it up, even when she was grown up, right?"

"Yeah." Trudy rolled her eyes. "She just stopped letting me read it."

"Do you—"

She shook her head. "I don't have it. And I don't know where it is."

"Sweet said you gathered up Anna's things. You don't remember—"

"Of course not!" Trudy shook her turbaned head. "That I wouldn't forget."

I pressed, though. "I saw your aunt, she said she had your mother's things. She didn't have the record, but do you think *she* could have the diary?"

Trudy thought a second, then emphatically shook her head. "You could ask her, but I can't imagine it. Anna leaving her most private thing with our mother?" Her lips fluttered. "I don't think so."

"It's like the acetate, and the diary—she died, and they just disappeared," I said.

"They weren't in L.A. when she died."

"And—"

A trace of uncertainty in Trudy's eyes. "And what?" she said pointedly.

"Her—Anna's death."

"What about it?"

"Sweet seemed—" I couldn't say the words that I was thinking so loudly: *Suspicious. Dubious. That it was explained.* "What do you think?"

"She died, Dink." Like that Trudy's mouth twisted. It was like she'd touched a hot stove and leaped back. *"My beautiful sister fuckin' died!"*

I recoiled from her outburst, even as I felt all the passion behind it myself. But I didn't know what else to say. We sat there for a few long minutes, then in a voice that didn't convince even me, I said, "Well, Trudy, you've been—"

"Don't patronize me, Dink, just 'cause I'm sick. Don't do that—"

"I wasn't," I started to say, but maybe I was: Going to thank her for talking to me in the state she was in.

"Listen," Trudy said, putting her hand on mine. "I want to help you. If it's true about Manny—well, anything I could do about that—"

"I have to find the demo disc," I said. "And the diary."

She shook her head. "I don't think you're—"

"But I'm going to try."

"I'm sure you are." A pause, then: "O.K., count on me," she said pointedly, "to do anything I can."

Her look at me then was wide-open, winsome, in an odd way younger than she'd seemed before. After our talk, there was more color in her cheeks. She absentmindedly touched the edge of the gold scarf atop her head.

"You, too," I said. "Anything I can do."

That skeptical light went back in her eyes.

"Damn you, Trudy," I said, emotion now bursting in me as if out of nowhere—though of course I knew just where it came from. "I mean it. And . . . I can't believe you've been so pissed at me for thirty years."

She was silent then, yet her gaze held mine. I saw it again, that girl who had made me jump all those years back. "Not just pissed," she said softly, mostly to herself. "Not only pissed at all."

✳ ✳ ✳ ✳ ✳

I PAID THE CHECK and walked Trudy a couple of blocks to the subway she'd take back to Brooklyn; and then I was on my own again. I went back to the hotel. Two messages. One from my sister, Nancie, the other from Jimmy Devine.

I called the memorabilia man as soon as I got up to my room.

"Yeah," he barked. Even after I introduced myself, he kept barking in a voice that mumbled rough, like a cement mixer, *Yeah? Yeahhhh? Yeahhhhhhhhhh?*

I remembered more about him. Devine was *the* Top 40 king for a while, running the playlist at WMAC, the power-house AM station in New York City; you wanted your song on the air, you made sure you saw Jimmy. I know that when Princess and I were first getting going, we always sent some-one to him. Later, about '64, he had some trouble, though I couldn't remember exactly what, just that he was abruptly out of a job. I'd heard he became a big-time boozer, and from his voice it sounded as if he still was. I was a little surprised, I guess, that he was even alive.

"You just called me back. I'm Dink Stephenson—"

"Yeah?"

"Dink Stephenson. I wrote with Princess Diamond. *Perfect Dreams? He's So Bad*—"

"*Yeahhhh?*"

I didn't know what to do, so I just plunged ahead. "I'm calling because I'm told you're an expert in early rock arti-facts. I'm looking for an original demo acetate of *Love Will Cut You Like a Knife*. You know, the last Annas' song."

"I know it, yeah," he went. "Great record." Ah, progress.

"You remember we wrote that, Princess and me?"

"So, yeah?"

"Well, have you ever—do you know—well, I'm looking for Princess's and my original acetate demo of—"

"Don't exist."

"It doesn't—"

"*Exist.*" The word hissed from the phone, as if he'd spit it out.

"Are you sure? I—"

"Listen, buddy, let me tell ya. I got my finger on everything out there. You want an unsealed first-state stereo Beatles butcher cover, there's only twenty-some out there, I know where nineteen of 'em are. You want the gun that shot Sam Cooke? You want the one-off red copy of Elvis's Christmas LP, I know where that is, too."

"This would've been—"

"I know, Anna Dubower had it—Punky Solomon gave it to her," he growled. "That was over thirty years ago, buddy. Nobody seen it since." A pause. "Hey, you got any Annas stuff yourself? You know, market in her's taken an amazing jump." Suddenly his voice had cleared. "You got any pictures? Any of her old things—"

I was shaking my head; then I said no.

"You sure?"

"Yes."

" 'Cause I know guys'd pay a pretty damn penny for anything. Specially around her death. I sold one guy a copy of her death certificate, man, that was a dynamite score."

"Her . . . death certificate?"

"It was a copy, but it was an official one. Had the L.A. Coroner's Office stamp on it. Man, that was sweet."

"What did it say on it?" I heard myself asking.

"What do you mean?"

"Cause of death—"

"Fuck if I know," Devine burst into the phone.

"You don't—"

"Listen, I didn't even look at it. You think I'm some fuckin' *ghoul*?" He cleared his throat, like rocks tumbling in metal. "And anyway it was all some medical mumbo jumbo. Hell, you know how she died, don't you? Weren't you there?"

I gave my head a faint shake, then said, "No. I was in New York."

"Yeah, well."

"O.K., could you—I really gotta find that acetate demo—"

"I told ya, boyo, it don't exist." Devine coughed his throat clear. "Got a lot of copies of the record, though. You want any of them?"

I shook my head, then said, "I don't think so." I had two pristine copies at my apartment in Scottsdale.

"You ever look close at it?"

"What?"

"That record's got a little secret, pal. You know that?"

"What do you mean?"

"In the deadwax, pal. Come to the shop sometime, I'll show it to you." The deadwax—he meant the record's runout groove. It was my record, and I didn't know of anything unusual there; probably just the common matrix numbers. "You oughta look there, pal. Yeah, yeah, *yeah*."

"Sure," I said. I was getting damn sick of this guy. I didn't believe him, either; I felt in my bones that our demo acetate had to exist. Anna *must* have given it to someone; she'd never have thrown something like that out. "Really," I went on, "about that demo, if you ever hear anything. . . ." I felt my heart sink. No, I couldn't talk to Jimmy Devine any longer. I just let that last word hang there and hung up.

Shit! It was Sunday afternoon and I'd just shot everything I had. Monday, Sandy would have to meet the judge and make a case for postponing the trial while we pursued the lost acetate. Did I have *anything* he could work with? I couldn't see it. And I couldn't see where to turn next.

I was lying down on my freshly made-up hotel bed, my shoeless toes wiggling aimlessly, my hands behind my head. What I thought I was doing was trying to think—think of something, anything—but there was nothing there to work with, and so I just lay there. Maybe, I told myself, Sandy would have done enough already to pull Judge MacIntire in our favor. Maybe, I went on, if we lose—and lose badly— maybe Punky will let me talk to him about those last few months of Anna's life. I knew nothing would ever come out of Manny Gold, especially if he'd . . . if he was behind what happened to Anna. But Punky, he was still sort of my friend, wasn't he? Hadn't he told me about SilverTone being torn down, alerting me to the last chance to find my ring. Maybe he would remember if somehow the acetate of *Knife* had ended up back at SilverTone; hell, maybe he still had it and was laughing at me right this minute. If he won big, would he tell me? Would I even want to know?

But I did need to know more about Anna's last days, and I despaired of that. Who else could I talk to? I lay there in my room and watched the ceiling and had no idea how much time passed.

When I finally got up, I saw the note from the desk with Devine's phone number and, above it, Nancie's. I sighed. I felt bad about how I hadn't seen her since I'd been back in New York. Maybe I should go visit now. Would that cheer me up? Probably not. Still . . . she was my sister, and she'd been after me for weeks to go see her in Queens.

Oh, Nancie. Over the years, although I kept helping Nancie with money, we'd fallen to calls mainly on holidays and birthdays. They'd been sweet and cordial, but we'd lost the gift of being able to so easily slip into deep news of our personal lives. As far as I knew she was doing fine in the apartment we grew up in. She also had a job she loved, with the city in protective services for children, and whenever I spoke with her, she always said things were just fine. Of course, I always told her things were fine with me, too, in Arizona. Just dandy. And that was that.

I dialed her number even before I actually decided to call her. "Hey, Sis," I said when she picked up after half a dozen rings.

"Let me guess," Nancie said. "Santa Claus? The Easter Bunny? The Ghost of Ed Sullivan—"

"Sorry," I told her. "I've just been—"

"Oh, Larry, come on, it doesn't matter. I'm just glad you called." A slight pause. "So when am I finally gonna see you?"

"Well, I was—if it's not too late, I could come out tonight."

She didn't miss a beat. "Tonight'd be great. Can you be here by seven?"

"If I don't get lost—"

"If you don't—"

"That's a joke. I'll be there at seven. Should I bring anything?"

"Nope. I'll have a good meal all set for you. Seven it is. And, Larry, it's the F train, you know."

I smiled. I hadn't been back to our old building in almost thirty years, and maybe that was a little of why I'd been avoiding my sister, too. I didn't have bad memories from there, much to the contrary, but I knew there would be powerful memories of my mother (they'd never caught the robber who shot her), and I'd been wallowing so deeply in the past simply with the trial and what I'd been learning about Anna.

What I didn't expect was how regular, comfortable, just normal it seemed to be on the train to Queens. Once we got through the tunnel and the old stops started coming up, I flashed easily back to those first bold forays into the big city across the river; Princess's and my first trips in with our sheet music and demo reel-to-reels clutched in our eager hands. I had a glimpse of myself at eighteen, with my whole life so hopeful and yearned for, and it startled me.

The memories piled on as I walked down the block of apartment buildings to our old place. It looked exactly the same, reddish-brown bricks, white windowsills, gray concrete entryway. There was a new buzzer system, and when I rang upstairs, a voice I didn't recognize asked who it was.

"It's Dink," I said tentatively.

"Dink?"

Oh, damn, did I have something wrong? "Um, this is Larry Stephenson. Is this the—"

"Oh, *Larry*!" the female voice called. "O.K., here's the door."

That was surprise number 1. My sister didn't answer the door; instead it was a tall, long-necked woman with long, straight gray hair and a high, patrician forehead. "Hi, I'm Barbara Castell," she said, holding out a hand.

I shook it, then asked, "Is . . . Nancie here?"

"Still in the kitchen." She raised an eyebrow. "I have to say, she never cooks for *me* anymore like she's doing tonight."

"Hey!" my sister said a minute later when she wheeled herself into the living room. "Lar, you look great." She rolled right up to me. "I like your hair that way, that brush cut—very distinguished."

"You're looking great, too," I said, and she did. She had gray hair also, but expensively cut and falling in layers to her shoulders. Her face had widened some, but her skin was warm and glowing. And her smile was a million bucks. "I can't believe it's—"

"Well, you've always known where *I* was," she said, with just a faint, no doubt well-deserved sardonic touch. "But I'm so glad you're here." She was all brightness now, clearly sincere. I found myself just smiling at her. My younger sister, crippled, glowing in front of me. I was a little light-headed. "And you've met Barbara?"

"Indeed."

"Barbara lives here with me."

I turned and smiled at her. "Oh, so you're a—"

"No, silly," Nancie said, "not a nurse or helper or anything." She wheeled over to the tall woman and took her hand. "She *lives* here with me."

All right, it took me a second to compute, but then I shot

through with joy. I guess during our holiday phone calls I'd read *I'm doing fine* as *All things considered* or *Since I'm stuck in this damn wheelchair.* . . . But this warm, easily domestic home? I bubbled up with a giddy joy. Go, Sis, go!

Dinner was a roast chicken, subtly spiced Caribbean style, with a grain I wasn't familiar with called quinoa and a melange of quirky vegetables that Nancie said Barbara always picked up on Saturdays at a farmer's market. It was easily the best meal I'd had since I'd been back in New York. After general chat about Nancie's job (she still loved it except for budget-cutting problems) and Barbara's (she worked for Lincoln Center, at the Metropolitan Opera), and my hinting that I wasn't sure I'd be returning to Arizona but that I didn't really know what else I could do, well, all that was just a way into talk of the trial.

"I've been following it in the papers," Barbara said. "That guy, Punky Solomon, there's still interest in him. And Anna Dubower—"

"Yeah," Nancie said. "It amazes me sometimes, that sweet girl I knew all those years ago, and people are still obsessing about her."

"I probably shouldn't say anything about this," Barbara said, "but one of our best young composers is thinking of using her as the subject of an opera—"

"Really?" I exclaimed.

"Well, it is a pretty good story," she said. "Young girl sings her way to stardom, starts slipping, makes one great record that nobody gets, then dies. Along the way she gets raped, then pregnant, then—"

My sister leaned across the table and tapped her friend on the arm. Barbara gave her a look, then nodded, and that's when she stopped speaking.

But I'd heard her loud and clear. She had blithely thrown out facts that I'd with the greatest difficulty dug up, and passed them across the table as if they were common knowledge. But they weren't. How could she know? Had Nancie told her? But then how had Nancie known? . . .

"Um, dessert?" my sister said, wheeling away from the table.

"Nancie's made a wonderful peach pie," Barbara turned to me and said confidingly. "Don't tell her, but I've already sneaked a slice." She looked with a smile to the kitchen. "One, two, three—" Then she flourished out a hand, and at just that second, my sister called out, "Barbara! What the hell?"

"I'm sorry, dear," she said. "It was just so . . . perfect."

Well, the pie got carved up all right, and with some vanilla ice cream on it, it was wonderful.

"So how *is* your trial going?" Barbara asked. "Seems like you should win easily."

"Well, I'm not so sure. We're still optimistic, but we're a little shy in evidence." I shrugged. "I've spent all weekend trying to track down this demo acetate that Princess made of *Knife*." I turned to my sister. "I've seen Sweet, her mother, and even Trudy—saw Trudy just this morning."

"God, Trudy Dubower!" my sister cried. She narrowed her eyes. "How did *that* go? Didn't you have a fling with her back when?"

I nodded, then Barbara spoke quickly: "But I thought you were engaged to *Anna* Dubower."

"He was," Nancie said. "Well, almost."

"Oh, right," Barbara said.

"Yeah, I've been digging up the past something fierce," I said. "To no avail, though. Can't find the damn demo record." I shrugged. "My attorney is going to have to go finesse the judge tomorrow, make her think we can dig the record up if we just have another few days."

There was a quick, sharp glance between Barbara and my sister, then Nancie said, "Do you think you can?"

Another shrug. "I'm not sure where to look anymore. It

Robert Dunn

seems that Anna brought the disc back here when she came East—you remember, Sis—and nobody saw it again in L.A. But . . . nobody in her family has any idea where it is."

As I explained this, I caught more sharp glances between the two women. Their eyes were lit up like telegraph keys. Finally, Barbara shot out one last questioning glance, and my sister gave an almost unnoticeable nod then said, "And how much do you need that acetate?"

"I really need it."

"And if you knew that somebody actually, um, possessed it, you'd ask them right out for it."

"Of course." I didn't have a clue what she was getting at. "Of course I would. As I said, I really, really—"

"Did you ever think—" Nancie started to say. "Did it ever cross your mind to ask *me* about it?"

I shook my head. "Why would I have asked you?"

"Oh, because I knew Anna back then. You remember, we became friends after that night you brought her over. Did you know I saw more of her back—"

"I don't remem— When?"

"Oh, I don't know, you were off doing something. She'd come over, and we'd talk. She'd take me down to the park, push me along by the water—"

"I never knew any of—"

"We were quite close, Larry. She told me *everything*."

My head was spinning. "I didn't know that."

"But," Barbara said pointedly to me, "you could *ask* your sister about that record, right?"

"I . . . could—"

My sister's companion was nodding, with the kind of vivid encouragement you'd use with a child you're trying to get to speak some first words. She even beckoned with her hands, trying to draw me out.

But I was a numskull. "I could ask my sister—what?"

Both of them hung on my every breath. Barbara kept

waving her hands at me. An odd thought: It was just like the way Jimi Hendrix uses his hands to draw out the fire when he's burning his guitar in the Monterey Pop Festival movie.

"O.K.," I said hesitantly, "I could ask my sister if—" I turned to Nancie, and I suddenly got it. "Nance, do you . . . do you *know* anything about the Annas' demo record?"

She didn't move for a long moment, then she whispered, "Yes."

Barbara kept beckoning me on with her hands.

"Do you . . . is it somehow possible that you actually *have* the record?"

I think I was holding my breath. It looked as if Barbara was, too. Finally, my sister closed her eyes, rolled her chair back a few inches, then said softly, "Yes, Larry, I do."

✳ ✳ ✳ ✳ ✳

MY SISTER EXPLAINED. "Anna gave me the demo record, and she said that I could give it to you someday, but only if you asked for it—asked directly. I'm not sure why she said that, but she seemed to have some real reason. It's like she was looking far into the—" Nancie stopped, as if she'd heard what she was saying, then shook her head. "Well, I thought it was a little silly, but then it didn't seem as if the disc meant anything to anybody, so I just held on to it. Then when your suit came up, I thought it might be helpful to you, but I remembered Anna's conditions. I thought you'd come see us right away—"

"I'm sorry," I said. "I was—"

"It's all right, Larry. Doesn't matter. You're here now. And—" she gave me a bold smile "—you asked."

"Can I see it?"

My sister was already wheeling herself backward, spinning, then heading into the bedroom. As she left us, I saw something bright in Barbara's eyes again; that same child-encouraging eagerness, then a wiggle of her Hendrix-like fingers.

Then it clicked. Of course she knew Anna's secrets. They had her diary, too.

My hand flew to my chest. I called out, "Um, Sis, if I ask to see her diary, too, can you show it to me?"

Nothing from the bedroom. Barbara was fighting to keep a straight face. My sister was gone for the longest five minutes of my life. When she wheeled back into the living room she had a black wax disc in her lap, and beside it a girlish pink-and-blue book, clad in a waxy plastic with a raised figure of a '50s girl in a ponytail and a bold golden clasp.

I took the record first. "Do you still have a record player?"

"Mom's," Nancie said, and nodded to the corner of the room where the family Philco console stood. It was heavy mahogany, with an inch-thick lid that opened over an old-fashioned record changer. The demo disc was, if I remembered correctly, set at 45 RPM, but unlike a normal 45 it had a small hole. I set it carefully on the spindle and clicked the play button.

I heard the piano first, Princess's full chords bashed out on that old upright in our office building, then her lilting voice and my fumbling harmonies. It was *Love Will Cut You Like a Knife* just the way we wrote it—and the way Punky recorded it. My memory was right: There were a couple different chords on the released record, and the words had changed in one line of the bridge, but that was it; though the sound was thin, tinny, with a weird echo hovering like fog over the whole thing, there was no question that I was hearing *Knife* as it finally was released.

I was pinned to my chair, couldn't speak for a minute after the fade out. Barbara got up and lifted the needle off the Philco. Then I told them, "You don't know what a lifesaver this is."

"Oh, we can imagine."

"I just—" I was about to say *Wish I could've had it earlier*, but my sister and her companion gave me a look, and I realized it was in truth just my good fortune I'd shown up tonight and followed Anna's instructions.

"Larry?" Nancie said, concerned.

"Oh, nothing." Then I reached for Anna's diary. "Can I—"

"You asked me for it," my sister said. "That was all she wanted." She held out the book. "It's all yours." She handed it to me, and I took it gingerly. It was too large to fit in a pocket, so I simply held it before me, as you would a missal in church.

We said our goodbyes, I swore I'd see them soon—and meant it; not even considering the discoveries, I'd had one of the best, most delightful evenings I'd known in ages—then took the subway back to Manhattan. Nancie had fixed me up with a well-constructed Lord & Taylor shopping bag, and in that I carried my near sacred objects back to the hotel.

It was about 9:45 when I got there, and I immediately called Sandy at home and told him what I'd gotten—told him about the disc, that is.

"That's fantastic," Sandy said. Then, as if he could peer magically into my room, he added, "Anything else?"

I hesitated. The diary was sitting right in front of me, but I didn't want anyone to know I had it until I'd at least looked at it. "Not at the moment." A pause. "Don't you think the demo will be enough?"

"I think it will blow Solomon and Gold out of the water."

"I'll see you tomorrow," I said.

"Yeah, don't be late. This is gonna be great!"

There her diary was. I'd set it on the desk next to the TV; propped it up so that its cover faced me. The embossed cartoon girl on it was wearing blue pedal pushers and a black-and-white-striped sailor blouse. Her blonde hair rose high above her forehead before being tugged back in a ponytail, and she was sitting next to a portable record player and held a black disc in her hand. She looked the perfect picture of *American Bandstand* innocence.

What was I afraid of? Why did I spend the next hour sitting there on my bed just staring at the diary? The answer was obvious, of course. Finally, I called down to the bar off the hotel lobby and asked if they could send up a small bottle of Scotch and a couple cans of Coke. I wasn't much of a drinking man, but I was remembering that night in London when Scotch and Coke was John Lennon's drink of choice; it seemed appropriate. The room service guy knocked, I tipped him grandly, cracked the bottle, popped the top of a can, poured both into the water glass out of the bathroom, took a long sip—it was kind of gross, like expecting wine but getting Kool-Aid—then sighed and opened the book to the first page.

Chapter Twelve

THE PAGES WERE mostly white with a pale pink tinge at the borders; the writing started off in purple ink, then went to blue or black. I recognized Anna's penmanship; I'd gotten a couple letters from her, nothing special, and remembered her personal style, headlong, firm printing, each letter perfectly articulated, with girlish flourishes—a small flower dotting an *i* here, a heart dotting one there—and occasional flurries of dots in the margin, as if she were tapping the pen against the paper trying to decide what to write next. Each entry was dated; there were weeks, even months between entries. The diary started in 1960, when Anna was 17, and the last entry was on Christmas Day of 1966, less than two weeks before her death. I simply noted that last date; I wasn't about to start at the end here—I planned to read every word in order. Though I did note that at the end her punctilious style had broken down—some of the words looked haphazardly scribbled—and there were none of the girlish touches.

I also was curious how Nancie had gotten the diary. If Anna had left the demo record with her when she was in New York in August, how did my sister get a diary that ran months later? I took a deep breath, another pull at the Scotch and Coke, then dove in.

The first thing I saw was how each entry was addressed to a Jennifer or Jenny.

Oct. 16, 1960: Dear Jennifer, I miss you already, dearest. I'm gonna start this new diary so I can keep in touch with you. Its gonna be my secret. Maybe someday you'll read it. I want to make it the book of my life.

Nov. 24, 1960: Dear Jenny, Its Thanksgiving, and I can't believe youre not with me. I woke up this morning really early. We're having turkey dinner around

*lunchtime because the girls and I have a show tonight—
its our first show since, well, you know. I was really
excited. Trudy worked on my hair all morning, and then
I worked on her hair. Sweet came over for pie, then we
all got in Marcos's Chevy and drove to the show.*

*It went great. We're called the Meringues, and we
whip up a storm, girl! The audience loved us, and I love
you. I'm really tired now. Good night, darling.*

I wondered who this Jennifer was; she seemed more
than just a made-up diary friend, but what else could it be? I
flipped through the pages, past entries mostly on high school
and the girls' music gigs, till I found a date that caught
my eye.

*Jan. 12, 1963: Ohmigod! Ohmigod! Jenny, dear, we
just got signed! To a real record company! With
Mr. Punky Solomon. He has a funny name, doesn't he,
but he's this hotshot producer, he did* Wading in the
River of Love, *which was just an* a-maz-ing *record.
You should hear it; I'm gonna play it now, and maybe
if there's some kind of miracle. . . . It is miraculous
music, dearest—it truly is!*

*So Mr. Punky Solomon's going to be working with
us. He brought round his whole team, including these
two songwriters, Princess and Dink. Princess is this girl
from Queens, a little older than me. Dink's a guy. He's
kinda cute and he's also really smart—you can see it in
his eyes. He knows all kinds of wonderful words. I'm
sure he did great on English tests in school!*

*Anyway, we're going to be making a record.
Princess and Dink are gonna write it, and
Mr. Solomon—you know, dear, he's not that much older
than me, but I think of him like a big grown-up, so he's*
Mister Solomon—*is gonna produce it. That means
he'll make it sound good—ready for the radio.*

Jesus, I hope you can hear our record someday.

Even if it doesn't get nowhere on the Top 40, it'll still be amazing. Imagine, me, Trudy, and Sweet singing on an actual disc!

Oh, yes, Mr. Solomon wants us to change our name. Just guess what its now going to be.

The next entry I noted was from the girls' first recording sessions, when Anna had had a run-in with the tympani player.

March 3, 1963 Dearest, we had our first real recording session today, and it was really exciting. I was standing in front of the microphone with the girls behind me and this whole orchestra—yes, Mr. Solomon's filled up the studio with musicians, just for us! Mr. Solomon's such a perfectionist, he spends hours trying to get everything right. And most of the time we just have to stand there. . . .

There was this one terrible moment. You know, darling, there are people out there who think that the color of your blood has something to do with who you are, and they think if you have anything other than white blood in you, youre somehow not, I don't know, all right or something. Anyway, this horrible little man at these big drums made some horrible comments about me. About—

Darling, this is important. We all have all kinds of blood in us. We have Daddy's blood and Mommy's, and hers is black and red and, who knows, maybe purple like my pen here. All that wonderful blood makes us who we are—makes us strong.

Anyway, some people can't see that, and this man started saying things, and, you know, the cute songwriter Dink got so upset—even more upset than me—he went and jumped on the man. You should've seen him! He actually dived at him like he was on a football field!

I want to tell Dink how much he means to me. He stood up for me—for us! I have a very good feeling

*about him. I'm sure I'll be writing more about him in
our diary here. I think he's going to be a* special
friend. . . .

I'd totally forgotten that day. The recording was going
great, our song *Perfect Dreams* building to its furious final
crescendo, Anna wailing *"Oh, Ohhhh, Ohhhhhhhh"* over the
girls chanting, *"Dreams, dreams, dre-eee-eams,"* when
Punky burst out of the control room and waved the whole
thing down. It was like trying to stop an airplane—notes
kept coming, skittering along, until finally everyone fell
silent.

He went up to this tympani player he'd worked with
before. He was a short, barrel-chested guy with sort of
strange red-orange hair that stood straight up a couple inches, like orange blades of grass. He looked more like a long-
shoreman than a symphony player, though that's what he
was. He'd actually shown up in tails and tie as if we were
tackling Brahms.

The room mike was open, and we could all hear Punky
go, "You fucked it, man. That was one kicking-ass tune, but
you threw off the wrong beat right after the bridge."

The tympanist shook his head.

"Oh, you did, man, you did. I could play it back for you.
Biff, play it back."

The engineer poked a button, the tape whisked back
with that swift, skirling noise it makes, and the bridge came
in, then the string solo. We all listened closely. All we could
hear was the amazing recording.

"You see, right there!" Punky cried. I hadn't heard anything, and I turned to Princess, who lifted her eyebrows,
then shrugged. Punky went on: "Where're you from, man?"

"The New York Philharmonic."

Punky snorted. "Must be third string—fifth string. Moe,
where'd you get this guy, really." But as he said this, Punky
had turned his back on the guy and was walking back to the

control room. "O.K.," he said through the room mike when he was in with us, "let's do Take 2."

The second take roared like the first; was even better, since the players were learning to feel each other. *Perfect Dreams* cooked along until the string solo, when all of a sudden the rhythm went wrong.

Punky flew out of the control room. "O.K.," he shouted, "that one was on purpose." He was right up in the beefy tympanist's face; a face now red and hot. "What gives? You got a problem here?"

"I do," he said.

"Oh, yeah, what is it, pal?"

"It's you—you're just a little twerp."

Punky went up on his heels. He was actually half an inch taller than the drummer, but stringbean thin, and a creature of sunless rooms and scarred pianos.

"And . . . it's those dames."

That caught all our ears.

"They're fuckin' niggers trying to pass as white."

That startled even Punky. He said sharply, "What?"

I couldn't believe what I'd heard either. Something in me just flipped. I found myself out of the control room and heading toward the back of the studio room. I went past Anna, who looked startled, appalled.

"I don't mind playing with Negroes," the guy went on, "I mean, hell, it's 1963, but I can't stand it when they try to *fool* people."

And that was it. I just went off. I flew up the steps to the risers and dove at the goddamn racist. Punky, seeing me coming, was grabbing at me. I had my fists up and was focused on the asshole's chin. He had his hands up, and I started to throw a punch at him, when Punky hit my arm; I guess I lost my balance then, because I slipped to the side.

By then there was a cluster of people around us. My arms were pinned back by one of the bass players, and three guys were holding back the tympanist. Moe Grushensky came up and took quick control. He bellowed, "This is on my fuckin' dime. Get both of these shitheads out of here, right now."

So I was thrown out of the session. When I fully cooled down, I went back to the studio and rang the buzzer, but nobody answered. I stood there till I felt sort of foolish, then took the subway home to Queens.

I'd never heard from Anna about that day; never knew. Now . . . now I did.

I read on, but as the girls' career took off, I dropped from the picture. I skipped ahead as the Annas made their first records, got recognition, sold millions, got famous. The early breathless tone changed; Anna seemed more subdued, weathered in a way. She'd occasionally say Princess and I had written a good new song, but I saw no other mentions of us. She did wax pretty ecstatic about meeting the Beatles in Britain (and made a sly reference to John Lennon, a "very good friend I made"), but there were no references I could see to other men until I read the following:

March 8, 1965: I haven't told you much about boys because there hasn't been much to tell. I have all these fans out there, Jenny, and I get their love shouted up at me every time we play. I also have, you know, a lot of dates, but they're usually arranged by our publicist. There just hasn't been anybody special yet who looked like he might stick—until now.

Jenny, I hope its O.K., but I think I need to keep this kind of secret, so I'm just gonna call him "Him" for now. If somebody ever read this—and I'm going to hide it away every night from now on—it would just be too horrible. He's very important and powerful. And besides, its so new I don't want to jinx it. You can understand, I'm sure.

But, oh, darling, my head's all aswim, my heart all bumpety-bump. And just like that. Its a surprise, too. I

*never thought, well, I never even thought I liked Him—
like that. But I do.*

*There's another man that's bothering me, I didn't
want to write about him because he's so worthless, but he
has this thing for me, has for over a year now, and it
just rubs me all wrong. He's this little Mafia dweeb
who's always hanging around. Just like all those punks
up on Pleasant Avenue. Jenny, he's always bugging me.
I think my man knows and will do something about it—
at least I hope so.*

O.K., the Mafia dweeb had to be Manny Gold, who defi-
nitely was making a fool of himself over Anna in early '64; but
"Him"? I didn't have a clue. She was meeting a lot of new
people every day, of course, and she and the girls did have the
Number 1 record in the country, so she had to be meeting all
kinds of "important, powerful" guys. I could think of three or
four male singers—a couple Bobbys, a Jimmy, who knows
who else?—dying to get to her, and who knew what kind of
cigar-chomping creeps she was meeting at parties and such?
The Annas fantasy *was* in full bloom. I read on:

*August 13, 1965: We're on the Beatles tour! Its so
exciting. We're the opening act, and though all the kids
are there to see the four boys, well, its still awful exciting.
We get cheers, too, even though we haven't had a hit since
last year. Maybe this means we'll have a hit again. Mr.
Solomon keeps saying we will.*

*And my man? Well, He wasn't very thrilled about
us girls going on tour with the Beatles. Of course He
knows about John. But I'm a true-blue girl, princess. I
see John from the side of the stage when me and Trudy
and Sweet are out there, and I gotta say, he's still awfully yummy. But I've made promises and I want to keep
them—well, most of the time.*

O.K., maybe she had another fling with Lennon—they
were on tour. Not surprising that her mystery man was jeal-

ous. It didn't take long for his jealousy to erupt. (I also noticed that she started making some of her I's lowercase. I wasn't sure why.)

October 3, 1965: Oh, Jennifer, i can't bear it! I'm still in, oh, i don't know. He's—he's just so STRANGE. The more i know Him, the more, i, i. . . .

O.K., here's what's happening. We got home from the tour three weeks ago, and that first night I rushed to Him—I wanted to see Him so bad. But it was like nothing i ever—. He was so jealous and angry. He accused me of all kinds of terrible things. I tried to tell Him that nothing had happened, but he didn't believe me. i said over and over, "It doesn't matter. i'm home with you now!" But He wouldn't listen. Then He—

No, its too horrible to say.

I ran out of there. I swore I'd never go back. But then He called, and He took me to dinner, and there were flowers, and it was so nice, and, well, I went home with him to his amazing house.

I want you to know everything, darling. You'll never read this, its just for my eyes, so I have to tell everything—all the truth.

So I went back with Him. But things have changed. He wants me to do things now. Funny, funny things.

We go to a new room in his house. He says he had it made special for me when the girls and i were out on tour. There are funny books in that room, and closets with dress-ups and masks in it, and all kinds of . . . of funny things hanging off the walls. There is also medical stuff, a table with a stirrup and pokey things, and chains and even collars with studs like we used to put on the boxer we had growing up.

Jenny, i didn't really understand any of it, but He . . . He insisted, and we. . . .

Oh, darling, can you see the teardrops on this page?

✳ ✳ ✳ ✳ ✳

O.K., Jenny, I feel a little better. But why, oh, why do i let him do these things to me? i'm a big star, i don't need this. i really don't know how much longer i can put up with Him.

But then He does something that makes me, well, that horrible Manny Gold, the mafia worm, has been put in his place by my Man. i didn't even have to say anything. He did it all on his own. You see, sometimes i can't help but love him. Jenny, what should i do?

She'd named Manny Gold, so I was on the right track. But what was going on with the other guy? And what was up with his "special room"? My head spun.

There weren't any entries of consequence until the next spring.

March 27, 1966: Jennifer, O.K., its over. We both knew this was inevitable. But the horrible thing is that it wasn't me who did it, it was Him. How could He!

He thinks He's so important! He thinks He can just! Well. He didn't even do it in person, He sent one of his flunkies over with the message that he wasn't going to see me anymore. I'm tempted to give him his name now, but I never have, so I'd better. . . . O.K., I'm writing this all over the place. Calm down, Anna, calm down.

O.K., here's what I did. I called him up and said, "What does this mean?" He said, "Nothing, babe. Just time to move along." I told him he had a lot of, well, my language wasn't pretty, darling. But he just laughed and said, "Don't worry your pretty little head about it, babe. I'm not."

Damn right he's not. But I am. I hate the way He's treated me, like i was nothing, like i was just a worm. If I gotta, well, I'll do the best I can, but I'm never going to think of him in any other way than with con-

*tempt. C-O-N-T-E-M-P-T. One of those fancy words
that our songwriter sweetie Dink Stephenson would use.*

*And the horrible thing is, Jenny, the next day Manny
Gold came around again. He thinks he has a shot now.
I swear I've never done a* thing *to encourage him. Why
would I? But there he is, like a sick dog outside my door.*

*And yet I have this idea. Its pretty crazy, but I'm in
such a tizzy that I just might give it a try!*

That's when she went on the cruise to Bermuda.

*May 29, 1966: Jenny, I did my silly, crazy thing—
I went on a boat with Manny Gold. i know, i know!
Yeah, i call him a gangster, and he is that, but i've just
been feeling so, i don't know, miserable and stressed and
all, and he's* so *damn persistent, well, i thought, a
cruise, a cruise—how bad can that be?*

*Plus, He was on my mind a lot, and I thought that
going on the boat, if He heard about it, it would make
Him* crazy! *I love that idea: make Him crazy!*

*Manny Gold—God, what a mess. He tried every-
thing in the world, flowers, jewels, even proposing to me,
but I wouldn't—couldn't—do anything with him. I'm
sorry, Jenny, I just laughed out loud, though its not really funny. Its just that, well, in a way . . . oh, poor guy.*

But I did nothing *with him. I swear I didn't.*

Did I believe her—that she'd fended off Manny for that
whole week? I didn't know. But when I read an entry further
on, I felt more certain she had.

She also had a short entry when she first heard the *Knife*
demo, saying how she thought it was going to be a huge hit;
she loved the song, though Trudy and Sweet were less sure
about it. Then I skipped to an entry that shook me.

*June 4, 1966: Oh, God, He's back in my life. Yes, in
that way. I guess He heard about me in Bermuda and
it made Him jealous. And now—*

Oh, Jennifer, sometimes i think i'm just such a sap.

And the horrible thing is, i'm not sure i care for Him anymore. i think i'm more scared *of Him. . . .*

Let me tell you. We were recording this great new song that's gonna be a hit, and there He was. He took me out to dinner at Chasen's, this fabulous movie-star restaurant, and He introduced me to some of his friends, Dennis Hopper, who was in Rebel Without a Cause, *and Nick Adams, who has that TV show all the guys watch, what is it?* Johnny Something? *And they fawned over me. Guess I still got it, eh, Jenny, girl.*

We drove around after that, up on Mulholland. He wanted to park but I told him no. He was good, he lis-tened to me.

So maybe things are gonna be different. But I swear I'm not going to do anything *with Him, I've promised myself that. He can keep that closet full of weird stuff to himself and his prostitutes. I'm not going to be one of them!*

Oh, then, just to make me more crazy, Manny Gold's still after me. He was at the studio today, and, boy, you could cut the tension with a knife!

July 11, 1966: The record's coming along, but Mr. Solomon is such a perfectionist, well, we're still working on the backing track, which makes it boring for me and the girls. We just sit there. Then this a—hole Manny Gold comes in and starts rubbing my back, then tries to play footsie with me. I kicked him—yeah, I really kicked him. That just made him laugh. Mr. Solomon called out, "Quiet," but you know how he is, he's so wrapped up in everything when he's working, he doesn't see anything.

July 15, 1966: Oh my God! Jennifer, this is the worst *thing i've ever had to write to you about. This is. . . . Oh, i can't even bear it.*

i—. i—. i was hurt. Hurt by a man, by that *man. He—. He—. He did* horrible *things to me. i can't bear to write them. i'm here crying now, my mascara is running, tears are smearing my writing.* [It was true: Anna's blue ink was smudged on the page. I found it hard to make out a lot of the words.]

O.K., i got up, walked around. i'm better. i'm going to get it out.

Here's what happened. After a long day of recording Manny Gold said he'd give me a ride home, and like a fool i accepted. i don't know what i was thinking. i was really tired, i guess. The recording was going so well, me and the girls laying down our vocals, and i just felt—felt like everything was gonna be great!

i told Manny to drop me at the corner, but he parked and walked me to the door. i tried to lose him there, but he pushed open my door and followed after me. i told him to leave me alone, but he was in my room then. Thank God he was too stupid to lock the front door.

Inside my room i told him to leave. He just laughed. He came at me. i was getting scared. There was an ashtray there, filled with cigarette butts, and i picked it up and threw it at him. He just ducked. And laughed again.

Then he came at me. He's a little twerp but he works out and he was able to grab me. Jenny, i'm crying now again, tears are falling, i'm—

O.K., i have to get this down. Manny pushed me into the bedroom. He tugged at my clothes. He pulled at his clothes. i was screaming, but there was no way anyone could hear me, and so i screamed louder, but then he put his hand over my mouth, and put his other hand down there, and then he was on top of me.

They say that if—if this is happening to you, just lie back and don't fight, but i couldn't—I couldn't! I kicked him and scratched at him but he was too strong. He was too strong. . . .

And then I was saved. God, it was a miracle. Jenny, it was Him!

Manny was on top of me, but He was there, He must've come through the unlocked door, and there was this horrible fight. Of course He won. He had surprise and He had goodness *on his side. He told Manny if He ever saw him again, He'd kill him—and i know He could. Manny ran away like a dog with his tail between his legs.*

i was just lying there, my head was spinning, Jenny, so dizzy, dizzy, and then He—. He was right there next to me. Oh, God! i was so—. And He was—. I said i didn't want Him. All i wanted was to get up. i felt all kind of hurt down there, and i wanted to take a shower sooooo bad. But He was there, and i was—. And He—.

i let Him. i didn't fight Him. He—he had saved me. He—.

When it was over we were both embarrassed, i think. i took my shower and He lay there and i tried to think if i should call the police, but He told me no. He could take care of Manny Gold. Nothing to worry about.

i'm trying not to worry. i'm trying to take it all in stride, get back to work, think everything is normal. But i know its not.

Jennifer, i've changed—changed forever.

i can't tell you yet how and why. but i know it. my head's like a cloud, just wide open and full of white cotton candy. i float around a lot like a cloud—like a little white cloud.

O.K., writing this, I just chuckled. It was the first laugh i've had since—since this happened. I love you, darling. Sometimes I think writing to you is all that ever keeps me sane.

I leaned back, my head whirling. I could see it all, Manny Gold trying to rape her, and then the mysterious guy coming in and "saving" her, then forcing himself—*Himself*—upon her. What a fuckin' creep. It sounded to me as if she was raped *twice*. I couldn't believe it; had to set the diary down my hands were trembling so much.

Then I remembered something from a TV show I'd seen, that the only two crimes without a statute of limitations were murder and rape. I had the diary, the evidence right in my hands: Manny Gold clean for rape. I balled my fists. I was so angry, I—well, I couldn't do anything at that moment. And there were more pages of Anna's diary to get to.

> *August 24, 1966: Jennifer, I'm pregnant! i'd been—well, i just went to a doctor and he says that i am. Can you imagine that!*
>
> *Oh, i wish i was happy. But I have to be honest with you and say i'm not. Not at all.*
>
> *He has to be the father. That's the only explanation, since He's the only man who could have done it—right after i was attacked by Manny Gold.*
>
> *Do i want His baby? i don't. It—it just confuses everything. But will i not have it? Not on my life!*
>
> *So youre going to have a little sister or brother—no, I know its going to be a little sister. And i'm going to be—i don't know what i'm going to be.*
>
> *For now this is just our secret. Just you, darling. Its only been a month. The record is moving along, but Mr. Solomon is sooooooo much a perfectionist, i thought the girls and i had done the vocals, but it turns out we haven't even started to record the real vocals. i don't understand. Its getting to be all too much.*
>
> *Jennifer, darling, i'd give anything to give you a big hug right now!*
>
> *Aug. 26, 1966: Jenny, i couldn't stand it anymore*

and i just went home. i'm writing this tonight in my old bedroom in my mother's apartment—and oh, how close you are to me.

Why am i here? i don't even know. He became overbearing, and the song became insane—really, he was making me start to pull my hair out—and i just didn't say anything to anybody but went to the airport and caught a plane to New York, and here i am. Its so quiet, well, its noisy as hell, this big crazy city, but inside my head its starting to be quiet.

I'm still waiting to hear myself think clearly, then i'll know what to do—i hope. More tomorrow.

Aug. 28, 1966 Well, Jenny, not tomorrow, but the next day. A lot has happened, well, nothing *has happened, which is just what I want, but I mean something's happened, which is that I found out that Dink Stephenson is here in New York, too. His mother died, its so sad, and he's with his sister in Queens. And I'm going to see him tomorrow.*

I'm excited. I feel like a kid again, that bubbly and full of anticipation. There—that's a Dink word, wonder how he'd rhyme that. I have this thesaurus here, let's look. How about Relaxation? *Excitation? Assignation?????*

Sept. 1, 1966: Dear Jennifer, oh, my! My heart is beating so loudly, darling. I didn't realize how hopeless, how truly desperate I was feeling, but now I can see because I can see the end of it. I can see a way out!

Here's what happened. I called Dink thinking I'd just be seeing an old friend, but you know, I always had a crush on him, even when I was with Him, and maybe there was a little of that in my mind, but mainly, darling, i just felt i needed a friend so bad. And with Dink

I never felt he was anything but a friend—never felt he was out for anything. (I have to say, I suspect he had a crush on me, too, but unlike that creep Manny Gold, Dink never forced anything or pushed it.)

So what did Dink and I do? It was the simplest, most wonderful time in the world. We went and sat under a bridge. For hours. *Just sat there. Pretty soon my head was on his shoulder, and he was soothing me— he was reaching right into my soul, darling, and sooth- ing me—and it was like nobody had* ever done before.

I've always rushed so, and made so many wrong choices, and had so many wrong choices made for me, *but now I feel different—I'm not at all sure how, but I know I'm looking forward like the dickens to seeing Dink again tonight.*

Sept. 2, 1966: Oh, Jenny, I have sooooo much to tell you.

I had the best—yes, the very best—night of my life. It was so simple, though. It was like I've finally found myself a true home.

Of course I was with Dink again, and I met his sis- ter, who I just adore. Her name is Nancie, a funny spelling, don't you think, and she's in a wheelchair from some horrible disease, and she lives alone now except for Dink in this nice apartment in Queens. Its—I don't know—but it was just perfect.

It reminded me just enough of my mother's place, but it was bigger and laid out much better, but it was the right size—not like His house in L.A. Nothing too much, everything just right. I loved it. I loved Nancie. And . . . I (gulp) loved Dink.

I said it, too. It just came out of me. Yikes!

Is it true? I just took a big swallow, dear. My skin's

all tingly, like when I used to use Clearasil all the time. But I really don't know. Dink is sooooo—he'd be so good for me, I know, and right then I was all his, yes, I was, but there's this little voice inside me that makes me wonder if I was maybe just reacting to all the horrible stuff in L.A. . . .

But I—well, I was with him. I don't feel comfortable saying much more. Just that it was simple and sweet, and he was kind and gentle. Isn't that enough?

And then Dink took me up on the roof!

Can you believe it? You know how much I love that Drifters song, and how I used to go up to the roof here at momma's and just get away from everything. Well, it was like that. We climbed two flights of stairs and popped out onto that rooftop, and the stars were right there above us, and the whole city was glittering around us, and, darling, I was a bad girl up there. I was. I couldn't help myself. I wanted him again and I made him have me. So there.

And then—then he proposed to me.

I've never been so flabbergasted. I didn't expect anything like that at all. See how sweet he is! Any other guy woulda spent the whole day bragging on the phone to his friends. Larry—that's his real name—gave me his grandmother's ring.

I'm looking at it now. Its beautiful. I love it.

I know. You're asking the big question: What did I say?

I told him i'd have to wait. There I was on the roof, and I knew that I had this baby inside me, but Dink didn't know. I knew that Manny Gold had done a horrible thing to me, and then He had been in my life and that He'd still think He had a claim on me, and Dink didn't know. I knew that sooner or later this magical time with Dink and Nancie would have to end and i'd have to return to L.A. and finish Dink's wonderful song, and maybe he knew that, but i'm sure he didn't want to hear it. So i told him nothing.

Its going to be hard for him, and i don't want to lead him on, but darling, i just don't know if Dink is the man i'm fated to be with. Sometimes i think he's just too good for me. . . .

I'm going to think about everything. But, oh, dear, i also know i can't marry him yet. Can't even ask myself if i love him enough till the things he doesn't know about me are resolved somehow.

Oh, Jenny, do you think Dink will want me if that means he has to be the father of another man's child? Do you think that?

And would I have? At that time, when I was so young and full of myself, this could have been a dilemma; but I like to think that even then I would have been smart and clear enough to accept Anna *and* her child, whoever the mysterious father was. And it's with mortal certainty that I know now that a life blessed with Anna and her child—and, God's faith, our own children to come—would have been the greatest joy of my life. But . . . she never gave me the chance to know.

I read on:

Sept. 9, 1966: O.K., darling, I'm back in California. I'm a little surprised, too, but Mr. Solomon insisted, and my sister got on the phone and put on the press, even Princess called me. They all said the song needed me and it was time for me to lay down my vocal. And, you know me, I'm never one to not finish what I started.

But what a week Dink and I had! It was sooooo wonderful. Almost every night I went out to Queens, just me on the subway. Did anyone recognize me? I didn't want them to, so I put on a disguise—it was so much fun! You would've laughed to see me dressed like a cleaning woman! But I always took it off before I saw Dink.

And then we'd just be there. Me, Dink, and Nancie. What did we do? What normal people do. We ate dinner, watched TV, and then Dink and I would go to his old bedroom, with his tiny tiny bed. Now don't be embarrassed, sweetheart. Men and women do these things, even if they're not married. And for that week, well, I just couldn't bring myself to think about anything!

Then I left. (And you've just heard a big big sigh.)

I feel bad, i didn't tell Dink anything before i took off. I thought it might even be good for me to be back in California and think over his proposal and what I really, really need to do.

You should have seen how I showed off his ring, though. I think everyone at the studio was jealous. Especially your Aunt Trudy. Even He saw it.

But I can't talk about that.

I miss Dink something crazy, but, funny, I miss his sister a whole huge lot, too. They were such a fine family for me.

Do you think I'll ever feel . . . feel that safe again? (Oh, dear, a tear just fell on the page.)

Is it too cockeyed, Jenny, if I keep calling Nancie and sort of leave Dink alone for a while? It does seem crazy, but I know Dink's going to want an answer to his proposal, and I just don't have one yet. But Nancie, I know, will just love me for who I am. I might even tell her about my surprise—because I'm sure its going to be a girl!

Pray for me, my darling. Please, pray for me.

I read over this entry twice, three times; tried to parse out each word. I was in truth just looking for one thing: Anna's answer to my proposal. She'd never turned me down, and that was encouraging, but she also never said she'd marry me. From what I'd just read, it seemed she didn't know at all herself. I wanted to believe she'd have chosen that "safe" world she found with Nancie and me. Was I reading this correctly? I bit my tongue. Was her decision coming up?

I flipped the page of the diary. Now we were into that time when I'd lost most contact with Anna. I read on avidly:

Sept. 16, 1966: We're finally getting somewhere on the record. Mr. Solomon is being a nutcake as always, take after take, sing this syllable again—not that one, this one!—and lets go back to the fade out, can't you get more soul into it? He's working me ragged, working us all ragged. But its kinda great. Takes my mind off of everything else.

I still haven't told anyone else about what's inside me. Its going to be our *little secret.*

Sept. 22, 1966: Oooh, she's growing inside me, and the amazing thing, Jenny, darling, is that as my baby gets going, my singing is getting better, too. Mr. Solomon says we're finally getting close to how the record should sound, though you know as well as i do what a maniac he can be—that at any time he can tear up what's perfectly good and destroy it and make everybody start over again.

And: He still doesn't know! And I'm not telling Him!

So there. Its our secret. I'm thinking a lot about Dink, too, worrying about him. I called his sister Nancie to see how he's doing, and she says he's all right, though he seems a little lost right now. Oh, Jenny, that broke my heart. I told her i miss him, but for now i thought we should keep apart. She said, 'He loves you, you know.' And I—I told her that he'd proposed. She didn't say anything for a moment—i guess it was a surprise to her—then she said she was glad to hear it, she'd love me to be in the family. That was soooooo nice to hear. But I just can't decide about it now. i hope Dink understands. Nancie says he will.

So that's all the news.

Oct. 2, 1966: Mr. Solomon says one more week. He promises—well, we know how much that *means. He also is saying that He wants to start things up again. i can't, Jenny, you know i can't, but I don't know how well i can fight Him off—He is the father of my child.*

Darling, i don't know what to do. He's pushing. It makes everything uncomfortable. But i can't do anything till the record is finished, i'm just praying that it is next week. Then maybe i'll go back to New York and see my friends. . . .

Oct. 10, 1966: Jennifer, the record is done! It was the most glorious day. We all gathered in the control room and heard it. Its SOOOO BIIIIIIIIIIIIG! I can't tell you. Mr. Solomon's a genius, even if he's a crazy man. And that gives me a kind of hope for it all. . . .

Oct. 12, 1966: Oh, darling, its all changed so fast. The record is going to the place that presses them up, and all the musicians said goodbye, and then I told Him I'm planning to go back to New York, and He said why? and I didn't say anything, but you know how He is, and He finally got the whole story out of me, about me and Dink on the roof, and He went ballistic. He said He'd *marry me. Right then, right there!*

Well, I was flabbergasted. And the amazing thing, Jenny, was that there was *a time when that was all i ever wanted to hear. But i was such a girl then. I'm not a girl now, I'm a mother-to-be.*

O.K., O.K., i can't hold it back any longer—i told Him. I was telling him i couldn't marry Him, that Dink had proposed to me, and He wouldn't listen. He just kept saying, 'Dink? Dink Stephenson? Are you fucking kidding?' I told him I wasn't kidding. (I was holding my ears.) And he kept yelling. And then I just blurted it out. . . .

Well, i guess i was thinking that He wouldn't want me with a baby inside me. He wouldn't want to be tied down like that. So i told Him—I told Him.

He got very quiet. i guess He was thinking whose baby it was. Maybe he thought it was Dink's. I heard Him mutter something like that under his breath, and that He'd kill him. I sort of shook my head, but i don't know if He got it. Wouldn't He know it could be his, too?

Finally, he was sooooooo quiet. And, darling, for all the time I've known him, I've never made Him so quiet. It was a strange feeling, like I was a little bit in control for once. I liked it. It was the way I was feeling with Dink and his sister, that I could have some things the way I wanted them to be. That they were not into controlling me but LOVING me.

I could tell He was mad—furious. But telling him about your sister, well, he wasn't talking about marrying me anymore.

No, He only talked about my career, how i had the biggest record of all about to come out. I said I didn't care that much, and He—He hit me. Across the cheek. Oh, darling, it wasn't that hard, and He didn't really mean it. But He did it.

He never apologized. He just walked away, and i went home. Oh, Jennifer, i don't have to tell you that i cried myself to sleep that night.

Nov. 12, 1966: The record's been out a week, and nothing. Its not on the radio. Not on TV. Nothing. Its making Mr. Solomon insane. Its making me . . . well, its funny, dearest, but in a way I just don't care.

Nov. 28, 1966: I tried to call Dink for Thanksgiving, but when I called he was out, but I got his sister Nancie. She told me that Dink seems very worried about me, not hearing from me. He's been trying to call, but he keeps missing me, and she thinks in a way he's a little afraid. I said I understood, that he doesn't know what's going on in L.A. I also said that it still wasn't the right time for me to tell him anything. I just wanted to wish him a happy Thanksgiving. Nancie said he'd be back soon and that he could call me, but I told her it should just be our little secret that I called. She said she'd follow my wishes—she's great in that way.

And Mr. Solomon? He's only thinking about the record now. He's trying to get me interviews, and he's thinking of sending me on a tour. I think he's desperate. I'm not going on any tour, not with your sister inside me, and i think he knows that, but he doesn't seem to care. He's getting the whole machinery working. One of these days there's gonna have to be a blowup about it. I'M NOT GOING ANYWHERE!

Dec. 15, 1966: What do they want from me? Its not MY fault the record's deader than a doornail. I did just what they wanted me to. Just what Mr. Solomon wanted me to.

But I'm drawing the line here. They want—no, its too terrible for me even to write about. Especially to you. They . . . they want me to do what i will never do.

I won't. No. I won't. Never. I don't care if I have to run to Mexico to hide. Or to New York. What's wrong with me? I wish i could just tell Dink i'm ready to marry him—God, that would solve everything—but i'm just too confused inside. Its not just . . . but would He have Dink killed, like He said? Would He really *do that?*

He might. He really might. So that's another reason. . . .

At night now i'm starting to hate myself. I can see what they want, its not just Mr. Solomon, its all *of* them. *He's got Rich Armour, the drummer Eldred Smith, and even Princess Diamond involved. They're all just* thinking about the record—*yeah, right.*

Dec. 25, 1966: Darling, i missed you so much today. This has been the worst Christmas of my life. I spent it alone because i'm afraid of everybody. i mean it. Even my sister and Sweet. Even them.

i don't know who to trust anymore. Everybody says they're just looking out for me and the group and the record, except the record's a disaster, the group is dying, and i'm only trying to do what's right.

i got scared and i called New York. i wanted to talk to Dink so bad, i realized what a horrible stupid mistake its been not talking to him. He's always been such a good friend—such strong support. And I—I was all ready to tell him about what's inside me, even if its really His. Why don't i have more courage?

Anyway, Dink wasn't there, and i had the longest talk with his sister Nancie. God, I think she's become like the best friend I have. I can tell her anything. And did. She told me that i had to do what i believe is right. She said that if i could just get myself to New York, she was sure i'd be all right. i—i want to believe her—

Well, its Christmas now, i'm going to try not to think anymore about this. But every noise i hear spooks me—just now i jumped half a foot when the wind outside blew a tree branch against the window.

You can see, this is the last page of the whole diary book. Just think, Jenny, I filled it all up! There must be something good about me after all.

Here's what I told Nancie I'd do, I told her I'd send her my diary for safekeeping. i also told her that if anything happens to me, well, if ever in the future Dink asks about me, she can show him the book.

But what am i thinking? Nothing's going to happen to me. I'm going to have my baby and then I'm going to be nothing but a good mother to her.

And darling, no matter what happens, you have to know that I—I love you.

And there, on the last page of the pink-and-blue book, the diary ended. I set it down, and my head was spinning with more questions than I'd had before. What I really was burning with was trying to figure out who this man she called only "He" or "Him" could be. Why wouldn't she name him? How powerful was he? And if she didn't feel she could name him, what other secrets was she keeping from even the privacy of her diary?

Then I noticed how light I was feeling; how my back muscles had relaxed, how buoyant and oddly hopeful I was. For the time that I'd been reading the diary, Anna was in the room with me, her voice and her spirit *right there*. It was more than eerie: I'd been totally back in 1966.

It was with a small, almost electric shock that I realized where I was and that my love had been dead for over thirty years. I sipped the vile Scotch and Coke, lost to my upended thoughts and harsh yet beautiful memories; and that was how the night passed.

Chapter Thirteen

FIRST THING MONDAY MORNING I shook off my hangover, then shook off the lingering stink of dread and called Sandy Kovall to ask him if he had a portable record player.

"I do, actually," he said. "It's the kind a lot of record collectors have, a yellow Fisher-Price Big Bird one—"

"Big Bird?"

"From *Sesame Street*."

"I know, but a kid's player?"

I could see Sandy shrug over the phone. "In this digital age, they're still easy to come by."

"Well, I'm worried about how . . . how decorous that will be—"

"Dink, you don't—"

"I have it, Sandy. It's right here."

"Right *there*?" His tone shot up an octave. "The acetate? The one that Princess wrote on?"

"There's her writing right on the label."

"Jesus! How'd you get it?"

"I'll tell you everything when I see you outside the courtroom. But, Sandy, I got it."

"Damn!" was all he said.

When the trial was gaveled to order, Sandy went straight up and offered the disc into evidence. Punky's lawyer, Donald Furtie, threw up his hands and shouted, "Objection!" and he, Manny's lawyer, Sandy, and Judge MacIntire disappeared into her chambers. I sat alone at the plaintiff's table. I couldn't take my eyes off of Manny Gold.

He had a rim of fat along his jaw, a pudginess that spoke of too much bad food for too many years, and the beginning of wattles under his chin. His eyes were a milky, distant brown, and his skin around them carried a tinge of yellow.

His ears were fat, like a pig's. He carried his usual smirk on his face, and even with Princess's record and the certainty it would surely bring to the trial, his look said, *Hey, it's only money—and it wasn't mine in the first fuckin' place.*

Then I thought of what he'd done to Anna, how I had evidence he'd raped her. The power was strong, sweet: I could so easily wipe the smirk off his face.

I got up then, as if I were stretching, then sauntered the few feet between the plaintiff's table and the defense table, where Manny and Punky sat. Manny was focused straight ahead, as if on nothing, though Punky looked up at me with that friendly, noncommittal mien he'd maintained since the trial had begun. *Hey!* his raised eyebrows seemed to say.

Hey, I went back. But I didn't want Punky, just Manny. I was standing right by him, but he still wouldn't acknowledge me. Finally, I tapped him on the shoulder.

He looked up, glaring.

"I have it," I said softly, but loud enough for both of them to hear. Punky lifted an eyebrow, but Manny just sat there, with a clear Fuck You on his face.

"No, I really do, you shit," I said. "Not the record. I have her diary."

It took Manny a minute to even react; Punky was faster. He whirled in his seat. "Her—"

"Diary," I repeated.

"So who fuckin' cares," Manny said.

But it was Punky who insisted: "Whose?"

I simply smiled. "Anna's."

Now the little asshole reacted. It still took a long minute, but I could see Manny begin to think, or do what passed for thinking with him; and then he pursed his thick brows and actually wrinkled his forehead, and I could see his thoughts turn back through the years: *Anna Dubower's diary, which means she wrote it when she was alive*—duh!—*which means it*

*probably would cover the last year of her life, which means that she
probably wrote down just what I—*

And there it was, like that: The smirk melted off his face.

But in truth it wasn't what Manny had done to her that
had kept me up half the night before, my thoughts career-
ing through dreams and half-awake rampant speculations,
all the while burdened with the question: Who was the man
who made Anna pregnant, and what did he have to do with
her death?

I was losing interest in what was going on in the judge's
chambers. All I was thinking about was Anna and her last
days.

Who could tell me more? Obviously not Manny, even if
I wanted to blackmail him, which wasn't my style. He probably hadn't been there. Punky? He'd certainly have some
idea, wouldn't he, but even if he *seemed* friendly, I was suing
him; and would he open up to me? I could only ask him who
the mystery man was as a last resort.

I kept thinking I could find out from Anna herself. I'd
been thinking about her diary, how it ended on the last page,
still two weeks before she died. Had she started a new one?

If she had, who would have it? Trudy? Sweet? Neither of
them had even spoken of Anna's main diary; they probably
didn't know about that, so what would they know about a
final one? Anna's mother, passed to her Aunt Cheryl? Cheryl
hadn't gotten the record, for the now obvious reasons, but I
hadn't known to ask about a diary. She'd be my first call
when I got out of the courtroom.

Then I remembered one thing Anna had written: How
Princess had been "involved" at the end with trying to get
Anna to sell the record, and by implication, her pregnancy.
Was there any chance that she? . . .

The attorneys and the judge came out from the judge's
quarters. Judge MacIntire quickly made this announcement
from the bench: "I'll be allowing this old recording into evi-

dence." A pause, then a look at Sandy. "Of course, counselor, you'll be recalling your witness Michelle Diamond to vouch for its provenance."

"Yes, Your Honor," Sandy said, smiling.

Down came her gavel, gently kissing the felt pad. "Then we're in recess until Wednesday morning at 9 a.m."

✳ ✳ ✳ ✳ ✳

I WANTED TO SEE Princess, but something else was nagging at me when I got to Midtown about six that evening. I made a quick detour, stopping in at that record mart near the hotel, Colony. I was hoping to find the guy I'd talked to on the phone, Jimmy Devine, and when I asked for him at the counter, the clerk said he was in the back by the sheet music.

He was blocky, with heavy eyebrows and thick arms, bulging under a well-faded, stretched-out STYX T-shirt. His hair was half gray, half red, and combed straight back over a wide forehead; slicked back with oil like juvenile delinquents did in the days of James Dean.

I walked right up to him, held out my hand. "I'm Dink Stephenson."

He was holding a stack of sheet music and didn't bother to set it down. "Hey, bro."

"I'd like to talk to you. Is there anywhere we can—"

"Man, I told you everything on the phone. Can't you see I'm working."

"Hey, I found it." I cocked my eyebrow back. "It does exist."

It took him a second to remember what I'd been looking for, but then he stopped, his eyes sharp. "That fuckin' demo you were buggin' me about?"

There was a bitter vibe coming off this guy, and I stepped back; but then I nodded and maybe just for a second *I* had the smirk on my face.

"No fuckin' way."

I smiled; remembered my Wayne and Garth. "Way, dude."

"Listen, come on, in my office." He'd already started toward a nondescript white door that read EMPLOYEES ONLY, and I followed. He took a seat behind a well-scarred wooden desk piled from edge to edge with purchase orders, old blue-and-white paper coffee cups, gum wrappers, you name it. He put me in a slat-backed wooden chair next to the desk. There wasn't even room for my elbow.

"O.K., spill."

I told him just enough about the record and my sister and the day in the courtroom to get him salivating. "So that means *you* own it?"

"I don't know that. I don't know who owns it, in truth."

"But when it leaves the court, it goes back to you?"

"I guess so."

His eyes, a little bloodshot, flashed like a lightning storm had blown up behind them. "And you're here because you might be in the mood to—"

"I haven't gotten that far."

"I know a guy on the Coast, man, he's creamin' now, just because this fuckin' disc exists. I know him. He don't even have to know I could get it for him, just that it fuckin' is out there—"

"This the same guy who bought Anna Dubower's death certificate?"

Devine shook his head. "Nah, it's a whole other guy. This guy's into the music." He shrugged to say, It takes all types.

I leaned toward him, over the mountain of detritus, and set my mouth tight. "Here's my deal. I'll only entertain the *possibility* of letting you *look* at the demo acetate if you tell me everything you know about her death."

"I told you, I don't—"

"No, no bullshit. You wouldn't sell anything like a death

certificate without running a Xerox on it. Right? And I bet you and your ghoulish pal know a fuck of a lot more about it, too." Devine hung silent. I pressed on. "That's my deal. Right there."

Devine was silent for a long moment, then he shrugged with a What's it off my skin? vibe, and I knew I was in. "I don't have it here," he told me.

"But you can get it—quick?"

"I can have it for you tomorrow."

I nodded; guessed that would be O.K. "But what do you remember?"

"What do you know?"

I shook my head. "I hate to say it, but I know almost nothing. I—I was having a hard time. I sort of tuned out—"

"It wasn't suicide."

"They said it was just an accident, but I never heard what kind. Drugs?"

Devine was impassive. "Sort of. But not what you think."

"She wasn't taking anything, far as I know." But of course I hadn't been there those last five months.

"She wasn't, you're right."

"So drugs, how does that—"

"I wasn't there, Bud. I just know what I read, what I saw."

I leaned forward so far I was hovering halfway over his desk, right in his face. "And that was—"

"Wait till tomorrow. I'll get you the copy. You can read it for yourself. Like I said, and I wasn't lying, it was a hell of a lot of medical mumbo jumbo."

I was sitting there staring at him, thinking, Come on, just a little more, when he did something extraordinary. He reached out and gently touched my shoulder. "Dink, no matter what happened, she's dead, bro. Over thirty years now." His eyes opened wider. "Man, I feel for you." He half-kneaded my shoulder. "Listen, I loved her too, man, though I only met her once, at some fuckin' promo thing with Punky Solomon. Even then, I only saw her from afar. But she was—she was really something. Lit up the fuckin' room." His smile and nod were solemn, sacred; gesticulations out of our holy church.

Hearing him say this triggered the thought that had been in the back of my mind when I turned in to the record store. "You said something about the record of *Cuts Like a Knife* having a little secret—"

"You haven't checked that out yet?"

I shook my head.

"Here, come with me. This'll give you something to chew on."

We were up then, and away from his desk. He led me to a room with thousands and thousands of 45s, all in olive-green jackets, lined up in shelves alphabetically. It didn't take him long to come to the Annas, between PAUL ANKA and THE AQUATONES.

There were copies of all the girls' records, even the ones that didn't sell, and my head went light when I saw the red and black label of Moe Grushensky's Black Dog records, then the blue and yellow of Punky's own San Remo. There it was, the Annas' whole history before me; and it comes to me now that I didn't really have to write any of this, could just have put copies of all the black seven-inch discs in a nice package with three cute girls, one with the fieriest of cat's eyes, on the cover, and *there!*: You'd have the whole saga, or at least all that truly mattered, in your hands.

Devine pulled out a copy of the final record. "Here," he said. "Take it—good faith gesture, bro."

He'd said something about the secret being in the dead-wax, but I couldn't look at it then. My hotel room was only a couple blocks away, and I knew I needed to be there, with a drink in front of me, before I tried to figure out what he was getting at.

"I'll be here tomorrow afternoon," Devine said. "Stop in any time after two." He reached out and shook my hand; tried to crush my hand in his. I squeezed back at least as strong, then beat it out of there.

I held the record carefully, my thumb on the rim, my middle finger pressing the side of the hole. It was that same gingerly way I'd always treated my records, these magical pieces of plastic that held the music in their grooves. And I couldn't look. I really needed that drink. As I walked down to 47th Street, I kept thinking, *Drugs?* What could Devine have meant by that. He agreed that Anna hadn't been using any narcotics, and yet they'd had something to do with her death. I racked my brain, couldn't think of anything.

As I rode up in the elevator I felt the pull of the record. It was a clean, unplayed copy of *Knife*, and the overhead light slanted across its pristine vinyl. I wanted to look so bad, but more than knowing, I knew I had to do it right: sit down by the window, make a drink—could I face another one of those Scotch and Coke memory drinks?—and then in the light of the setting sun put on my reading glasses and look at that black band circling the blue-and-yellow label.

And that's just how I did it, the ridiculous Scotch and Coke sweetening my mouth. I lifted the disc like a chalice before me and saw the tiny scratch marks in the deadwax catch the orange light like little flickers of fire; I set my reading glasses just right on my nose and tilted the record till what was inscribed there was unmistakable. What I saw threw me back in the chair like a shot. There in the dead black wax were five marks: PS + AD.

* * * * *

I WAS STILL LOST to the implications when an unknowable time later there came a loud knock on the hotel door. I wasn't expecting anyone; didn't know who even knew this was where I was staying. My first thought was not to answer it, but the rapping was insistent, and finally I got up and opened the door.

It was Manny Gold, and behind him the man I'd spent the last hours obsessively turning over and over in my thoughts, Punky Solomon.

"Dink, hey," Punky said. Manny was silent, but he looked angry. Punky, as usual, looked as if he were flying way above it all.

"What do you—"

"Oh, just a little visit," Punky said. Both men pushed through the door.

"Can you do that?"

Punky frowned. "Because of what, the trial?" He shrugged, ran his hands back through his spiky blond hair. "Why not?"

I took a step back. "So what do you want?"

Now Manny spoke up. "You started fuckin' with me today."

"Hey," I said. I knew Manny from years back; he was going to try to intimidate me, but I'd had none of it then, and I wouldn't take it now. "I'm *suing* you. What do you mean, 'Today'?"

"You know, motherfucker." He took a step toward me, growling low. He was so obvious. I simply shook my head.

"Punky, what's he want?"

"What do you think?" Punky kept that vague, diffident smile on his face; kept pushing back his hair.

Then I got it. "No way."

"Where is it?" Manny said, and he started around my hotel room.

He was after the diary, of course, and I guess I really wasn't surprised that he was there. I was surprised, though, that Punky was with him, though now I had a pretty good idea why he'd have almost as much interest in Anna's words. But to show up with Manny? I remembered the shoving match in court. I thought they were enemies.

Punky must've read my mind, because he gave a wink toward Manny, now groping toward the chest of drawers, and said to me, "I figured he needed some moral support."

"Yeah, right," I said, then regretted it. Punky couldn't know what was in Anna's diary, and thus he couldn't know how much *I* knew. "Like you two are long-lost buddies," I added, trying to cover myself.

"Hey, we *all* go way back, don't we, Dink." Punky smiled vaguely. "Your little suit here has been like a reunion." He shrugged. "Even Princess was there. I have to say, in a weird way I've actually been enjoying it."

Manny was pulling out drawers, tossing my underwear and shirts on the floor. I looked at him and shook my head.

"Let him do his goomba shit," Punky said coolly. Then with his eyebrows he added a very clear: *And then we'll really talk*.

"You're really not mad at me, are you?" I said then.

Punky froze for a second, then considered my unexpected question. He spoke slowly, for Punky Solomon, *very* slowly: "You know, Dink, I'm really not. I don't need the money from *Knife*, and it's cool that it's getting all this attention again. And, you know, this whole trial thing has gotten me out of the house—"

Was he kidding? He had a sparkle in his eyes, and I couldn't tell. My best guess: Half kidding in a way that reveals.

I held out my hand. "So no hard feelings?"

Manny left the chest of drawers and moved to the closet. He was rifling pockets on my jackets there.

Punky didn't waste a moment; held out his hand, too, and gripped mine tightly. "Nope, never has been. I always liked you, Dink, you know that."

I said, "I always liked you, too, Punky." I'd caught just a whiff of condescension in his tone. "And *you* know that."

He smiled, right up with me. "Right."

"Dink, where the fuck is it?"

I looked over at Manny. He was sweating a little now, a fine sheen on his forehead, teardrops of sweat by his ear. "I don't know, Manny. Where would *you* keep it?"

"Fuck you. Tell me."

I rolled my eyes, looked to Punky—appealed to Punky. The producer didn't do anything, and Manny fell to his hands and knees and looked under the bed.

"He wants it," Punky said.

"I know." Then I focused tight on Punky. "How about you?"

He took a long moment to shrug, then said, "Well, I will say I'm sort of curious about what Anna wrote." He let another vague smile slide out.

"I bet."

"You've read it, of course."

I didn't even answer.

"How far up does it go, sport?"

I didn't answer that, either. I didn't have to. Punky gave a tight nod, then said, "I see."

"I don't fuckin' think it's here," Manny called out. He was in the bathroom now, looking behind the toilet, I think.

"Keep looking," Punky said. He gave me a wink as Manny clattered into the closet. Punky lowered himself onto the bed, stretched back, then put his hands folded behind his head. He couldn't look more relaxed. "So, Dink, what've you been up to all these years?"

I kicked my head a little to the right, then said, "My life."

Punky frowned. "Come on, we used to be friends. I heard you were teaching high school. Is it in California?"

I didn't answer right away. Manny clattered in the closet. "Arizona."

"You like it there?"

"I like the kids," I said.

Punky pursed his brow. "It's not the money then, right?"

I shrugged. "Doesn't hurt. But, yeah, I still do pretty well with royalties from our tunes." The last two words made Punky smile. "But I'm helping support my sister, too."

"The one in the wheelchair—good for you."

"So what have you been doing all these years?" I peered at Punky. "Like that scar on your cheek. How'd you get that?"

Punky gave out a big laugh. "On safari in Africa, if you can believe it. I fell on a stick. It was like a spear."

"Africa?"

"I've spent a lot of time traveling—"

Manny popped his head out of the closet and said, "I don't think it's here."

"You said you could find it. Keep looking!" Punky said, then winked at me again. I sort of got it now. He was actually enjoying chatting with me and wanted Manny to keep busy while we talked.

"Just traveling?" I asked, when Manny got down and brushed his hand again under the bed. "No music?"

"Ah, the million dollar question!" Punky's eyes lit up. "Everyone wants to know if Punky Solomon's gonna make a record again. 'Has he lost it?' 'Has time really passed the boy genius by? . . .'"

I waited.

"Dink, there's a lot of hours in the day—" He shrugged. "You gotta do something."

I began to hear what he was saying. "So you're actually doing some music?"

He held fire a long moment. We could hear Manny grunting as he stood there trying to figure out where else to look for Anna's diary. Then Punky said, "I guess it's in my blood, Dink." He suddenly held my gaze sharply. "You know, the computers they got these days, amazing what just one person can do—"

My head flew back at least an inch. "You're still making records?" My voice rose, too.

He gave me a got-me shrug. "Yeah, I've made dozens—maybe more."

I moved toward him. "Real Punky Solomon records?"

"Well, they're on hard drives now, but I guess so."

"Has any of it come out?"

Punky didn't answer right away, then shook his head.

"How come you haven't released them?" Just thinking of what I was hearing made me jazzed, right there and then. "Man, I can't believe—"

He held up a languorous hand. "Oh, you know what'd happen if I did." A thin smile. "I'd get crucified. 'PUNKY SOLOMON SECRET TAPES: ONCE AGAIN HE BETRAYS HIS PROMISE.' It'd be a fuckin' firestorm. No thanks."

"I'd love to—I mean, when this is all over—when I'm in L.A., maybe come by and. . . . I mean, just me—"

"Sure," he said. He gave me that vague smile again. "That'd be cool."

"Punky, the fuckin' diary ain't here," Manny declared. "I'm good at tossing rooms. It ain't here."

Another wink at me. "Of course it's not here, you moron," Punky said sharply. "I told you we couldn't just come in and get it." He turned back to me. "You've put it somewhere, right?"

I simply shrugged. Manny was standing next to us, his face red, burning.

"Some place safe?" Punky paused. "I sure would have."

Manny glared at Punky. "So what do we fuckin' do now, Mr. Boy Genius?"

"Come," Punky said to both of us. "Both of you guys sit down.

Neither of us moved.

"All right. Listen, Dink, I was pretty sure you wouldn't keep anything as sacred as Anna's diary just lying around, right?" I didn't answer. "What, the hotel safe?" Nothing. "Well," he went on, "it really doesn't matter. The thing is, Manny here needs that book—*really* needs it." I looked up at Manny, who glared down at Punky stonily. "So we're prepared to make a deal. We'll throw the towel in with the lawsuit if you give us the diary."

I took awhile to answer, not to decide what to say, just to let them squirm. "You're going to lose anyway."

"Yeah, but you really don't ever *know* that. Anything could happen. The judge can hate Princess's voice on that demo you came up with. She can see the truth: That I put my body and soul into that record. Maybe she'll give the verdict to me for that—"

"And me?" Manny insisted.

"Hey," Punky said sharply, "shut up."

"*Fuck you!*"

Punky rolled his eyes again.

"So you never know, Dink. But listen, you'll win for sure. We'll also—Manny, said he would—that he'd pay your court costs. You'll walk away with the record, the royalties, and it won't have cost you a dime."

Again, I took my time. "All for the diary."

Punky shrugged. "Simple as that."

"And if I don't go along with your 'deal'?"

"The diary can't ever come out, Dink. You know that."

"Say it doesn't come out—"

"But how could we ever *know*. How can old Manny here ever sleep well again." Punky turned to Manny. "You still sleeping like a baby, sport?"

"Fuck off."

"I'm not going to do it," I said. I was thinking about having Anna's—*my* Anna's—secret writings in their hands. Nothing would be worth that. "I'm gonna take you at the trial, and I'm going to keep the diary." I turned to Manny. "And you're always going to worry about what you did to her."

"What *I* did!—" Manny blustered. "Anything she said is a fuckin' lie—"

"And," I went on, ignoring him and facing Punky straight on, "you're going to worry about what *you* did to her, too."

That caught it. Like that, the air in the room changed, grew hotter, stuffier—or so it seemed. Punky took his time, rolling his blond head from side to side, stretching out his hands, cracking his knuckles; then he said, "There can't be anything about *me* in her diary—"

"You shit," I said under my breath. "The whole fuckin' *book* is about you."

Punky's features were pinched, pained. "You'd really have to show it to me, Dink."

"No I wouldn't." I felt a hot swell rise up in me, and the next words just flew out. "You got her pregnant. And for all I know, *you fuckin' killed her.*"

Punky froze. He flashed me a slanted, dark eye, but when he spoke, his voice couldn't have been calmer. "I'd have to see it, Dink, I really would."

"What's that?" Manny said, boring in at me. He fumbled inside his coat. "What are you sayin', man?"

"It's all right, Manny," Punky said, standing then. "Come on, let's go." He took a step toward the door. "He's not going to do anything with the diary, I know it." A glare, though pleasant enough, at me. "Are you, Dink?"

I was suddenly sick of both of them, Punky's false friendliness, Manny's eruptible vulgarity, the low-lying threat in the room. I told them what felt like the truth. "Probably not."

Punky lifted his chin to Manny. "You see." He went to the door. "Come on."

Manny didn't move for a second, then he followed Punky, who opened the door to my room.

"See you on Wednesday in court, sport," Punky said. "And if you change your mind—"

I shook my head. "I won't."

Punky gave me a nearly beatific smile. "I know you won't. I also know I can trust you. You were always the good guy, Dink. Anna . . . Anna was always holding you up to me like that." The tiniest smirk danced in the corners of his eyes.

Manny had stopped inside the room, getting wound tighter and tighter, but Punky took his arm and pulled him with him through the door. I stood where I was, a million thoughts popping in my head, then went to close it. At the click of the latch into the jamb I was awash with relief.

I was still by the door when I heard a sudden rush of arguing in the hallway. I couldn't make out what Manny and Punky were saying, just the rough and clashing tones. I heard Manny mostly, yelling. Punky was quieter.

I was reaching to lock the hotel room door when it kicked in at me. The edge of the door hit my forehead, knocked me back. I was dizzy for a second. Then both men were back in my room. Manny, behind Punky, had a small black pistol pulled.

"I want the goddamn diary," Manny said. "I'm not leaving without it."

I looked at Punky, who glanced at the pistol, then made a *Nothing I can do* gesture. "I think he means it," he said.

"Damn right I do." Manny moved the gun over so it was pointed at Punky. "Want to see what it says about *you*."

"Oh, nothing that interesting, right, Dink?"

"I heard what Dink said, that you're all over the book." Manny had one of his heavy eyebrows cocked up.

"That's not true." Punky turned to me. "Dink, I think you'd better show it to him—"

I shook my head. "This is some trick, right guys?"

Nothing between the two men. Manny said, "I wouldn't count on that, buster."

"Buster," Punky went, mouthing the word more than saying it. He kept the light, amused smile on his face.

I looked down at the gun. I didn't know how many men Manny Gold had killed—and I didn't know how deeply he was still in that game—but I knew he had more than a little blood on his hands. Still, none of this seemed quite real, and in truth I wasn't feeling worried at all. Maybe it was Punky's unconstrained blithe vibe that kept me light, too.

"Dink, listen to me," Manny said, curiously earnest. "We're old friends, too, you know. I know you never thought much of me. You were like Anna like that, you never bothered to see what made me good. But don't underestimate me. That's one thing I can say about her, *she* never did."

I shook my head; didn't know what he meant.

"She didn't belong with you," he went on. There was something a little unleashed in his talking now, his words jumping out. "She was uptown, East Harlem . . . *street*, man. Not fuckin' Beverly Hills, or even Kew Gardens. She should've been mine. I was the only one who understood her. I—"

Punky interrupted. "You *still* think that?"

"Yeah, fuckhead, and when I see that diary, I'm gonna know it for a fuckin' fact." But for his bluster, Manny looked over at me. I guess he wasn't so sure, because his eyes queried mine.

"There's a lot of interesting stuff in it," I said blandly, then glanced at Punky to remind him what I now knew.

"What does she say about me?" Manny said.

I didn't speak for a moment, then said, "Well, since I'm not going to give it to you, I'll tell you. She said you raped her—"

"That's a fuckin' lie!" The gun jumped up in his hand, but neither Punky nor I flinched.

"And that Punky came and saved her."

"That's not true, too."

"There's more."

"More lies?"

"About Punky," I said. "You know, it's sort of funny. Here we are over thirty years later, and we're *all* still in love with Anna."

"What do you mean?"

"Oh, Punky loved her, too." I looked down at the man on the bed with his hands behind his head. "Right?"

Punky looked at me with hooded eyes, but didn't say anything. Then softly: "Manny, listen. I told you, Dink isn't going to let the diary get out, I know he isn't. Why don't we just split, let this whole thing go."

"No, man!" Manny turned on Punky. "I want to know what she was saying about you."

I knew I shouldn't say anything, but I was stricken then with a flood of rage at Punky, for all those years he was supercilious, all that ego, and then what he—or should I say *He*—did to Anna. "Punky made her pregnant."

"He—" Manny gave his head a violent shake. "You think *he* knocked her up?"

"Sometime after you—"

"That's impossible, man. She was *my* lover."

"That's not what she wrote."

Manny was growing more agitated. "Bullshit. I don't know what kind of—" He paused. "She said it was *Punky's* kid inside her?"

"That's what she wrote, yeah."

Punky shook his head. "It's not true."

"Damn right it's not true," Manny cried. "I know all about her kid. The kid was mine."

"She had no question," I said flatly. "None."

"And it wasn't yours?" Punky said in his cool tone.

"Timing," I said, shaking my head. "Impossible."

"I don't believe it!" Manny sputtered. "All these fuckin'

years! She was carrying my kid—*mine*." A glare at Punky.
"Not *his*."

"She wrote that after you raped her, Punky was there.
She felt grateful to him. They'd—well, something had been
going on for years, and right then he took her—"

Punky simply shook his head again, as if it were all lies.

"You know," I said, "I *could* get the diary if you don't
believe me."

"Oh, fuck," Punky uttered. "Listen, this is too crazy
even for me. I'm out of here—"

"Don't."

"What?"

"Don't move!" Manny barked. He flourished the pistol.

Like that, Punky was set off. Later I understood it must
have been Manny's giving him orders that did it. "You
fuckin' loser!" Punky cried. He took a step toward Manny,
then lurched for the gun. When Manny moved back, Punky
threw his fist at Manny's cheek. He nipped his chin. Manny's
hand flew to his face. His eyes glared. Punky jumped at the
pistol again, but Manny was too fast for him. He stepped
back, then brought his arm up quick, pistol in hand, and
clapped the black metal barrel against Punky's ear.

Punky flew back. "Oh, shit!" He swiped his hand at his
ear. "Damn you! Don't you know *you* fuckin' killed her."

"What're you saying?" This caught Manny; he was still
rubbing his chin. Even in his flabby face his black eyes were
funneled down tight and hard. He gave his head a wide
shake. "I wasn't anywhere around her when she died. You
had me banished from the goddamn studio, from her fuckin'
life—"

Punky still cupped his ear. "No, man, it was you. You got
it started. You raped her, you pig. I was there—I fuckin'
saved her."

Manny was shaking his head. "But you cut me out. I
didn't have anything to do with her dying. Are you crazy?"

"How did she die?" I said softly. I thought I was only thinking this, but the words were heard.

"I told you," Manny insisted, turning to me, "I don't know." Then back at Punky. The gun went up. "But he knows. Tell us."

Now Punky was hesitant. "I don't know anything you don't—"

"You were there, man. I know you were there."

"I'm hearing drugs were involved," I said. "But Anna wasn't taking drugs." I shook my head. "I don't know what that means."

Punky shook his head. "I don't either." His tone wobbled a little, and I wasn't the only one who clearly felt he was lying. "Tell me, what does the diary say?"

"It ends too soon."

Punky raised his arms then, extended them out from his body, as if to say, *See*. When he spoke he was calm again, that preternatural, old-hipster cool. "Listen, we're not getting anywhere. Come on, Manny, like I said, let's just split. Friends again, eh? Leave Dink the book. You won't use it against Manny, will you?"

I shook my head. "I don't think so."

"So, there. See. We're good." Punky turned his light, unruffled smile from Manny to me then back. But I could see residue from his being hit by Manny, too: a new tightness, a quiet anger. "We're good, right?" Punky said again.

But Manny wasn't calming down, and it was much more vivid. There was fury in him, unchecked. I could see it shoot through his tight black eyes, glints of angry silver; lightning strikes.

"So we're good?" Punky repeated with quiet insistence. He started to the door.

Manny, not ready to leave, reached out to grab Punky's shoulder, but before he could touch him, Punky whirled around, then erupted. He half-balled his fist, then threw a punch as hard as he could at Manny's chin.

Manny's eyes flashed; he was fast and experienced, and he twisted away from Punky's hand, then came up glaring. *"What the—"* he cried. He had his pistol up, right on Punky, against his chest. I could no longer see Manny's face, he was turned from me, only inches from Punky.

"No," Punky said, fighting to stay calm. "Manny, don't."

But Manny couldn't hold himself back. Through tight lips he said, "This has been a long time coming, bro."

Punky simply stood there. I couldn't say he was quaking, or even that worried. But the way it felt in the room, Manny had it: Something long blocked, long festering, had broken open.

Punky held his courage. "You're right," he said, stepping up to Manny. The gun was tight against his chest, his chin inches from Manny's. "So what're you gonna do about it?"

"Hey, guys, come on." I moved around so I could see both men clearly. There was violence in both their faces. "Let's cool it."

Manny ignored me. He took a step back and brought up the pistol, right in Punky's face. He held it firmly between his two hands, tilted slightly to the side. His left elbow was a tight fulcrum against his chest. There was no hesitation or ambiguity in the gesture. "I'm gonna get to the bottom of it. I'm gonna fuckin' finally understand what happened to Anna—"

Punky stood his ground.

"It may not be in that diary Dink says he has," Manny hissed, "but I *know* you were there, man. So what the fuck did you do to her?"

"I didn't—"

Manny's eyes were loud as sirens. "How did she *die*, Punky?"

Punky raised his hands slowly, let them bounce lightly on the air between them. "Come on, put the gun down."

Manny didn't move.

More hands. "Come on, Manny, O.K., put it down." There was a new light in Punky's eyes, though I didn't know what it meant. He gave a quick nod. "O.K., listen, I'll tell you what I know."

"You fuckin' better," Manny said. The pistol didn't move from Punky's face. "Tell it to me now—to *us* now."

That surprised me, that Manny acknowledged me like that. I felt a strong twist of that tie between us, the way we'd all cherished Anna Dubower. I also wanted desperately to know what Punky was going to say.

"I didn't kill her," he told us straight. "I wasn't even there."

"She was alone?" I said.

Manny looked startled that I'd spoken, but then gave me a nod, meaning, All right, just ask the right questions. I gestured back that I would.

"No," Punky said. "I'm not sure."

"She didn't kill herself—"

"Good God, no."

"Then what happened?"

"We had to—" Punky winced, just a flicker. "We *needed* to fix the situation."

"What the fuck does that mean?" Manny's gun didn't waver.

"We had a problem." Punky was speaking faster. "Nobody was playing *Knife*, you remember?" A nod to me. "And it looked like the whole thing was going to fall in on us. We had to make a new record, had to get the girls out on the road, had to do something. But then—then she got—"

"Pregnant," I said.

Punky turned to me. "I really did always think you did it, Dink. She came back from New York, with your ring on her finger, and she seemed so ... up there." His eyes glanced upward, toward what I couldn't tell. "So happy."

"I didn't," I said. "I told you, when I was with her, she had to already be—"

"Fuck that," Manny barked. He shook the gun at Punky. "I want to know how you killed her."

"Manny, I didn't." Punky's blond spiky kid's hair was drooping now, as if he'd just come out of a very humid day. Right now, up close like this, it looked thin, bleached; and in that instant he seemed a man getting old. "We just had this . . . situation—"

Manny scowled, then thrust the pistol a couple of inches closer to Punky's head. "I don't like that fuckin' word."

Punky still didn't flinch. "Well, we had to do something—"

"About her being pregnant by you?" I said.

"It wasn't going to help anything."

"She was thrilled, in her diary," I said, "about that. She'd—" I thought then about Jennifer, to whom she'd written the whole diary, but decided that had to remain my secret. "She had reasons to want to have the baby. Didn't she tell you that?"

"She said all kinds of things," Punky said. He brightened slightly. "She was a chick, you know."

"So what did you fuckin' do to her?" Manny cried.

Punky took a deep breath. "We just tried to solve the problem—*her* problem—"

I got it then. The realization hit me like a rampant wind; I found myself actually leaning into it. Drugs, Jimmy Devine had said, but not her drugs—drugs administered by a doctor, if it even was that. Anna died in 1967; legal abortion wasn't common till the '70s. Of course, Punky would be plugged in to the hot Hollywood abortion docs, but it was still way out of the public eye—and dire things happened all the time. Like somebody being given the wrong anesthesia, or too much, or any of dozens of other slipups. It hardly mattered. Anna must've gone under. She never woke up.

"The doctor did it, if it even was a fuckin' doctor," I said.

Manny turned to me; he still didn't understand. "Punky got Anna an abortion. She never made it."

"You made her kill my kid?" Manny cried.

"It wasn't your kid," Punky said.

"But you did make her do it," I said. "She didn't want to. Her diary made that crystal clear."

Punky didn't say anything.

"You made Anna kill *our kid*?"

"*It wasn't your—*"

But it was too late. Manny didn't move, just braced the gun tight against his chest and pulled the trigger. The gun was only a foot from Punky. I heard the explosion, whirled away from it. A second later I heard him fall to the floor.

I ran. I just ran. I got the door open in a second, then flew down the hallway, saw a red-lit EXIT sign, and plunged down the stairs. My heart was beating furiously. My breathing seemed out of sync, faster than the rest of me. I flew down the stairs two at a time, almost tripped but bounced against a wall and caught myself. The stairwell threw me out onto 47th Street, and I ran to Times Square, where I found two policemen sitting high in the saddle on their bay-colored horses. "There's been a shooting," I cried. "At the Hotel Edison." They looked at me incredulously for a moment, then I gave them my room number. The room key was in my pocket and I brandished it. I also looked down and for the first time saw the blood splatters on my shirt; I guess they saw them, too. That convinced them. One pulled out a thick black walkie-talkie and spoke into it. Less than a minute later I heard sirens. Police cars pulled up in front of the hotel; another slid to a stop in front of me. A sergeant came out with a black-leather notebook. "Sir," he said, "come with me. We're going to have to have a long talk."

Chapter Fourteen

THE TRIAL WAS POSTPONED the next morning. There wasn't a lot of precedent for this—one defendant shooting and killing the other—and Judge MacIntire simply called an indefinite recess. My case seemed beside the point, but Sandy assured me that I'd soon be getting my full half of the royalties of *Love Will Cut You Like a Knife*. Lawyers. I simply shrugged.

The story was huge in the tabloids for a week. Manny had fled my hotel room before the cops got there, and even though they quickly cordoned off the area, he'd gotten away. Each day pictures of Manny, Punky, Anna, the three girls in beehive mode, Princess, and even a small, unflattering one of me crept into the *Post* and the *Daily News*. The MANNY-HUNT, as the front pages had it, went on, but after a week the story faded from the papers. Manny Gold is still uncaught.

Princess's play, *Angel's Trumpet*, opened in the middle of the frenzy. The papers were all over that, too. Even the *Times* review couldn't resist.

> The same week that Michelle (Princess) Diamond's name came up in regard to the infamous rock 'n' roll murder at the Edison Hotel—her former writing partner, Dink Stephenson, watched their former producer Punky Solomon be shot—Ms. Diamond's first rock musical opened on Broadway. There are no murders in "Angel's Trumpet," no violence of any kind. Instead, the play follows the private dreams of a young man from a small California town as he plans to, then does scale the heights of early rock 'n' roll glory.
>
> There will be some who see in Stephen Green a character based on the late Mr. Solomon, but I'm

afraid that the real model is far more interesting than Ms. Diamond's creation. . . .

This is not to say that there aren't stirring songs in "Angel's Trumpet"; Ms. Diamond has already proved she can write or co-write immortal tunes such as "Perfect Dreams" and "Love Will Cut You Like a Knife," but in "Angel's Trumpet" she forsakes the pithiness of her early pop hits for longer, more pretentious numbers. The climactic number, "Angel's Trumpet," will remind some listeners of the more bombastic moments of Led Zeppelin, especially their classic "Stairway to Heaven."

The good news is that many of the tunes climb that long stairway successfully. The less good news: the book of the show dematerializes along the way. . . .

I went out to stay with my sister and Barbara in Queens. They were thrilled to have me, and although I was still shaken by what I'd witnessed, I was hardly as far gone as they seemed to want me to be. They treated me gingerly, fed me rapturously, mothered me, and in every way made me feel like I was about fifteen again and well looked out for. I didn't do a whole lot. The police asked me to stay around in case more questions came up, and then there were the reporters, though after that first week they began to disappear.

So I had a lot of free time, and no particular purpose. This was a little strange, but I was happy for the rest. I slept late, rode the subway into the city and took long walks, especially in neighborhoods I didn't know well, and ate every kind of food under the sun. It was a curiously relaxing time, and I just went with it. Then Princess called.

She was irate, and let me know right off.

"You ruined it!" she rasped into the phone. "Damn you, Dink, you wrecked it!"

"I did not," I said clearly. I knew she meant her reviews; that everyone had Punky on the brain, not her musical. "I didn't shoot him—"

"But you didn't stop it."

That question caught me; it was the one thing I'd worried myself over, had I provoked things? Could I have backed the whole wild escalation down? How much was I to blame? "It was so crazy, Princess. I couldn't, really."

"Oh, I bet you could've. I bet you were playing Manny and Punky like all get out!"

"Why are you saying this?"

"Oh, I know you, Dink. You like to think you're a simple guy, that you don't manipulate anybody. It's not so simple, boyo."

I took a deep breath. I wasn't so self-deluded that I didn't wonder if there was truth to what she was saying, but I was never going to admit it, certainly not to her. "That's not right. You weren't there."

"Not so you read the fuckin' papers, I wasn't there."

"I'm sorry for that—"

"Well, yeah." Princess's furious breathing slowed. "O.K., Dink, I feel better. Had to get that off my chest."

"Thanks."

"Don't get sarcastic on me. You're just lucky you didn't play 'em so far they both shot *you*."

"Not much chance of that."

"Oh, I don't know. I can think of half a dozen people right now who would like to shoot you."

What was she talking about? I felt my hands flutter against my pants. Did Princess remember my paranoid streak? Oh, yeah. Was she playing it now? In spades. Just like her, too.

"Hey, I'm not taking that bait," I said.

"I'm not fishing."

"Then what are you doing?"

"Just giving you shit." She laughed then, deep and throaty; and I knew everything would be all right.

"Hey," I said a moment later, "I'd like to see you. Why don't you come on one of my walks with me."

"Your walks?"

"Yeah, walks. That's what I'm doing all day. Walking around Manhattan."

"Where do you start?"

"Where do you want to start?" I said.

The phone was silent a moment, then she said, "Meet me at the theater, about five. We're putting in a couple of small changes, should be done by then."

"Deal," I told her.

Maybe *I* was manipulative, or maybe I just knew what I needed to know. It was those last months of Anna's life that were still haunting me. O.K., Punky's there, and he gets her to have an abortion, and she dies. But . . . the diary had said that Princess was there, too.

I went to the Minskoff Theater a little early. Princess had left my name with the guard, and I was able to get in and see them run through some of the musical. What I saw I liked. It was a Cinderella-type tale set in a small town in California. The set was a house at the edge of the ocean. I wondered how much it actually looked like Punky's birthplace. And the boy who dreamed the big rock 'n' roll dream was inspired. He had that singular mix Punky had: great ears, and furious, unstoppable ambition.

"Looks like fun," I said to Princess when she noticed me in the back of the theater.

"You see any fuckin' Led Zeppelin in it?"

I rolled my eyes. "Well, the boy's older sister does look a little like Robert Plant."

Princess laughed, then said, "I never noticed; that must be it. Hold on. Let me get my coat."

A couple of minutes later we were walking west along 45th Street.

Princess still had that New York way of walking, swift

strides skating around slower passers-by, and I scrambled to keep up. I thought of asking her to slow down, but I knew her. She'd say, Sure, then not slow a wink.

We got to the Hudson and turned south, heading down by the piers there. It was a cool day, with a faint mist that came and went. The wide river stretched gray and murky beside us.

"So what do you want to know?" Princess said, as she plowed ahead over the macadam walk.

"I don't want—"

"Dink, come on, I know you know a lot more about Anna's death than you did before." She glanced over at me, her lively brown eyes dancing. "But you don't know it all."

"All right," I said reluctantly. "You nailed me again."

"I've been married three times," Princess said, "but sometimes I still think you're my true husband."

"Lucky me," I muttered under my breath.

"What was that?"

"Nothing."

"I'll bet." She laughed loudly. "And no, that wasn't a proposal."

God forbid, I thought—this time only in my own mind . . . I hoped.

"Yeah, that'd make *me* turn pale, too. Hah!"

We headed down through the 30s. "So?" I finally said.

Princess tilted her head to the side, then said, "So, what exactly do you want to know?"

"I never saw Anna after that early September in New York. She wasn't in contact with me. It was pretty awful. I thought she got to L.A. and forgot all about me—"

"Not true."

"That's what I found out from her diary."

"I heard about that diary. The police have it, right?"

"A copy of it. I still have the original."

"Safe, I trust."

"Oh, yeah." What I didn't tell Princess was that the book was right there with me in the shoulder bag I carried. Punky had been right: I'd had it in the hotel safe. But now I wasn't letting it out of my sight.

"Well, what I remember," Princess said, "was Anna was thrilled with your proposal. She loved your ring. Showed it off at the studio—"

"And evidently left it there," I said, thinking of how only a month or so back I was digging my hands through the rubble on Sunset Blvd.

"That was later—after Punky went to work on her."

"Manny insisted that she loved him, but he wasn't there at all, was he?"

"Totally out of the picture. Punky had him banished from the studio—"

"What was going on between them? I mean, besides Anna."

"Even I don't know the full extent of that, but it was business of various kinds all the years we knew them. Do you know about the records?"

"What records?"

"The ones that conveniently fell off the backs of trucks that Manny and his friends ran. The ones that Punky himself sold to distributors—"

"Punky was—"

"Yeah, stealing from his own record company."

"That doesn't make any—"

"Dink, you've been away from the biz for thirty years. You don't remember: It's all about bookkeeping, tax scams, even real estate. For a lot of those guys, the music itself—" Princess threw her hands up into the air "—that's piffle."

I shook my head. "But not Punky," I said emphatically.

Princess was silent a moment, then agreed. "No, not Punky. Still, he always did what he had to do." She shrugged. "And Manny was very useful. He did a lot of things for Punky. Question is, what did Punky do for Manny?"

I waited a second, then said, "You tell me."

"It was more for the guys behind Manny. Besides the records that fell off the trucks, Punky would run tens of thousands more and simply give them to Manny's friends."

"Why?"

"He owed them." Princess shrugged.

"I never knew all this."

"Well, it wasn't that much of a secret, but you had to be looking for it. I guess you never did."

"I—I think I wanted to think things were, I don't know, purer—"

"Ever the romantic, eh, Dink?"

I let that go by. "Did Anna ever—"

"Oh, Anna, she was a romantic, too. She did what she had to do, sure—"

"Like what?"

"Oh, the girls would play certain clubs, special dates that Manny would set up for the 'backers.' The girls would go along."

"So?—"

"Yeah, not a big deal." Princess looked over. Our hurtling down the pathway had slowed; I found it easy to match Princess step for step. "I don't know of anything else."

This was a relief. "And Manny—did he ever get anywhere with her?"

"Not as far as I know."

"Did you know—" I hesitated a little, but figured it would all come out soon enough if the police let the diary out (which they'd sworn to me they wouldn't, but I wasn't *that* naive). "I think Anna was pregnant way back. Did you know that? When she was seventeen—"

"Really?" Princess shook her head. "No, I didn't know."

"In the diary, she's writing it to her daughter. What I think is that she had an abortion but never forgot the girl—that's why she was so freaked in her diary when Punky wanted her to have another one."

Princess nodded. "That makes sense. Anna fought the abortion as much as she could—"

"When did it come up?"

Princess squinched her forehead. "I think it was in November '66. The record was tanking, and Punky wanted the girls to work harder, try to save it—"

"He said something about that last week, before—"

"Yeah. Well, there was one morning when Punky took Anna aside in the studio, and she came out of it crying. Deeply sobbing. I went up to her, tried to help her. When I asked what was wrong, she said that Punky wanted her to do something really horrible."

"Did she say what?"

She shook her head. "She wouldn't tell me. The other thing about Anna, you know, in a way she was a sort of prude—"

"I know," I said. "I wouldn't use that word, though. I'd just say, what? More modest than you'd think. Some true values." I shrugged.

"O.K." Princess stepped up the pace. Chill gusts of wind caught us, made us wrap our jackets tighter. "Anyway, that was the first time I really worried about her—"

"Anna?"

"Yeah. I started trying to keep a close eye on her. Befriend her as much as possible."

"Why didn't she ever—" Something caught in my throat; this was going to be hard to ask. But I pushed myself. "She took so long to call me. Why?"

"I think—it's hard to say, but I think it was a lot of things. When she was with you in New York, I think it was like a dream to her—or came to *feel* like a dream. You know how

Punky was, how he'd make everything around him so, well, Punkyfied. He did that to her. He got Anna totally caught up in his dream—*his* hallucination. That's that thing I tried to get in *Angel's Trumpet*. And you know, in truth, it excited her—Punky excited her." She shrugged in a way I took to mean: Didn't he excite us all? And didn't he excite the world, too?

"Do you think she ever ... ever took my proposal seriously?"

Princess didn't answer right away, and we kept walking. She even sped up a little more. Then she finally said, "I just don't know, Dink. I think—I think if anything, she wanted things to be perfect. She sure as hell didn't want to burden you with her mess—"

"You know, she was in contact with Nancie—" I said this half-distractedly. There was something I was trying to hold on to. I couldn't say what it was—it was nothing more than a tingling inside me—and all I could feel was the effort to cling to it.

"That must've been one of the ways she stayed close to you then."

"Maybe," I said softly. And it was funny. Something flew out of me right then, I felt it rise out of my mouth and my eyes, off my arms and my shoulders, and simply sail away. I looked into the red and orange sunset sky but saw nothing.

"And then, Dink, she was just too far gone."

That brought me back. "What do you mean?"

"Punky was messing with her head. I could see it. He had a way into her that—that I couldn't do anything about."

"It was Punky's kid inside her. The diary makes that clear."

"I didn't know that then," Princess said. "I thought it was yours—that he was trying to get rid of *your* baby." She shuddered. "I never dreamed it was his own."

"I know." I found I was walking faster now, a quiet fury kicking my steps along. And Princess was keeping up with me. "It's pretty—

"Fucked up. That must've been how he got inside her head. 'Anna, but it's my child, too. How could I do anything to hurt *our* child?'"

We were both silent then for a long while. We were walking past Chelsea Piers, swept along in a tide of joggers and Rollerbladers, and we just kept quiet, lost to our own thoughts.

Princess broke first. "Damn it!" she said. "Dink, I tried—I really did try—to save her. I was her confidante. I knew what Punky wanted. I—I just didn't—" She stopped speaking for a second, then startled me with a tear on her cheek. "I couldn't save her."

I reached out to touch her shoulder. She shuddered again.

"Oh, Dink, it was so horrible. Punky knew this guy in El Segundo—El Segundo, for Christ's sake—who he said was a doctor. I don't know. It was this small rundown apartment off an alley a few blocks from the beach. The guy looked like a surfer, peroxided hair and all. Could've just been a surfing buddy of Punky's.

"He had a room in his apartment set up like an operating room. He had an assistant, another bottle blonde, in a nurse's uniform that didn't fit—it was way too tight. I remember thinking at the time that she looked more like a hooker than a nurse—"

I interrupted her. "So you were there? You were actually there?"

"Anna insisted. Punky didn't want me to come, but Anna threw a fit. So, yes, I was there."

I was silent. So Princess had lied to me before. But I knew I was hearing the truth now.

"They took her into the 'operating' room. Punky and I

sat out in this other room. There was a TV. I remember, *Guiding Light* was on. I've always hated fuckin' soap operas, but that was the one on the black-and-white TV.

"We sat there, not speaking. Punky had that smile—you know his blank smile? *I've got a secret.* He had that secret smile on his face the whole time. I finally couldn't take it, and I told him I was going to take a walk. I went down to the beach, watched the waves for a while, but then something came over me. It was like—oh, Dink, it was like I heard Anna calling me.

"I rushed back to the place. When I got there, I pushed into the 'operating' room, and there was Punky, the so-called nurse, and the guy performing the—the guy doing it. They were all running about, shouting, and there—there—"

And Princess stopped. Stopped talking, and stopped walking. There was a wooden railing along the path, and she went over to it, gripped it tightly with both hands, and leaned over it. She swayed, and then she was sick, right over the railing. I stood next to her, put my arm over her shoulder, felt her quaking body fall into mine.

Through gushes of tears she spoke. "She was just lying there, Larry. There was a tube in her mouth, and she had on this sort of dingy white robe, and it was all crumpled up below her waist though it was oddly straight and prim above it. She had a slight smile on her face, and at first I thought everything was all right—that the deed was done and she'd come through it fine.

"But she didn't move. I stood there, and slowly it began to dawn on me, and I looked for movement, a hand, a leg, then just a whisper of breath coming out of her nostrils . . . anything!

"But . . . but she didn't move."

The tears were building, and I held Princess tight, and she swayed, then looked as if she'd be sick again but held herself back; and finally she seemed to relax into my body. The tears slowed.

I didn't know what to say. I had nothing to say. So I just stood there, my old writing partner—my oldest friend, in truth—sobbing and clinging to me; and we looked out over the small whitecaps of the Hudson, the normality of the Circle Line ship plying its round-the-island route, the people jogging and strolling around us. I held her as tight as I could. I hoped it could do some good. I wasn't sure it would.

Finally, I said, "Punky fixed it, didn't he? With the coroner?"

"Yeah. I don't know what it cost him. I do know the guy was a huge fan of the Annas." Princess tried to laugh then, didn't really get it, but what came out was close. "Can you believe it: The L.A. coroner was a big fan of the dead woman. The public autopsy simply made it death from accidental overdose." She kept shaking her head. "I think there was another one, though, that told more of what really happened, but pretty soon, you know, it wasn't that much of a story. It wasn't like the girls had had a recent hit or anything. Anna was an icon of an already-past age. The press didn't get that far into it—"

"She barely got written up in the New York papers."

"Not like now, eh?" Princess tried to laugh again, and was more successful. She was clearly coming back to herself.

"A solid week of headlines. Well, everybody who was a teenager then now runs the media."

"You got it, Dink."

"And there was a murder."

Princess gave her head a shake. "I can't believe Punky's dead." She grimaced tightly. "Fuckin' Punky Solomon—"

"You know, he said something surprising that night—that he was still making music."

Princess's voice rose. "You mean, records?"

"That's what he said. 'Real Punky Solomon records.' He mentioned a computer, doing a lot of it himself; said it was all on his hard drive."

Princess had stopped, her tweezered eyebrows flying. "Dink, this is amazing."

I felt the swoop of her enthusiasm. "It is, sort of, isn't it?"

"If somebody—if we could get our hands on that music—God, that would be a great tribute to Punky, wouldn't it?"

"Do you think anybody would care?" I spoke coolly. "It's not hip-hop. It's not Mariah Carey."

"I'd fuckin' care," she said. "I'd love to hear Punky Solomon today."

"I'll talk to my lawyer, Sandy. He's pretty plugged in to the old music scene. Find out who's handling Punky's affairs."

Princess nodded. "I think, I just think that would be the best thing we could do for him."

"Short of catching Manny Gold."

"Yeah, there's that." Princess looked somber. "But not much we can do about that. He's probably in Brazil or Venezuela or something."

"I keep thinking he's out in Scottsdale, Arizona, watching his life drip away—"

Princess got that, gave a sympathetic smile. "Probably."

We'd come to a place in our walk, I could feel it, where everything had been said—almost everything. I felt as close to Princess now as I ever had. She seemed to again be my friend.

"So what're you going to do now?" she asked. "I mean, we could walk around the whole island, but—"

"I've nearly done that already."

"Go around again?" Princess lifted her eyebrows, gave me that pointed look that I recognized from all those years back.

"You see a song title in that?"

"*Twice Around the Island*?" She half-shook her head. "I don't know where it goes."

"I was thinking, *Go Around Again*."

She was silent for a while, but I could hear the wheels turning. "There might be something to that. *Sometimes, you don't know when / You just gotta go around . . . again.* What do you think?"

I laughed. "You want to do your next Broadway show with me?"

I meant it as a joke, but Princess said, "It was pretty damn lonely, writing *Angel's Trumpet* all by myself. Who knows, maybe we could give it a shot—if the damn show doesn't end my career—"

"Well then, there, *that's* something I could be doing."

"Cool." Princess smiled. She slowed down, and I slowed, too, then she threw her arms around me. "O.K., old pal, I'm bailing here." She lifted her eyebrows. "You going out to L.A.?"

"For Punky's memorial?"

She nodded.

"I guess I have to, don't I?" The actual burial had been handled expeditiously, in the Jewish manner; as soon as the police released the body, Punky was flown by a special cargo plane to L.A. and put to rest in Forest Lawn, not that far from Anna herself. Now there was going to be a memorial service at Forest Lawn. The New York cops had made it clear that they wanted me to stay close, though I guessed they'd give me permission to attend the service; I just hadn't yet asked. What I told Princess was, "I'm not sure yet, probably."

"Well, see you there." She touched my shoulder gently, then said, "Nice walking with you, pal."

I laughed. "Likewise."

She gave me a warm smile and headed to the curb, then stuck her hand out for a cab. A minute later she was gone.

We'd gotten as far south as Canal Street, right by the Holland Tunnel, and I cut east across Canal, pretty soon hit-

ting Chinatown, then turning south till I came to the opening to the Brooklyn Bridge. It was about 6:30, and the sun
was still in the sky, turning the bridge cables a glinting gold.
I didn't have a place in the world to be, and so I kept walking. I always loved walking across the Brooklyn Bridge, sus-
pended above the traffic as cars made their busy-bee noises
zipping over the water. I walked, simply lost to myself, not
thinking at all of that odd feeling that something had flown
out of me. I also wasn't yet admitting to myself where I was
going, though in truth I knew.

When I got across the bridge the evening shadows were
sweeping up the brownstones; plane trees gathered what
light there was within them and let it out as blue-black shadow. I didn't know this area all that well and was glad when I
found a subway. By then there was no diffidence about
where I was heading. I checked the bank slip I'd written
Trudy's address on, then looked at the subway map. She was
only three stops away.

It was a three-story row house, with a plain brown facade
capped by a golden frieze; tear-shaped planters were
beneath each window, holding flowers. I climbed the stoop
to the front door and stood there a second. An arcing fanlight
above the door was lit with a buttermilk yellow glow—it
looked like somebody was home. There was a big brass
knocker as well as a doorbell button. The knocker seemed
more in spirit with the house, and I gave it a couple claps.

I'd talked with Trudy that morning and told her I might
come see her, but I said I was pretty strung out from Punky's
murder and wasn't sure what I was doing, so I didn't want to
make any definite plans. She said she understood totally; if I
wanted to visit, just show up. Well, here I was, just showing up.

The door swept open, and Trudy stepped out and cried,
"Oh, Dink, it is you—I'd almost given up on you. I'm glad
you're here. Come on in." She stood aside and beckoned me

over the doorstep. I went into the 19th-century-looking foyer, lamps shaped like candles glowing, and saw another woman there. For a moment I thought it was one of Trudy's daughters, but then I stopped, thunderstruck. God, she looked just like her. The same brunette hair with mahogany tones, the same lively face, the same cat eyes, the same full, rich mouth. For a second I thought it was Anna herself. . . .

But this woman looked to be in her late thirties, and was chicly dressed in well-cut wool slacks and a white silk blouse. Her smile to me was large and radiant.

My jaw must've dropped—I know I was simply paralyzed there—because she gave a small, lifting laugh, then held out her hand and said, "Yes, I'm Jennifer. Anna Dubower's daughter." Then she leaned in and kissed my cheek.

✳ ✳ ✳ ✳ ✳

WE SPENT THE EVENING going over it all. I'd brought the diary to show Trudy, but I knew now that I had to give it to Jennifer, to whom it had been written, even if her mother had never expected her daughter would actually see it.

We were sitting in Trudy's front room. She had a pale-blue turban wrapped around her hair, and her complexion held more color than when she'd met me those few days before. When I asked her how she was, she answered right away: "I feel pretty good."

"Great," I told her. But there was no sense that anything really had changed.

When Trudy had brought in herbal tea for everyone, I reached in my bag and pulled out the pink-and-blue book.

Jennifer's eyes grew round and huge. "Is that—"

"Here," I said. "It's addressed to you." When I held out the diary to her, my hand shook, I hoped imperceptibly. "I never—*never*—thought you'd see it, though."

"Me neither, Mr. Stephenson."

"Call me Dink."

She nodded, then took the book. She held it gingerly before her and didn't open it. Then I saw her hand shake.

"From what I read," I told both women after a moment, "I didn't think—well, that there actually was a Jennifer—"

Trudy pursed her brow.

"The way Anna puts it," I went on, "well, I just didn't think she was—" No, I couldn't say it, it was too awkward.

But Trudy knew what I was saying. "She talked about doing that," she said, bringing a hand to her chin. "I was right there with her. I even found a guy in the Bronx who would have—" Trudy took her hand and dabbed her eye. She reached out and took her niece's hand. "But at the end, she couldn't do it. She wanted you to be born, dear, even if she couldn't keep you."

"So she put you up for adoption?"

Jennifer nodded. "I ended up in Wisconsin, outside Milwaukee." She smiled. "Nice people. They were the only family I knew."

"Back then, you remember," Trudy said, "if you were adopted, that was it. No contact with the adopting family. They wouldn't even let you know who the birth mother was. It was all very secret."

Jennifer nodded again. "But when I got older—what was I, Aunt Trudy, about twenty?—well, it had become easier to find out who your real parents were, and I went at it. I was— it was amazing to find out who my birth mother was, but then I found she was dead, too." She patted Trudy's hand. "Luckily, I was able to find my aunt."

"You've been following my trial, right?" A tight nod from Jennifer. "Everything that happened—"

"It's really horrible," she said.

"Yeah, I—"

"I know," Trudy said. "I can't believe it either."

That kept us quiet for a long moment, thinking of Punky, of Anna, of all the dead.

"So this leaves me—I hope it's all right, but I just have one question left—"

Jennifer glanced at Trudy, who nodded, then said, "You want to know who Jennifer's father is."

A tight nod back.

"A guy from the neighborhood," Trudy said. "His name was Sal. There wasn't anything huge there, Anna was just a teenager, and—" Another glance at Jennifer.

"She got pregnant." The daughter shrugged.

"Sal fixed tires. Best we can find out, he died in the early '80s of emphysema."

"So what do you do now?" I asked Jennifer.

"Entertainment law." She laughed. "Aunt Trudy here was great. She got me through college—helped pay for it when my parents couldn't." Sweet nod to her aunt. "I'm managing a few bands."

"Yeah, one of them just cracked the Top 10," Trudy said.

"Congratulations."

"Thanks."

"So what are you going to do now?" Trudy asked.

I shrugged. "I'm not sure."

"Back to Arizona?"

I shook my head. "No, time for something new.

That hung there for a long while. Then I had an idea that burst brightly before me. "Punky's memorial, it's this Friday. It's in L.A., and I'm flying out. Trudy, I think you—"

She touched her turban, then said softly, "I have a treatment—"

"Can't you get away, Aunt Trudy?"

She sighed. There were deep, parchmentlike lines on her face. "I should be there, shouldn't I?"

I nodded. Jennifer said, "I'd like to be there, too."

"Tell you what," I said. "I'll get us all tickets. We can fly out in a couple days, stay through the weekend." I smiled. "Use some of the new royalties I'll be getting from *Love Will Cut You Like a Knife* to pay for it."

"I'll try," Trudy said. She looked suddenly tired, and I got up to go.

Jennifer walked me to the door. "It's been—"

I reached in and took her arm. "I know. This is . . . it's just—"

At that moment she looked even more heartbreakingly like her mother, the same deep-character face, the same arcing brows, sweet rose-flushed cheeks, fiery eyes, flows of wild brown hair. She was the way her mother would have looked if she'd lived ten more years; if, in what I knew now could only have been a whole other world, she'd have been my wife, raising our ten-year-old daughter. . . .

But nothing like that was said. That's where we left it, both of us nodding, lost for words.

Chapter Fifteen

THE MEMORIAL SERVICE was by Punky's gravesite at Forest Lawn–Hollywood Hills, and it was jammed. I was surprised, but the *L.A. Times* had made much of Punky's death, and the local radio stations had been playing his records over and over, and on this beautiful early May Friday morning, the glades of the funeral park were thronged. There were even dozens of cops there to direct traffic.

I hadn't been to many memorial services, and you always think of skies lowering and overcast, a fine mist, and everyone in black raincoats. Couldn't've been more different here. Half the guys wore Hawaiian or Cuban shirts, women were in shirtwaists with sandles; there was the occasional black hat, but more mourners wore baseball caps, the women with their hair pulled discretely through the openings in the backs.

Bright as it was, the whole thing depressed me. It wasn't just Punky's death, or how close I'd been to it, but more the final end of his talent; the way that his work itself had stopped—short of the mysterious recordings Princess was still trying to locate—thirty years before. I guess, as with the Beatles up to Lennon's murder, there had always been the hope that there would be more music, another single so pure and compelling to sweep all the mindless dance-pop off the airwaves. Now Punky's legacy was fixed.

So was my place in it. The media were requesting interviews, but so far I'd declined. I could just tell that they wanted blood and gore in a New York hotel room, not *Perfect Dreams* or *The Truth Is in the Air* erupting out of a Hollywood recording studio.

I'd hoped not to be recognized, not that anyone ever knows what the *songwriter* looks like anyway, so I'd taken a place quite a ways from the gravesite, up a hillock. Trudy was next to me, Jennifer a few feet in front of her. It hadn't been easy for Trudy to get away, but Jennifer had worked on her, and finally her doctor okayed the trip, with the provision that she'd get a treatment in L.A. She had one scheduled for later that afternoon, after the service.

The traveling together? A little awkward at first, our history swimming around Trudy and me, and Jennifer, Anna's spitting-image firecracker, leaving me a little off-guard; but I have to say, once we'd buckled in on the plane, something innately comfortable kicked in: It was that feeling that was just like knowing each other forever, and we read, chatted, watched the movie as if there were nothing unusual with us at all. The surprise, for me, was in the lack of anything surprising.

Up where we were the rabbi's words floated up in spurts. We'd hear a sentence like "This proud man, this amazing creative force," and then we'd miss the next three. Not hearing the eulogy didn't bother me—I knew what *I* thought about Punky Solomon—and the women weren't asking to move closer, either. We were all silent, of course, lost to our own dreamy thoughts and memories.

I looked over at Jennifer. Her mother was buried only a few lots over from where Punky was being laid to rest, and I'd had the limo driver I'd hired stop at her gravesite. I hadn't explained why we were stopping, but when we pulled up, Jennifer had drawn in a tight breath. Trudy leaned over and touched my hand, then gestured for Jennifer to get out alone; and so we'd let her niece commune in her own way with her mother's bones.

Jennifer took things deeply. More than once on our trip I'd caught her being silent, contemplative; and I felt I was looking through her to a deep, crystalline pool inside. These private glimpses were entrancing. I wondered what she was thinking now as the rabbi's obsequies floated up to us as evanescent as soap bubbles.

There was one more surprise: the short man with the ring of gray hair around his shiny red scalp and the triple chins, in the front row in a shapeless suit. It was Punky's father, down from San Remo. He didn't look like a resistance fighter or a former mobster; no, just a kind, simple old man. Guests behind us pointed him out. One of them asked the other what he'd done, and believe me, I was all ears. The other said Mr. Solomon had been San Remo's candymaker; that he'd handmade chocolates, nonpareils, luscious gooey hearts for Valentine's Day for everyone in his small town.

At the end of the service, as we were walking past the grave, I went up to him and took his hand.

"I loved your son," I told him.

His eyes were bright. "Thank you, sir," he said, traces of Eastern Europe still in his accent. "And you are?"

"Dink Stephenson—"

"Ah, the songwriter." He bowed his head, then slipped me a sly smile that could have been Punky's own. "You and Princess: very nice tunes." He nodded deeply. "Very, very nice tunes."

I was telling him how sorry I was when Trudy came up and touched my arm. "Is it all right if we go?" She pointed to her watch. "I've just enough time to get to the hotel and out of these clothes before my treatment."

"Jennifer?"

She was staring intently down at the gravesite, but she half-nodded and said, "I'm good."

We were silent on our way back to the limo. When we were inside, Trudy said, "I'm amazed so many people turned up."

"Me, too," I said. "But, you know, Punky always got press, even when he wasn't doing anything. And people love that old music more than ever."

"It still seems like another lifetime—or two or three—to me," Trudy said.

Jennifer put a hand on her aunt's arm. "Sometimes I wish—" Her voice trailed off.

"Dear?"

"Oh, just that I could've seen it. You and my mother up on that stage with Aunt Doris, that big hair, those screaming crowds. It all seems . . . so innocent."

"I'm not so sure," I said softly. "The innocence. That's just Hollywood. They make it look that way."

Trudy nodded, too. "Not to say it wasn't great, but, look, you got gangsters, little dictators like, well, you know who, and, I hate to say it, dear, but your mother was *anything* but innocent—"

"Maybe, but I just—" Jennifer closed her wide eyes. "I just wish I could have seen it for myself."

We were silent till we were back at the hotel. Trudy and Jennifer went to their room, I to mine, to change, and then I met them both in the lobby.

"You don't have to come with me," Trudy said.

"I'll be happy—" both Jennifer and I said. We looked at each other and laughed.

"No." She gave her head a firm shake. "It takes forever, and you'll just have to sit there and wait." She started toward the door. "I can call for a taxi."

I looked questioningly at Jennifer, she back at me, then she said, "Dink, let's give her a ride to the place. We'll just get an idea how long she'll be there and return in time. Aunt Trudy, would that be O.K.?"

"You don't mind?"

"I have an idea," Jennifer said, nodding. "It'll be fine."

So that's what we did. The hospital was near Century City. When Trudy went in through the glass doors, Jennifer jumped into the front seat of my rented Audi and said, "O.K., show it to me."

"Show you what—"

"That old L.A. Whatever's left. When you and Anna and Punky Solomon were out here making records."

"That was thirty—"

"I don't care. I just need to—this is a once in a lifetime thing, Dink. Let's just drive around, tell me what you remember."

I sighed. Everything, the trial, the discovery of Anna's diary, Punky's death, had pulled me back to the early '60s; and now Jennifer's request simply seemed to follow. I headed east on Olympic, then turned up to Santa Monica Boulevard. What was left from the mid-'60s? The occasional restaurant, a nondescript stretch of buildings—not much else. The L.A. I'd known had been minimalled out of existence.

"I don't really—" I started to say. "There's not very much—"

"It's all right," she said. "I'm getting some of it just being with you. The way your eyes are searching it out."

"O.K.," I mumbled. I turned north to Sunset. I knew where I was going, and so what if it was just a hole in the ground waiting for another minimall? SilverTone Studios had been the center of it all—our true home. I thought of how I'd hopped the fence that night a month or so ago. No need to do that again. Still, maybe I could conjure up the place for Jennifer.

I parked across Sunset. The fence was still up, though the foundation for the shops was set now. Five Hispanic workers, bareshirted with red bandannas over their heads, were pouring concrete.

"See," I said to her. I knew I didn't have to explain where we were.

She opened the car door and got out on the sidewalk. I turned my head to look carefully at the traffic, then when there was a lag, opened my door and got out, too.

She stood there, her hands on the hood of my rented car, staring across the street. She gazed out with all the intensity she had, trying, I figured, to conjure up the plain stucco building, the next-door car wash, the tiny waiting room, the glass-enclosed control room, the acoustic-tiled studio itself—not even rubble and dust now.

"I'm trying to hear it," she said. "That record, that sound. . . ."

I cocked an eye at her as she strained forward.

"And I think I am."

"Jennifer—"

She pointedly didn't acknowledge me. I felt this profoundly intense silence in her, around her. It felt a little like church, when everything hollows out, the air around you silvered with reverence. I heard the slip-slip of cars on Sunset Boulevard, the tumble of the cement mixer across the road, the whine of a plane overhead . . . and then I heard nothing; I heard just what Jennifer heard.

It wasn't anything as corny as a record playing in my head, or the swells of Punky's sound, but there was something there. We don't know a thing about how the present lies on the past, and how the past blooms into the present, and we caution our suspicions and intimations with the sharp rap of reality. So it wasn't as if I were actually hearing sounds from thirty-some years before, and I don't believe Jennifer was, either; it was that we felt the thrum of the underlying *complexity*, the tight braids of desire and will and hunger and triumph strung even on this forgotten corner in the dead part of Sunset Boulevard.

She wanted her mother. *I* wanted her mother. Manny Gold and Punky Solomon had wanted her mother, too, as did the world, which still cherished her beautiful large eyes, her towering beehive hairdo, her streaming vitality—and the records that caught it all.

On this broken land they'd been born.

We stood there for an unknowable length of time, I following Jennifer's lead, taut in her intensity, until finally she simply gave a quick nod, then got back into the car.

She said: "Why don't we go pick up Aunt Trudy now."

Coral Press publishes fiction about music.

If you enjoyed *Meet the Annas*,

We're sure you'll like our other novels.

Robert Dunn is the author of *Pink Cadillac—a Musical Fiction*, which was chosen for the prestigious Book Sense 76 list, *Cutting Time: A Novel of the Blues*, and *Soul Cavalcade*. *Meet the Annas* is the fourth in his series of novels tracing the history of rock 'n' roll, blues, and R&B. More info and Annas' pictures and music at www.coralpress.com.

Dunn has published poems and short fiction in *The New Yorker*, *The Atlantic*, and the *O. Henry Prize Story* collection. He teaches fiction writing at the New School in New York City, where he lives. His band, Thin Wild Mercury, plays often in Manhattan. More info: www.thinwildmercury.com.